CODE DEAD

A SAM TAYLOR THRILLER
BOOK 3

BEN BALDWIN

Copyright © 2025 Ben Baldwin

The right of Ben Baldwin to be identified as the Author of the Work has been asserted by them in accordance with the Copyright, Designs and Patents Act 1988.

First published in 2025 by Bloodhound Books.

Apart from any use permitted under UK copyright law, this publication may only be reproduced, stored, or transmitted, in any form, or by any means, with prior permission in writing of the publisher or, in the case of reprographic production, in accordance with the terms of licences issued by the Copyright Licensing Agency. All characters in this publication are fictitious and any resemblance to real persons, living or dead, is purely coincidental.

www.bloodhoundbooks.com

Print ISBN: 978-1917705493

"Everyone dies sometime, it's just death comes quicker for some."

*To my mum and dad,
For every book you ever gave me and everything in between…
Thank you.*

"La muerte es segura, pero su hora es incierta."

— A traditional Spanish proverb.

("Death is certain, but its hour is uncertain.")

REPATRIATION OFFICE

The Foreign Office's repatriation department is tasked with returning the citizens of the UK back home. Whether missing, wrongly incarcerated or deceased, the department will bring them back

ONE

THE SPANISH COASTAL town of Jávea sits on the easternmost peninsula of the Spanish Mediterranean coastline. To a visitor standing in the centre of the long bay upon which the town was nestled, the juxtaposition of traditional and contemporary Spain would be impossible to miss. Even the spelling of the town's name was a battleground of historical customs. The town's traditional Valencian spelling of Xàbia was still prevalent as graffiti sprayed across its civic buildings and local traffic signs in a determined protest against the changing world. Its vandalism a silent resistance as the local population continued to hold on to its past. But to an unwary visitor, it was in the town's geography that the differences of the traditional and contemporary movements could be most clearly seen.

To the south lay the contemporary Arenal, with its thriving seafront of bars, restaurants and shops. It was the centrepiece of contemporary Jávea, attracting thousands of tourists to its soft sandy beaches. From there the landscape was transformed into the land of the villa, as row upon row of newly-built residential streets spread inexorably from the seafront until they reached up all the way to the slopes of the southern headland of the town's bay. Here at the headland's plateau the expansion of foreign investment had reached its peak as tourists flocked to purchase the prime real estate. Nowadays, the entire headland was a sea of holiday homes, with swimming pools covering all of the land right up to the clifftops that overlooked the sea. Its effect had been to make the entire rocky southern headland of Jávea a permanent bastion of the new contemporary Spain. A physical monument of brick and mortar facing out towards its northern brother.

Not that the traditional northern end of the bay needed any helping hand in its own man-made geographical markers. Nestled under the imposing mountain known as *el Montgó*, the northern side of the bay was dominated by the old town of Jávea. Like the contemporary Arenal, the old town expanded outwards from the seafront. But unlike the tourist-centric south of the bay, the old town had grown round a thriving fishing port. Countless generations of families had found a living from its sheltered harbour, until even today its fleet of ships continued to provide a home to the town's small fishing fleet. Moving up from the harbour, the town had evolved over the years as narrow streets became replaced by modern tarmac-covered roads. Here, the town was a true mixture of old and new as the local residents tried to adjust to the ever-changing world encroaching upon them. A visitor could happily walk through the narrow side streets and still find hidden reminders of medieval remnants embedded within the architecture yet still on the same corner find the latest high-street storefront.

It was from the old town from which the three men drove out of late that summer's evening. The August sun was beginning its descent in the western sky having spent the day baking the bay's inhabitants. Even to the car's three occupants, all of whom were locals since birth, the day had been unseasonably warm. Now as the small hatchback made its winding way out of the old town and up the steep slopes of *el Montgó*, all three felt sweat prickling under their clothes. The car's engine revved noisily as the driver dropped a gear to compensate for the angle of the road ahead and all three were pushed backwards by the vehicle's momentum. It was not a comfortable journey in more ways than one.

The car seemed to relax slightly as they turned the final corner of the climb, before reaching the flat plateau of the northern headland of the bay. The noise of the engine fell to a more comfortable level as the driver was able to move back up the gears, allowing their speed to increase. Around them the green foliage that somehow managed to grow in this challenging environment at least gave them some shade from the setting sun. Even having lived their lives under the mountain's shadow, none of the car's occupants had ever considered how the tree roots could find the nutrients in such rocky ground. Or how the large bushes could possibly survive in the dry parching summers. But survive they did and incredibly, the entire bay stayed green the whole year round with both citrus and olive trees thriving across the bay.

"Turn left here," grunted the man in the passenger seat, pointing to a side road that led away from the main thoroughfare.

The driver, already knowing their destination, bit his tongue and allowed himself to be directed by the older man. He turned the small car onto the narrow sunken road which ran beneath the rocky foliage. The huge rock face of *el Montgó* rose before them as the car bumped its way along the road. Gripping the steering wheel tightly the driver tried not to think of what was awaiting them at the end of their journey. Both his companions were old hands at this and while the summons had been unwelcome news on this summer's evening, neither were unduly worried. Their driver, on the other hand, struggled to understand why his body allowed his mouth to be so dry, but allowed for his neck to be completely covered in sweat, though it might have been because he was still young compared to his companions and this evening's trip was the first time he had been summoned to meet the Chief.

Suddenly the foliage around them disappeared as the car drove through into an open car park at the end of the road. The young driver had to quickly bring down the sun visor to shield his eyes from the rays now driving into his face.

"Keep going. You cannot park here," one of his companions grunted.

The driver's foot had involuntarily left the accelerator in response to the momentary loss of vision. He shook himself back together before steering the car to the far end of the stone-covered parking. Only two other cars were parked up ahead and even these were a conflicting image of the types of vehicles a person could buy. To the right stood a rusty blue pickup truck, the white Toyota branding now barely visible from the years of use. The blue-painted exterior was covered in dents, chips and scratches as if the owner had used it as a battering ram more than a mode of transport. Yet next to this heap of metal, its black exterior polished to a radiant shine, stood an immaculate Jaguar F-Type sports car. The thick metal alloys seemed to shimmer in the late-afternoon sun as the new arrivals parked up beside.

Stepping out of his driver's seat the younger man couldn't help but stop and stare longingly at the machine he had just parked up alongside. The difference between his own small hatchback to this work of art was as great as comparing chalk and cheese. Standing there he reached out a hand to touch the metalwork when the gruff voice of his companion stopped him.

"Mateo, we are late."

Mateo withdrew his hand from the gleaming car and swiftly placed it in his jeans pocket. The three men followed the path that led away from the gravel car park and began the final climb to the peak of the mountain. All three were soon breathing deeply as they stumbled across the rough track that took them ever steadily upwards. Even at this height, the heat of the day seemed to make the air around them stale as their lungs tried to keep the oxygen flowing. Sweat was now dripping down Mateo's lowered face as he watched the feet of his companions ahead of him, carefully stepping so not to lose his footing on the loose rock.

Time seemed to stand still as the young Spaniard trudged along the mountainside. Any other time he would have been grateful to have had the opportunity to stop a moment and take in the view of his hometown. The entire bay seemed to shine under the rays of the lowering sun, giving the whole scene a picturesque feel. As if a photographer had already ran the image through his editing suite ready for the glossy magazine cover. That this beautiful corner of Spain was his actual home had never meant more to Mateo than at this moment in his short life.

The three companions walked round one last bend in the path and stepped out onto an open ledge that protruded from the mountain top. While not quite at the summit of the seven-hundred-and-fifty-metre-high mountain, they were still high enough to have an uninterrupted view of the entire Jávea bay. To their left the bright-blue Mediterranean ran on, out towards the horizon, and would eventually meet the island of Ibiza ninety miles away. On their right they could take in the entire bay with its two distinct areas clear before them. But it was to the centre of the ledge that all three men looked, where two equally distinct men now sat perched on two boulders opposite each other.

Closest to the three new arrivals sat a tall thin man whose lank grey hair sat untidily down to his shoulders. He was dressed in a pair of torn, dirty blue jeans with a raggedy well-worn T-shirt which seemed to hang off his thin frame. Opposite this scruffily dressed individual was sat a man so different in appearance he could have arrived from a different planet. This man looked younger than his companion and wore his long brown hair tied to the back of his head in a top knot. His pale complexion was smooth and cared for when compared to his ragged, weather-worn companion. A perfectly groomed growth of stubble covered the lower half of his face. Like his companion this man was tall, over six foot but that was where the comparisons ended. This second man was well-built with thick strong arms bulging against the tight polo shirt. Two strong legs could be seen protruding out of a pair of cream chino shorts ending in a bright-white pair of trainers. His companion, on the other hand, wore a pair of threadbare leather Jesus sandals, dirty and uncut toenails clearly visible under the frayed ends of his jeans.

"You're late," the grey-haired man commented as the three newcomers edged their way forwards.

Now standing closer to the two men, Mateo was surprised to see the grey-haired man seemed younger than his appearance had first suggested. Below the scruffy exterior he could see a pair of dark-grey eyes peering out from a sunken face. Mateo shivered as the man's piercing eyes seemed to look deep into his very soul as he cautiously followed his companions forwards. The dark-haired man had yet to even turn round to face the newcomers let alone offer any kind of welcome.

"Sorry, Chief, we had to wait for traffic," offered the more senior of Mateo's companions.

The man called Chief pulled a face and indicated the man in the polo shirt. "My friend here seems to think we have a problem."

None of the three newcomers replied.

"He thinks we are becoming distracted by our other activities. That they are making us sloppy."

Again none of the three newcomers spoke. Instead, each man fidgeted nervously as they stood before this strange raggedy man.

The Chief continued in his slow drawl. "He feels that we are now making mistakes, which is impacting on his business." Then repeated, "He feels that there is a problem."

Somewhere over the bay a bird of prey let out a shrill cry as it surfed through the hot air waves. Not that any of the five men on the high mountain top noticed. Instead, a tension had befallen those unfortunate enough to be stood amongst the rocks and boulders.

The most senior of the three newcomers cleared his throat. "I do not understand, Chief, all of our operations are succeeding. We are seeing our profits only increasing across all streams."

The grey-haired man let out a hollow laugh. His long greasy mane seemed to bounce on his shoulders as he did so. "You hear that? My men seem to disagree with you, Major. They are happily making a profit. No doubt making me thousands of euros along the way."

Only now did the man referred to as Major turn from staring out to sea. He twisted on the boulder he had perched on to look at the three newcomers. Mateo felt his breath catch in his throat as he saw the face of the second man. It was a narrow high-cheeked face with a sharp nose protruding from underneath thin eyebrows. But it was the eyes that shook the young Spaniard. Two dark-brown eyes looked at him with such venom that he felt they were more fangs than pupils. Their gaze seemed to chill his very blood.

"Then let them make you thousands more, but you can say goodbye to my hundreds of thousands. Because of your sideshows we now have unfriendly eyes all over us and I don't like it. We are days away from the next shipment and I have to spend my time worrying about whether you and your men would rather be conning old women from their life savings." The man called Major spat the unaccustomed Spanish words in an English accent. His voice was low and deep to go with his large frame.

The Chief shrugged. "What do you want me to say? I have a business to run just like you."

"But not at the expense of our business," Major snapped back.

Mateo guessed this argument had already been played out before they had arrived at the clifftop.

Major continued. "Because of your people's incompetence we now have British law enforcement all over us–"

"Ex," interrupted the Chief. "Ex-British law enforcement. Remember, he is now retired."

Major raised his eyebrows and waved his hand nonchalantly out to sea. "Whatever, but he's still out there and what's more is he is now looking into us. How did this happen?"

The Chief seemed unmoved by his partner's tone. He simply leant backwards on his own boulder, resting his weight on the palms of his hands. "Somebody messed up."

7

"Somebody messed up," Major mimicked with scorn. "Then you better sort it or I will sort you."

"Fine. Mateo, come over here." The Chief looked towards the youngest man there and waved him over with a friendly smile.

Mateo, his knees barely having the strength to stand, somehow began edging towards the man they all called the Chief.

"You see, Major, young Mateo here was the one responsible for ensuring we left nothing behind at dear old Mrs Sheridan's house but unfortunately he forgot to lock up behind him…"

Mateo had now lost control of his nerves and his whole body began to shake as he looked at the Chief's tanned face. He tried to blink away the sweat that was pouring into his eyes.

The Chief continued. "…which allowed some of the more industrious neighbours to question whether little old Mrs Sheridan had actually fallen down her stairs all by herself."

Mateo tried to look over his shoulder at his two companions but neither of the more senior men would meet his eye. His right leg was shaking uncontrollably now.

"I'm sorry, Chief, I did not mean to but I forgot."

The Chief ignored the plea and looked past Mateo to where Major had returned to looking out to sea. His sandalled foot kicked a small pebble off the edge of the cliff to attract the Englishman's attention.

"What would you like us to do?" the Chief asked in a voice that suggested he couldn't have cared less about the answer.

Major moved his gaze away from the blue waves and rubbed his eyes. Without saying a word he stood up to his full height, towering over the frightened Mateo. The unpitying brown eyes looked down upon the young man. Mateo forced himself to meet the taller man's gaze and saw only disdain looking back at him. Then, without any warning, a huge hand grabbed the front of Mateo's shirt and in one fluid movement flung the unsuspecting boy from the precipice. The four remaining men stood in silence as Mateo's screams echoed up the cliff face before ending in a dull thud as the body broke on the rocks below.

"Well, that's one way of solving the problem," the Chief said with a sigh, scratching his stubble-covered chin.

Major gave the cliff edge a final glance to see the end results of his actions before returning his gaze to the remaining new arrivals. His brown eyes scanned the two men, daring either of them to question the violent fate that just befallen their companion.

"I take it you drove here in the boy's car?" asked a relaxed Chief.

"Yes, sir," the two men said.

"There we go, another suicide has tragically occurred on *el Montgó*. May our departed comrade rest in peace," the Chief said with a chuckle.

Major eyed his companion with disdain. "That's not the end of this, there are still many loose ends to tie up."

The Chief nodded. "We can do that."

The huge Englishman took a step closer to the seated Chief and looked down. "That includes the octopus. We don't need it anymore, not for the main show."

Chief's lined face dropped, a look of shock took over his rough features. "Really?"

Major bent over the grey-haired Chief until his face was a mere inches from the man's face. "Really. There can be no more problems. Plus, we don't need it anymore, it's just another liability."

The Chief's shoulders dropped underneath his baggy T-shirt. He waved his arms in exasperation but did not argue the point. "I'll sort it."

Satisfied, Major moved back from the Chief and returned to his perch on the boulder overlooking the simmering Mediterranean. Behind them, the sun was setting quickly now and lights were beginning to appear across the wide bay below. The lank-haired Chief slowly rose to his feet and stretched out his skinny arms. "Is there anything else we can do for the great le Central organisation or have we done enough this evening to please our lords and masters?"

"The next shipment is due in a few days, I expect your little sideshow to have been closed down by the time it docks."

The Chief shrugged. "It happens."

Major twisted on the boulder. "One last thing. You need to take better care of the shipment. You lost too much last time, we can all afford to lose a few on the side but there's only so much we can turn a blind eye to."

"It's all just stock and everyone loses stock," replied the Chief nonchalantly.

Major ignored his business partner. For all of his rough exterior and non-existent manners the Chief was the best in the business. If he had to put up with the smell then so be it. It was why he always insisted on their meeting outdoors, it saved on cleaning the Jaguar.

The Chief scratched at an itch down his back before indicating for his remaining men to follow him back down the mountain. Strolling down the path and just far enough away for the seated Major to pretend not to have heard he called out, "Well, he's a miserable bastard, isn't he?"

Ignoring the insult, the Englishman stared out beyond the horizon. Somewhere out there in the middle of the sea a rust bucket of a fishing boat was making its steady way towards them. Within its hold was money, pure bloody money and he was going to be swimming in it.

TWO

SELWIN BIRKS SPENT his last living day in the paradise he had built during his retirement. Ever since he had moved out to the Spanish town of Jávea, with his now deceased wife eighteen years ago, he had never looked back. Like most days he awoke to a sky already warmed by the early sunrise. He would start his daily routine by swimming two hundred lengths of his outdoor pool before sitting on one of the sun loungers to let the rays dry the moisture away. Resting the back of his head in his hands, he looked down at the tanned body before him. For a man of nearing eighty his limbs were still strong, his torso still fairly trim. Apart from his liver, he was quite confident the rest of him would have been in pretty good shape. A career in MI6 had seen to his liver, no one could have seen the things he had and not have enjoyed – no, required – a few stiff drinks.

Twenty minutes later his body was dry and ready to begin the next part of his morning routine, a breakfast of porridge and freshly squeezed orange juice. Even in the height of summer, he still insisted on the hot bowl of oats to start his day. His late wife could never understand the obsession, but had long since given up the argument in the years leading to her death. The orange juice was more understandable. The fruit locally sourced from a

Spanish farmer who had spent every morning standing on the same street corner for twelve years. Whatever the weather, the oranges were always somehow plentiful.

Breakfast finished, Selwin jogged up the white tiled stairs to dress for the next pillar in his daily routine. A round of golf on the local course was without a doubt the highlight of the morning. His swing may have lost some distance, but he was still generally able to win the standard ten-euro sweepstake. Dressed, he skipped down the stairs back to the entrance to the villa. Picking up his car keys he paused for a moment to look at the portrait of the two women in his life smiling up at him, the happy faces of his wife and daughter giving him the usual pangs of regret and sorrow at not being able to see them in person. His wife would have been gone five years come December. She had been a lot younger than him and it should have been her spending her autumn years alone mourning him, not the other way round. The other face was even younger and it was this face that Selwin would have given anything to have seen today. His daughter had always been beautiful. An enchanting smile shone out of a face full of life. Hazel eyes glinted in the camera's flash as the full lips stretched out into wide cheeks. Selwin touched the glass with his thumb before leaving for the door.

"Damn it," he snapped to the empty villa before heading back into the living room.

Reaching down, he picked up his leather-bound diary and slipped it into his back pocket. While his memory was still fairly sharp, it did not hurt to have the filled pages to hand. Heading back towards the exit he unlocked both the sturdy internal PVC door and then the thick wrought-iron gate, which acted as the first line of defence for the building. All of the villas around him were the same, every window and door equally secured. Each covered in the heavy iron railings to lock down the building while the inhabitants returned back to their home countries. Not that Selwin had set foot in the United Kingdom for many a year. But any added security was welcome, especially in his former line of work.

Or was it still former? He mused on the thought as he walked round the well-watered garden and down to the waiting car. Had he not fallen back into the old ways over the past few weeks? Wasn't he even now heading to meet with a contact that very afternoon? His wife would have had a few things to say about it all. She would have told him to stop being a stubborn old sod and to leave it for the new generation. But that was easier said than done. He had been asked personally for help and he could not just turn away those in need. His daughter would have called it playing to his ego, but what the hell, neither of them were here to understand.

Seventeen holes later Selwin was walking down the final fairway looking up at the imposing *el Montgó*, standing guard over the entire bay. The eighteenth hole had been strategically placed allowing golfers to play directly towards the mountain and most importantly, the highly sought-after nineteenth hole with its ice-cold beer. Behind him, his playing partner continued his hacking of the green-keepers' carefully cultivated course as the sweating retired accountant struggled to finish his round.

"I love that mountain," Selwin commented, as his partner once again managed to only succeed in hitting his ball a matter of feet.

"Not as much as I'll love walking off this goddamn course today," grunted his partner.

"It took me a while to be able to see the elephant in the rock, but now I can't not picture it as anything else."

"You should have tried actually wearing your glasses, Selwin. Oh yes, get on that green you little bastard." The final words were directed at the little white ball that had finally found the required destination.

Selwin chuckled and stared up at the giant mountain, mentally tracing the contours of an elephant's head and tusk in its rock formations. It all added to the mountain's persona as it stood watchful over the bay's inhabitants.

"Looks like our French friends are struggling to find their balls?" The retired accountant laughed, pointing at their playing companions for that morning, as they searched the grass.

The lean figure of Selwin shook his head in bewilderment. "The fools are looking in the wrong place. They would be best giving up and learning racquetball."

"But where would we get our daily ten euros from if they did!" gloated the accountant.

Selwin had to wait for all his playing partners to take their putts before finishing his own round. The satisfying sound of the ball nestling in the plastic cup had automatically sent his taste buds working at the expectance of his cold beer, but that would have to wait. He shook the hands of his playing partners and promised to meet them later in the clubhouse bar. Instead, he strode from the course ahead of his ambling companions and ignoring the entrance to the terraced bar, followed a tiled slope which led down inside the clubhouse depths.

Stepping through a glass doorway, he entered the white-walled corridor which ran under the main building. Frosted glass doors led off from both sides to unseen rooms beyond. The heat of the midday sun now faded as the concrete walls kept out the stifling temperatures. Striding briskly along, the sound of his studded golf shoes echoed down the long corridor which only added to his tension. Reaching the far end, Selwin stopped in front of a wall of metal lockers, their rectangular doors all securely fastened to one side. Scanning the metal doors, he reached up and inserted a small key into the lock of one before removing the contents. Checking he had everything he relocked the small door into place, then turned back the way he came. Walking confidently along the corridor, he paused outside a frosted glass doorway with the words *green-keeper* stencilled across it. Checking the contents retrieved from the locker a final time, he knocked twice on the glass door and entered.

Less than an hour later, Selwin was stood back outside under the Spanish sun. He leant on the metal railings of a narrow footbridge over a large pond that was built to one side of the clubhouse. Below, scores of golden fish swam around him in search of food. Black terrapins lay flat on the floating boards, taking in the heat. Behind, his friends waited for him to join them in the air-conditioned bar. The thought of a well-earned beer was now overwhelming his desire to watch on, as his guest drove out of the busy car park. Their conversation, while not long, had certainly left its impression. Selwin had seen much in a professional life that had taken him all around the world, but he had never expected to find something like that here. The idea of it made him shiver, even in the summer heat. There was danger in the air, but it was still far enough away not to concern him that much. Instead, he waited until the car had driven off before heading back inside to join his companions and the newly won ten euros.

Selwin Birks left the golf course later that afternoon and drove back to his villa on the south side of the bay. His wife had chosen the location when they had first arrived in Spain. She had instantly fallen in love with the town. The thought of spending their retirement together in the bay of Jávea had made even Selwin's pain at a reluctant retirement seem lessened. Situated on the plateau of the southern headland, the villa benefited from all-day sunshine and still received some of the cooling sea breeze. Then during the winter months, when the temperature dropped to the point that even the English dressed in full-length trousers, the villa had still felt exotic. Selwin's mind drifted back over those winter nights with his wife and he wondered again what she would have made of everything. The years had not lessened the pain of losing her.

Taking the back roads through the rows of orange trees, Selwin wondered whether he should ring his daughter and tell her what he was up to. Not that she would have approved, but at least it would have been someone to share in what he had uncovered. It may even be enough to tempt her to come visit him again.

"No chance," he said aloud to the empty car.

Tilly had not spoken to him for over a year now and he

doubted she would want to come all the way back here just to hear about his retirement case. But still, the thought felt good and he allowed himself to be distracted by the hopes of what could happen and the memories of times gone by. She would always be that little, snub-faced girl he had held all those years ago. His mind was still occupied with the bittersweet images as Selwin brought the car to a halt outside the whitewashed villa. Stepping out, he let himself back inside the villa, throwing his keys next to the photo frame, before running the diary to his safe upstairs.

The afternoon was passing by now and he decided to have an early dinner. After pottering around in the kitchen, he carried out the plates and bowls to the patio that overlooked the pool. Even though he had lived alone these past few years, he still always made the effort when it came to mealtimes. Setting the plates onto the tablecloth, he returned twice more with a cheese platter, salad bowl and a bottle of unopened red wine. It was only when he was returning on the fourth trip, did he notice the intruders. He stepped out onto the patio above the pool to see three strangers staring up at him. Their tanned faces looked blankly at him like three lions eyeing up their prey. He had spent a lifetime in this world and recognised in an instant what was happening. It was a hit squad and he knew what they were here to do.

Adrenaline shot through his body and his heartbeat began to quicken. The instinct to turn and run inside was screaming at him, but the logical part of him knew it was too late. He had been wrong, the danger had indeed been closer than he had guessed.

"I take it you're not here on a social visit?" he called out to his uninvited guests.

The three newcomers did not reply. Instead, they spread out further to encircle him.

Selwin nodded and bit his lip. He already knew what they were going to do and he tried to steel himself to face it. But he couldn't just let them have it their own way.

"I don't suppose I can offer you a drink?" he asked.

The nearest intruder shook his head.

"I thought not, you don't mind if I do? Just a final glass?"

Selwin did not wait for an answer. Instead, he picked up the unopened bottle of wine and poured himself a glass. His lips felt the liquid pass over onto his tongue and then down into his throat. Not the worst vintage to have as his last drink, he decided. Turning back to his would-be killers, he raised his glass.

"What's it to be then? I take it you're the accident squad I've been hearing all about. Although you will find I'm not a little old lady, so it will have to be something a bit cleverer than falling down stairs."

The three intruders again did not reply. If they were surprised by Selwin's knowledge they did not show it.

Selwin took another sip from the glass and groped behind him on the table. Finding what he wanted, he gripped tightly as he tried to steady himself. Over the years he had faced death many times in his line of work. He had seen friends killed before their time and had even ended a few himself. He had then watched on helpless as his own wife had died in the cruel grip of cancer. But now faced with the certainty of his own mortality, he wasn't quite sure if he had the strength to do what was required. His hands felt clammy as he gripped the two items which while he knew would not save him, would at least make his attackers' jobs harder.

One of the intruders moved towards him and placed a foot on the tiled steps that led up to the patio where Selwin now stood. The man was a stranger to Selwin, just a nameless face in a lifetime of encounters, yet this one would be the last. He swirled the wine in its glass, remembering they had been a retirement present from somebody or other. His wife had insisted that they brought the glass set over here with them.

"It's good stuff," he told his killers and raised the glass again in one hand. Then raised the cheese knife in the other to point at the approaching man.

The man paused in his stride for a moment to take in the shining blade. He evaluated the danger and shrugged it off. They still outnumbered the old Englishman three to one, it would not be a problem.

"I don't think it will be much use to you, señor," the approaching Spaniard said menacingly.

Selwin let out a brief smile, pleased to have had this one last score against his enemies. "I don't know about that."

The retired spook turned quickly and stepping slightly backwards into the villa, he threw the glass of wine, not at the approaching attacker, but at the far white wall of his living room. Glass fragments and wine covered the pristine surface of the wall staining it crimson. Next, he kicked out at a vase which stood next to the entrance, knocking it over. The three Spaniards, suddenly aware of what the old man was doing, dashed forwards, but were checked by the flash of the glinting knife.

"Careful, gents, I'd hate to cause a mess."

The three intruders continued to step forwards together and slowly began to encircle Selwin. *In for a penny*, thought the older man, before gritting his teeth. He plunged the cheese knife deep into his leg. The pain was incredible, far beyond what he had expected. He stumbled backwards into the living room, but kept his balance. The three attackers, looking to move forwards, froze in shock, their plans having been disrupted beyond repair. Selwin, seeing their uncertainty, pulled the knife from his flesh and before anyone could get to him stabbed the blade into his abdomen. Pain was now filling his mind, he began to lose his balance. He thought he had fallen to the floor, but could not be certain. Somewhere near him, he could hear the anguished voices of his attackers arguing about what to do with him. *Let them try to make this look like an accident*, he told himself as his life crept away.

Suddenly both the voices and more importantly the pain seemed to stop. He was alone in his mind when from nowhere a picture appeared. There were two smiling faces looking up at him, but this time they were moving. They were laughing, excited to see him. Now, finally, he was able to reach out and touch one of them.

THREE

REPATRIATION OFFICER SAM TAYLOR pushed back into his seat and closed his eyes. It wasn't that he disliked flying, in fact at times he rather enjoyed the feeling of being shut off from the rest of the world. Sat there in the compressed environment, thousands of feet in the air, it could be relaxing to know he could switch off from everything and just let the powerful jet engines fly him off to wherever. But then there was the landing. Again, the logical part of his mind told him that the chances of anything going wrong were near enough zero. Yet he still felt an uncontrollable urge to close his eyes every time the plane landed. It all came down to his limited understanding of physics. He understood the concepts behind take-off – lots of thrust, big wingspan and moveable flaps all resulted in the lump of metal getting airborne. It was no different to sticking his hand out of a car window and surfing the wind. Yet nothing he had read explained in a simplified way how tonnes of metal could be safely brought to standstill after travelling hundreds of miles thousands of feet in the air. So, as the fasten seat belt sign came on, his eyes were firmly closed.

"It's a bit late to have a nap, Mr Taylor, we will be landing in a moment," said a feminine voice above him.

Opening his eyes, Sam stared up at the pretty flight attendant who had spent much of the journey back from Norway in friendly conversation with him.

"Old army trick, sleep when you can," he replied, feigning a yawn. The idea of telling this regular flyer about his irrational fear was too embarrassing to contemplate.

The flight attendant shook her head in exasperation. "After spending hours sat here doing nothing, you now decide to go to sleep?"

"I wasn't doing nothing, I was finding excuses to speak to you."

She blushed and gently patted his shoulder before walking past him to the end of the cabin. Sam watched on, surprised by his own boldness at replying in such a direct way. True, he had only been speaking the truth, he had spent most of the flight trying to find excuses to chat to the red-haired beauty. But still coming out with a line like that? He would be lucky to be allowed to fly again with the airline. Yet she had also found excuses to come and chat to him on the two-hour flight. Something greatly helped by lack of other passengers on this early flight from Oslo. Sam had counted twenty-two other travellers on this morning's flight, allowing all of them to have a row to themselves as they flew into London.

The droning voice of the captain came over the plane's speakers instructing the cabin crew to complete their final checks. Sam received another smile from his new friend as she moved past his front-row seat. Feeling the plane bank slightly, he looked out of the oval window to see the sprawling city of London below. In the clear summer morning air, he could see the River Thames making its way through the historic city. Somewhere down there would be the Foreign Office, his workplace for the past few years since leaving the army.

"See anything interesting?" the feminine voice said.

Sam turned and saw the uniformed attendant, her checks now complete, had taken the folding seat opposite him. "Just checking if I can see the office."

"What is it you do?"

"Nothing that exciting, I work for the government. Just a regular civil servant."

She raised a trimmed eyebrow at him. "Do all regular civil servants transport dead bodies in the holds of aeroplanes?"

Sam shrugged, not surprised at her knowing about the deceased businessman somewhere below their feet. "I was away when they were giving out generic work laptops."

She shook her head. "Come on, what do you really do?"

"I'm a repatriation officer, which in practice means I help bring people back home. Take our friend down below. He was found with an ice pick up his... well, somewhere it shouldn't be."

The stewardess grimaced. "I don't think I want to know."

"You did ask," teased Sam.

Somewhere behind them an alarm buzzed as another passenger pressed for attention. Sam's new friend looked past him and pulled a face, but was saved by a more senior attendant, who, seeing his colleague was again talking to the tall, handsome man on the front row, went instead.

A silence fell between the pair of them and Sam watched as the woman opposite crossed and uncrossed her arms a few times.

"I'm sorry, I never asked your name," Sam said.

"Joanna." She reached out a hand.

"Sam."

She smiled and flattened her skirt over nylon-covered knees. "So, Sam, have you got anyone waiting for you when we land?"

Sam gave a dry laugh. "Nope, unless I'm very unlucky."

Joanna gave a friendly smile and waited expectantly for Sam to get the hint.

Eventually he asked, "And you?"

"Oh no, totally single." She paused again then asked, "Did you say you were in the army?"

"I did, I was a captain in the Royal Military Police. Seven years in uniform."

Joanna's colleague returned with a face of thunder. "Joanna,

I'm sorry, that slob in row eleven has just vomited everywhere, I'm going to need your help."

"Damn it. Well, Captain, I'll have to catch you later."

"I look forward to it."

Watching the tightly uniformed Joanna set off down the cabin Sam settled himself back into his seat and again closed his eyes. A thought occurred to him – she had known his last name. He had not told her so how had she known? A flutter started in his chest as he realised she must have looked him up on the passenger list. *Steady, Taylor, try not to embarrass yourself,* he mused.

Joanna did not return for the rest of the flight, leaving Sam disappointed not to have been able to continue their conversation. Instead, as the plane came to a halt outside the terminal, he could only get a glimpse of the red-haired stewardess at the rear of the cabin. A blast of warm air came into the plane's interior as the pressurised door was unlocked and a high-vis-clad ground crew could be seen entering the plane. Sam tried one last time to see Joanna as he made his way out of the plane, but the only staff on hand to wish him goodbye was the senior attendant and a white-shirted co-pilot.

Easy come, easy go, he thought to himself as he wandered into the airport to join the queues of people waiting to get through the passport checks. Instead, the near hour waiting to get through the border security queues only added to his regret. Not that he would have had the courage to have actually asked the girl out, but it was a nice daydream. Eventually getting his passport scanned by one of the newly installed automated machines, Sam walked through into the luggage reclaim hall. Thankfully, the deceased businessman would have already been collected by the local undertakers, allowing Sam with just his carry-on to walk through.

At the end of the hall he suddenly noticed a group of blue-coated attendants walking past the waiting crowds, the sound of their high heels pitching loudly on the polished floor. Sam immediately spotted the tall frame of Joanna towards the back of the group. A sudden surge of adrenaline pulsed through his veins. The old internal battle between caution and adventure began to work up inside his head. He had barely seconds to make up his mind before the fast-paced group would be beyond hailing range. *Let it go you fool*, the more cautious voice in his mind told him.

Instead, Sam jogged a few steps and called out, "Hey, Joanna!"

The entire group of attendants stopped and turned to stare at him. What they saw was a tall, broad-shouldered man with light-brown hair loosely lying to one side. A handsome, chiselled but friendly face suddenly flushed as numerous eyes turned their gaze towards him.

"Sam?" Joanna asked, slightly embarrassed in front of her colleagues.

Internally cringing at his actions, Sam rubbed his stubble-covered chin. "Yeah, sorry. I don't suppose you'd–"

Joanna suddenly beamed and cut him off. "Yes, I would, give me your phone and I'll give you my number."

Sam, grinning like a fool, handed over his phone. Speaking a bit quieter now he apologised for asking her out in front of her friends.

"Don't be, half of them will be jealous as hell. Every one of them had spotted the handsome Yorkshire man with the deep-blue eyes before we'd even taken off."

She handed a deeply embarrassed Sam back his phone. "Make sure you message me, Captain. I'm on a long-haul flight for a few days but will be free for dinner when I'm back."

"Yes, ma'am," Sam replied and watched as the group of flight attendants resumed their march through the reclaim hall, his eyes lingering over the tall red-haired woman at the back of the pack, whose figure he decided was perfectly suited to the blue uniform.

Today was definitely going to be a good day, he mused as he continued his way through the arrivals hall. He looked down at his green-ringed Rolex. Ten thirty in the morning and with the whole day ahead of him. After a good bit of breakfast he could look forward to planning on where he would be taking the beautiful Joanna. Even better than that, he would soon be home and back in his own bed. There was almost a spring in his step as he walked round the final corner into the main arrivals hall. All around him people were greeting loved ones and he felt good listening to the hum from the crowd.

Again he relished the bright start to what was going to be a good day and then he saw the two faces waiting for him in the crowd. The two faces were well-known to him, their presence could only mean bad news. It felt as if the balloon of happiness he had been carrying had just popped with a loud bang. He had definitely hit the ground hard. Making eye contact with the two waiting faces, he gave a brief nod of recognition before continuing to follow the crowd round the barriers and into the open concourse. The pair followed, keeping their distance as Sam strode towards a purple-fronted coffee shop. Finding a table in the corner he fell into one of the seats and waited. His two watchers made their own way through the crowds before taking the two seats opposite.

Sam leant back, crossed his knees, folded his arms and asked, "Right, so who's dead?"

The new arrivals looked back at him in bemusement until the eldest of the two, a silver-haired man with a white goatee beard answered. "No one you know, so relax. We are here for business purposes only."

"I don't see how that is better news," Sam replied coldly.

"How was Oslo?" asked the second of the new arrivals, a slim-framed woman with a narrow face and dark-blonde hair. She asked the question in a soft Irish accent.

"Don't give me that, Emma, you know it went fine. What are you and the old man doing here? It certainly can't be good."

Emma Read, head of the repatriation office, looked at her companion, the retired diplomat Sir Jeffrey Doyle, who shrugged before standing up. "I'll get us some coffee."

Sam and Emma watched as Sir Jeffrey left to join the queue for beverages.

"So come on, give it to me, what is it?" Sam asked his boss. "It's never going to be good if the grim reaper is here as well."

Emma's face softened and she leant forwards to rest an arm on the table. "We need you to fly out to Spain, there's a rather tricky case that requires a certain type of tact."

Sam let out a sarcastic chuckle. "And you picked me?"

"You speak Spanish and you know how to look after yourself. So yes, I picked you."

Sam did not dispute Emma's assessment. It was true he was a fluent Spanish speaker and after surviving some of his previous cases, he couldn't dispute his ability to somehow come back in one piece. Since joining the repatriation office he had been shot, kidnapped, beaten and blown up all in the name of the service. He had faced off with drug gangs, international arms dealers and the Russian secret service. Sometimes he thought he would have been safer staying in the army.

Rubbing the bridge of his nose he asked Emma, "I don't have a choice, do I?"

"Not if you don't want to upset the old man."

The old man was Sir Jeffrey Doyle, the man who had looked after both their careers. Sam had known him since childhood as a strange friend of his grandfather's. It had been the wiry old diplomat that had arranged for Sam to join the Foreign Office, after being forced out of the military. He may as well have been family.

"Christ, that makes it worse if he's involved."

Sir Jeffrey Doyle claimed to be retired, but after a lifetime balancing his career between diplomacy and espionage, Sam found it hard to believe anything his mentor said.

"Still, Spain though?" said Emma, trying to change the subject. "In August, by the sea? I mean, you've been to worse places."

"Great, I'll save you some tapas," said Sam sulkily.

"Sir Jeffrey said you looked too happy when you walked into the arrivals. I take it the Oslo assignment went well?"

Sam was saved from answering as the aforementioned knight of the realm reappeared with a cardboard carrier of hot drinks.

"I take it you've told him everything and he's all signed up ready to go?"

"Only the basics. I thought you'd be better telling him the details," answered Emma, taking her coffee from the carrier.

Sir Jeffrey retook his seat, rubbed the top of his thighs and studied Sam. A pair of bright eyes twinkled behind his gold-rimmed glasses as he looked over the younger man.

"We'd like you to fly out to Spain as soon as you can," the retired diplomat told him shortly.

"Yes, I got that bit. Are you going to tell me why?"

Sir Jeffrey looked to Emma whose face made it clear she was not going to help. "Last night a retired former MI6 agent was found deceased in his villa. The local police are suggesting suicide, but the whole situation stinks."

"How so?"

"How many people do you know commit suicide by stabbing their torsos with a cheese knife?"

"I mean it's not your usual method, I'll grant you that," admitted Sam. "Unless he was a practising samurai performing a hara-kiri suicide ritual?"

Emma let out a wry smile which was quickly hidden. Sir Jeffrey did not see the humour. He raised a hand and pointed a finger at the Yorkshireman. "Don't start with any jokes, Sam. Selwin Birks was an old friend of mine and I do not believe he would have committed suicide. Especially not like that."

Sam quickly raised his hands in apology. "I'm sorry, it's been a long day already. I don't get on well with early flights."

"It's not just the cause of death which is worrying us," Emma began. "He also had a stab wound to the thigh and it looked like there had been some sort of disruption within the house. In any other situation it would have been classed as a murder, but the pathologist who arrived at the scene is adamant the angle of the knife is more suited to a self-inflicted wound."

Sam's curiosity was triggered. "Interesting. Have the local police offered any other explanation?"

Emma shook her head. "Nothing, they've been pretty useless so far."

There was something missing, thought Sam, something they were not telling him. It all seemed to be very urgent, rushed almost. He could not see any reason why this couldn't have waited until Sam had been able to return home, get a good night's sleep before setting off the next day. What were they playing at ambushing him at the airport?

"Then what do you want me to do? Why don't we just let the local authorities wrap everything up?"

"We need you to go there and stand over the investigation, shake a few trees, see what you can find. Then we also need you to stay at Selwin's villa, just while everything is taken care of."

A light switch was suddenly turned on in Sam's mind. He finally realised why there was all the urgency, why both Emma and Sir Jeffrey had travelled out here to meet him at the airport.

"This Selwin bloke," Sam said, looking Sir Jeffrey directly in the eye, "you said he was a retired former MI6 agent, yes?"

Sir Jeffrey shifted uneasily. "I did."

"How retired are we actually talking?"

FOUR

SIR JEFFREY DOYLE sat back in his chair rubbing his chin. He looked carefully at his young friend as if weighing him up, debating what he should say. Eventually he caved in. "Selwin was like me, officially retired from the service and had no access to anything of interest nor was he under any orders whatsoever from anyone in the government."

"But?" said Sam, knowing there was always a but when it came to the former diplomat.

"But for the first time since he retired he had been in contact with some of his old colleagues in the service."

"Here we go, are you going to tell me the old fool got himself killed?"

Sir Jeffrey snapped, slamming his hand on the table. "He was no fool, Sam Taylor. Selwin Birks was a bloody good man and I don't need to hear any of your *chat* this morning."

Sam felt a wave of shame wash over him. "I'm sorry, Jeff, I misspoke."

The old knight nodded, then relaxed slightly before continuing with his story. "We don't know what he was doing over there in Spain, but we find it highly suspicious that we hear nothing from him for years and then weeks after he puts in a routine information request he ends up dead. I don't like it."

"How routine was this information request?" Sam asked.

"Absolutely bloody boring," added Emma. "It was a request for financial details for a list of deceased pensioners living near him. I looked through it all this morning and found nothing of interest, expect they all died out there in Spain and all of natural causes."

"What type of financial details?"

"Bank accounts, savings, investments, wills, that type of thing."

Sir Jeffrey took a sip of his coffee. "Not one of them showed anything interesting, well, not to us anyway."

"But you think they were of interest to Selwin?" surmised Sam.

Sir Jeffrey nodded. "I do. That man was old school. He didn't waste time on wild fairy tales. That means he must have been onto something and that something I think killed him."

Sam eyed Emma, hoping he could read into her mind as to whether she thought their old mentor was perhaps losing it in his old age, that this whole case was just a bit of nonsense.

Emma guessed Sam's thoughts. "I know what you're thinking, Sam, and this isn't just from Sir Jeffrey – the head of MI6 has personally asked that we handle it. She was recruited by Selwin years ago so she's got a vested interest."

"Bloody hell," Sam said. "Why can't she send one of her people then?"

"Because Selwin wasn't an active agent. If she sends one of her team then she will have to explain to the Spanish authorities why she had an active agent working under their noses. Think of the political minefield there!"

"Great. So it means we get to clean everything up."

Emma laughed at him. "You're the one who always moans about never going anywhere hot. I thought you'd like some days by the seaside?"

"Again, I'll save you some tapas. Why do you want me to stay at the man's villa?" Sam asked, wondering at the strange request. Normally he would have stayed at a local hotel when away on business, somewhere he could abuse the service's expenses policy on alcohol.

Sir Jeffrey cleared his throat and looked uncomfortable. "It's like I said, Selwin was old school, he wasn't the biggest fan of computers, anything he may or may not have found is likely to have been kept in his villa."

"And you want me to try and find it."

Emma answered, "Yes, we've arranged for a police presence to be kept around the villa for a couple of days, but I think we'd all sleep a bit better if we knew there was no incriminating documentation left lying around for anyone to find."

"How do you know his killers – if there were any – didn't find anything?"

Again Emma answered, the Irish brogue as strong as ever. "Simple answer is we don't. They may have found something they shouldn't, but I'm hopeful they didn't. We think they were disturbed as a neighbour heard some noises and found Selwin's body still warm."

"You mean you're crossing your fingers?" said Sam doubtfully.

"And all our bloody toes," admitted Sir Jeffrey. "But that's now your problem."

Sam ran his hand through his light-brown hair. His happiness of earlier now well and truly vanished. The thoughts of going back to his flat and sleeping in his own bed seemed like a distant memory.

"Anything else I should know?" he asked resignedly.

"Selwin's got a daughter, Tilly. She was in LA but is travelling to the villa as soon as possible. She knows all about her dad's past career and will be able to help you search the villa," Emma told him, pulling out her phone. "I've had you booked onto the next flight to Alicante which departs in just under three hours. As you know, you won't be needing any accommodation so it's just a rental car you will be picking up when you get there."

Sam rubbed his eyes trying to get his mind into gear. He suddenly realised he was hardly dressed for his destination. "Hang on, I've just got back from Oslo. I've got nothing with me for a Spanish summer." He indicated the three-quarter zip jumper and chinos he was currently wearing. "I'm going to bloody melt."

Emma gave him a pitying look. "You have my permission to expense some clothes when you get there if you have to. Any other excuses?"

"Plenty but I'm guessing you don't want to listen?"

Sir Jeffrey stretched out his arms and stared at the pair of them. The two people sat round him were his legacy to a service he had spent his entire career working for.

"Right then, I guess we best let you make your way back through the airport," he said with a mischievous grin.

"Thanks for that."

Emma swiped her finger a few times over her phone's screen. "I've just sent you over everything we have and I'll have Lucy Marsh book you a rental for when you arrive."

Sam looked up. "What about Hannah, where is she?" Hannah was Sam's favourite analyst back in the office. The bright, pretty brunette made coming into the office worthwhile. The only problem was everyone knew it, including Emma, even if Sam had no idea they all knew.

"She's on holiday," Emma replied, her voice a little softer. "Her boyfriend has taken her somewhere exotic for a fortnight."

"Lucky girl," said Sir Jeffrey, a slight teasing edge to his voice. "I wonder if he's going to pop the question?"

"Well, she did get her nails done," warned Emma, more for Sam's benefit.

Sam's day was getting worse.

Sir Jeffrey noticed the look that had crossed the younger man's face. "Cheer up, you miserable bastard, you're going to sunny

Spain. Perhaps if you're lucky there may be a pretty air hostess on your flight?"

Sam departed from his companions a short time later, heading through the airport's maze of buildings back towards departures. Already his mind was ticking back into work mode. The gears began to move round as he considered what lay ahead. He was intrigued to read the police report into Selwin's death and how they had come to the conclusion of suicide. Surely even the local police found the circumstances strange? It must have been a brave pathologist to make such a bold call. Moving on through the departure hall, he quickly checked in to his flight and headed towards security. Joining the back of the queue, he got into line behind a couple wearing matching honeymoon T-shirts. The thought of Hannah potentially getting engaged made his mood sour again. He tried to lessen it by thinking of seeing Joanna again on his return, but somehow it just wasn't the same. Forcing the thoughts out of his mind he could not see how this day could get any worse. It was only when he had sat down at the back of the day's second airplane and the group of intoxicated women on a hen party to Benidorm took their seats all around him, did he realise he had been completely and utterly wrong.

Just over two and a half hours later, Sam handed back the bright-pink cowboy hat to the hen party, then tried to pretend the entire flight had not happened. On balance, he had definitely preferred the empty flight from Oslo, with the friendly cabin crew, compared to the party atmosphere that had surrounded him on this trip. Exiting the plane was equally uncomfortable as walking down the plane's steps to the tarmac below he was greeted by the mid-afternoon heat. It had been eleven degrees when he had left the Norwegian capital this morning. Now, still dressed for colder climates, Sam was walking in a nearly forty degrees oven. Sweat was pouring down his back as he entered the air-conditioned airport. After picking up the promised rental, Sam turned the car's air conditioning to full, then followed his phone's navigation out of the third airport of the day.

The small screen promised a drive of a little under ninety minutes, as Sam settled into his seat to make his way through the traffic. He skirted round the main town of Alicante following the motorway north. To his left, the rocky outcrops of eastern Spain towered over the motorway, the jagged cliffs leading up to countless individual mountain tops. All were covered in green shrubbery which seemed to cling on like ivy to an English country house. To his right, the bright-blue Mediterranean reflected the afternoon sun, making it seem to glitter as the rental hatchback sped down the motorway.

Turning a corner, the sprawling city of Benidorm stretched out ahead of him. Huge skyscrapers shot out of the ground into the sky above. Hotels, apartment blocks and offices made up a skyline more akin to cities in America than this corner of Spain. He wondered where the hen party had ended up and was pleased not to have had to share any more transport with the well-oiled group. Forty minutes after passing Benidorm he left the motorway then followed a winding road which ran along the contours of the hillside. Now on either side of him were lines of orange trees, their fruit a mixture of ripe oranges and unripe greens. The long day was taking its toll on Sam – more than once he had to rub the tiredness from his face as the afternoon wore on. All he could do to keep his mind focused was hope that the villa's bedrooms had air conditioning.

Sam drove the hatchback over a final hilltop which overlooked a wide-open bay. Checking the map he felt relief at finally arriving at the town of Jávea – the effects of the long day were now catching up quicker than he'd like to admit. Peering through the windscreen he saw the outline of the huge mountain that overlooked the entire bay. Based on his limited reading in the airport departure lounge he guessed this must be *el Montgó* – even while driving he could spot the distinct elephant shape in its rocky formations.

Fifteen minutes later, the satnav announced its final direction as Sam steered the car onto the residential street. Rows of villas all with high-walled gardens ran along either side of the street, their whitewashed buildings tinted slightly orange in the waning sunlight. He had no problem finding Selwin's villa, the waiting police car was more than enough of a clue. Pulling the car to the kerb he brought it to a stop directly in front of the green police car and cut the engine. Ahead of him two uniformed officers stared out from the front of their vehicle. Sam gazed back and hoped that someone had a least told them of his arrival or this was going to be one short visit. Deciding to break the ice first he opened the door and stepped out onto the path. The breath caught in his throat as even in the early evening the heat felt oppressive. He desperately needed a change of clothes.

"*Hola,*" he called to the watching police officers who reluctantly made to move out of their vehicle.

Both officers were young men whose idea of police work had not been to spend their entire shifts parked outside a deceased Englishman's villa. Sam tried to give his most friendly smile as the two stepped towards him adjusting their belts complete with holstered firearms.

"*Hola,* señors," Sam repeated. He had been speaking Spanish almost as long as he had English, his paternal grandfather having arrived in England having fled Franco's Spain.

"Who are you?" the first officer asked in Spanish. He eyed Sam suspiciously, taking in the unseasonal get-up the Englishman had chosen to wear.

Sam reached out a hand. "Sam Taylor, I believe you were expecting me?"

Neither of the officers took the offered hand. Instead, the same officer gave his partner a look before turning disdainfully back to Sam.

"You're late. We were told to expect you three hours ago."

Sam shrugged. "There must have been a mix-up. My plane only arrived three hours ago."

The explanation seemed not to have impressed the two officers. Instead, the second officer reached into a pocket and threw

Sam a set of keys. "Your people said you will be staying here, yes?"

"Yes, is that a problem?"

The officer seemed not to care one way or another. "If that is what they want then that is up to them. We will be here all night if you want anything."

"Have there been any developments with the case?" he asked them.

The two officers looked at each other, unsure of what to say.

"Come on, I'll only find out tomorrow from your superiors."

Eventually the second officer spoke. "The pathologist is adamant Señor Birks killed himself."

"You don't sound convinced," said a bemused Sam.

The second officer went to speak but catching his colleague's eye he fell silent.

"Okay, I understand. I'm already looking forward to meeting this pathologist of yours," said Sam before looking down at the key ring, then he stopped – there must have been over fifteen keys fastened on. "Christ, I bet you need less keys to get into Fort Knox."

The officer laughed and waved an arm at the black iron gates that led into the villa's garden. "Welcome to the world of holiday homes, their owners keep them locked down when they are not in the country." He reached out a hand indicating for Sam to pass back the keys. "It seems the owner who lived here had his head switched on because if you start with this one you can work your way round clockwise door by door."

Sam took the indicated key and inserted it into the gate's lock, opening it wide.

"Cheers. Any other useful tips?"

The first officer spoke. "Sleep in the left-hand bedroom downstairs, that's got an air-con unit that actually works."

"Thank God for that," said Sam with a sigh. Then thinking about his stomach he asked the two officers, "I don't suppose you can recommend anywhere to get some food?"

"There's a pizza place just up the road, give them a ring and they can deliver." The officer paused, clearly wanting to say more. "Your Spanish is very good."

Sam laughed. "Thanks, although I'm guessing you're only comparing that to the drunken tourists you normally have to arrest?"

The two officers grinned. "Good point."

Leaving the two policemen to sentry duty, Sam made his way towards the villa's entrance. Around him, well-watered grass grew neatly along the pathway. A lemon tree was growing to his left, its fruit not yet ready for picking. Nearing the main building Sam looked up at a two-storey villa, its orange-tiled roof overhanging the whitewashed walls. A porchway covered the entrance above which spelt out in individual lettered tiles *Villa Esmerelda*. Stepping onto the tiled porch he walked past a large statue of a boxer dog sat looking out over the garden. He absent-mindedly reached down and patted the ornament's head.

"Easy boy, that's a good dog," he told the dormant figurine.

Taking the next key on the ring he unlocked a heavy metal gate which clanged against the wall as he pushed it to one side. He went to open the main door but stopped – something had caught his attention. Looking upwards he saw a gecko hurrying across the painted surface, scurrying quickly up to the safety of the pillared rooftop.

"Leaving so soon?" he asked the vanishing lizard. Perhaps it was a sign of things to come? Looking back later, Sam was adamant it had been a missed sign.

FIVE

STEPPING inside the villa Sam found himself in a darkened entrance hall, the evening's light limited by the blinds over each of the windows. To his left ran a wooden cabinet with a glass bowl to one side of a single glass photo frame. Flicking a light switch Sam picked up the framed photo to study the two faces smiling up at him. Based on the report on Selwin Birks he had read while in the airport, Sam guessed the two women must have been his wife and daughter. The wife looked to have been a good few years younger than the deceased Selwin, her face still fairly youthful. But it was the daughter that really caught Sam's eye – the full-faced blonde-haired woman seemed to emanate from the print.

Returning the glass frame onto the cabinet he continued to make his way further into the villa's interior. To his right a door opened to a large kitchen area, black granite work surfaces covering the white cabinets. Sam stepped in and casually opened the fridge door to find a limited choice of edibles. There seemed to be more beverages than food, but with the hot weather and single widower occupant it did not surprise Sam. After the day he'd had Sam would be making a dent in the bottles of beer stacked to one side. But for now he grabbed an ice-cold bottle of water and carried it out of the kitchen into the open living room. Three sofas were placed round a wooden coffee table, a glass surface shining under the lights. A widescreen television was fastened to the wall above a gas fire which seemed rather redundant in a climate such as this.

Sam's eye was immediately caught by an ugly red stain to one side of the room. Directly above a dining table and chair set was the dull remnants of what the police, having found the open bottle, knew to have been a glass of red wine. His deep-blue eyes lingered on the strange stain on the painted wall. He tried to imagine what could have happened to have resulted in such an outcome. Now standing there in person the idea of Selwin Birks committing a run-of-the-mill suicide seemed almost laughable.

A rumble from his stomach brought his attention away from the wine stain and he remembered the promised pizzeria round the corner. Finding the number online he dialled up and ordered three pizzas to be delivered as soon as possible, the idea of improving Anglo-Spanish relations increasing the quantity. His order safely placed Sam continued to explore his new surroundings. At the far end of the room wide patio doors were locked down behind thick metal sliding gates. Making his way along the key ring he unlocked the gates then pulled them open. A new wave of warm air blew into the building as Sam stepped onto the covered patio, the former owners having added glass windows to the concrete arches to make a type of conservatory for the colder months.

Standing there, Sam realised this was the exact spot where they had discovered Selwin's body. Looking down, he saw markings on the tiles which he guessed had once been covered by a rug, which was now probably in a police lock-up being scientifically tested. He noticed two stands guarding either side of the patio doors, one with a vase, one without, having been found smashed next to the body. Another door led out to an uncovered area of patio and further on, steps led down a garden, then down to the pool area. Standing still, Sam had seen enough, the heat from the conservatory windows was becoming unbearable. Back inside he found two double bedrooms separated by a bathroom. The advice from the officer in the car had been spot on as the room to Sam's right was as warm as the conservatory. Uniquely for this building someone had left a window open in response to a broken air conditioning unit. It did at least make Sam's decision for his own sleeping quarters easier, finding a fully functioning air conditioning unit in the adjacent room.

Coming back out of the bedrooms Sam looked directly at a set of tiled steps that led to the first floor. He debated about continuing the tour but decided it could wait. It had been too long a day. Instead, he walked back into the living room and fell onto a sofa. He spent the next few minutes trying to work the television until he eventually found a channel showing an old British sitcom. Just as Sam felt his eyes begin to flicker under the day's fatigue did the doorbell sound. Wearily standing up, he half-staggered to the door to receive his pizza delivery. Afterwards, placing one box on the cabinet, he quickly ran into the kitchen to grab a couple of beers, then, with his hands full, wandered out to the waiting police car.

Both sets of eyes followed him as he walked down the garden path. Sam gave his most friendly smile as he leant forwards then offered the two boxes of pizza and bottles of beer.

"Hungry?" he asked as the car's front window opened.

The two officers looked up at him quizzically for a moment before eagerly accepting the proffered food and drink. There was a slight pause as they looked at the beer bottles before Sam shrugged.

'Hell, I'm not going to tell anyone.'

But it wasn't enough and the two bottles were reluctantly handed back. Sam instead twisted one bottle's cap and drank the chilled beer.

"Okay, now that we are friends can we at least share names?"

"I'm Officer Mata and this is my colleague Officer Picque," the man called Mata answered.

"Great, I'm Sam Taylor, nice to meet you."

"Did you find anything interesting inside the villa?" said Mata.

"Nope, just that the call on the bedroom was an outstanding suggestion."

Picque smiled. "I take it you do not like our weather?"

"I'm beginning to think I complain about whatever climate I'm stuck in."

The two officers chuckled.

"Tell me the truth, what the hell's really going on here? I've looked inside, I've seen the stain on the wall, it's a murder scene in anyone's book. He certainly didn't kill himself, did he?"

Mata and Picque looked at each other, unsure of what to say, the conflict of toeing the political line versus the human nature of wanting to tell the truth.

Eventually Picque answered. "We do not know ourselves, we are just ordered to stay here and watch over the building."

Sam raised an eyebrow. "You're going to tell me the uniformed rumour mill hasn't been in full gear? Come on, humour me, what's the consensus about what really happened?"

Mata scratched his head before answering. "We agree with you, a suicide doesn't smell right does it?"

"Then why is your department determined to push it on everyone?"

"We are not the ones pushing it," the officer replied curtly.

"Who the hell is then?"

"Our pathologist."

Sam nodded and remembered the report. "The same man who said the knife wound was self-inflicted?"

"Yes."

"He may be right but surely it's your responsibility to still explore the circumstances? Find out what caused a man with no history of depression to suddenly end it all?"

Picque swallowed a bite of pizza before replying. "He was a

widower whose remaining family had nothing to do with him. I can't imagine it was a happy existence."

Sam thought about that for a moment. It may be plausible but with the timing of the information requests something more sinister seemed more likely. He was about to tell the two officers his thoughts but stopped – he realised none of the Spanish authorities would know about Selwin's recent dealings.

"Fair enough, I'll be interested to speak with your commissioner and see their thoughts."

"You'd be better meeting the pathologist."

Sam rubbed his face. "Ah, so it is the good doctor running the show."

The two officers exchanged further glances, their body language betraying their awkwardness.

"Let's just say he's quite vocal for a pathologist," answered Mata cautiously.

"Sounds ominous."

"It is fair to say he likes to push the boundaries of his remit."

"One of those people who've watched a few too many true crime series and think they know it all?" joked Sam.

"Something like that but in this case, it involves someone who could embarrass us all if it ever went to court. Imagine if he gives an alternative cause of death compared to our own case."

"I see," said Sam.

The role of a pathologist could be a vital piece of evidence in any case and if the police's own doctor was not playing ball then the case may as well be closed before it even went to court.

"I'll make sure I give this doctor a visit then."

Sam turned to leave when Officer Picque called out, "Make sure you have a look upstairs, the old guy kept an office in one of the rooms and a safe in his bedroom. Perhaps the daughter will be able to help you find something when she arrives tomorrow."

That was news to Sam. He knew the woman was on her way and at least now he knew when to expect her. Perhaps this time tomorrow he may even be able to check into a hotel or better yet be on a plane home. He left the two officers and returned to his own pizza, still warm in its cardboard box. Finishing it swiftly he decided to give the first floor a quick look-over. The tiled stairs led up to a small landing with two doors leading off to either side of him. To his right the door led into the main bedroom. An en suite lay to one side while built-in wardrobes ran down one wall. A double bed faced out onto a balcony which looked out beyond the garden over the rest of the sloping headland. Sam unlocked the iron bars that locked the patio then stepped out to look over the scene. The previous owners had chosen the location well, the south-facing villa would have the sun all day long. A gentle sea breeze could be felt blowing in from the unseen Mediterranean providing a cooling sensation as he stood still.

Locking the balcony back up Sam returned to the bedroom and noticed one of the wardrobes had been left open. Peering in, he noticed the aforementioned safe fastened to the floor in one of the corners. Its thick iron casing looking impregnable to Sam's eye, he wondered if Selwin had kept his findings in there. Sir Jeffrey had said the man preferred to do things the old-fashioned way. He would have to warn the daughter in the morning not to let the police have anything confidential or potentially embarrassing to the government.

The small home office was even less revealing to Sam as he gave it a once-over. A desk faced out of the square window looking over the street below. A filing cabinet stood in one corner with only one drawer filled with the personal documents of the deceased owner. Not even a computer was left standing on the desk – instead, there was only a leather resting mat holding a blotting board and a couple of pens. Sitting in the single chair Sam saw faint lines on the blotting paper where Selwin's pen had imprinted through whatever he had been writing on. If the daughter could not provide any light on her father's musings, then this was going to be a long case, thought Sam. He swirled the chair round a final time to see if he had missed anything of importance but only a framed photo of a golf course hanging from one wall caught his eye. The imposing outline of *el Montgó* overlooking the green fairway.

Sam sighed, rubbed his face and returned downstairs to check in the kitchen for something stronger than the empty beer bottle. Opening a few cupboards his face lit up as he found the former spy's liquor collection.

"Well, Selwin, you certainly had some taste in gin," muttered Sam as he pulled out the blue Tarquin's Cornish gin bottle.

Searching the rest of the kitchen he made himself a strong gin and tonic adding plenty of ice to combat the waning day's heat. Cutting up a fresh orange he dropped in the slices and went back into the living room to wait out the rest of the evening. Darkness seemed to fall quickly around him and after another gin he decided to call it a night. After a final check of the villa to make sure all of the entrances were relocked, followed by a glance at the still parked police car, Sam headed to bed. The air-conditioned room sent a new wave of fatigue over him – within moments he had stripped down to his boxers and had fallen asleep on the nearest bed.

Sam woke with a start in the early hours. Lying there he felt the sweat drip down his spine onto the sheets. It took a moment for his senses to kick into gear and assess his surroundings as he remembered where he was. For a blissful moment he had forgotten he was in a stranger's house in the middle of Spain. No, not just a stranger but a deceased stranger who had been killed in the very building he was trying to sleep in. Sitting up, the sheets fell from his chest as he rubbed the sleep from his eyes. His mouth felt dry from the previous evening's alcohol and he cursed himself for not bringing in a bottle of water with him to the bedroom. Climbing out of the bed he stood up and stretched his limbs, the after-effects of the two flights had stiffened up his weary muscles. What he would have given to have been wrapped up in his own bed at this moment in time.

Instead, Sam walked out of the bedroom into the main hallway of the villa and switched on the light then stopped. A man was standing halfway down the stairs ahead of him. For a moment both men just stood there staring, the shock of the discovery freezing them to the spot. Sam blinked the sleep from his eyes and looked up at the stranger. A gaunt-looking face stared back at him, in the centre of which was a snub nose that looked to have been broken more than once. The man was dressed in a black shirt and trousers, his bearded face was still trying to decide what to do now his presence was known.

Sam spoke first. "If you're looking for the toilet it's behind me?"

The intruder did not reply.

"I'm going out on a limb here and saying you're not Tilly Birks?"

The intruder still did not respond. Instead, he leapt forwards from the staircase. Sam spotted the movement in time to reach out one side and fling the cabinet's glass bowl at his attacker. The bowl hit the man's face, pausing his momentum for just a second, giving Sam a chance to follow up his projectile. Still in just his boxers he threw his elbow into the man's jaw sending him staggering back. Sam followed up with a kick to the knee but without wearing any shoes, only hurt himself more than the intruder.

"Jesus Christ," he gasped as the pain shot up his foot.

The two of them had moved into the living room as the intruder gained the advantage. He threw a punch into Sam's stomach, forcing the air from his lungs. Now doubled over, Sam stumbled past his attacker, bouncing off one of the sofas. This time a booted foot did make contact but it was against the back of Sam's own knee and he fell forwards onto the other sofa. He tried to turn to somehow get back into the fight but found himself disorientated by the previous blows. His stomach ached, his leg was on fire but he found his feet to see his attacker coming forwards again. This time the blow came in from a straight jab to the face sending Sam backwards. He tipped over the sofa's arm, bounced off the cushion and fell onto the coffee table smashing the glass surface.

"Shit," Sam groaned as he lay trapped on his back between the metal frame of the coffee table.

Trying to get up he looked for his assailant but the room was empty. Whoever the man was he had gone.

"Yeah, you better run, you bastard," stuttered Sam. "I was only giving you a head start."

Slowly, careful not to step on any shards of glass, he climbed out of the now destroyed coffee table's frame. Gingerly finding his feet he tasted blood dripping down from his nose. *Who the hell was that?* he wondered. Whoever it was had certainly made a quick getaway. Suddenly he remembered the police car outside, hoping against hope they may have heard the commotion. Tiptoeing over both the glass from the table and then the broken bowl he headed for the door. Opening the locks he pulled the thick door open, then pushed out the metal gate to see an empty street. The police car with its occupants had vanished.

SIX

STANDING in the open doorway in nothing but his underwear, the only sound Sam could hear was the incessant chirping of insects calling out to the night. Ahead of him, beyond the garden gate the street was bereft of any sign of the missing police car. Sam swore, he could taste blood inside his mouth. Worse than the beating he had just taken was the sickening thought that Officers Mata and Picque had left him to it. Had it not been them who suggested sleeping in the one bedroom whose window was closed? Now standing there he realised the intruder must have climbed in through the other bedroom's window, all of the other possible entry points had been firmly locked down. *Christ*, he scolded himself, he'd been so stupid. Ever since he had arrived in Spain he had been too busy treating the whole experience as a holiday when he should have recognised the dangerous situation he had landed himself in. A trickle of fear began to creep into his mind as he looked out into the night. He suddenly felt extremely vulnerable stood there on the porch.

Moving quickly, he turned back inside then firmly shut both the gate and door, securely locking each in turn. Next, switching on all of the rooms' lights he surveyed the scene in front of him. Fragments of broken glass lay all across the floor where both the glass bowl and coffee table had separately smashed. He rubbed the remaining sleepiness from his face then flinched as he touched his bruised cheek. The blow had cut the inside of his mouth and he tentatively poked around inside to assess the damage. While his head was sore the throbbing in his knee was causing the most concern. The blow had badly bruised the back of his knee causing him to wince in pain as the adrenaline ran its course.

"Bloody hell," he called out to the now empty villa.

The Rolex on his wrist showed the morning had ticked past four am but he was in no mood to return to bed. Now limping he decided to make a start on the clearing up of the glass which covered nearly the entire ground floor. He tiptoed over to a storage cupboard under the stairs, retrieved a dustpan and brush then gingerly began the clear-up operation. After painfully crawling around on his hands and knees to retrieve the final shards he poured the contents into a bucket then fell into the nearest sofa.

Closing his eyes he leant back then ran his hands through his hair. A weariness was returning, making its weight felt through his tired limbs but any thought of sleep was quickly pushed out of his mind. He realised the opposite bedroom window was still open and worse, he had not even bothered to check what his intruder had been up to upstairs. Muttering curses on everyone from Emma Read through to the deceased Selwin Birks, he forced himself up to his feet for a final effort. Still limping he started by finally locking the open window which had allowed his intruder access. Had the two police officers been in cahoots or had it been coincidence that the intruder had known about the one open access point in the villa? Someone had known. Worse, someone had planned it.

Leaving the room to its mysteries he headed upstairs, the pain in his knee forcing him to take each single step one painful movement at a time. Reaching the landing he first turned to stare into the study on his left. The cold grey light of an early dawn was filling the room giving it an eerie silence. Not much had changed since his search of the night before, only the filing cabinet seemed to have been touched. All three of its metal drawers were left at differing angles as the intruder had rifled through each of them. *But looking for what?* Sam wondered. Knowing only the top drawer contained anything, Sam gave the contents a brief study but without knowing the exact details of what was originally stored within it was pointless task. Perhaps the daughter would be able to make a better assessment.

The bedroom was nearly exactly as he had left it with only the wardrobe door left ever so slightly ajar, betraying the intruder's movements. It all pointed to a fact which Sam had feared the moment he had realised how the intruder had managed to get into the villa. A normal intruder searching for something would have torn up both rooms in his search. Every drawer, cupboard and piece of furniture would have been searched. But whoever this intruder had been he had known exactly where to search. He had somehow been briefed about both the safe and filing cabinet. Someone, most likely as part of the investigating team that had originally searched the place, must have told him where to look. The thought made Sam shiver. Both of the officers below had known about the safe's location. In fact, Officer Picque had even suggested Sam search it out for himself. Perhaps it had all been an elaborate attempt at giving themselves alibis?

Studying the iron box he noticed scratches around the locking mechanism where someone had tried to break it. A poor attempt, thought Sam. He guessed the plans must have changed when they learnt of Sam's planned presence in the villa. The original plan must have been to wait until the main investigation team had left the property and for whoever was involved in all this to have returned at a later date. Unfortunately for them and Sam, his presence downstairs had put a major dent in their planning. All of this thinking had finally brought a weariness back into Sam's mind, driving him to return downstairs. Calling first into the kitchen he searched the freezer for an ice pack which he wrapped up in a discarded tea towel. Still limping he returned to the now cold bed that he had left less than an hour ago and lay down. Carefully he placed the wrapped-up ice pack directly under his hurting knee before falling back into an uneasy sleep.

Sam was awoken by the sound of a door slamming shut. The loud crash of the iron gate clanking into the wall seemed to vibrate through the villa. A filtered sunlight covered the room through a pair of flimsy curtains, betraying the morning. Hearing more noises he quickly threw off the bedcovers and still only in his underwear, crept to the door. The sudden movement made his knee groan underneath him but he put it out of his mind. Beyond the closed door out of the bedroom footsteps could be heard on the hard tiles. Straining his ears he tried to work out exactly who or what had just entered the residency, but came up short against the thick concrete walls. He tried to look around the bedroom for some sort of weapon to defend himself yet beyond a rolled up pair of trousers his options were significantly lacking.

"Bloody hell, here we go again." He cursed himself for not thinking ahead earlier that morning, to at least make sure he was armed for any potential round two.

A new noise entered his ears, this time the sound of wheels being dragged across the floor. What the hell had they brought with them this time? he wondered. In this still drowsy state the only thing he could think of was something to try and crack open the safe. A temptation to stay and hide in the room lingered in his mind, but he knew it was pointless. He would only be placing himself in a trap for his enemies to prise him out of. The footsteps echoed again, more loudly this time, as if the owner had moved into the living room. Giving the bedroom a final desperate once-over for something, in fact, anything to use in defence, he spotted his discarded boots. They would have to do. Crouching, he picked up one boot and put it over his right hand as a makeshift boxing glove. It would certainly leave whoever it was outside something to remember him by.

Now using his free left hand he gripped the door handle and took a deep breath to steady his heart rate before gently stepping out into the hallway. A new figure had entered the villa, its tall slim shape stood with its back to him in the middle of the living room. Spotting the blonde hair tied firmly to the back of the skull he relaxed slightly. A woman now stood before him and sensing his presence, turned calmly to face him.

"Well, they don't advertise this kind of service when they try and sell you a villa holiday," she said without missing a beat. A pair of bright eyes scanned Sam's near-naked form standing there in his boxers, with his right hand entombed in his boot. "They said someone had been sent to look after the place, although," she paused, a glint in her eye, "I wasn't quite expecting this welcome."

Sam blinked the sleep from his eyes. Slowly he began to recognise the woman in front of him. She was older than her picture placed on the sideboard by the entrance, but it was definitely her.

"Tilly Birks?" he asked.

"In the flesh." She reached out a hand. "Sam Taylor I'm guessing?"

Sam dropped the boot then took her hand. "How do you know that?"

"One of Dad's old friends rang me yesterday to explain the situation, someone called Jeffrey?"

"Yeah, that would be him."

Sam studied the woman in front of him. A round face which looked ever so slightly more drawn since her photo had been taken stared back at him. The hazel eyes and full lips had, however, not changed. Her beauty had only seemed to have grown with the years. He tried to guess her age. She was certainly older than him, over forty perhaps?

Tilly Birks looked around her deceased father's living room

then spread her hands. "So are you going to tell me what happened here?"

Taken aback, Sam asked, "What do you mean? Has no one told you?"

"What, that my father died? Of course they did. No, I'm asking what happened here, more specifically what happened to you?"

Confused, Sam's mouth moved but no words came out.

Tilly shook her head. "And they told me you were good. Something clearly has happened here. For a start the table's broken, something that had not happened in Dad's attack. There's a bucket full of broken glass by the door and empty glasses in the kitchen. So that suggests you were drinking my dead dad's booze and smashed up the place."

Sam raised his hands shaking his head desperately. "No, it wasn't like that–"

Tilly interjected. "Relax, I don't think that either, your sudden appearance all armed with what looks like a boot, added to your damaged knee and bruised face suggests something else entirely."

A slightly shell-shocked Sam was struggling to keep up with this new arrival into his life. The night's events, added to the long day yesterday, was surely taking its toll. "I was attacked last night, someone broke into the villa."

The older woman nodded. Taking a seat she looked up at him. "That makes more sense. How did they get in? This place is like Fort Knox when it's locked down."

"That's what I said but someone left a bedroom window open."

"Someone as in you?" she said, a slight tone of inquisition in her voice.

"Hell, no. I was the one who got a beating, remember?" Sam, his senses clicking into gear, decided to keep his suspicions on how the window came to be open to himself for now.

"Evidently. Are you okay?"

"I'll live."

"Did they take anything?"

Sam shook his head. "Not that I could see but I'd appreciate it if you'd give it the once-over?"

Tilly nonchalantly waved him away. "Later. I've just crossed a continent and an ocean to get here. I think I deserve breakfast first, then you can tell me everything you have planned." She paused, looking him over again. "Perhaps after you've had time to get dressed, as much as I do enjoy the view."

The realisation that he was still standing there in nothing but his boxers caused Sam to hurriedly attempt to cover himself up. Clasping his hands over his crotch he felt himself flush with embarrassment.

Tilly laughed. "Mr Taylor, seriously, it's nothing I've not seen before, so stop being a prude and put some clothes on. I'll make us some breakfast and you can tell me everything in more detail."

Ever so slightly impressed by this new arrival, Sam gratefully returned to the privacy of the bedroom to be faced by his next problem. Opening the suitcase the old challenge of being suitably dressed reared its ugly head once more. The best he could do was a pair of chinos to go with a new polo shirt, it was going to be a sweaty day ahead of him.

Heading back into the hallway of the villa, he found Tilly busy in the kitchen rustling up a breakfast out of the leftover bread, fruit and cereals.

"Stack what you can on that tray and we'll eat outside on the patio," she ordered him as he entered.

"Yes, ma'am," said Sam as he fitted the mixture of plates, glasses and cutlery onto the tray.

Tilly had already opened the patio doors, allowing Sam to walk straight out into the refreshing morning air. A slight breeze tickled the garden's foliage around him, disturbing the small number of leaves lying across the tiles. Ripples expanded their way across the blue waters of the pool. It was hard to associate the peaceful environment around him with the events of the past couple of days. This villa in the heart of the Spanish Costa Blanca, had certainly seen more than its fair share of violence.

A round table had been set out by his new companion, a fresh new tablecloth was being held in place by a jug of orange juice and place mats. Laying the tray down, he finished setting up the table before taking a seat facing outwards over the peaceful scenery.

"One thing about Mum and Dad, they always had good taste," commented Tilly as she carried her own tray out onto the patio. "They originally wanted a sea-view villa, one of those that hang over a cliff edge but soon realised this was the only place to get all-day sun."

"It's a nice place, I can see the appeal of retiring out here over our wet and cold country."

She shrugged, taking the seat next to him. "It can still get pretty chilly in the winter over here. Don't let the summer season fool you." Tilly eyed Sam's outfit. "Although it looks like you have already come dressed for the winter season."

"Don't ask, this time yesterday I was on a plane coming back from Oslo. A slightly different climate. Then duty called and here I am."

Sam looked over Tilly's own outfit. She was certainly better dressed to their environment than he was. Two well-toned, tanned legs protruded from a pair of white shorts, while a dark-blue tube top revealed her bare shoulders that were only covered by a white cotton shirt tied in a knot across her torso. Now in the bright light of the Mediterranean sun, Sam could see his host had definitely aged well compared to the younger woman in the original photo.

"And what is duty? That man from the foreign office gave a bit of an explanation."

"I'm what's called a repatriation officer, which basically means I help get our fellow countrymen back home safe."

"You're a bit late in my father's case then," she mused while pouring them both a glass of fresh orange juice.

"We also make sure everything is done correctly, support the local police or individuals in trouble."

A mischievous smile flashed across her full lips. "Well, since my father's no longer in trouble that must mean I need watching over."

"Maybe," parried back Sam, not quite sure how to take Tilly's seemingly overly relaxed personality. For someone who had just lost their last parent she seemed pretty chirpy.

"Relax. I know why you're here, it seems Dad got himself into some bother before he died and you're here to find out why. Don't worry, I'm all on board, in fact I'd have been disappointed if they hadn't sent anyone."

"By *they* you mean MI6?"

"Well, the government. What happened to Dad was clearly foul play and between us we need to find out why."

Sam nodded along, happy to have found such a willing ally. "Sounds a good plan." He paused then asked the question he had been wanting to ask. "I may be being out of place here but if I said you seem pretty relaxed about all this, would that upset you?"

Tilly paused in cutting up one of the apples. "Fair point and well put. I think it just comes with the profession."

Unsure, Sam asked, "Yours or your father's?"

"Perhaps both. Dad had always been very frank about the risks from his past life, although I guess we thought he would have been past all that in retirement."

Now gently as he was unsure of his footing, Sam asked, "And are you involved in any spook work?"

"Christ, no, I'm a doctor back in LA. I see death all of the time. Spend enough time around death and it soon becomes second nature."

Not quite believing her, Sam decided to move the conversation onwards. He knew there would come a time for further questioning on this strange father-daughter relationship.

"Where do you suggest we should start then? I had planned

on visiting the police headquarters this morning and visiting the mortuary afterwards if you wanted to come along?"

"Yes, I'm up for that. Apparently I have to make a formal identification so I'd be glad of some company. My Spanish is non-existent," she admitted in between mouthfuls.

Now picking up a slice of toast for his own breakfast Sam asked, "Also, before I forget, you know the safe upstairs. I don't suppose you would be able to open it? I'd be curious to see what's inside. I'm hoping there should be some papers the service sent over, some of which I'd like to keep out of our Spanish friends' hands."

"Yeah, no problem, I'm not sure what he keeps in his study. I'll be interested to see for myself."

Sam stopped spreading butter across the toast's surface and looked up. "Don't you mean in the bedroom? The safe is in his bedroom wardrobe."

Tilly Birks chuckled, shaking her round face. "Mr Taylor, you will need to up your game if you're entering the espionage arena. That safe is purely for show, Dad kept anything of importance in a secret, very well hidden safe."

SEVEN

ALEX COOMBS WOKE up early that morning. Even with the morning's planned events, she was still expected to complete her normal routines. Not that she really minded. Having worked for the Kane family now for the past six months, the morning routine had become almost second nature. True, this morning was slightly different, as she had to leave the family's villa before most of them had even woken up. First, she needed to prepare breakfast, set the table with all of the required cereals, pastries and fruit mixtures the family enjoyed for their first meal of the day. Next, she would quickly tidy up the kitchen, disposing of anything left over from the night before, which thankfully was very little. Then finally for that morning, she would creep into the children's rooms to set out their set of clothes for the day ahead.

That was the trickiest part of that morning's routine. She had been explicitly told not to wake up the children if she was wanting to enjoy that morning's planned excursion. Although whether the warning had been in jest or a genuine risk to her plans, she wasn't keen to find out. Creeping round the darkened room, she soon realised there was nothing to worry about – both children were completely out of it. Their little chests were rising in tune to the deep breathing that signalled a secure sleep was still being enjoyed. *Strange*, mused Alex, normally the children needed very little in the way of waking. The slightest of noises was generally enough to bring them back round to the land of the conscious. Not that Alex was complaining. If this was the day they chose to sleep in, then happy times.

Leaving the two sleeping children, she ran back to her room to collect the small bag she had prepared the night before. Checking her watch, she still had a few minutes before she was expected and so quickly looked at herself in the long mirror on the wall. A tanned face stared back at her from under dark-brown hair, which she had tied up in ponytail. She was dressed in a small white T-shirt above a pair of denim shorts, while underneath she was already wearing her bikini, ready to make a quick change into her wetsuit on the boat. Twisting round, she couldn't help but stare at the long, firm, twenty-two-year-old legs protruding out from underneath her shorts. The shorts would leave a tan line but what else could she do? Her employer would probably appreciate the loss of the shorts. Alex wasn't sure about how his wife would feel.

Alex had already caught Chris Kane – like most men – staring at her youthful body on a number of occasions, yet to be fair to the guy he had never crossed any boundaries. In fact, he had been a perfect employer, no, an absolute gentleman the entire time she had worked for the family. She had heard of worse families to work for, lecherous old men who took a delight in feeling up the hired help. She had even known friends in the business who had suffered much worse. So far, her own experiences with both of the Kanes had been nothing but enjoyable. From living in the basement of their London town house, to joining them on their regular trips to Spain, where Mrs Kane's family were originally from. In fact, this very clifftop villa had been in Mrs Kane's family for years. To top it all off, even the children were well-behaved, at eight and ten years old the workload in keeping them entertained was barely worth the wage she earned.

Accepting the risk of tan lines she shouldered her bag and headed back to the kitchen. The room looked over the pool area and beyond that straight out over the sparkling Mediterranean Sea. It was a stunning home, the building embedded into the clifftop, providing the inhabitants with a perfect environment to spend their days. Alex, her excitement building for the morning's trip, bounced into the kitchen and picked up a fresh croissant from the plate she had set up earlier.

"Be careful, Alex, if you have too many of them then Chris will need to adjust the weight belts," a voice called out from the doorway.

Alex looked round to see the stick-like frame of Mrs Kane watching her.

"Ha, I'll help him carry some of the air tanks when we get there to burn it off."

Sofia Kane shook her head at the younger woman as she came to join her by the table. Alex's other employer was the very definition of glamorous, from her hair and make-up to the jewellery that adorned her, she was always on point in her appearance. Today she was dressed in a long, maroon-coloured dress which seemed to cling to her narrow body as she moved. The dark-haired Spanish woman of the house picked up the jug of orange juice and poured the pair of them a glass. "Chris is on his way, he's just getting the keys for the boat."

Alex just nodded in response.

"So you're quite the diver then?" Sofia asked.

Alex must have had this conversation with all the family at least half a dozen times. It had been worth it as without it, Chris Kane may never have offered to take her out for a dive. He had finally kept to his word and arranged to take her that morning. "I don't know about that, but my dad ensured I got all my qualifications almost as soon as I was able to swim."

"Then you will enjoy the Granadella, the diving there is particularly good. Have you prepared the boys' clothes for later?"

Alex confirmed that she had.

"Good, I'm going to take them out while you're gone. I'll show them a few of the places I used to hang round."

"Surely not all of the street corners in Jávea?" a male voice called out as Chris Kane walked into the room.

Chris Kane was tall like his wife, but where she was all skin and bone, he was athletically built. Thick strong arms were hanging out of his shirtsleeves, while a pair of stout legs were straining against his surf shorts.

"All of the wrong places," Sofia agreed. "If I grew up in England then you would have had to arrest me for everything me and my brother used to get up to."

"I still could, you know," mused Chris. He turned to look at their young au pair. "Are you all ready to go, Alex?"

"Ready to go, boss." She smiled back. Alex had grown a habit of affectionately calling Chris 'boss'. In some ways it helped keep their friendship formal.

"Don't forget to get me some oranges on the way," Sofia reminded them. "And I want the fresh ones so you better call on your way to the boat, I don't want you leaving it till later. Diego will be out by now so make sure you get in there early."

Chris went over and kissed his wife's cheek. "Hey, we are already running behind, we should have been on the water at dawn and Diego's stall is out of the way."

Sofia Kane gave her husband a scowl. "Chris, get me the damned oranges and remember the solicitor will be calling you at some point. So unless you're actually underwater make sure you answer it this time."

Chris Kane gave his wife a nonchalant wave as he walked past her, only stopping by the doorway to blow her a kiss. "Señorita, have I ever told you I love your Spanish fury?"

A flurry of Spanish expletives greeted his sarcasm and Alex quickly followed Chris from the room. Joining him in the family car, Chris drove them away from the villa and the southern headland back down into the main Jávea bay. Reaching a crossroads he turned to his passenger.

"What do you think? Shall we get the oranges later? She will never know."

Alex shook her head, fearful of Mrs Kane's wrath. "You know you'd be risking it leaving it until after, he could be sold out by the time we get back."

"We could just get some from the supermarket, she can't tell the difference once they've been juiced."

Alex gave him a bemused look and Chris got the hint. He turned left and headed inland to the street corner where Diego sold his locally grown oranges. Their fruit collected, Chris drove the car back towards the seafront. They talked about the morning's upcoming dive and what they hoped to see while underneath the waves. She had always enjoyed Chris's company, he could be funny, charming and insightful all in one go. There had been more than a few times she had found herself jealous of Sofia in finding such a man.

Chris drove the car to the small marina situated just behind southern Arenal and parked up next to the local dive centre. Rows of bright-white boats were moored along a jetty. Standing up out of the car, he waved, then called out to one of the dive masters milling around outside. The Spaniard called back before heading inside to fetch the pairs of pre-booked dive tanks.

"I'll go and ready the boat if you're okay to bring the stuff from the car?" he said.

Walking round to the back of the car she opened the boot and collected their bags then headed after Chris, who had already boarded the boat. The words *Foxy Sofia*, an homage to Mrs Kane, were painted across the boat's rear. Stepping from the wooden planks of the jetty and onto the boat's deck she peered around the medium-sized craft. She was stood at the stern of the vessel looking into an open cabin that led down to a deck consisting of a small kitchen, bedroom and bathroom. Chris was standing on the bow pulling in the ropes that kept the boat tied to the jetty.

"Watch out, Marco's bringing up the tanks."

Alex turned to see a pair of local dive masters each carrying two of the heavy air bottles between them towards the small boat.

She had to step aside as Chris reached up to take all of the heavy bottles down in turn, ready to be fastened to the deck.

"You have everything else?" Marco called down.

"Yes, everything's locked up in my storage. I think we will be good to go. Can you release the last line?"

Marco gave him a friendly salute before bending down and releasing the *Foxy Sofia* into the water's current.

"*Adios*, Marco," Chris called to the watching dive masters as he took the boat's helm. Steering the boat into the centre of the gentle current, he skilfully guided the craft through the marina's channel into the open ocean. He turned to Alex who had been standing to one side as he had prepared the vessel for launch. "You can relax now, Coombs, there's no kids to worry about here. You can get yourself up front and enjoy the sun. There's a few cushions or towels in the locker up top and there's drinks in the fridge down below if you want them."

Alex, happy not to have to spend her morning babysitting, gladly took up the offer, climbing up onto the white-topped bow of the boat. Bending down, she opened the aforementioned locker and pulled out a blue towel which she laid out ready to lie on. The morning sun was already beginning to feel hot, even with the sea breeze that was surrounding them. Chris had navigated the boat out into the open water and was beginning to open the throttle of the boat's engines.

"It's going to get a bit bumpy in a minute," he called out from behind the glass window protecting the boat's controls. "You may want to lie down."

Taking the offered advice, she dropped down to the deck, quickly took off her white T-shirt and stretched out. Even with her eyes closed she imagined the wandering eyes of her employer looking over her bronzed body. The thought pleased her – if she could attract a man like Chris with his gorgeous wife, it boded well for her future quests for her own husband. After a few minutes she felt brave enough to remove the denim shorts until all that remained was the skimpy bikini. If Chris was watching –

no, that was a stupid question, he would definitely be watching – he did not say anything. Instead, steering the boat past the southern headland, he navigated round into a narrow bay which ran inland to a pebble beach. Either side of the vessel, jagged cliffs rose out of the water, their peaks dotted with villas built into the rocky outcrops.

"We will moor up on the red buoy for the first dive. It goes straight down to a few corals which generally have some big squid and eels," Chris called out to her as he skilfully manoeuvred the boat towards the bopping buoy. "Come and see if you can pull in the rope so we can fasten on."

Alex did as she was asked, climbed to her knees then crawled to the side of the boat. Once secured, she stood up and walked back round to the stern where Chris was pulling out the rest of the diving equipment he kept stored under one of the boat's benches.

"I'm going to set you up with Sofia's equipment, it should all fit. I've got a spare computer for you as well for our decompression stops," he told her as he merrily arranged their equipment. Stopping for a moment he noticed her bikini-clad body. "I've laid her wetsuit up over there."

A few moments later Alex was zipped into the snug wetsuit and was helping to finalise setting up her equipment. She checked the tank, then the buoyancy control device jacket and regulators which Chris had put together for her. Two flippers were fitted securely round her feet and a weight belt now hung round her hips. Next, spitting into the eye mask, she leant over the side of the boat to wash out the saliva, ensuring the plastic would not fog up while on the bottom. Finally she fastened the loaned dive computer to her arm, the grey numbers ready to monitor her descent into the depths.

"Ready for the BCD?" Chris asked, hefting the heavy jacket with its tank fastened on the back.

"Hell, yes! I'm sweating like a pig in this wetsuit."

Chris laughed. "I'll have to wash it before I give it back to Sofia then."

He lifted the jacket for Alex to pass her arms through, then helped her fasten first the Velcro strap followed by the clip and zips. Gently Chris guided her to the side of the boat.

"Regulator all working okay?"

She checked both of the mouthpieces then inflated her jacket. "All ready, boss."

Chris smiled down at her, a wide boyish smile which seemed to cover his entire face. "You look like the all-action girl you see in the movies."

"Damn right, now hurry up so I can cool down."

"Why don't you just drop in? You can wait for me in the water, I'll only be a few minutes."

Alex, the sweat now dripping underneath the warm wetsuit, readily accepted. "Hell, yes to that. Am I clear to go?"

Chris peered over the side. "All clear."

Alex beamed up at him, pulled down her mask then grabbed her regulator. "Honestly, thanks for this, Chris, I've been looking forward to it all week."

"Get on with it, you big softy. I just needed an excuse to get out of the house."

Placing the regulator in her mouth she crossed her arms, held her mask in place and fell backwards. Immediately the blue water assaulted her senses as she rolled back amongst the bubbles. Within seconds the buoyancy in her inflated jacket brought her dark-brown hair back to the surface. She spat the regulator out and lifted up the mask from her face.

"Hurry up, boss, the fish will have gone by the time you get in."

Chris, halfway through zipping his wetsuit, stuck up his middle finger. She laughed and allowed herself to lazily lie on her back over the gentle surf. Looking along the cove she could see the pebble beach nearly two hundred metres away, still empty, the day's tourists yet to arrive. One gentle lap of the boat and Chris was still not quite ready. He had hefted his equipment to the side of the boat but was still not sat on the edge ready to fall back into the waves. Alex watched as his athletic frame bounced around the deck.

"Right, I'm coming," he suddenly called to her.

"Yeah, yeah."

Chris Kane moved towards the boat's side then stopped. A ringing noise had erupted from the boat.

"Oh, Jesus, it's the solicitor," moaned Chris, who debated for a moment, then turned to the ringing phone. Answering, he placed his hand over the mouthpiece then spoke to Alex. "Right, you go down and I'll meet you at the bottom. Just follow the rope down and head north following the rock face, it forms a semicircle which you just have to follow. Keep making your way round and I'll catch up."

Disappointed, Alex asked, "Are you sure?"

Chris sighed. "It's an important one, if I don't then you know my life won't be worth living."

Alex laughed and waved goodbye. "Yeah, I'm not sure it's worth it. I'll see you at the bottom, boss."

Reaching down, she found her buoyancy control to let the air out of her jacket. Slowly gravity began to take hold of her and she felt the slow pull of the water bring her under. As her head left the surface she dropped downwards into the blue depths. Using the anchored buoy's rope she guided herself down to the bottom until she reached the sandy floor. Around her the looming rock faces that gave a home to the entire ecosystem rose above her. Fish of various shapes and sizes were already becoming increasingly braver in their curiosity as they approached her. Careful to avoid the stinging black sea urchins, she squeezed twice on her buoyancy control until becoming weightless, floating above the aquatic world. This is what she had always loved about diving, it was the closest she would ever come to visiting another planet. By sinking a mere twenty-five metres below the surface she had arrived in a different world full of life and colour.

Kicking her legs round, Alex looked up at the shadowy hull of the boat above, but could see no sign of her diving partner.

Her father would have scolded her for diving alone, calling it unnecessary bad practice. Yet he wasn't here to give her the lecture, so deciding to take Chris's advice and not to waste her own storage of precious oxygen, she kicked on into the murky depths. Floating along the reef she could never understand how some people found the whole experience of diving claustrophobic. To her the blue murk that surrounded her seemed to stretch on for miles. Who knows what could be out there looking back at her.

Forty minutes later she had arrived back at the rope that would lead her to her own world of dry land. There had been no sign of Chris through the entire dive. She guessed he had spent so long on the phone that he'd simply wrote off this first excursion, they had a second tank each anyway for a further dive. Following the diving computer's directions she took her first stop at ten metres and then a second at five before breaking the surface just below the bow of the boat.

"Oi, Chris, where were you? You missed a huge octopus down there," she called up to the boat.

There was no answer. She swam round the stern where a small gate opened up to the swimming ladder.

"Hey, did you fall asleep or what?"

Still there was no answer, so pulling off her flippers and throwing them up she began to slowly climb the unsteady metal rungs.

"Seriously, boss, I could do with your help right now," she called, trying to keep her balance.

Eventually Alex had a clear view of the deck, but Chris was nowhere to be seen. Guessing he was probably down below, she quickly disposed of her diving gear before unzipping the wetsuit, allowing it to fall to her waist. Chris's own gear lay untouched on the deck.

"Seriously, Chris, this isn't funny," she called out to the empty boat.

A fear began to creep into her mind causing goosebumps to form on her arms. She shivered in the hot summer sun. Stepping cautiously forwards, she moved towards the hatch that led to the small cabins below. Taking each step one at a time her knees began to shake and walking became tough. Raising a trembling hand she pushed the first door to the boat's tiny bedroom open and screamed. Lying on the bed, swimming in a pool of his own blood was Chris Kane, his throat split open to the world.

EIGHT

TILLY BIRKS STOOD up from the breakfast table and led Sam back inside the villa. Heading upstairs she first pushed open the bedroom door and slipped into the en suite. Sam followed to see her crouching behind the unit that housed two sinks, in front of a mirror that covered most of one wall.

"Watch where your eyes wander to," she warned Sam in a flirty voice as she laid down then angled her body under the sturdy furniture.

Sam ignored the warning, watching with amusement as her slim frame contorted itself to reach under whatever it was Tilly was hunting for.

"Don't mind me, I'm just here for the experience," he told her, grinning to himself.

"A gentleman would have volunteered to do this for me," Tilly grunted, still trying get a grip of something out of Sam's sight.

"Not if he knew what he would be missing out on," mused Sam to himself.

"Got it. Christ knows how the old man ever got to it. Must have been a flexible old sod."

"Pensioners' yoga?" suggested Sam.

"Ha, only if it was on a golf course," said Tilly, rolling from under the unit. She held up a long narrow key. "Safe number one."

Standing, she strode into the bedroom and opened up one of the inbuilt cabinets. Kneeling, she threw out a number of well-worn leather-strapped sandals, then fitted the key into its lock. Turning the key until the metal safe opened, she stood back to allow Sam to take the first look.

"There you go, I bet you dinner tonight you won't find anything useful in there."

Sam moved past her to kneel down in between the wardrobe's wooden doors. He reached down into the safe's interior and searched. His hands moved through the open air banging against the cold metal on either side.

"Finished yet?" Tilly called out from where she stood above him.

Ignoring her, he stretched further into the safe's depths, feeling his fingers brush against something soft. He ran his fingers over the object, feeling a leather covering over a flat surface. Finding the item's edge, he gripped it then lifted it out of the safe's darkness and into the daylight.

"What is it?" said Tilly.

Sam turned the leather-bound book in his hand then opened the cover to reveal the first page. Spread across it were rows of photos that had been printed out and then stuck to the page. The pair of them looked down to see a far younger version of Tilly Birks smiling cheerfully up at them. Each photo showed the young girl happily making her way through childhood, her parents also appearing at random intervals amongst the photos of family holidays, birthdays, Christmases and other family gatherings. The book was full of them.

Gently Sam passed the book on to Tilly. "I'd say he kept his greatest treasures in this safe."

Tilly did not reply at first. Instead, she gently fingered the pages, her eyes gazing over her memories.

"You would never make a good doctor, Mr Taylor, you would

be far too sentimental but I do appreciate the thought. I didn't think my dad had it in him to be honest." Reaching the last page she firmly closed the family album shut. "Well, something to look at later."

Sam raised an eyebrow.

"Don't give me that puppy dog look, we've a job to do. Was there anything else in that box or can we move on to the real stuff?"

"There was nothing else," said Sam with a sigh.

"Very good, now let me show you a real safe." She placed the album on the bed, then turned from the room to set out across the landing into the study.

A curious Sam followed wondering what this secret safe would or even could reveal. He had been bemused at the finding of the family album, the sentiment behind the bound photos had made Tilly's clinical exterior crack just a little.

"Right, Mr Detective, can you tell me where you would hide a safe in here?" Tilly challenged him.

"Not a clue, I've already tried and failed in that endeavour," admitted Sam.

Her hazel eyes gleamed with the joy of knowing more than her companion. "One thing my dad loved probably even more than me was golf. Although why I had no idea, what a stupid sport. In fact, I bet you play it."

"Not since I was a teenager."

"Yes, well, all you have to remember when it comes to my dad is if it's important then it's on the golf course." She turned to the painting of the local golf course hung on the white wall. Reaching out, she took hold of the wooden frame then lifted it free from its hanging.

"Now that's a safe of a retired spy," said Sam with a chuckle.

The pair of them looked at the safe embedded into the painted wall. Its edges had been completely fitted into the concrete leaving barely a lip to give its presence away. The whole device had been securely fitted behind the painting, which without

Tilly's knowledge would have remained hidden. Unlike its counterpart in the bedroom, this safe was state-of-the-art, there would be no simple key to access its secrets. Instead, a keypad had been fitted to one side of the opening lever.

"I hope you also know how to open it?" Sam said.

"Me too, it has been a while," admitted a concerned Tilly.

Sam watched on as she started to press a combination of digits on the keypad. Electronic beeps followed as her finger pressed the rubber buttons down. The first attempt failed, as did the second.

"I'm hoping it doesn't have an automatic shutdown if you have too many failed attempts," muttered Sam.

"No shit, Sherlock," answered a visibly flustered Tilly.

The doctor stepped back a moment. Putting her hands on her hips she looked at Sam. "I'm struggling to think what else it could be."

"There's no point looking to me for help. There must be a failsafe way of getting inside in case the battery on the lock fails?" he suggested.

She dismissed the suggestion. "No, it's connected to the mains. I can only think of one other possibility."

"How confident are you? I'm serious about it automatically shutting down if we get it wrong too many times."

"There's only one way to find out," Tilly said, pressing four buttons.

The sound of the electronic lock moving open echoed around the room, causing both of the occupants to relax again. A relieved Tilly opened up the metal door before peering inside.

"That's more like it," she announced, reaching inside to remove the contents then placing them on the desk. "What do you think of that?"

Sam stepped closer and looked down at the safe's contents spread across the work surface. What did he think? The question was well put and he was unsure what to say. Placed neatly on the table were three passports, four bundles of cash, one pistol with two spare ammunition clips, a set of keys, something that looked like a giant black pen and a small pocket diary.

"I have no idea," admitted Sam, picking up the passports.

There were three, two of which were British and Spanish passports containing a photo of Selwin. It was the third that caused a surprised Sam to raise his eyebrow again.

"Look here." He showed the document to Tilly. "It's a Spanish passport in your name. Looks like he was planning for a rainy day."

Tilly nodded and pointed out the bundles of euros. "Twenty thousand euros as well, that would definitely help on a rainy day."

Sam next looked at the pistol. A Walther PDP Compact nine millimetre, the square-shaped metal looked almost ugly with its sharp corners but in the right hands it was a deadly weapon. He looked inside the mechanism and rechecked the safety before handing it over to its new owner.

"Interesting choice," said Sam as Tilly took the weapon.

"Why? Dad always liked his Walthers, I remember him taking me to the range when I was younger to fire a few rounds."

"So you know how to use it then?"

She gave him a withering stare. "Yes, I do, thank you and I'll be the one looking after it."

Sam moved on and picked up the next item from the collection. Realising what the giant-looking pen actually was his eyes lit up.

"You can keep the gun, I'm keeping this bad boy."

Tilly frowned as she looked at the device Sam was holding. "What the hell is that?"

"Watch this," said Sam, flicking a switch on the side. Tilly stepped back as a long metal pole extended out of Sam's hand.

"This is a telescopic baton or expandable baton depending on who you ask."

"A what?"

"Basically a retractable stick, you see the police use them

during crowd-control operations. I bet you can leave a nasty bruise with one of these. I've always fancied trying one out."

Tilly sighed. "Boys and their toys."

"Bit naughty of your dad to have one though, they are illegal back home," he told her as he pushed the extended metal back into the handle.

"You can keep it for next time someone disturbs your sleep. I bet you can fit it in your boxers," she teased.

Sam pocketed the device, quietly pleased with his discovery. *Boys and their toys indeed*, he mused. He next picked up the small keys from the desk.

"What is it about your family and keys?"

"Don't ask, I sometimes think it's an addiction."

Unlike the main house keys there were just two small silver ones on this ring, both with the number eighty-nine etched on their heads.

"What do you think they open?" asked Tilly.

Turning them in his fingers Sam replied, "I was going to ask you the same thing. Based on their size I can only guess they open something small like a drawer, cupboard or locker. Is there anything in the villa like that?"

"Nothing that would require keys, there's only these two safes."

"And the importance of the number?"

"Eighty-nine? I've not got a clue."

Sam placed the keys back on the desk, completely stumped by the mystery of what they opened.

"That just leaves the diary," commented Tilly, picking up the small book.

Leaning in, Sam watched as Tilly skimmed through the pages. "I wonder why he kept it in the safe. Anything interesting?"

Tilly did not answer at first as she continued thumbing through the pages. Reaching that week's pages she stopped.

"There's names on here. Look, even on the day he died."

Sam took the diary and read the last days of Selwin's life. The first appointment had been on the Monday with an L Fernández. Then nothing on the Tuesday but on the Wednesday, the day he had died, Selwin had plans to meet a C Sheridan.

"Do you recognise any of the names?"

"Nope," Tilly answered honestly.

Sam looked back through the diary. "Look here. Wednesday was the second time he had met with Sheridan. He'd met them the week before as well."

"That's if he actually met with them?" suggested Tilly.

"What do you mean?"

"He died on the Wednesday, who's to say he wasn't to meet them until later that day? There's no time written down in here."

Sam nodded. "Good point, I wonder if he kept any phone numbers inside?"

Searching through the rest of the pages he failed to find any telephone numbers, but on reaching the final few pages he paused. On the spare blank pages at the end of the book a list of eight names were scrawled in an untidy hand.

He held up the diary. "I recognise these names, they are the same ones he asked his old workmates to look up. They were all in the report I was given before I flew over."

Tilly took the small book and looked at the names. "Interesting. It's a shame we can't link them to one of the appointments he had prior to his death."

Sam shook his head. "I think we can make an educated guess."

"What do you mean?"

He motioned to the diary in her hands. "What day last week did he meet with Sheridan?"

Tilly looked into the diary. "Tuesday?"

Sam pulled out his phone and brought up the case report Emma had sent him the previous day. Flicking through the documents until he found when the information had been sent to Selwin, he answered, "He put in the information request that same afternoon. I don't think he met anyone else that day, yes?"

"Nope, nor the day before."

"Then we can take an educated guess that it had been something from his interaction with this C Sheridan which led to him asking about these names, yes?"

Tilly thought about it for a moment. Sucking in her cheeks she looked out of the window to the street below. "I guess it's all we have to go on at the moment. I take it neither you nor your team found anything interesting on the names he provided?"

"Nope, I read the whole report in the airport. They were pretty average people, the only common trend was they were all dead. I mean that and the usual, they were all living out here so had that going for them."

"That could be something, it's a pretty small community out here so they will have had other things in common which they wouldn't even have thought about."

"Such as?" asked a curious Sam.

"Well, a doctor for a start, I feel like I see the whole town back home. I know more about the community than any of the gossips."

"Good point."

"I'm willing to bet most of the expats who live out here all use the same companies. Word of mouth is a powerful tool, I bet these old biddies are all sheep when it comes to dealing with the locals."

Sam considered Tilly's point for a moment. The argument made sense, a good English-speaking business who could earn the trust of all these pensioners would have a loyal customer base for years. "I'll have the guys back home have a deeper search and see if we can't find any links."

Putting the bundles of euros and passports back into the safe, but keeping everything else, the two of them returned to their breakfast table. Stepping back out into the open air Sam immediately felt the heat prick at his skin. It wouldn't be long before the sweat returned.

Tilly noticed his discomfort. "I think I'll have to take you shopping later, otherwise you'll melt."

"I honestly don't know how people live in this heat," Sam said with a sigh, sitting back in his chair. He poured himself another glass of orange juice to try and combat the rising temperature.

"You'll acclimatise eventually," Tilly said, laughing and dropping the diary on the table. "Right, now we've got all this where does it leave us?"

Sam scratched his stubble-covered chin while he considered the question. "Well, I think we are in agreement that your dad did not commit suicide of his own free will. If it was even suicide."

Tilly nodded. "Agreed."

"We know he was looking into this list of names and we guess it was something to do with this Sheridan person."

"I concur."

"Wow, bringing out the medical terms now?"

"Shut it before I shut it for you."

Smiling, Sam continued. "I think we can say something about this list got your dad killed and I think that's what we've got to somehow get to the bottom of. Find the connection, find the killers. Preferably without the same thing happening to us."

"Is that a risk?"

"Almost certainly. Look what happened to me last night. Especially since I'm not sure we can trust the police."

Tilly looked up from her breakfast in surprise. "We can't?"

"I'm not convinced," he admitted before telling her about Officer Mata's and Officer Picque's disappearance during the night.

She looked at him, concern etched on her face. "Jesus, that's a worry. Do you think they were in on it?"

"I don't know, I hope not. It could just have been a coincidence that it happened when they were gone but I don't like too many coincidences."

Tilly pushed a hand under her shirt and rubbed her bare shoulder. "What did the old fool get himself into? Seriously, this is supposed to be a town full of retired people. My mum literally dragged him out here to get away from all of that, now look where it got him."

Sam laughed and ran his hand through his hair. "I wouldn't get too worked up. It's just a normal day for me. I'm just pleased I've not been shot at yet. I've not even told you about the pathologist."

Her hazel eyes widened. "What about the pathologist?"

"Let's just say I'll be interested in your professional opinion on him. It seems he's a bit of a player in all this."

Tilly shook her head in bewilderment. "Is there anyone we can actually trust in all this?"

"At the moment I'd say that's a negative. When I was in the army we'd have said our list of allies is pretty thin."

"You were in the army?"

"Captain in the Royal Military Police."

"Impressive – and you still got beaten up last night?"

"I was literally in nothing but my boxers, plus next time I'll have your dad's expandable baton to knock some sense into whoever it was."

Tilly put down her glass on the table and looked around her deceased father's garden. The greenery was in full bloom, the neatly planted flowers colourful in the simmering sun. The lush grass glinted under the light as the water from the morning's sprinklers evaporated into the air.

"Right then, we better get started, if it's just us two against the world we might as well crack on."

Admiring the woman's drive, Sam pushed his chair back, stood up and put out his hand. "Doctor Birks, shall we begin?"

Tilly took the proffered hand and stood up. She was almost as tall as Sam, the pretty face set stern, ready for the day's events.

"Indeed we shall, Captain Taylor."

NINE

SAM DROVE the pair of them down from the southern headland, then across the bay to the old town, where they planned to start by visiting the police station. Tilly sat in the passenger seat, her head bent over Sam's iPad, studying the list of names requested by her father. A list of names they were now pretty confident had killed him.

"I was right about the connections," she told him, tapping the screen.

"You were?" replied Sam, concentrating on the road ahead.

"Well, in terms of their solicitors, all of the financials relating to their estates were prepared by a firm called *Dos Árboles Verdes*."

"Two Green Trees?" translated Sam.

"Perhaps we should give them a visit?"

"Maybe, I'll still ask the office to delve deeper. I'd like to go in knowing everything first. Was there anything strange in any of the wills?"

Tilly shook her head. "Nothing that springs to my mind, only that…" She trailed off, flicking through the documents on the screen. "Yes, none of the estates I can see on here have any references to property. That's peculiar, for most of these people the biggest asset they would have had would have been their homes, but there's nothing in their documents referring to them."

Sam took the car round a corner before answering. "I never noticed that. I wonder why that is?"

Tilly turned off the iPad and threw it onto the back seat. "Could be a variety of reasons, one for your office to find out, I think."

The maps application on the phone directed the car along the main road that crossed the length of the bay, the local police station being situated in the heart of the old town's centre as it rose up from the seafront. Around them the late-morning traffic was making the roads busy.

"Not the sleepy seaside resort is it?" Sam commented as he parked into a queue for the traffic lights.

"There always seems to be a buzz around Jávea. In the summertime it's all the holidaymakers renting summer lets or staying in hotels, then in winter all of the expats from across Europe descend back in their hundreds. In fact, Dad used to say the restaurants could be busier in winter."

"What do you think you will do with the place now he's gone?" Sam asked cautiously. He was still unsure how his companion was taking the recent loss of her father. While she had so far shown a tougher exterior to the events that had hit her family than he had expected, he was still worried of any cracks appearing.

"I'll have to sell up. It's a bit too far to fly from LA for a short break on the Costa Blanca, isn't it?"

"You don't fancy coming home? Even moving back to the UK?"

"Hell, no, as long as you can turn your nose up to the insurance system, working in the American healthcare system is far more rewarding. I make nearly twice as much as I would at home and with thirty per cent less hours."

The traffic lights turned green allowing Sam to proceed to the phone's route. "I take it there's no one else left on this side of the pond?"

"Nope, it's just me left now," said Tilly, looking out of her window.

There may have been a slight change in tone but Sam couldn't be sure.

"What about back on the other side of the pond? Any family over there?"

Tilly raised her eyebrows in exasperation. "I can tell you were a policeman in a past life. What's with all these questions? Normally someone would have bought me a bottle of wine before examining my lifestyle."

Now Sam laughed. "Touché. I'll wait till a time when you've got a glass in front of you then."

The phone vibrated as it directed them to turn left into the town's police station where Sam was stopped by a line of metal bollards fitted into the ground. "Looks like we will have to park up and walk back."

Driving on past their destination Sam pulled into the first side street to park the small rental car. Turning off the engine he looked at Tilly.

"How do you want to play this?" he asked her.

She looked back him quizzically. "What do you mean?"

"Well, we may find ourselves on the opposite side of the argument to our friendly European law enforcement officers and I'm not sure they will take kindly to being contradicted."

"Oh I see, I take it you don't want me to walk in and piss everyone off demanding they find my dad's killer?"

Sam grinned then rubbed his chin. "I mean if that's what you wanted I'd of course follow your lead. But I'd suggest we perhaps be a bit more gentle, let's see what they have to say. Try to gauge who's pulling the strings."

"You mean the pathologist?"

"Maybe, I just get the feeling something else is going on here and I don't want to burn any bridges until I've got a clear view of the land."

Tilly climbed out of the car. "Agreed. I'll play it nicely. I take it you don't want to mention your visitor last night?"

Sam opened his door and joined her on the street. "No, I think we can keep that to ourselves for now."

"I really don't know what you're worried about, it's not like I can kick off a fuss."

Sam eyed her, highly doubting the downplaying of her apparent ability to kick off. "And why's that?"

"I can't speak a word of Spanish."

"Hmmm, I'm sure you would be able to find a way. Tell me you've left the gun in the car?"

"Do I look like I'm going to walk into a police station with a loaded gun? Relax, it's in the glove box next to your little baton toy."

Rejoining the main road the pair of them walked along the pavement up to the local police station. To their left they had a view of the bay stretching out from the old town's hillside. Ahead, the white-stoned station drew closer until they could see its details clearly. The building was a square modern design with the corners jutting off at various angles making the different rooftops look lopsided. A mixture of rectangular and square windows were fitted into the stone, adding to the unsymmetrical styling. Three flags hung flat from three poles just outside the main entrance. Sam recognised the blue and gold of the European Union alongside the red and yellow of the Spanish national flag then was slightly stumped by the third. Red and yellow stripes ran horizontally from a blue stripe running down the left-hand side.

Tilly noticed Sam's gaze. "The al se'ɲeɾa, or the Royal Senyera. It's the flag of the Valencian region."

"Impressive knowledge, Birks."

"Thanks to a boring but very well read father."

They climbed up a set of concrete steps towards the glass doors of the reception. Sam looked on hopefully, praying for the building to be air-conditioned, his back already damp. Reaching the final step he went to pull open the glass door then seeing the approaching officers hurriedly stepped back, pushing Tilly out of the way.

"Hey, what are you doing?" she demanded but was immediately answered as a group of green-shirted officers ran out of the building, their faces stern.

"I wonder what that's all about?" she asked.

Sam watched as the group ran to a line of parked cars which immediately blared to life, their blue lights flashing menacingly.

"It never rains but it pours," he muttered.

"What?"

"Never mind, come on," he told her, heading into the building's reception area.

A wave of cold air hit him like a welcome hug, embracing his body as the air conditioning made its presence felt. Sam could have cheered as he felt his body temperature immediately start to fall to a more comfortable level.

"Crickey, it's cold in here," complained Tilly, rubbing her arms.

"Don't start," Sam warned as he walked to the reception where a middle-aged man looked up to greet him.

"*Hola*, how can I help you?"

"We've come to meet with the commissioner, we are expected. Sam Taylor and Tilly Birks, we are from the British government."

The man gave no reaction to the announcement of their representation of the British government – instead, he asked them politely to take a seat while he called it in. Doing as they were told, the pair of them sat on a line of plastic chairs facing into the open reception area. Sam watched as a range of people went about their business. Most of those around him were out of uniform, dressed in formal work attire. Three more officers came running out of a doorway to follow their colleagues urgently out of the main entrance.

"Well, something's rocked the boat," commented Sam dryly.

"I'm glad I'm not at the end of it," added Tilly.

Sam began to respond before having his attention drawn to the station entrance once more where unlike their colleagues heading in the opposite direction, two officers walked inside. Recognising them from the previous evening he stood up, a red mist descending over him, the memory of the lost fight with the unknown intruder erupting in his mind and his warning to Tilly to keep the peace completely forgotten.

"Hey, you two, where the hell did you go last night?"

Officers Mata and Picque looked over at him, shock at his tone of voice etched across their faces.

Sam marched over to the uniformed men then repeated, "Where the hell did you go?"

The officers gave each other a bemused stare before Mata answered. "We were called to a disturbance, there was a fight at the Arenal."

"What happened to protecting the villa?"

Officer Picque answered. "It was not our decision, anyway you were there. Nothing happened, I can see you are okay. What, did you expect for us to babysit you?"

Sam was about to reply then stopped, he remembered no one but he and Tilly knew about the intruder. At the very least publicly the two officers seemed to have been clueless, what they knew privately was a different matter. He stared at the two men, trying to read their implacable faces. Two sets of brown eyes stared defiantly back at him.

"It would have been nice to have had some warning," he muttered.

"It was two am in the morning, we thought you'd prefer the sleep," Mata responded coolly.

Sam felt a hand on his arm as Tilly spoke gently. "I think we can talk to the commissioner about the villa's protection."

As she began to pull him away from the two officers Sam couldn't resist a final tester.

"I've managed to fix the air conditioning in the other room by the way, I should be able to sleep comfortably in there tonight. I found the other room not to my liking."

Neither of the officers replied, instead with a final shrug of their shoulders they turned away and headed off to start their shifts.

Sam felt a firm blow on his arm as Tilly punched him. "What was that for?"

"What happened to playing it cool?"

"Fair point but I bought those two pizzas and for all I know they set me up for a beating."

Tilly raised her hands, wiggling her fingers to mock him. "Oh wow, a pizza. Well, that could turn even the most ardent criminal."

Sam ignored the jibe. Instead he sat back on the plastic chair to stew over the two officers. Someone had known about the open window, whoever it was last night had been told how to get inside, he was certain of it.

The sound of doors being pushed open and footsteps pounding over the polished floor caused them both to look up. Entering the reception area, dressed in an immaculate green uniform was a middle-aged woman. Short, with narrow cropped grey hair over a hard face, Sam could tell immediately from the woman's expression that this was the town's commissioner. He had seen enough commanding officers in his time to recognise the aura of confidence and authority within this woman. There even seemed to be a slight march in her footsteps as she walked towards them.

"Señor Taylor? Señora Birks? I am Commissioner Ana Moreno. Welcome to Jávea." She greeted them in English. Reaching out a hand she turned to Tilly first. "Señora Birks, I am truly sorry about your father, it is a terrible tragedy."

"Thank you."

Next, the commissioner turned towards Sam. "Señor Taylor, I am most grateful for your help in this matter. Please believe me when I say me and my officers will be happy to offer any support you may need."

"Thank you, Commissioner, I appreciate that."

Ana Moreno gave a brief smile then indicated for them to follow her further into the station. "Let us talk in my office. I'm sure you have quite a few questions."

"Well, she seems nice," whispered Tilly as they followed the commissioner out of the reception.

"Don't count your chickens just yet, I'm sure there's time to upset her."

Reaching her office, Moreno opened the door and beckoned the pair of them inside. "Would either of you like a drink?" she asked as they each took a seat round a coffee table in one corner of the large office.

Both Sam and Tilly declined the offer, instead Sam indicated the long glass window which looked over the bay and out to sea.

"Not a bad perk of the job."

"It does have its moments. Before we start, let me apologise in advance for my English – it is not my strong suit."

"Don't knock yourself," said Sam. "Probably better than my Spanish."

"It is definitely better than mine," added Tilly.

Sam cleared his throat, these polite exchanges were beginning to bore him. "Commissioner, could we discuss the case please? I'd be interested to hear where you and your teams have got to."

Moreno's eyes flashed over Sam, weighing him up. "I'm afraid we don't have much of an update. At the moment we are still treating it as a suicide."

"Really?"

"Yes really, Señor Taylor. Our pathologist has been quite clear in his assessment that Señor Birks injured himself." Moreno said the final words softly while giving Tilly a sympathetic glance.

"Come off it, why would my dad kill himself in such a way? I trust you know what he did in his professional career? Surely if he was going to kill himself he would have found an easier way to go?"

Moreno leant back in her chair clasping her hands together as she did so. "I completely understand your point of view and at first I was in complete agreement with you."

"At first?" said Sam.

"Yes, at first I found it hard to comprehend the method in which Señor Birks chose to end his life So I had a secondary post-mortem completed by an external pathologist from the next town. He concurred with our own, Señor Birks killed himself."

Sam gave Tilly a sideways look – the news about the secondary post-mortem was new. It was one thing to have one suspect pathologist covering up a murder but two independent assessments?

Not quite ready to accept the commissioner's word, Sam continued. "What about the rest of the scene, the broken vase, the spilt wine?"

Moreno shifted uncomfortably. "Yes, well I understand what you're saying but the science…"

"The science doesn't mean anything without context," snapped Sam. "There's nothing else to suggest that this was a suicide."

"Apart from the fingerprints on the murder weapon? Perhaps the question should be what is there exactly that suggests it *wasn't* a suicide?"

Sam found himself without an answer. There was no actual evidence to suggest any foul play in Selwin's death. The only thing driving any other hypothesis was pure gut instinct.

Moreno attempted to break the silence. "Look, we are aware that this doesn't exactly look right and we are happy to keep all options open."

"Which means?" a sceptical Sam asked.

"Which means we will give you any support you may need."

"Which basically means you're leaving me to it?"

Again the commissioner shifted uncomfortably. "We only have

limited resources here as you can appreciate I'm sure. It's a busy time for us with the summer tourists, the fiesta this weekend and now we've just had word of another murder." She stopped, then flushed, realising her choice of words.

"A murder?" said a shocked Sam, ignoring the commissioner's Freudian slip.

"Yes, we've just had word this morning. As you can imagine I can't tell you any more at this moment in time. In truth, I don't know any more myself."

Sam ran his hand through his hair, a range of thoughts flying through his mind. He couldn't help but wonder if this murder had anything to do with Selwin's killing. He was sure he'd find out more as the day went on. In the short term he had to concentrate on Selwin's death.

"Back to the original case, does this mean that you can offer us nothing in relation to investigating Señor Birk's death?"

Moreno shook her head. "Only what we've already provided, if we find or learn anything more I will ensure you are the first to be told. In the meantime you are welcome to carry out your own inquiries with my complete blessing."

So that was it, mused Sam. The local authorities were distancing themselves from the case and by simply allowing Sam to crack on with his own efforts they were protecting themselves from any future pushback. On one hand, the apparent disregard to the murder, for that was what it was, irked him. On the other, he could just about understand their position – if the science said one thing then Moreno would be hard pushed to contradict it.

"I take it you will allow us access to anything we need?" asked Sam, his tone cold.

"Yes," Moreno answered. She bit her lip as if in debate about whether to say what was really on her mind. "I understand this will be all very frustrating for you both, especially you, Señora Birks, and I'm truly sorry. But please believe me when I say my hands are tied. I – like everyone – have to answer to someone. You need to understand there is more than just my voice that is heard by those in power."

"You mean your pathologist," guessed Sam.

Commissioner Moreno did not answer the question directly. "For what it's worth, I do not believe Señor Birks killed himself of his own free will."

"That makes three of us," added Tilly.

"You will find there is more than three of us," Moreno said. "Please do not make the assumption that me and my team are fools. I am quite aware there is something happening in my town. But my own hands are tied."

Sam gave the diminutive commissioner a long stare, taking in the sharp uniform, the obvious years of service. The last admission had been given freely, said almost as a warning to them both. Or potentially a plea for help.

"Your hands may be tied, Commissioner, but mine are certainly not."

TEN

ANA MORENO STARED at the two foreigners for a moment as if trying to weigh them up. Her lined face looked strained, thought Sam, sitting there, as if a thirty-year career had been compressed into only a few years of service. The commissioner eventually broke the silence by standing up and indicating the door.

"I thank you for your sentiments, Señor Taylor. If you don't mind, I must return to oversee this latest incident."

Sam, knowing he wasn't going to get anything else from this interview, took the hint and rose from his seat.

"Can I ask what your next course of action will be?" asked Moreno.

Sam eyed Tilly then answered. "I think I'd like to speak with your pathologist. I'd be interested to hear his side of things. You know, see the science and all that."

Tilly added in support, "And I need to officially identify the body."

Moreno gave the briefest of smiles in approval of their plans. "I think that would be a good place to start. Yet, allow me to give you a piece of advice. Doctor Serrano can be a little, er…" She trailed off, trying to find the right world. "Difficult – he is very dedicated to his job."

"So I've heard. I think I understand the situation."

The commissioner began to lead them towards the door. "Doctor Serrano has many friends in this town, some even higher than a police commissioner."

Sam and Tilly nodded along, both getting the unspoken message hidden amongst the words. Ana Moreno, like the majority of people, had to report to someone and Sam would have been willing to bet that that someone was friendly with Doctor Serrano. Nothing more was said beyond mere pleasantries as the commissioner escorted them back down to the reception area. As they stepped into the public entrance she stopped and held out her hand.

"I wish you more luck than we have had, my friends," the hard-faced Moreno said.

Sam took her hand and clasped it tightly. "Me too."

Tilly took her offered hand, then they all headed their different ways – Sam and Tilly back towards the foreboding glass doors, which the Yorkshireman knew would mean back into the Spanish sauna. Reaching to push the door open for them both, Sam found himself moving backwards to avoid oncoming traffic. Four uniformed officers were hurriedly marching a young woman up the stairs towards them. Sam paused to allow the group to push past. There seemed to be an unspoken tension amongst the four officers as they guided their prisoner up the stairs and into the reception area. All four seemed to be bristling with excitement as they physically moved the girl between them.

"Out of the way," one of the officers snapped at Sam who, having already given more than enough space, neglected to move any further. Instead, he nonchalantly moved his gaze over to the prisoner.

The young woman would in normal circumstances have been quite the looker, thought Sam. But now, caught between the firm grips of these officers, the girl looked dishevelled. Tears were running down her face which seemed consumed by terror. Her bright eyes were now glistening as they looked about for help. The girl's attire only added to the pathetic scene, a white T-shirt barely covering the bikini underneath.

Between the sobs her hoarse voice was heard pleading in English. "Please help me. I didn't do it. You have to believe me."

The final word came out as a moan as she was half carried, half dragged into the station. Sam looked over to Tilly, the same look of pity as his etched over her face.

"The murderer?" she asked him in almost disbelief.

"They come in all shapes and sizes," answered Sam truthfully. Over the years he had seen many unlikely killers. However, something about this girl did not suggest she was a murderer. But then again what did he know?

"Come on, if you're interested I'll message the office. She was clearly English so no doubt my department will be hearing about it soon. I'll drop Hannah a text and she will be all over it."

Sam paused at the automatic use of Hannah's name, he had forgotten she was on her romantic break. The thought twisted in his stomach.

"Well, someone will be able to tell us. I've no doubt I'll be dragged back here. As I said when we came in, it never rains but it pours."

The two of them walked gently back to the car, careful not to over-exert themselves in the midday heat. Once safely back inside the air-conditioned car Tilly asked Sam what he had thought of the morning's events.

"Bloody painful," he answered honestly.

"What do you mean?"

"Where do you want me to start? For one we are clearly on our own on this, the police won't have or can't have anything more to do with it. Everyone seems to have been outmanoeuvred by this Doctor Serrano."

"I'm looking forward to meeting this doctor," said Tilly.

Sam chuckled. "Careful, Doctor Birks, you don't want to go upsetting the good doctor too soon. You can leave that one to me."

Tilly scowled and looked out of the window. "What's the plan then?"

Sam shrugged still watching the road. "Let's just start by going and meeting the man. If we can shake a few trees, all the better."

Tilly turned her head back to his. "I keep thinking about that girl they brought in. She looked terrified. I don't think I've ever seen anyone look like that before and I've worked on the emergency ward."

Sam cast his mind back over the slim, scared figure trapped between the police escort. "I'm sure it will work itself out." He then let out a brief laugh. "She wasn't exactly covered in blood so it may turn out to be a mistake."

The local mortuary was housed in the main medical centre in the next town along the coast. Sam, choosing to follow the scenic tour, guided the car over the direct route over the northern headland and the foothills of *el Montgó*.

Indicating the mountain he asked, "Have you ever been to the top?"

Tilly tilted her head to stare up at the peak. "Once, there's a car park along here where you can find the path that goes to the top. It's a tough walk but worth it."

Sam, conscious of his warm attire, replied, "I'll take your word for it."

Like most western medical buildings the *Hospital de Dénia* was square and clad in white. The large building hardly needed the large sign welcoming visitors to its gates, mused Sam. It was as if all the architects in the west had gone through the exact same design course, until now it seemed every hospital was the same template of white, square buildings.

"Right, so this is my territory, Captain," warned Tilly as Sam parked the car. "You will be best following my lead."

"And do what, act as your translator?" said Sam sourly.

"Now wouldn't that be nice?" Tilly flashed him a wide smile. "Come on, let's shake a few trees."

Sam did as he was instructed and followed Doctor Birks into the hospital. She seemed to automatically know where to go from the moment she entered the building. Without even stopping to ask for directions or to get Sam to translate the signs, she walked briskly through the main entrance, down the first corridor then down a flight of steps.

"Have you been here before?"

"No, but the first rule of these places is to put the morgue in the basement. Out of sight, out of mind. No one needs to see all of the ones you lost while trying to save the rest."

Stepping out of the stairwell they paused to decide on the next direction. The windowless corridor stretched off in both directions with only a small blue sign offering any direction.

"*Mortuorio* that way," said Sam helpfully.

Heading right, the two of them walked down the empty corridor, the only noise echoing from their feet on the hard floor. At the end of the corridor they came to a small waiting area where a nurse sat at a desk busily typing away at her computer. As the two new arrivals stepped forwards through the seating area the typing stopped and two heavily made-up eyes flicked up to greet them.

"*Hola*, can I help you?" she asked in Spanish.

Sam, ignoring Tilly's earlier instruction, answered back in Spanish. "Señor Taylor, here to meet Dr Serrano and Señora Birks here to identify her father. I think we are expected?"

The nurse's narrow face warmed at his introduction, almost forcing a smile from her firm expression. "Ah yes, we were expecting you. Normally someone from the police would accompany you for the formal identification but we've been advised Doctor Serrano and I will suffice."

Sam looked at Tilly and spoke in English. "She said it's just her and the doctor for the identification process."

Tilly nodded. "Fine with me."

There was just the slight hint of hesitation in her voice, thought Sam, as if the realisation she was about to see the body of her father was finally hitting home.

"Are you okay to continue, Señora Birks?" the nurse asked cautiously, also noticing the hesitation.

Sam repeated the question to Tilly.

"Of course I bloody am, and if you ask me that again I'll give you a kicking far worse than the one last night."

"We are not fighting already?" asked an English-speaking voice from behind them.

Sam and Tilly swirled round to see a short, bald, bespectacled man looking up at them. A round face smiled warmly at them in greeting. Standing there in his white lab coat, Sam couldn't help being reminded of Doctor Bunsen Honeydew, the green scientist from *The Muppet Show*.

"It is a curse of my profession that while I must say it is a pleasure to meet you both I am sorry to do so," the pathologist said. "I'm sorry, a professional joke. Although I'm sure you two are more than used to dealing with pathologists in your line of work."

Neither Sam nor Tilly replied.

"Anyway, let me begin by offering my sincere condolences for your loss, Miss Birks."

Sam noticed it had been the first time that day he had heard anyone use the English prefix, the man's English was damn near perfect.

"I'm sure you've guessed I am Doctor Serrano and this small corner of the hospital is my domain." He gestured to the nurse still sat at the desk. "And this is my assistant nurse, Señora Diaz. Shall we begin? I'm sure with your medical background, Miss Birks, this will seem quite familiar."

"Apart from the fact that it's the body of my father, yes, and you can call me Doctor Birks if that makes it easier," replied Tilly, tersely reminding the good doctor of her own medical authority.

Doctor Serrano put on a look of embarrassment before reaching out to take Tilly's arm. "Of course, how clumsy of me. Please allow me to take you in to see him."

The small doctor guided Tilly past the reception desk and through a pair of double doors. Silently Sam followed along with Nurse Diaz who gave him a searching look before moving past him. Entering the sterile room, Serrano guided Tilly to a line of metal refrigerated drawers, each with small name tags fixed to their handles. The sight reminded Sam of the countless mortuaries he'd seen in his career. He had grown accustomed to the soulless metal fridges. Watching on, he couldn't help but wonder what was going on in Tilly's head. He guessed a complex debate between the professional mind that had seen death a thousand times and the personal feelings of seeing her deceased father.

The Spanish doctor gently released his arm from Tilly's, placing her to one side of the first drawer. He made a pretence of reading the drawer's outer label before returning his gaze to the Englishwoman.

"Are you ready, Doctor Birks?"

Tilly gave a tight nod of acceptance. Sam held his breath, his eyes entirely on the woman in front of him.

Doctor Serrano unlocked the drawer then pulled out the stiff body of Selwin Birks, covered only by a thin white sheet. Everyone in the room held their breath a moment as they reset themselves for the next part. The pathologist slowly reached up to one end of the cloth, took a corner in each hand before cautiously pulling it back to reveal the grey face of Selwin Birks. Sam, still watching Tilly, saw the slightest flicker within her set features as her eyes looked down over the face below her. Tilly did not speak, instead she gently placed the palm of her hand on her father's forehead then removed it.

"That will do, Doctor," she said to the waiting Serrano. "You can put him back inside now."

Doctor Serrano bowed his bald head as he returned the sheet back over the dead man's face. Pushing the corpse back into the fridge the Spaniard relocked the door and turned to look at his guests.

"I can only offer you my deepest condolences," he said to Tilly.

"You can offer me more than that, I'd like to read your medical report if you will. I understand there was an English one written as well?"

Doctor Serrano's eyes twinkled behind his glasses, his face giving nothing away to his true thoughts. "Of course, I expected you to ask that. I'm sure you will be aware that my findings have been supported by an independent doctor."

"So I hear, but I think you can understand why I'm sceptical about your hypothesis of suicide? My father, even if he was suicidal, I'm sure would not have chosen such a method."

Serrano spread his arms out. "Who knows the thoughts of our loved ones in their desperate final moments. Suicide is not something acted upon by a sane mind."

Tilly took a step forwards and Sam could see for the first time a sense of strength within her. "While I understand you are speaking as a medical professional, I am still the daughter of the man you are referring to and I would ask you to consider your words."

Serrano, slightly taken aback, bowed his head. "Of course, please follow me. I suspected you would like to read the report and I have left an English copy on my desk over here."

Sam watched as Serrano guided Tilly to a desk on the opposite side of the room, where he pulled out a chair for her to sit on. Then, reaching over, he passed her a file of papers.

"Please take all the time you need."

Expecting to be waiting a while Sam began to wander around the pathologist's lab, looking at the various signs on the walls and at the tools of the doctor of the dead.

"Have you been working here long?" he asked Serrano.

"Six years this November."

"Enjoy it?"

Serrano shrugged. "It is not a job you enjoy, it is one you either find interesting or you do not sign up for."

"Now that I understand. Not a job for the weak-stomached."

"No, and I have seen inside enough stomachs."

Sam let out a brief smile at the jest. Time to shake the tree.

"From what I understand, Doctor, you seem to have been pretty successful in your time here. Your reputation preceded you long before we arrived."

"I do my best," acknowledged Serrano.

"Is it standard practice in Spain for a pathologist to be so heavily involved in a police investigation?" asked Sam.

"I only do what I can to help," replied Serrano, becoming wary of where Sam was going.

"Sorry, I only ask as I've never heard of a pathologist going over the police's heads in a murder case." Sam was shooting in the dark here. Commissioner Moreno had not quite admitted to Serrano going over her head, only hinted at it.

"Is it a crime to be friends with the mayor? To help save valuable police time in chasing dead ends when the science is absolute? Then yes, I admit to it all."

Sam was about to retort when Tilly interrupted him. "I wouldn't bother, Sam. The doctor is correct in his findings. I can see that here with the angles and depths of the lacerations. I don't dispute that his hypothesis is scientifically accurate." She said the words almost bitterly.

"My thanks, Doctor Birks," said Serrano, now smiling at Tilly who, slightly pale, continued reading the report.

Sam, deflated, decided to move on to another track. "I have another question for you, Doctor, one which is slightly off-topic."

"Go on."

He reached into his pocket and pulled out the small diary that once belonged to Selwin Birks. Flicking to the back pages he read out a few names.

"I don't suppose you remember any of these names do you, Doctor?"

Doctor Serrano fidgeted uncomfortably and moved round to lean on one of the cabinets. "Yes, I remember a couple which stand out. But I see many cases, Mister Taylor, as you can imagine they all merge into a blur."

Sam, now walking back round the laboratory, continued. "Yes, I can understand that, but help me out, do you remember if they all died of natural causes?"

Doctor Serrano did not reply immediately, instead he rubbed his chin in thought. As he did so, Sam noticed for the first time since they had entered, Nurse Diaz standing to one side of her boss looking strangely at him, an odd look in her eyes as if she was trying to answer his question by facial expression alone.

The pathologist finally answered. "Yes, I'm quite sure. Obviously I can check them out for you to be one hundred per cent certain if you'd like?"

Sam, expecting the answer, shook his head. He gave Nurse Diaz another glance but could not quite read the expression etched on her face. He wished he could get Tilly to notice. Still walking around the room he paused at the remaining drawers which held the mortuary's deceased. Next to Selwin he read the name of Mateo Blanco and was surprised by the date of birth written underneath.

He pointed at the label. "Bit young to be in here?"

"They come in every shape, size and age as I'm sure you're aware," answered Serrano sadly. "This one is also a suicide, he was found at the bottom of *el Montgó* a couple of days ago. We are just waiting for his family to raise enough money for a funeral. I hear a local businessman has offered to pay the costs."

"I'm sorry to hear it," said Sam, moving on.

Doctor Serrano, seeing Sam's movement to the next drawer, continued. "And in there is one of your countrywomen, a tragic case. Mrs Carla Sheridan, seventy-eight, died from falling down her stairs just the other day. Left to die all alone in her home. It is very sad."

Sam had not heard the final words, instead his mind had

jumped to life at the corpse's name. Carla Sheridan, it was too much of a coincidence. He didn't need to check the diary to be sure, Sam already knew the last person Selwin Birks had been scheduled to meet on the day of his death had been a C Sheridan. Now they were here together again, only this time in death.

ELEVEN

CARLES CASILLAS STEPPED onto the bridge of the old fishing trawler, stopped and then waited nervously for his captain to notice him. He felt the rusting metal boat beating its way through the soft Mediterranean surf beneath his feet, as they made their way ever closer to their destination. The thick iron hull gently rocked under him as they headed further northwards, the days since they had first left the calm waters of the Jávea Bay having now all blended into one. Standing there on the bridge of the vessel carrying him home, he felt his knees shake slightly. Clenching his hands to calm his nerves he allowed himself to take a few steps to steady himself. In front of him, embedded in the wooden control panel, the navigation screen flashed up their position as they crept closer to the Spanish coastline and their home port.

For at least the twentieth time on this voyage alone, Carles promised himself this would be the final trip, that as soon as they were back home he would tell the Chief he wanted out. It wasn't as if there were no other opportunities within the scruffy bastard's empire. He had worked for the Chief nearly his entire life, from boy to man. But now something had changed, he had seen things he could not now unsee. He was no longer able to just forget and move on with his life no matter how much he wanted to.

"Have you checked on the cargo, Carles?" the captain, finally noticing the younger man, asked gruffly.

"Yes, sir."

The captain, a gruff old sailor used to the hard lifestyle of the trawler, grunted in reply. "And?"

"And everything is okay, well, it is still the same as yesterday. There are still the same problems below."

"Which means we are still going to lose some more units."

Carles shifted on his feet nervously. "We are doing our best, sir. But it is too cramped, too full."

"But you're not the one having calls with the Chief having to explain why his profits are down." He shook his weather-worn face in disgust. "We took on too many this time, I told him we were overloaded, but does the hairy oaf ever listen?"

Carles remembered the scene at the African port and the looks on the crew's faces as they'd seen the amount they would have transport on this crossing. All around them the chaos of the port town had been battering their senses as they tried to accomplish their mission. Angry words had been exchanged, made even more threatening by the language barrier as both sides tried to put their arguments into broken English. The captain had stoically tried to stand his ground with one of the locals, but had been met by only the round muzzle of the AK-47 held to his face.

The captain now looked away from Carles and stared forlornly out of the salt-covered glass windows of the bridge. "How many trips is this now for you, Carles?"

"This is my fourth time to Africa. Although I've spent years sailing for the Chief."

"And how many units have you seen us lose while at sea?"

Carles bit his lip as he considered the question. He had flinched at the captain's use of the official terminology the crew were supposed to use when describing their cargo. A cargo which was now stored beneath their feet in the boat's groaning hold, that would have once been filled by thousands of fish. If the captain had seen his crew member flinch at his words he chose to ignore it.

Carles eventually answered. "I think at least three or four per trip."

"There you go, it happens. Trust me, it is best not to think about it, just keep your mind focused on the money."

Now that was a fair point. Carles would make more on this trip than he did in six months working on the fishing fleet. He even had to spend less time at sea to earn it. That fact alone had been enough to pass him through the previous journeys. Still, the thought of what they were actually bringing into the country made him queasy.

The captain could see his words had had no effect on his younger shipmate. He shook his head and checked his watch. The afternoon was passing by and even when floating in the middle of the sea, the summer sun was intense. The limited breeze that buffeted their small boat made no difference to the sweat-covered crew. Deciding to bend the rules slightly, he walked to the back of the bridge to a small fridge fixed to the floor. Returning with two cold beers he handed one to Carles and opened his own.

"My friend, let me tell you something, life is all about making yourself comfortable. You live, you scrape by and then you die. Everything else you do in between is up to you. All these fools who spend their lives worrying about good and bad, God and all the rest have only themselves to blame. Look at me! This is my thirteenth trip for the Chief, I make seven more and I retire years before I would have done if I'd stayed catching fish."

Carles just drank from his beer bottle. The captain's words sounded hollow.

"Whatever, we will be back in Jávea in two days and the cargo will be someone else's problem. I bet within a month you will be looking at your bank balance and counting down the days until you're back here with me." He gave a deep cackle which seemed to screech from his throat. "Strippers don't come cheap, my friend."

Carles did not take the bait. Instead, he shuffled his feet slightly and waited for the older man to get over his attempt at humour.

As the laughter ended Carles asked a question he had been pondering for a while. "What actually happens to the cargo when we dock? Where does it all go?"

"How the hell should I know, and more importantly, why the hell should either you or I care?"

"But you're not even interested?" Carles persisted.

"You can get yourself in serious danger asking those sorts of questions, boy. Some things are just better unknown." The captain saw Carles's face and, realising he wasn't going to drop the subject, drained his beer. "Look, boy, we load the cargo onto the lorries, the men in suits count the units and we get paid. There's nothing else to it."

"Apart from whatever is at the end of the supply chain," Carles said bitterly.

"I'm warning you as a friend to let this go. I don't know what has gotten into you, boy, but this isn't worth it. I called you up here to help you see sense, you know what could happen if you don't let it go." The final three words were said slowly, a warning to Carles.

"But–"

"There's no buts, Carles. I've warned you as a friend but now I'm telling you as your captain, leave it. It is not worth dying for."

These final words had gone beyond a warning and into a threat. Carles realised he had pushed too far this time and decided to take a step backwards. "I'm sorry, sir, it's just a wandering mind."

The captain studied the younger man, casting his eyes over him as he attempted to decide whether his words had done the trick. "Very well, go below and help prepare tonight's dinner. You can tell that oaf we have for a cook that I don't want another curry this evening."

Carles, realising he'd been dismissed from the bridge, took the hint.

"And make sure we open the Italian red, I don't want any more of that French piss on my table," the captain called out as Carles gratefully rushed out into the open air.

Now standing on the boat's deck, Carles was surprised to see his hands gripping the metal railings, his knuckles white with the tension. Inside, he could feel his heart pounding against his chest, he was struggling to keep control of his breathing. It was as if another man had left the boat's bridge, that the control he had felt while in his captain's presence had fallen into the deep blue sea.

"Steady, Carles," he told himself.

The captain was right about one thing, the warning was unnecessary for a man who had worked for the Chief for as long as he had. So what should he do? He was one man alone in the middle of the ocean. He tried to put the thought out of his mind and headed towards the galley, where almost certainly a drunken cook was trying to find the correct end of a frying pan. For the next hour he helped prepare the crew's evening meal, all the time allowing his mind to wander down to what was held in the boat's hold. Why, after all the other journeys, had he suddenly decided to grow a conscience? It was a question he asked himself as he cleaned up behind the boat's alcoholic cook. Sure, the money was good, the days short, and the work easier, but still, there was no point in wondering – he knew why and he cursed himself for it.

Why did he have to look inside? Three whole journeys he had managed to avoid having to go into the hold himself, instead leaving it to the other crew members. The closest he'd been to the cargo had been to watch the discarded units being tossed out to the open waters and the murky depths below. He cursed himself. There again he had used the same terminology used by the rest of the crew to describe what they were carrying. It was nothing more than a poor attempt at managing their psychology. A cheap trick by the Chief in order to somehow distance themselves from the act they were partaking in. It made him sick.

"I'm going to get some air," he called out to the cook, who just ignored him as he fought with the boat's oven.

Free once more, Carles stepped out into the ship's mess where two of his fellow crew members were sat watching a battered television. Like the cook before them neither reacted to his presence. Grateful for these small mercies Carles felt the prickle of temptation begin to take hold. The voice in his head told him to walk away, to find anything else to take his mind from what was below. Walking out of the mess he had meant to head back outside onto the main deck, to let the fresh sea beat out of him this dangerous temptation. But when faced by the metal staircase he found his feet descending the rungs. Instead of feeling the salt air of the Mediterranean he felt the close, stuffy air of the lower decks. Landing on the metal floor of the lower deck he paused, checking to see if he was alone. To one side of him the door to the engine room was slightly ajar. He peered in but could see no one inside. Steeling himself, he set off in the opposite direction. The historic smell of fish filled his nostrils as he quietly made his way to the wrought-iron door that led into the main hold.

Reaching the end of the passage he checked again to see if anyone else was around. The fear of discovery felt even closer now as he stood there next to the door. He moved to open a small window that allowed him to see once again the cargo which had led them across the sea. A cargo which had seen them stowed away in one continent and would eventually disappear into who knows where inside another. Whatever the captain or the Chief said to try and palm him off, he knew that the only thing driving this damned venture was money – blood money. Peering through the dirty glass into the dingy hold beyond, it took a moment for his eyes to adjust to the gloom. Again he checked behind him to see if any of the crew had followed him or were on their way out of the engine room. He was alone in the boat's depths. Turning back to the window he peered again into the hold but this time he knocked gently on the iron door. Moments later a pair of eyes looked back at him through the glass.

TWELVE

STANDING FROZEN IN THE MORTUARY, Sam felt a surge of excitement as his mind made the connections between the two dead bodies. A feeling which was quickly replaced by discomfort over what this new information meant. Whatever Selwin Birks had discovered about the list of names within his diary had not only got him murdered, it had also killed Carla Sheridan. It was if the spectre of death was circling ever nearer to him as he made his way through this strange landscape. Looking over towards Tilly he could see that she, too, had made the connection between the two deceased bodies. She had replaced the report onto Serrano's desk, her eyes wide at the new information.

"How do you know she had fallen down the stairs?" Tilly asked suspiciously.

Doctor Serrano simply batted the question away. "It is natural to presume such a cause of death when a body is found at the bottom of a staircase, is it not?"

Ask a silly question, expect a silly response, thought Sam.

Tilly, however, was not amused. Pursing her lips, she stood up from the desk chair and marched over towards the exit. "Thank you, Doctor Serrano, I have no further questions. While I cannot find anything wrong with your professional findings I have serious doubts about your judgement. If you honestly think my father's death was a suicide then I'm glad they only trust you with the dead bodies and not the living."

Impressed, Sam had to struggle to stop himself from laughing. Tilly, her opinion thoroughly expressed, made her way to the exit, violently pushing the doors out of her way.

"I'd apologise for my companion's behaviour, but I think she summed up everything quite well, don't you?" he asked the shocked pathologist.

"Grief is a difficult emotion to control," Serrano answered limply.

"Apparently so," said Sam, glancing past the doctor to where Nurse Diaz was still staring at him intently. He tried to think of a way to get rid of Doctor Serrano so he could speak to her privately but failed. Instead, he followed Tilly out of the lab back into the mortuary reception area.

"Come on, I need to get out of here," she told him the moment he stepped out.

"Now that is not a suggestion I'm going to argue with."

The pair of them set off back down the corridor in silence, both desperate to ask the other their opinion of what had just happened. Sam's mind was trying to process everything from the list of dead people all the way to the body of Carla Sheridan. Somewhere amongst the fog there had to be a connection. Selwin Birks had known it and that had got him killed. He wondered how close the ever-moving spectre of death was now.

Tilly only broke the silence as they stepped back into the afternoon sunlight. "I'm literally shaking, I'm so angry. I wanted to hit that smug bastard so much."

Sam gave his companion a gentle pat on the back. "You did well, it can't have been easy seeing your father like that."

"Yes, that was harder than I expected." She paused. "But I meant because of the report. Everything he wrote was correct. From the angles of the lacerations, to the depth of the blade, everything he said is medically correct. Pathologists around the world have studied all kinds of wounds, the level of knowledge now available proves what he said beyond doubt."

Shaking his head in disagreement, Sam said, "We already knew the science was against us before we arrived. It was never about disproving two separate pathologists, it was about trying to understand the man."

"And have we done that?"

Sam shrugged. "No. At least we now know who C Sheridan is."

"You mean, was?"

"Whatever, but I think it's safe to say whoever killed your dad probably helped old Sheridan down the stairs as well."

"I don't disagree with you, but how does it help? We still have no idea why."

"Patience, my dear doctor, one step at a time. What about the rest of the deceased, all of the names from your dad's list? Isn't it strange that they would all be done by the same pathologist?"

"Not if it's a small department. People die every day. There's nothing strange in that. The question is whether they died from natural or unnatural causes."

Sam was about to answer when he heard footsteps behind him followed by a voice calling his name.

"Señor Taylor! Please stop."

Sam and Tilly turned to see a flustered Nurse Diaz running after them into the hospital car park.

Reaching them, she tried to speak between deep breaths. "I'm sorry, I could not speak with you downstairs."

She spoke in soft Spanish words, ensuring only Sam could understand.

"Don't worry. Look, stop and catch your breath," he told her as she placed her hand over her chest.

Diaz shook her head then looked behind her. "I'm sorry, I don't have much time, he will soon notice I'm missing."

"Serrano? Why would he care if you came outside?"

"Because I think you know the truth, something is not right here."

Sam's body tensed. He moved closer to the nurse. "About the deaths? They were not all natural causes, were they."

Diaz again shook her head. Her face looked pale, her eyes wide in their sockets. She was frightened, gripped by a fear only a person facing death could imagine.

"You can tell me. I can help you."

"What's going on? What is she saying?" asked a confused Tilly.

Sam waved her away. "Señora Diaz, please, if you know something we can help you."

"What's happening here is awful, I can't do it anymore. People are dying and I am stuck here right in the middle of it."

"I know, well, we've guessed and more than that we can help you. Protect you from Serrano. You just need to trust us, tell us what you know."

Diaz moved back from Sam, her thin frame looking pathetically small under the uniform. "Not here, not now. I have proof, I have everything you need but I can't give it to you here."

"Then tell us where and we will be there, whenever suits."

The Spanish nurse thought for a moment before answering. "This evening when I finish here, there is the Moors and Christians festival in Jávea. Meet me there during the parade at ten by the Hotel Miramar, there's a fountain opposite. Do you know it?"

"No, but she will." Sam thumbed towards a confused Tilly.

"Thank you, meet me there this evening and I'll have everything for you." She stopped, looking over her shoulder and then around the deserted car park. "But please do not tell anyone, Serrano is not alone in this."

"I won't, you can trust us." He looked at Tilly then back at Diaz. "Does this include what happened to Señor Birks?"

"Yes, everyone, all of the names and more you do not know about. He's like a demon spreading his claws into everything."

Tilly, at hearing her father's name, tried to interrupt. "What about my dad? Sam, tell me."

Ignoring her, he asked Diaz, "Why don't you come with us? Leave now?"

"I can't. I've hidden all of my papers in the office and at home. I'm sorry, I have to go back. Ten pm outside the hotel, please be there."

Nurse Diaz pulled away from Sam then hurried back inside the hospital without a second glance. He watched as her small figure disappeared into the vast medical building wishing she had not returned to the waiting Serrano.

"What the hell was that all about?" demanded Tilly.

"I'll explain in the car," said Sam, dismissing her, his mind even more confused.

Walking back to the rental car he looked around the car park to see if anyone could have witnessed their conversation. He could only see a single man reading a newspaper while sat in a black Mercedes. He felt an urge to go back into the mortuary, to protect the nurse as she collected her evidence regardless of the protests from Serrano. Yet what good would that do apart from put Diaz in danger? Who knew who else was involved, it couldn't just be the doctor. There had to be a bigger picture. If they alerted Serrano then they'd lose any chance of finding the others.

"I know where she's talking about," said Tilly after he had explained what had just occurred. "It's near the harbour on the front, it will be packed with people watching the festival parade. The whole festival celebrates the Christians ejecting the Moors out of the area. Lots of fancy costumes, swords, drums, you name it. You're lucky – it's pretty impressive. I wonder what she's going to show us?"

"Hopefully something that helps us nail Doctor Serrano and brings us one step closer to whoever killed your dad."

"And if she doesn't?"

"I'm still thinking on that."

Sam drove the pair of them back over the steep headland with its looming mountain back down towards Jávea Bay. His mind kept drifting back to the mortuary and Nurse Diaz, a growing concern gnawing at him.

"What do you want to do now?" asked Tilly. "I can book us a table in a great little local restaurant in the old town, not far from where we are supposed to meet our new friend."

"Sounds good but if we've a few hours to kill I know where I'm going," he said, looking down at his green-ringed Rolex.

"Where?"

"The best clothes shop in town, I've had enough of being dressed for a Scandinavian climate."

A grinning Tilly directed Sam through the old town and across the bay towards the tourist-filled Arenal. Taking him to the crowded seafront, they bypassed holidaymakers as they went to and from the sandy beaches. A loud buzz seemed to echo around the place as people enjoyed themselves, blissfully unaware of the troubles of the two companions as they walked down the front. Halfway down the public walkway, Tilly pushed Sam into a trendy-looking beachfront shop whose façade was covered in wooden panelling and surfer-type scenery.

"You're kidding, right?"

"Just shut up and leave the styling to me."

"You do know I've a reputation to maintain as an anti-fashion campaigner, right?"

Exiting the shop later, Sam at least felt more acclimatised to the hot weather, dressed in a pair of cargo trousers and shirt. Other changes of outfits were now folded inside the two paper bags he carried as they walked back down the Arenal, the receipts safely stored, ready to be sent back to the office. Tilly had tried and failed to make him give up his boots.

"You can't kick someone barefoot. Trust me, I know," he told her, thinking about the previous night's attacker.

"When are you planning on kicking someone?" she pushed back.

"On this case probably pretty soon."

Relenting, she had taken him to an ice-cream parlour where the two of them took their orders to go and sat on the low wall that ran along Arenal. They sat in silence as they ate, watching the world go by. Sam looked to his left to see a family of four had sat next to them. Two small blonde-haired girls were sharing a chocolate-covered waffle, smears of Nutella all over their pretty summer dresses. Noticing him staring, they looked at him cautiously, unsure of this strange man. He forced out a smile then hurriedly gazed back out to sea, shuddering at the mere thought of having to look after children. Give him night-time intruders any day of the week.

"Fancy a drink?" Tilly asked, breaking the silence.

"I'd kill for a gin and tonic about now," admitted Sam.

As he stood up from the ledge Sam felt his phone vibrate. Retrieving the device he saw Emma's name flash up on the screen.

"Bugger, it's my boss."

"She may have an update for you."

"Or to give me additional problems to worry about, more like."

Preparing himself for the worst he answered the phone. "Taylor's tapas delivery."

"Your sense of humour knows no bounds, does it?" the Irish accent clipped back at him.

Sam covered the phone's microphone. "She can't stop laughing," he told a disbelieving Tilly.

"I have news for you," Emma said. "You're not going to like it."

"When do I ever? You never ring to say, 'case closed, I've got you a ticket home', do you?"

"There's been another murder."

"I know. I saw the prime suspect being brought in, English girl by the looks of it," he replied, thinking of the frightened woman being dragged half naked into the station.

"Yes, yes, Alex Coombs, she was the au pair for the victim."

"Don't you mean nanny?"

"Au pair is the posh way of saying it these days. Anyway, the victim's name was Chris Kane, does it mean anything to you?"

"Nope, let me ask Tilly."

Tilly shook her head.

"I thought not but Chris Kane was an MI5 officer, who according to the local police had his throat cut by young Miss Coombs this morning while on his boat. The pair had gone diving, the boat being two hundred metres out at sea."

"No, she didn't," answered Sam calmly.

"Excuse me? How the hell do you know that?" asked a surprised Emma.

"I saw her today being brought in, she did not have a speck of blood on her."

"She could have cleaned herself."

Sam shook his head. "Have forensics found anything?"

"No."

"Then she didn't do it."

Sam could picture Emma's face at the other end of the line, a mixture of frustration and, he hoped, admiration. "Look, trust me. Call it intuition. Remember, I've seen enough killers and she isn't one of them."

"Well, you can go and find that out for yourself, you're wanted down at the station. You've been given permission to speak to her."

"You think the two deaths are connected – Kane and Birks?"

"Don't you?"

Sam thought about it, the deaths of one retired MI6 agent and one active MI5 agent in the same town within a matter of days seemed too coincidental. "You're probably right, yet I can't see how if Kane was actually killed by his au pair. Bit of a stretch of the imagination."

Emma brushed past the last comment. "Anyway, you can decide for yourself when you get to the station. As you can imagine MI5 are kicking off big time here, they don't like it when one their own dies abroad. Gives them the jitters. They are already talking about sending one of their officers over. I've told them that's our job, for all the good it will do. There's a wife out there as well, perhaps you should go see her."

Visiting a recently created widow was not high on the priority list for Sam. Reluctantly, he promised he would find time to call in.

"Great, I've got one dead MI6 agent who we know was murdered but no one else agrees with us. Now one dead MI5 agent who apparently was killed by his au pair, who this time we don't believe actually did it. Oh, and somehow they are both connected. I'm beginning to think we are the cynical ones, Emma."

"I'm Irish, I was born cynical. I don't know what your excuse is."

"Touché, I'll let you know how I get on."

Sam hung up on his boss back in London. He ran his hand through his hair as he considered this latest news. Surely whatever was going on here had not managed to kill another member of the British secret service? At least Selwin Birks had been retired, this Chris Kane had still been active. He tried thinking back to the young woman's face as she was forced into the police station. He had instinctively felt then that she had been innocent. Could she have killed Kane for a reason completely separate to their own problems?

"It's like you said this morning, they come in all shapes and sizes," Tilly reminded him as he finished retelling his conversation with Emma.

"I know but still, if you cut someone's throat you generally get covered in blood. You saw her this morning – she didn't have a speck on her."

"It could have been under the T-shirt or the police had already removed it?"

"I guess so."

"How far out to shore did they say the boat was?" asked Tilly.

"About two hundred metres."

"So someone could have swam to the boat and killed him?"

Sam dismissed it. "Without the girl seeing them? No, I doubt it."

The afternoon was beginning to pass, some of the families with smaller children were leaving the beach. The bars around them were starting to fill, groups of customers taking advantage of the early happy hours to order fruit-filled cocktails. Sam watched as one waiter served a table with glasses of ice-cold gin and tonics – the longing for a drink itched at him.

"I've got to go to the station," he told her.

"Rather you than me, you can drop me off back at the villa so I can get ready for the evening."

"Oh, Christ, the bloody nurse," Sam said. "I had almost forgotten about her."

That day's afternoon may have begun to fade but Sam suddenly felt his day had hardly started.

THIRTEEN

SAM TAYLOR ENTERED the police station alone this time, having dropped Tilly back off at her father's villa. Where before the bright modern building had looked welcoming with its promise of air-conditioned rooms, now it carried a slight air of foreboding. Inside these very walls was the next piece of a jigsaw puzzle that had already claimed lives and now may have claimed another. Waiting in the reception area, Sam tried to imagine what possible links this latest murder could have had with Selwin Birk's death. The more he thought about it the more he hoped that the police were actually correct and that the au pair had in fact done the killing.

"Señor Taylor?" a voice called out from across the open reception.

Commissioner Ana Moreno walked confidently across the polished tiled floor towards him. She was accompanied by a younger woman dressed in a dark pantsuit and a white blouse, open at the top. Bright-blonde hair had been tied back in a long ponytail which hung past her shoulders.

"Commissioner."

Moreno gave Sam a brief look up and down, taking in his new outfit. "I take it you've become accustomed to the local climate."

If she thought Sam was feeling self-conscious dressed in shorts amongst these formally dressed officers, she had another thing coming. "Definitely, I'm hitting the beach after this."

Moreno pursed her lips. "Indeed, can I introduce you to the lead detective in this latest case? Elsa Vega."

"Detective." Sam greeted the newcomer then asked as they began walking, "What's happening with the case? London told me a brief summary but I'd like to hear the latest directly from you."

Commissioner Moreno indicated for Vega to answer as they walked into the main building. "The deceased male – Chris Kane, a financial crimes officer with your MI5 – was found deceased in the sleeping cabin of his boat this morning. The prime suspect, a Señorita Alex Coombs, and the deceased had gone for an early-morning dive off the Granadella beach, a cove beyond the southern headland." She added the final explanation for Sam's benefit then continued. "Señorita Coombs claims that she had gone into the water before Kane who was distracted by an expected phone call. Kane then indicated that Señorita Coombs should dive without him. She then returned to the surf exactly forty-one minutes later, claiming to find Kane already deceased."

"How do you know she was underwater for exactly forty-one minutes?"

"We recovered her diving computer at the scene."

"What happened then? How did you guys find out?"

Vega continued to take the lead in the recounting, speaking in a firm, confident voice. "A passing diving boat heard her screams, one of the crew jumped aboard and piloted the ship into harbour. We were waiting for them, having being radioed by diving crew."

"At which point you took Señorita Coombs into custody?"

"Yes, it was clear there could have been no one else involved."

"Really? How so?" asked Sam, a slight mocking tone in his voice which Vega ignored.

"The boat was empty, there was no one else aboard. Señorita Coombs admitted as much. The only other explanation is another boat could have moored up, but again Señorita Coombs told us she did not either see or hear another boat while at the bottom."

Sam, having dived before, questioned this. "How deep was she not to have heard anything?"

"At most, twenty-five metres."

Sam nodded along, at that depth Alex Coombs should have heard any motor engine approaching. He was beginning to agree with their assumption that the au pair had been the killer, her own honesty only adding to her presumed guilt. Trying to find anything in which to find a hole in their case, he asked about a motive.

"Well, we are still working on that, she is an extraordinarily pretty girl, he may have been planning on trying his luck, she said no and then it turned physical."

Sam for the first time felt Vega stumble in her explanation. "And your evidence for that?"

"Coombs denies any sexual relationship and yet we did find champagne and condoms in the cabin where Kane was found."

"Lock her up now then."

At these words Commissioner Moreno stopped walking. "I sense you have some doubt about our hypothesis."

"Only a gut feeling," said Sam honestly. "I agree it's hard to see an alternative suspect. But I saw the woman this morning and she didn't exactly scream 'killer' at me."

The two Spanish women gave him a pitying look.

"Because she's a woman?" asked Moreno, her face filled with sarcasm.

"Maybe, but also I would have thought the girl would have at least been covered in blood?"

"We thought about that," snapped Detective Vega. "We think she killed Kane and then dived."

"That would make her one damn cold-blooded killer. She fights off an unwelcome sexual advance from her employer, cutting his throat. She is then straight-thinking enough to think 'sod it, I'll go for a quick dive'?"

The two officers did not reply so Sam continued. "If you're right and there was a fight between the two of them, has anyone found any bruising on either party?"

Moreno answered. "No, that is a fair question. Our mutual friend Doctor Serrano is currently completing his post-mortem. I'm sure we will get an opinion from him soon enough."

Sam's mind drifted back to the mortuary in the hospital's basement and thought of the panicked face of Nurse Diaz. Would this latest body throw a spanner in her plans to meet them later?

"There were no signs of force found on Señorita Coombs. I was in the room as the forensics team did their analysis," Detective Vega told him.

"Not the most waterproof of cases, is it?" teased Sam, thankful not to be the one investigating.

They had followed a corridor to a staircase which led down to the cells. Vega scanned her passes, allowing them to enter, waving at a bored-looking guard as they moved into the cell block. Eight grey metal doors, four on either side of the room, stood forebodingly ahead of them.

"Now we are here what is it you want me to do exactly?"

"Talk to her, we are arranging for an English-speaking lawyer but thus far she has been willing to talk to us without."

"And look where that got her, a five-star accommodation." He rubbed the corners of his eyes with finger and thumb. "Are you planning on charging her?"

Moreno shifted from foot to foot. "We will wait until we get a full forensics and post-mortem report."

"Great, I look forward to that conversation. Last thing, back to the dead man, have you spoken to the family yet?"

"Yes, I went this afternoon," said Vega.

"Thank God for that. Right, let me in and I'll have a chat with her. You know anything she tells me will be confidential, right?"

"Yes, of course."

"Has she eaten or drank since she was brought in?"

Vega shook her head, the ponytail flicking behind her. "No, she's refused everything we've offered."

Sam reached into his pocket, retrieved some euros and gave them to Vega. "Send someone out and get her something edible, not something from the police kitchen."

Vega looked at the thirty euros in Sam's hand, an expression of disdain on her face at being sent on such a menial errand. She seemed about to refuse the request when Moreno injected.

"We will sort something," she told Sam, taking the money herself. "I'll have it brought to her cell immediately."

"I'll have a Coke Zero while you're at it, please." Not quite a gin and tonic on the beachfront, he mused, but it was better than nothing. "Right, anything else before I go in?"

The two officers replied in the negative and Detective Vega walked Sam towards the locked cell. She checked through the spy hole, called down to one of her colleagues to release the central lock, then pulled the wrought-iron door open. Stepping into the small cell, Sam saw the bedraggled figure of Alex Coombs sat on a low bed, huddled up in one corner. She had her thin arms wrapped tightly round her knees, drawing them up against her chest. Since Sam's first sighting of her that morning she had changed into a simple T-shirt and trousers combination while her old clothes were being forensically tested.

"Perhaps a couple of chairs to sit on?" suggested Sam.

Vega agreed and left them alone in the cell.

Switching back to English Sam spoke gently to the young woman nervously eyeing him. "Would it be selling you short by saying you've had one hell of a day?"

"You're English?"

"Last time I checked."

Alex began to release her knees from the tight embrace of her arms. "Are you my lawyer?" she asked, looking at his shorts and shirt.

"Nah, I never had the brains. I'm from the British government.

As your good luck and my considerable bad luck would have it I was in the area on another case."

"Are you here to get me home then?"

Sam now shifted uncomfortably. best to rip the plaster off, he decided. "No, I'm afraid not. As you already know, our Spanish friends have you as their prime suspect for your employer's murder. I don't think I'll be able to get you home for some time."

Her brown hair dropped to her chest, tears falling down her cheeks. "I don't know what else to say, I told them everything."

Yes, and in doing so gave them more ammunition to charge you, he mused but kept his thought to himself.

"We can cross that bridge later, you've not been charged yet so the pressure is on the uniforms to build their case. If we are lucky we won't even have to cross it."

A knock on the door announced the return of Vega carrying a pair of chairs. "We've sent someone out for your food order."

"Cracking, I'll leave it with you to make sure it's chilled."

Vega's face flushed at Sam's comment as she left the cell, the door clanking loudly as she slammed it shut.

"I don't know about you but my TripAdvisor review will be mentioning a distinct lack of customer service," said Sam, trying to bring a little humour into the small room. He took one of the chairs for himself while pushing the second towards Alex who instead remained sat on the bed.

"Who are you?"

"Sam Taylor, Repatriation Office. It's my job to make sure you're treated fairly."

"I didn't kill him, Mr Taylor. I swear it."

Sam raised a hand, calming her down. "I know, I know, but let's just take it from the start – and it's Sam, don't worry about formalities. I'm not your lawyer but let's see if I can help. Start at the beginning."

"It was this morning."

Again Sam raised his hand. "No, right from the start. I'm right in thinking you worked for Mr Kane?"

"Yes, I've been their au pair for the last six months. Until today it's been the best job I've ever had."

Sam listened quietly as Alex spoke. In any other circumstance the brunette would have been very beautiful. But here in this small square cell she looked pathetically young in Sam's eyes. He had met prisoners in all sort of cells across the world, a mixture of the guilty and the innocent. The more he listened to Alex's story the more confident he felt in her innocence.

"And Mrs Kane?" asked Sam as Alex reached the part about breakfast that day.

"Sofia."

"Sofia, what was she like to you? I'll speak bluntly but did she ever seem upset to have a younger woman in the house? Jealous even?"

Alex shook her head, the tears now drying up as her mind concentrated on retelling her story. "No, she's always been lovely, they both were."

"Brave woman letting her husband around a potential rival," Sam mused.

"Not all men think with their trousers."

"Point taken. Go on, what happened on the boat then?"

Alex went through the rest of the events of the morning, from the dive masters handing over the tanks all the way to the last-minute phone call from the solicitor.

"Do you know what the call from the solicitor was for?"

"No, something to do with property. Mrs Kane's family have a lot of property out here."

"Lucky them," said Sam, crossing his legs on the chair. "What about Mr Kane, did you ever speak to him about his job?"

"No, both of them never brought their professional lives home. Well, at least around me."

"Do you know what Mr Kane did as his profession?"

"Yes, he worked for the government, a financial crimes expert or something."

Alex's body language had opened up as the conversation had

progressed. She was now sat on the edge of the bed, her feet firmly on the floor as she spoke. A small flicker of life was returning to her youthful face.

"He never told you anything else about it?" probed Sam. "Or did you ask any questions?"

"No."

A knock on the door interrupted them and a police officer stepped in with a paper shopping bag. Without a word he handed it over to Sam then left them to it.

"Now they tell me you've not eaten since you were brought in," he said as he looked into the bag's contents. Two filled baguettes were wrapped up along with packets of crisps, chocolate, some small fruit and to Sam's delight, cans of ice-cold Coke Zero.

He picked up one of the cans, the condensation soaking his fingers and passed the bag over. "All yours, if you don't eat at least some of it I will be very insulted. The sod didn't even give me any change."

Alex cautiously took the bag, looked inside then said, "You're not a normal police officer, are you?"

"Ha, I told you I'm not even police or a lawyer, I'm just someone who tries to help out where I can. You've no idea the trouble it gets me in," said Sam, opening the can.

"Thank you then for trying to help."

"Don't thank me yet, I've still got to ask you some questions. You can start by finishing up with what happened when you returned to the surface."

Alex, now between mouthfuls, finished her story right up to arriving at the police station. She spoke about the panic at seeing the body, at being frightened still.

"I was so scared I just screamed, I didn't even try to see if he was still alive," she admitted.

"You probably did the right thing, it means there should be nothing from you for forensics to find. What about the boat, did you notice anything different from when you left it?"

"Apart from the dead body?"

"Apart from the dead body."

"No, not that I noticed but I was hardly thinking straight to look for anything like that."

Sam scratched at the stubble on his chin, thinking. "Have you any idea if the Kanes had any enemies?"

"No."

"If you didn't kill him who do you think did?"

She stopped eating, her defences suddenly up.

Sam saw the response. "No, sorry, I wasn't accusing, it's just I need some kind of other hypothesis to look into if I'm going to help you."

"No, I'm sorry. Chris seemed to be liked by everyone."

"Well, this is a tricky one and you're adamant nothing ever happened between you and Mr Kane? No misplaced physical contact, no comment here or there?"

"No."

Again the repeated single syllable word, thought Sam, pondering on what he had so far gained from this interview. At this stage his best guesses would all have pointed at the woman in front of him. But there were just too many gaps in the picture for Sam to be convinced. The woman for one just did not seem the type. Then there was the actual forensics of the crime. Unlike in Selwin Birk's case the science did not match the police's view – so far no blood or DNA from Chris Kane had been found on the woman.

"Then at this moment we are going to have to wait until the police have completed their investigation and we know all the facts," Sam told her. "Note the word 'facts'. At the moment everyone is working off too many presumptions."

Alex's shoulders dropped at Sam's words. "I don't think I can do this, Sam."

Sam rose from his chair to sit beside her on the bed. "You will be surprised what you can do. One day you will look back on this as just a bad day."

"A very bad day. I can't stop thinking about Sofia and the boys. What must they be thinking?"

Probably that you killed their dad, thought Sam but kept it to himself. "Try not to think on it, that should be for the actual murderer to worry about."

He squeezed her hand. "Keep your chin up and let me give you some advice – I wouldn't speak to the police again until you have a lawyer. I'll tell the officers it is under my instruction so you don't get a hard time."

"Thank you."

"Have you spoken to anyone back home? Family or friends?"

"No, there's only my mum and I don't want to worry her."

"Let me know if you'd like me to speak to her. If you need me at all you just have to tell the officer on guard."

"Thank you."

Sam rose to leave but stopped, an idea coming to mind. "Alex, random question, does the name Selwin Birks mean anything to you?"

Like the rest of the interview Alex replied in the negative.

"What about Carla Sheridan or Doctor Serrano?"

"I'm sorry. I've never heard of them."

Sam shrugged. "Don't worry about it, it was a long shot. Keep your chin up, Alex Coombs, and I'll be in touch."

Leaving the stricken girl in the cell he helped the officer carry the chairs out. Detective Vega was waiting for him in the small office at the end of the cell block, Commissioner Moreno having left for more urgent business.

"Anything useful to tell us, Señor Taylor?"

"Yes, you can tell whoever went to get the food they can keep the change."

Vega gave him the stare only a woman could give a man trying to be funny. "And about the case?"

"You better get yourself some extra staff in as you will be working overtime on this one. The girl in there didn't do it."

Vega sighed and stood up from the desk she had been sitting on. "I told Moreno you'd be no help."

"Whatever, I take it you will be continuing to investigate all leads?"

"Obviously."

"And I'd like a copy of the forensics and post-mortem reports sent to my office as soon as you get them."

"Fine."

Sam began to walk towards the stairs and the freedom they offered when a thought struck him. "Alex said the last she saw of Chris Kane was him answering the phone to his solicitor?"

"Yes," replied a curious Vega.

"Did you check the story?"

"Of course, we found Kane's phone on the boat."

"So Kane was killed between the time he hung up the phone and when the dive boat heard Alex's screams, yes?"

"Yes, I guess so." Vega was now thoroughly confused.

Sam grinned. "Have a look at Alex's diving computer."

Detective Vega was still not following and Sam rolled his eyes. "The computer will have time-logged Alex's every move. I bet it will show Alex twenty metres deep by the time Kane ended the call. It means that Alex could only have killed Kane in the limited time between resurfacing and the diving boat arriving. That computer gives the woman a perfect alibi – it's hard to kill a man when you're twenty metres under the sea. It also blows a hole in your 'she killed him then dived to clean off the blood' theory."

Vega looked completely shocked, the realisation of Sam's logic having ruined her day's work. She tried to regain her composure. "It still means there could have been time, we would have to check the facts."

"Not if she dived in to clean off the supposed blood. Bad luck, Vega, let me know when you plan to release the woman. You can keep her overnight while you cross-check everything, in this town it's probably the safest place."

Detective Vega spluttered a half-hearted response, but Sam

ignored her – another thought had entered his mind, something which sent a shiver down his spine. He almost feared asking the question.

"I don't suppose you know who the solicitors were that Kane spoke to?"

Vega stopped trying to argue about the diving computer. "Dos Árboles Verdes, why?"

Sam swore, he had found a connection.

FOURTEEN

SO THERE WAS a connection after all, the same solicitor at the heart of Selwin Birks's murder had also been working for the Kanes. Not only working for him, they were the last people to have actually spoken to the dead man. It could, of course, mean nothing – just one of those random connections between two people which would normally have been completely irrelevant. But Sam knew better. He could feel it. He knew this connection meant something.

Detective Vega was still staring at him, unsure as to why this answer could have triggered such a response. "Does this matter?" she asked tentatively.

Sam considered the detective before answering, he decided not to share his thoughts with the Spanish officer. "It's probably nothing, forget it."

Vega's face clearly told him she did not wish to forget it, the brown eyes narrowed as she glared at him. "You do know the more we share the better we can work together, yes?"

"It's easy to forget we are working together sometimes," he responded coldly, the memory of the disappearing police officers from the night before fresh in his mind. True, while Moreno and to be fair, Vega, had been more than supportive today, he still decided on caution.

An insulted Vega refused to say another word as she escorted Sam back to the reception. Not that he minded the silence, his mind was back on the merry-go-round as he tried to wrestle with everything. What could have resulted in both the deaths of Selwin Birks and Chris Kane? He had always enjoyed a good puzzle although this was beginning to feel extremely one-sided. Saying his farewells to the still furious Vega he walked back to the car. The late-afternoon sun had turned golden as he drove back across the floor of the bay and back up to the southern headland. It gave the whole area a hazy cast which seemed to fit with his mood. A fatigue was beginning to creep up on him which was not helped by the thought of their late rendezvous with the mortuary nurse still to come that evening.

Tilly Birks was waiting for him as he wearily walked up the flagged pathway into the villa's porch. The round tanned face split into a warm smile as she opened the door.

"I was beginning to think you'd decided to return home."

"I considered it."

"You look worn out, go and sit down while I get you a beer."

Sam did not need to be told twice and gratefully dropped his weight onto the sofa's cushions. He rubbed his eyes only to open them again when he heard Tilly walk back into the room. She had changed outfit since he had last seen her – gone were the shorts and shirt to be replaced by a deep-blue jumpsuit which hugged at her slim frame. A jumpsuit which Sam couldn't help but notice was both incredibly short and low-cut. She held out an ice-cold beer bottle to Sam which he took gratefully for its cooling effects.

"How'd it go?"

"Well, she's innocent, I can tell you that."

"Do you know that or is it a guess?"

Sam recounted his visit to the station and his audience with the incarcerated Alex. He explained his theory on the diving computer and his expectation of a clear forensic report.

"Even our friend Doctor Serrano will have trouble connecting her to the body," said Sam with a sigh, taking another deep swig of the bottle.

Tilly had taken a seat on the opposite sofa, her long legs now crossed. "And so is it connected to Dad's death?"

He told her about the solicitor.

"Christ, first the pathologist and now the solicitor, who else is on it?"

Sam gave a dry laugh. "Slow down, it is only a guess. I do think it's too much of a coincidence but we need to not jump into anything just yet. Let's take it one step at a time."

"Which means Diaz."

"Yes, Diaz."

The two left the villa to head back towards the old town. Sam, now changed into a pair of chino shorts and T-shirt, had still refused to give up the boots, much to his companion's chagrin. Driving back along the bay, the roads had filled with traffic as the crowds headed towards where that night's fiesta was due to take place. Tilly spent most of the journey telling him about the fiesta, its parades and fireworks.

"There's hundreds of locals all dressed up, marching through the streets, towards the port where they're congregating for the fireworks. Throughout the lead-up there will have been re-enactments and mini-parades. It's a real big deal here."

"I thought they just did bullfighting here when they fancied a party," said Sam, concentrating on the road ahead.

"Well, they do but not all the time. I've never watched a proper bullfight, I've seen one where the poor animals get pushed into the sea."

"*Bous a la Mar*," added Sam, remembering the event from somewhere in his memory.

"That's it, makes me cringe at the thought."

"It's why I always support the bull, I'm always on the side of the underdogs."

Tilly laughed. "I can see that."

Parking on a back street they walked in the warm night air, under the glow of the lamps. Ahead of them Sam could already hear the faint sounds of the fiesta growing louder with each step. Tilly led him through the streets, expertly avoiding the moving crowds until they crossed over a road and entered another back street, this one running parallel to the seafront. She stopped on the corner in front of a pair of wooden doors under an overhanging black sign which read *Azorín*.

"One of the benefits of living out here is you find out all the best local restaurants. I'll bet we are the only English people in here tonight."

She led him in and waited by the door until a middle-aged waiter arrived to welcome them.

"*Hola*, I'm Selwin Birks's daughter, we have a table booked?"

The waiter looked back, confused.

"I'm Selwin Birks's daughter."

There was still confusion, leaving Sam to step in with his Spanish.

"Oh yes, we have a table booked for you," replied a relieved waiter.

"Did he say he knew me?" asked an eager Tilly.

"No."

With a slightly deflated Tilly tailing behind, they followed their waiter past tables all filled by customers enjoying their evening. Taking a seat in their corner table, Sam looked over to the bar where there seemed to be as much Real Madrid merchandise as there was bottles.

"*Hala Madrid*," Sam said to the waiter who, appreciating the gesture, nodded amicably then left.

"So you're a football fan then?" asked Tilly.

"Good God, no. I'm just trying to be friendly after your efforts at the door."

She blushed before burying her head in the menu.

A bottle of wine appeared for Tilly while Sam stuck to beer. Sam let his night's companion order for them, and who immediately ordered the house chicken paella. He watched the beautiful woman in front of him, her round face smiling as they spoke of family, childhoods and their varying professions. He answered all of the usual questions that occurred when the subject of his military career came up. Then he turned the tables on her and questioned her on why she had left for America.

"Why not?" she parried back at him. "I had no connections left at home, my parents were already living abroad so I decided to follow suit."

Sam raised his eyebrows slightly and took a drink.

On seeing this Tilly seeing immediately challenged him. "What's that look for?"

"There wasn't a look."

"Yes there was. Come on, say it."

"Well, I was just thinking you may have been running from something or someone?"

Now it was Tilly's turn to raise her eyebrows, her eyes widening in mock shock. "No, Mr Taylor, I was not running from something or someone, thank you. I'm presuming by someone you mean a man."

"Maybe."

"Well, I'll have you know I'm old enough not to worry about men – just because you are what – five, seven, maybe ten years younger than me, you think we all need a man to look after us."

Sam let out a laugh. "You're not that much older than me and no, I'm certain you don't need a man."

Tilly eyed him as the huge metal frying pan was placed between them, the bright-yellow rice steaming in oil.

"What about you then? You run off to the army and now what, are you a travelling undertaker?"

"I like that, a travelling undertaker, I'll have to use it in the future. But no, there's no one." He paused, thinking about Hannah and then he thought of the red-haired air stewardess. "Well, actually, I did get promised a date by a very attractive air stewardess just yesterday."

"Oh, of course you did, I can just imagine you trying to flirt with some unfortunate girl just trying to do her job," she mocked.

"Ha, well I've still not checked to see if she gave me her real number."

"There you go then, stalker it is."

The conversation continued in this vein throughout the dinner. For every joke Sam made, Tilly more than matched him. He was very quickly realising he was enjoying this woman's company. It was only after the paella dish had been cleared away did the conversation turn to the reason they were out.

"What do you expect or hope Diaz will bring us later?" Tilly asked Sam as he picked up his coffee.

"I hope a complete summary of everything that's been happening here, names and evidence of who killed your dad and preferably irrefutable proof that our friend Doctor Serrano is a piece of shit who's going to be locked up."

"Amen, but really?"

Sam swirled the coffee around in his cup. "I don't know, what can she give us? I'm hoping some insight into the list of names we got from your dad. She said it didn't she, that something wasn't right."

"Here's hoping then, she was certainly scared about it."

"Who can blame her? At the last count thirteen people have died."

"The ten names on the list, Sheridan, Kane and Dad."

The two of them went quiet as if by saying the number aloud it had brought home the reality of what they faced. It felt like they had opened Pandora's box.

"Come on then, let's see what more bad news we are going to get," said Sam, standing from the table.

Leaving the restaurant, Tilly led Sam along the back road before turning down a narrow passageway to the seafront. A walkway ran alongside a pebble beach, the surf gently pulling at the tiny rocks after each impact, creating a soft rumbling sound in the background. The pair were surrounded by crowds of people heading towards the port area of the old town, where bright spotlights could be seen over the roofs of the buildings. Somewhere, speakers had been set up and music was echoing over them. Sam, walking amongst the throng of people, could not help but be caught up in the atmosphere.

"In any other situation I think I'd say I was enjoying myself," he called out to Tilly.

"Got to love a good fiesta."

The pathway continued a little on past shops and restaurants all taking in a busy night's trade. Ahead of them the walkway opened up to where a main road, now closed, would host the evening's finale. A stage had been erected between the seawall and the end of the road where a band was playing to an ever-growing audience.

"The parade comes to an end here and the hotel's just around the corner this way."

Grabbing his arm she pulled him through the crowd, pushing their way through to the seawall.

"There's the Hotel Miramar at the end of the road."

They walked on past a white-walled tourist information centre, more cafés and restaurants until they were stood opposite the hotel. Sam spotted the promised fountain in an open space just across from the hotel's entrance and made for it. The main road to the port ran alongside where crowds had now gathered to see the parade's procession. There was no sign of Diaz.

"We are early, it's only five to," said Tilly, her voice reflecting Sam's own worry. For some reason he had expected Diaz to be early.

From somewhere above them the booming sound of drums thundered around the space. It was followed by the blare of trumpets calling out their challenge to the night sky as the crowds began to cheer and yell. The people around them all ran to the road to try and jostle for the best position.

"Talk about bad timing," groaned Sam. "How the hell is she going to get through all this now?"

More cheers moved their attention to across the road where it branched off a short steep slope, then ran under an archway between two buildings. The echo of the marching band was pounding through the covered gap of the buildings, its stone archway causing the sound to amplify. Sam stepped onto the stone ledge of the fountain to get a better look over the crowds as the band appeared from the tunnel. Another round of trumpets bellowed out to the night's sky. The effect of the music, mixed with his own anxieties was causing his heart to beat hard against his chest. Again he tried to spot the nurse amongst the crowd.

Now the band made its steady way through the archway, each of its members uniformly dressed in white shirts as they made their procession down the slope. Behind them strode a single man dressed in a grey fur cloak covering a gold tunic, held in place by a golden sash. Thick golden armbands were held tight against his biceps, while leather arm guards covered his forearm. At the slope's summit he stopped and took off his round brown hat to reveal a grey bandana. In his other hand he waved a short sword, its steel glinting from the street lights.

"I have got to get me one of those," said Sam to Tilly, who just smiled.

The man at the head of the procession let out a great yell and began marching down the slope playing to the cheering crowd. Behind him and dressed identically to their foreman came two lines of six men linked arm-in-arm, marching in unison, each man together stepping to the left and back to the right. They cheered in time to the music and were followed by another marching band feverishly playing their instruments.

"Bloody hell," muttered Sam, impressed with the effort that had clearly gone into this. "Who makes all the costumes?"

"That's just the beginning."

Tilly was right – after the white-shirted band came another line of linked marching men all dressed in yet another intricate costume, their weaponry polished to a dazzling shine as they moved. Next came the women who somehow had managed to outshine the men. Like their male counterparts they came linked together arm-in-arm. All were dressed in golden helmets which ran down their necks, complete with a cape beautifully sown with green and gold designs which hung down to the ground. Each was dressed in a short green-and-gold dress and calf-high boots.

"They look like Amazonians! Why wasn't I told about this earlier?" he called down to Tilly, who rolled her eyes.

"Just keep looking for Diaz."

Sam did as he was told and between watching the differing groups of warriors tried to keep an eye out for their missing nurse.

"It's gone well past ten," said Sam, becoming even more concerned.

The parade continued to progress along the road, blocking Sam and Tilly in amongst the crowd. The armoured warriors were being replaced by ever-brighter costumes. More women came, all marching together, their heads covered in feathery headdresses. Now, new lines of men, their faces painted yellow and their hair dyed pink, scowled at the crowd as they made their way forwards. Each was carrying an even more elaborate headdress of pink, white and gold. It was between one of these groups and another marching band that Sam finally spotted their missing nurse. She was standing on the opposite side of the parade route, tiptoeing on a stone-built wall underneath a group of low-hanging palm trees. Sam caught her eye and she waved to him from across the street.

"There she is," he cried out, and waved back. "How can we get across to her?" he asked Tilly.

"We can't, not until the parade's over."

Sam raised his hands and signalled for Diaz to wait where she was. Catching his message, the small-framed Diaz nodded and raised up a small satchel bag, pointing at it excitedly.

He looked up the street to where another band and a new group of costumed soldiers were making their way forwards. "How much longer does this go on for?"

Tilly shrugged. "It's Spain, they take their fiestas very seriously."

It was another twenty minutes before the final arrangement of costumed men marched past. Their shouts to the night air were matched only by the huge drums that followed. As they came past, the crowd began to snake in behind the last of the procession causing a rush of bodies. Sam, still standing on the fountain's edge, tried to keep his eye on Diaz but he soon lost her in the press of people.

"Come on, let's move," he told Tilly, stepping down.

Tilly tried to move forwards but she was going against the tide of the crowd. "We can't get through this, we will need to wait it out."

Sam reluctantly agreed, waiting until it was only the stragglers to avoid before moving forwards across the road. Pushing his way through, he headed directly for the palm trees with their green leaves shooting upwards to the darkened sky. A few people still mingled around, as most had now followed the procession to the gathering in front of the stage. Crossing the street, he stopped for a moment, surprised not to see Diaz moving towards them – in fact, he didn't spot her at all amongst the remaining people.

"Where did she go?" asked Tilly, standing next to him.

Sam didn't answer. Instead, he moved forwards, a sick dread pulling at his stomach. His eye had caught a shape under the low palm trees.

"No, no, no," he shouted, now running.

Diaz was sat prone on the wall's ledge amongst a pile of rocks, laid in between two of the thick tree-trunks which covered the area in shade, her face frozen in a mixture of shock and confusion. They both saw the dark stain expanding on her purple dress.

Tilly moved forwards and went to check for a pulse and in doing so dislodged the body from where it had been perched, causing it to fall lifeless to the side.

"Sam, she's been stabbed," cried Tilly, pulling her blood-covered hands away in shock.

People around them had finally noticed the dead body. Someone seeing Tilly's blood-drenched hands screamed. More faces turned to stare at them, somewhere a shout for the police was heard. A cold anger burning in him, Sam ignored them all. Instead, he knelt by the still-warm body, its eyes looking up at him and searched round her. Nurse Diaz, their one hope to finding out what was happening in this godforsaken town was gone and so was the satchel.

FIFTEEN

SAM LAY in his bed staring up at the white-painted ceiling. He tried to guess the number of different ceilings he would have woken up to over the years. From under canvas in Afghanistan, to cheap American motels, they all merged into one. The early-morning sun glowed warm upon the white paint – what little light could actually get through the iron railings, thick roller shutters and curtains did anyway. A wave of cold air tickled his bare chest as the air-conditioning unit continued its valiant attempts at making the room habitable. The room was silent, so quiet, in fact, he could almost still hear the ringing in his ears given to him by the dressing down both he and Tilly had endured at the hands of Commissioner Moreno and Detective Vega.

"Give me one good reason not to have you both locked up for murder!" screamed the blonde-haired detective as they stood round the commissioner's office.

"Because we had nothing to do with it," replied Tilly, attempting to rein in her own frustration. "We were only there to help Diaz in exposing the crimes being committed under your very noses. Crimes which she clearly felt too scared to tell you about."

"And much good it did her trusting you two then," sneered Vega.

"It's not our jobs to arrest your criminals," retorted Tilly.

Sam tried to block out the two women, the evening's frustrations having gone beyond mere words. Instead, he stared out of the office windows, down towards the port area, where the last of the fireworks had faded away against the night's sky. The image of Diaz's small body, left to bleed out amongst the palm trees, was still fresh in his mind, the thought of it making his insides turn. A cold-blooded anger was seeping into him. Whoever they were up against had crossed a line, this wasn't just a name on a report. Diaz had been a living, breathing human being who had come to him for help and he had failed her. He had not even known her first name.

"I had thought we were all on the same team, or did I misunderstand our conversation earlier, Señor Taylor?" The voice of Ana Moreno brought him back to the office.

"I never said we weren't, Commissioner."

"Then why did you feel the need to withhold this information from me today?" Moreno's use of *me* was clearly an attempt to try and guilt-trip him.

Sam was having none of it. "It wasn't my choice, clearly Nurse Diaz did not trust you and who was I to break that? I had no idea what she was bringing us."

"I gave you my own trust, I even expressed my personal doubts about Doctor Serrano but you still felt the need to do it your own way and now a good woman is dead."

Not just one good woman, mused Sam, *you could now add Diaz to the other thirteen bodies.* The conversation continued in the same vein as the two officers took it in turns to berate the two of them. Sam, having spent years listening to senior officers lecturing him could just switch off and let it pass over him. Tilly, however, used to being the main voice in the hospital ward, simply could not.

"How dare you shout at us for your failings. You've had months to try and get a grip of whatever is going on here and done nothing. My dad managed to learn more than you and it got him killed."

"And again he did not share it with anyone, you English seem determined to do everything alone," snapped Vega.

Sam let out loud yawn, stretched his arms and ran his hand through his hair, causing all three women to look daggers at him. "I think that's quite enough for today, shall we regroup tomorrow?"

Detective Vega looked like she would have been quite happy to continue the fight further into the early hours but her commissioner overruled her.

"I think that would be for the best," she agreed, bringing the conversation to a close and allowing Sam and Tilly to return home.

Now in his bed, Sam lay still, listening to the gentle breathing of Tilly in the bed next to him, her belief that it was safer for the two of them to be in the same room overriding any potential embarrassment. So Sam had jammed a chair against the door and moved the two beds to the opposite side of the room just for good measure. He did not fancy becoming body number fifteen. Leaving the still-sleeping Tilly, he silently slipped out of bed and crept out of the room. Closing the door softly behind him he moved through the empty villa, opening the main windows and patio doors to let in the new day. Setting up the breakfast table out on the patio he was soon joined by a tired-looking Tilly.

"Tough night?" he asked as she sat down rubbing the sleep from her face.

"That's putting it lightly, I feel like I barely slept at all," she said while pouring herself a glass of orange juice.

"I know what you mean, my mind's not stopped since I woke up."

"What the hell do we do now? It feels all such a mess."

Sam had been thinking of nothing else all morning. "I want to look into Chris Kane's death, there's a lot of holes there which we need to start filling."

"I can take you down to the Granadella beach where it happened if you'd like?"

"Sounds like a plan, I'll bring my bucket and spade."

Replacing the glass, Tilly shook her head. "You won't be needing them and after we've done that?"

"I will have to see Mrs Kane, you don't have to come but I'll need to pay my respects. I've asked London to chase the police reports as well."

"I'll come along, I don't mind. What about Dos Árboles Verdes, the solicitors? Surely we will need to understand what role they play in all of this."

Sam nodded along. "Already on it, I've pushed London to get me some answers on what they did for the original list of names." He paused, wishing Hannah was on point rather than enjoying her exotic romantic vacation. If anyone could have found something it would have been her.

"I can't stop thinking about that poor woman," said Tilly sadly.

"I know, with everything else going on it's not been the easiest of days."

"Is it wrong of me to blame myself? What if we had somehow managed to get to her?"

Sam brushed it off. "Then we would have most likely joined her on one of Doctor Serrano's mortuary tables. These people don't mess around, if you don't find them, then they find you."

"How did they know? How did they know she was helping us? What did we do wrong?"

"Could be lots of reasons, perhaps they caught her collecting the evidence, or she told someone else at the hospital." He paused again, thinking of the scene in the car park, he had been certain they had been alone. There had only been the man reading his paper in the car? "Or perhaps someone saw her speaking to us."

"I just feel we should have done more."

Sam ran his hand through his hair. "It's time we started getting on the front foot with these people, at least try to disrupt them."

Tilly Birks nodded, her round face gaining a little more colour. "Then I know where to start, let's see if we can work out how they killed Kane."

The two of them hurriedly finished breakfast, then Tilly left to get ready, leaving Sam to tidy up. As he was coming out of the kitchen he almost bumped into her coming down the stairs. She shoved a pair of blue swim shorts at him.

"Here, put these on. They were Dad's but they should fit, he was in pretty good shape."

"Is that a compliment? I do try to work out when I can."

She gave him a mocking smile. "I saw enough yesterday, those boxers did look a little tight."

Sam eyed the shorts, acutely aware of their limited length. "They are a bit small on the old leg front aren't they?"

Tilly rolled her eyes as she headed out of the rear of the villa. "I thought you didn't care about fashion? It's retro to have a pair of short swim shorts. I'm sure you're not worried about anything hanging out."

Locking up the building Sam carried a pair of towels out to the car, where Tilly waited for him, holding two swimming masks. The drive to the Granadella beach was not long. Almost as soon as they turned out of the housing estate Tilly was guiding Sam down a steep winding road which snaked its way along the hillside's contours. Sam had to really work the small car's brakes while he forced it round numerous hairpin bends as the road dropped towards sea level. From the moment they had begun the drive down it had felt like they had arrived in another country as thick fern trees covered one side of the road. To the other side, barely separated by square, white-painted concrete blocks acting as a low barrier, were sheer cliffs which fell to the sea below.

"Is this the only way down?" Sam asked Tilly as he carefully navigated another bend.

"From this side, yes – there's a smaller road that goes over the side and down into the next town but no one ever uses it."

"Can't be any worse than this death trap."

The road flattened out as they reached the floor of the bay where the ferns now grew either side of the tarmac.

"Do you see all the pine needles on the ground?" Tilly asked. "They completely carpet the area which has caused some huge forest fires. You could get some eye-watering fines for even thinking about having a barbecue around here."

Turning a final bend they drove down to the small inlet. Sheer cliffs surrounded the small cove, their peaks dotted with villas jutting out over the sea. A small collection of buildings faced onto a pebble beach, the morning tide beating against the stones. Sam parked the car outside an open café, a few early patrons stared out sullenly as the pair of them exited the vehicle.

"Friendly bunch, aren't they?" muttered Sam, looking at the scowling faces.

"Look at them, they are all old, probably retired fishermen hoping to come down here to avoid the summer tourists and now you've turned up."

"I'm not a tourist," said Sam, feigning hurt.

"You're dressed in swim shorts and a T-shirt. What do you notice about all the locals round here."

"Tell me."

"Even in the height of summer they all dress in trousers and jumpers," said Tilly, laughing and dropping their belongings on the pebble beach.

"I imagine London must be Arctic for them," started Sam, then he stopped, distracted as Tilly pulled her beach dress over her head to reveal what he thought could have been the smallest bikini he had ever seen. Her narrow, toned body, tanned from the Californian sun, seemed to have had the swimsuit moulded to it.

She caught his wandering eye. "Hey, careful you, don't go getting your imaginary cabin crew upset."

Sam gave her a grin before following her lead by taking his T-shirt off. Now it was Tilly who was giving him the once-over.

"I know what you're going to say and yes, as I said, I do work out every now and then."

"I highly doubt that, I was more interested in the bullet wounds in your left shoulder."

Sam looked over at his shoulder where two white scars still stood out against his skin, placed either side of his collarbone. He shrugged. "I walked into a couple of bullets in Amsterdam, it could happen to anyone."

"Clearly," replied Tilly, evidently wanting to ask more as she took notice of the other odd scars across his body. "I take it you don't watch where you're going quite often?"

"Hey, I'll have you know the warranty is still intact."

"You have an answer for everything, don't you?"

"Always. So what now?"

Tilly bent over and opened the bag she had been carrying. "Now we swim. According to the police, Kane's boat had been tied to the far buoy. I say we swim out and see how long it would take to get there. You can also swim to the bottom and see if she was telling the truth about being able to hear another boat."

"How do you know I can swim?"

"Honestly, do you ever just agree to something without saying something stupid?" She threw him a diving mask while putting one on her own head. "Now look, do try to keep up."

"Yes, Doctor."

Tilly walked cautiously towards the sea, carefully placing her feet on the larger stones to avoid hurting herself on the smaller rocks. Sam followed suit, unable to match the balancing act of the lighter woman. He found himself slipping on the stones, all rubbed smooth by the sea, each missed step hurting the underside of his feet. A splash came from up ahead and Sam took his attention from the obstacle course of a beach to see Tilly's head rising from the surf.

"When you get close enough just dive right on in."

"It looks a bit cold for my liking," grumbled Sam, waving his arms in an attempt to stay upright. He failed, landing hard on his bottom.

"Gracefully done," Tilly called out to him.

Returning a few choice words Sam carefully reached the edge of the water, took a few final steps before diving under the crystal-clear waves. The seawater took over all of his senses as he felt his head push through up to the surface. Breathing deeply to counter the shock of the cold he swam over to the woman waiting for him.

"Have a look below and see how clear it is, the cove is protected from the main currents that bypass the coastline here."

Sam put his head beneath the waves, seeing countless little fish swimming below them, although if he had been honest the bare kicking legs of his companion were far more interesting. They began to swim outwards, Tilly leading him through the surf. She seemed to glide through the water, her long limbs slicing their way into the sea until Sam was struggling to keep up. Noticing him falling behind, she stopped.

"Are you just hanging back to look at my bum again?"

"You got me, if it wasn't for those small bikini bottoms I'd be swimming like an Olympic athlete," he lied, trying to catch his breath.

Finally reaching the buoy Sam was grateful to tread water for a moment to recover. His chest was pounding from the effort. Thankfully there was little surf and he had no trouble keeping his head above the blue water.

"Right, head down and see what you think," Tilly told him.

"You don't stop, do you? You could have made an excellent drill instructor in the army."

"Shut it, soldier, and get down."

Sam focused for a moment, breathing deeply to fill his lungs with air then taking four long breaths he flipped over and dived. Immediately he was surrounded by the hazy depths, the rocky bottom appearing below him. Kicking hard he soon reached the first of the outcrops where he rolled over and looked upwards. He could clearly see the kicking form of his companion above him. He had been right – there was no chance Alex Coombs would not have heard or seen another boat from this depth. Whoever had killed Chris Kane had not used a boat, well, at least a motor-powered one.

Using the surface of the rock face, Sam kicked himself up towards the surface. Guiding his body in the right direction he broke the surface inches from Tilly's face, spraying her in the process.

"You bastard." She hit out at him. "I take my eye off you for one moment."

"Ah, sorry, I didn't see you there. Did you want to take a look?"

"No, my ears don't like me going too deep, I'll take your judgement on it."

"Whoever it was did not use a boat."

"So they swam?" asked Tilly.

"Must have, but in that case how did neither Kane nor Alex not see them coming?"

Sam thought on it as they made their way back to the shore. Whoever had killed Kane would have had to swim out here undetected and then in the small window of opportunity between Kane's call to the solicitor ending and Alex resurfacing, committed the murder. After which they would have swam back to shore. He explained his theory to Tilly as they sat drying on the stony beach, the heat of the day already enough to evaporate the remaining water from their skin.

"I mean it's possible," admitted Tilly.

"It's the only possible way," insisted Sam.

Tilly looked out to sea where a couple of boats had entered the cove. One in particular caught their eye, a huge catamaran, its two hulls supporting a large single sail.

"There is another option," she suggested. "Perhaps the killer had been on the boat the whole time. Hidden somewhere below?"

Sam thought about it. "It's possible but bloody risky – it wasn't a huge boat. What would have happened if they'd been spotted? I guess there would have been room. Still leaves the biggest question of who."

"That's one for you to think about later. What next then?" she said, standing up.

He raised a hand to shield his eyes to look up at her bikini-clad figure above. It was definitely a good view to have. "The widow, I need to see the widow now."

They left the beach, Sam over the moon to be back on firm footing. He would never complain about sandy beaches again. Walking over to the car they saw a new arrival had parked next to them. A shiny black Mercedes – something about it seemed familiar to Sam. Reaching their own car he looked round for the owners and immediately spotted them in the café behind, their faces distinct amongst the wrinkled pensioners. One was reading a newspaper while his companion smoked a cigarette and drank coffee. Neither paid them any notice.

"Looks like the average age dropped while we were off," Sam said, opening his door.

Tilly, busy with the bags, did not respond. Instead, the man smoking looked up, noticed Sam and gave a friendly wave of acknowledgment. Sam found himself returning it out of habit – it was probably nothing.

SIXTEEN

THE KANES' villa overlooked the Mediterranean from a clifftop just north of the Granadella inlet. Sam, now showered and changed from his morning's swim, parked the car on the gated driveway, then turned off the engine. He had done countless visits such as these, the quiet, ghostly houses comprising of family members dealing with emotions of shock and grief. There would be the hollow words that had to be said, even though their effects were minimal. It may have all become part of the same old routine, but it had not become any easier.

"I'm beginning to wish I hadn't come," said Tilly in the passenger seat.

"I'd have thought you'd have been more used to this kind of thing being a doctor, don't you knock off a few every day?"

"Yeah, but that's easy – you just tell them the medical facts, say you're sorry and move on to the next one. This is different. You have to talk about the emotional side of things."

"You can still stay in the car if you want," Sam offered, thinking it had been only a couple of days since her own father had died.

Instead Tilly came with him. Walking up to the dark-brown wooden door Sam went to ring the doorbell but instead found a brass knocker fixed to the wall. The metal had been shaped into an intricate-looking octopus. Hammering the metal down against the door it was opened by a tall, dark-haired woman dressed in a plain black dress. Sam, his knowledge of feminine ways of fashion minimal, was still taken aback by the woman. Her hair was stylishly fastened above her head, showing a soft long neck from which hung a large silver crucifix, small diamonds covering its surface. Her face was made up to perfection as if she was expecting to be driven to a red carpet that morning. He tried to guess her age, older than him yet younger than Tilly, mid-thirties perhaps? The whole image was that of a glamorous woman, not exactly a grieving widow.

"Mrs Kane?" Sam asked gently.

"Yes?"

"I'm Sam Taylor and this is my friend Tilly Birks, I'm from the British government. I'm so sorry to hear about your husband."

Sofia Kane nodded in acknowledgment. "His office said they would be sending someone. Did you used to work with him?"

Sam gave Tilly a confused glance. "No, Mrs Kane, I'm sorry, I did not work with your husband, I'm not from MI5. I work for the Foreign Office."

The woman gave a brief smile before guiding them inside. "Can I get you something to drink?"

Sam and Tilly declined the offer. Instead, they followed their host through the villa out onto a patio that looked out over a shimmering sea. Sofia Kane indicated for them to take a chair each around a small coffee table.

"How are you doing, Mrs Kane? I trust that you are being well looked after and kept up to date by the local authorities?"

"I am, thank you, Mr Taylor, my countrymen have been most supportive."

Sam frowned at use of 'countrymen', he could not tell whether it had been a subtle warning that this was nothing to do with him or a genuine use of the phrase.

"Well, I'm pleased to hear that, both you and your husband were British nationals and I'm here if you do need anything."

"I don't need anything." The brown eyes flashed, the body language defensive.

Sam was beginning to realise this was not going to be an easy conversation. He tried to change tack.

"I understand you have two children, Mrs Kane."

"They are out, staying with friends," she said flatly.

He rubbed the top of his legs trying to decide the best course of action. Tilly was sat quietly next to him, her face giving nothing of her thoughts away.

"I'm glad to hear you are being well looked after, Mrs Kane. I met with the police team who are investigating your husband's death."

"Murder, you mean murder."

"Indeed, my apologies – your husband's murder."

"And has anything changed or are they still thinking poor Alex killed my Chris?"

Sam frowned. "You don't think Alex killed Chris?"

"Of course not, don't be a fool. Do you really think that Alex cut Chris's throat in cold blood? That girl hasn't got it in her."

Sam gave Tilly a confused glance. Of all the things he was expecting the newly-made widow to say, this was not it. True, he had doubts himself about Alex's presumed guilt – in fact, more than doubts. Yet he still had expected Chris Kane's wife to have at least suspected the woman her husband had been alone with to have wielded the knife. But apparently not this time.

"I'm sorry, I had presumed that you would have shared the police's suspicions."

"I do not and I'm guessing neither do you."

"I don't," Sam answered honestly, deciding there was little to be gained in hiding it. "But it does leave us with a bit of a problem."

"Who did kill my husband."

Sofia Kane uncrossed and then recrossed her legs. She was

drinking from a small coffee cup, her little finger poking outwards. Sam wondered if this woman wasn't better suited to the French Riviera rather than the Costa Blanca.

"Correct, at the moment it would seem quite hard to suggest anyone else." Sam chose not to share his theories on elusive swimmers.

"It must have been something to do with his job – he worked in a role which made many enemies."

"I'm sure his people are completing all of the relevant checks back home as we speak," said Sam, not quite believing the hypothesis.

"Then at least we can ensure Miss Coombs is released, that can be something for you to work on, Mr Taylor."

Sam raised an eyebrow at the directive given to him but did not reply.

Instead, Tilly broke her own silence. "You seem very concerned about Miss Coombs, Mrs Kane?"

"Of course I do. She worked for me and my husband, we brought her out here, so it is only reasonable that I want to see her home safely."

"Even though the police think something may have happened or had been happening between the pair of them?" continued Tilly, almost needling their host.

Sam could feel himself cringing, *tin hat time*, he thought, expecting Sofia Kane to lash out.

Instead, she spoke quietly, the scorn evident in her words. "No, I don't think that, I knew my husband and he would not have done anything like that."

Nobody spoke for a moment. There was an awkwardness amongst them that Sam had never felt before. Normally when visiting the families of the recently deceased there would be a mix of emotions, from anger to sheer unhidden grief. Instead, there seemed to be nothing but an awkwardness between the three of them as if neither party really wanted to be near the other.

Sam decided to break the silence. "Mrs Kane, if you would

humour me, I agree Miss Coombs did not kill your husband and I can understand your suspicions about his work. Yet we are all stuck with if not Miss Coombs then who – and how did this happen?"

For the first time since he had met her Sofia Kane hesitated in her reply. Her mouth opened and then shut again before eventually she chose her words. "That is your problem, my priority is to look after the children."

"I understand, Mrs Kane, I'm sure these last twenty-four hours have not been easy. I take it your house has been searched by the police?"

"Yes."

"It has to happen."

"Does it?"

Christ. Sam was getting tired of this. Whatever sympathy he had for her loss, he was quickly losing it.

Sofia Kane drained her cup, placing it on the table. "So what now, Mr Taylor? What exactly is it you do now?"

"You'd be surprised how many times I get asked that question. I don't really know myself to be honest, I wasn't originally here to investigate your husband's death. You said London is sending someone over?"

"Yes, his office rang to tell me this morning. They will be working with the police to rule out anything connecting with his work."

"Ha!" Sam laughed. "That's what my job is! I must say I won't be sad to let someone else deal with it." He stopped as he saw the severer look of this widow in front of him.

Clearing his throat he added, "But of course, I will be still helping out." Changing the subject he asked, "There is one thing that may help me with another case I'm investigating."

"Yes?" asked Mrs Kane, her interest piqued.

"Your solicitors, Dos Árboles Verdes? What do they do for you?"

"They clean my pool, what the hell do you think they do?"

Tilly had to cough to mask a chuckle. *Ask a stupid question, get a stupid response*, thought Sam.

"Have you been a client of theirs for long?"

"My family have been a client of theirs for many years."

"Your family?" asked Tilly.

"Yes, my family. I grew up here, my family have a variety of business interests in the town."

Sam ran his hand through his hair. "What type of interests?"

"A variety." Again came the cold response, they were getting nowhere. Sam was beginning to miss the days of weeping inconsolable widows compared to this verbal dual.

"What about your husband's work, did he ever mention a Selwin Birks or Carla Sheridan?"

Sofia Kane's eyes narrowed. "What are you trying to do, Mr Taylor? You keep asking these questions which mean nothing to me and expect what? I have no idea who these people are. All I want is my husband to walk through that door and for me and my family to live our lives."

"Of course, I think it would probably be best if we left you to it, Mrs Kane, I'm sure you have many things on your mind at this time." He paused, trying to think of the right sympathetic words but the awkwardness of the brief conversation had driven it from him. The entire visit had been like pulling teeth.

For the first time since they had arrived Sofia Kane looked genuinely pleased. "My thanks, it is as you can imagine a horrible time for my family. Two children have lost a father, I have lost a husband – the least you can do is find the real killers."

The three of them stood. Tilly looked as if she wanted to continue the conversation but Mrs Kane gave her no opportunity as she led them back through the villa. The elegant frame of their Spanish host strode purposely across the tiled floors only stopping as they reached the thick brown door. Without even a backwards glance she pulled it open for them. "I trust you will keep me informed if anything changes?"

"We will," said Sam curtly.

"And you will ensure Miss Coombs is released?"

"We will certainly do our best."

Following Tilly out to the driveway he asked Sofia Kane a final question. "You will ask whoever your husband's office sends out here to reach out to me please?"

Sofia Kane considered the question longer than she should then eventually agreed that she would do so. Sam, just grateful to escape the strange atmosphere, left without thinking anything of their host's final words. It was not until he was safely back in the privacy of the car did he speak again.

"That was bloody awkward. I mean, I get her husband has just died but Christ, talk about spiky."

Tilly was more philosophical. "Grief hits everyone differently. Who knows what's going through her mind right now. Those poor children, they lose their father and their carer all in the same day. I wonder if she will take them back to England now or stay here with her family."

"Who knows, interesting to hear about her family being from around here. Makes you wonder what they do." He nodded over at the large villa as he reversed the car out of the drive. "I mean, you won't be affording a second house like this on just an MI5 officer's salary. Unless I'm very much mistaken and in the wrong job."

"Nor would it cover some of Mrs Kane's taste in fashion."

"What, the crucifix?" asked Sam, now back on the road.

"And the rings, the earrings, the furnishing, the dress. Honestly, that woman was like a fashion catalogue."

"I only noticed the crucifix, it was big enough."

"Because you are a man and clearly blind to taste."

"True on both accounts."

Sam's phone began to vibrate in his pocket before coming over the car's Bluetooth speakers.

"Sam, I take it you're still alive then?" Emma Read's Irish tones filled the car's interior.

"Just about, although if you're ringing me then I may not be for much longer."

"Very good," she responded dryly, clearly wanting to move the conversation onwards. "We've been looking into the finances of the list of names Selwin Birks requested before he died."

Sam saw Tilly move slightly as she heard her father's name but kept quiet.

Emma continued. "In particular the solicitors as you asked."

"Dos Árboles Verdes?"

"Yes, that's the one. Well, apart from the usual will-writing or odd services we've found only one thing that connects all of them."

"Go on," Sam said, eager to hear more.

"We had to put a few pieces together but it seems all the names on the list received a rather large payment into their current accounts from the solicitors. Generally landing into their accounts around anything between six months and six weeks before their deaths."

That sounds more like it, thought Sam, something more tangible than the clues they had stumbled across these past two days.

"How big are we talking?" he asked.

"Between one hundred and eighty thousand euros right up to seven hundred and thirty thousand."

Sam whistled. "So a fair amount, any ideas what it was for?"

"As a matter of fact we do, one of our analysts pointed it out. Up until then we'd all been scratching our heads a little."

Sam raised his eyebrows at Tilly and mouthed silently, "She's enjoying this."

Emma, completely unaware, ploughed onwards in her explanation. "They said that solicitors generally transferred the cash in a house sale. The analyst had just exchanged on their own place so had it fresh in their minds."

"That would explain why we never found any mention of property in any of the estates," mused Sam.

"Exactly, they had already sold them off! We think they all

signed one of those equity release deals whereby they sell off their homes, then are able to live in them until they die or something similar."

"And if the buyer, say, wanted to get hold of their property a little bit earlier, then they could have helped nature take its course by prematurely ending the occupant's life?"

"That's precisely what I was thinking," said Emma. Sam could imagine the smile at the other end of the phone.

"Are you able to see who now owns the land like back home?"

"Oh, Sam, I thought you'd never ask. Yes, we've done that for you as well, all the properties were bought by a company named Two Bull Industries. But apart from giving you an address and director's name that's all I can tell you. They've absolutely no public presence that we can see."

"Christ, well that's it then, isn't it?" said Tilly, sitting up. "These Bull people buy the houses off vulnerable pensioners, probably for a fraction of their real price. Then they wait a few months before bumping them off and making a profit. Doctor Serrano is certainly in on it, he will be the one making sure that any death is automatically written off as an accident or some natural cause. Who's to argue? They are just old lonely people in a foreign country. I bet that's what Nurse Diaz was trying to tell us about, she would have seen it all."

"Sam, who's that?" snapped Emma.

"Tilly Birks – she's Selwin's daughter," Sam explained hurriedly.

"I bet my dad found out about it and they decided to get him too. Oh, God, it makes me sick. I can't wait to see the police arrest all of the pieces of shit."

"Woah, slow down," warned Sam. "There's a way to go before we can start pulling out handcuffs."

"Indeed," said the voice on the phone. "This is purely speculation – just because there's a single link between these names does not mean anything. In my experience communities of expatriates living abroad generally all use the same trusted services or professionals. It becomes a tight-knit word-of-mouth arrangement."

Tilly blinked, remembering she had told Sam the exact same thing. "But still there's a connection, surely that means something."

"It does," said Sam, "and we will certainly look into it. But it still doesn't explain Chris Kane's death or who actually committed the crimes. You can also add in why was Carla Sheridan killed and how did they know about Nurse Diaz? We just need to slow down for a moment and check we are seeing the wood through the trees."

"I mean, I don't have the same Yorkshire way of words as Sam does, but I do pretty much agree with exactly what he said," added Emma.

"We also don't know if we can even trust the people we need to arrest the bad guys. I'm not sold on any of them."

"And remember that is just a single link, there could be many more we've not found between them all. They could all have shared the same dentist with a side hobby of murder for all we know," said Emma.

"My dad knew and they killed him," Tilly said bitterly.

Sam gave her a gentle pat on the leg. "One step at a time, we will get there."

Emma must have guessed the atmosphere in the car and her voice softened. "I wouldn't worry, there's two things I've learnt since working with Sam. One – wherever in the world you send him he will always find something to complain about."

Sam laughed. "True, it is too hot over here for me – and the second?"

"If there's a woman involved then he will almost certainly end up coming out on top."

Sam grinned at his boss's words, enjoying the humour, hoping Tilly missed the hidden meaning. "Damn right, boss. You forgot to add if you give me three gin and tonics I'll do anything for pretty much anyone." Then, remembering the day of the week.

"Hang on, it's the weekend, which poor sod have you dragged in to do all this?"

There was a momentary pause on the line before Emma answered truthfully. "Do you think I'd leave you all on your own out there? Just because you haven't got Hannah keeping her eye on you doesn't mean we are all incapable."

"You dragged the graduate in, didn't you?"

"Of course I did. Now get to work. I'll send you our findings now, including the address," said Emma, hanging up.

"We have what you'd call a different working relationship," Sam said sheepishly.

"I can see that. I take it she meant figuratively when she said you end up 'coming out on top'?"

Sam grinned, knowing full well what his work colleague had meant. "Of course, you know me – professional to the end."

The phone vibrated again with an email notification and Sam pulled over to flick open the message. Scrolling downwards until he saw what he wanted, he typed in the address to the phone's navigation application.

"Where are you going now? I thought we were going to see the solicitor."

Pressing the green go button, Sam connected the phone to the car display. "Why? We've got what we wanted from there. I've never been very good at dealing with the monkey."

Tilly frowned. "What do you mean 'dealing with the monkey'?"

"I want the goddamn organ grinder."

SEVENTEEN

THE ADDRESS EMMA had sent via email to Sam's phone led them away from the coast and up into the low foothills further inland. The journey took a surprisingly long time, as Sam had to navigate the narrow winding roads which snaked around the ever-steepening slopes. Around them, the mix of commercial and residential buildings that made up the bay of Jávea were being replaced by the countryside. They passed vineyards, the rows of grapes waiting to be picked, then rows of orange trees, their leaves a dark green in the sandy-coloured environment. Eventually the satnav began to count down the distance in yards, until the instruction came to turn down onto a white dust-covered track leading away from the road.

Sitting uncomfortably as the small rental bounced its way along the uneven surface, the two companions got their first glimpse of the Two Bulls Industries. It was not what Sam had been expecting to find. The address had led them to a large farmhouse situated on a wide plateau on one of the hilltops, its red-tiled roof pockmarked with holes. Around it stood an assortment of outbuildings in a varying degree of disrepair. In fact, the only thing that looked in good condition was a strange circular steel-framed construction that stood off to one side of the farm. Clad all around in odd-coloured wooden boarding, Sam could see the outlines of people sat round the circumference.

"A bullring," commented Tilly, seeing Sam's gaze. "A big one at that."

"It would explain the name then if they are breeders," mused Sam.

He drove the car past the bullring and parked in front of the run-down farmhouse, then looked about to see if anyone was coming out to meet them.

"Hardly a welcome party is there?"

Tilly laughed. "What were you expecting – banners and balloons?"

"Is your father's gun still in the glove box?"

Tilly eyed the closed compartment nervously. "Yes, why?"

"Pass it over, you never know."

Her hazel eyes stared back sternly. "No."

"No? Seriously? After everything that's happened?"

"I mean it, Sam. No, we won't go down to their level."

Sam ran his hand through his hair in disbelief. "Then at least give me the pop-up baton, it will make me feel better even if you want to take the high ground."

Tilly reluctantly handed him the telescopic baton then pointed out of her window. "Looks like we've been spotted."

Sam looked to where a casually dressed Spaniard was walking towards them from the bullring.

"The organ grinder?" Tilly asked.

Sam shook his head. "Nope, still a foot soldier."

Leaving the car they met him halfway across the open space between the buildings. Sam looked on to see a weather-worn face under a mop of thick black hair.

"Can I help you?" the Spaniard greeted them in a deep voice. A pair of unfriendly black eyes gazed out upon them.

Sam met the gaze head-on. "We are looking for someone in charge round here."

"We are not expecting you, why do you think you can just turn up here and walk right in?"

"I didn't see any keep out signs?"

"This is private property."

"Then you should invest in your security," replied Sam coolly. He was in no mood to play along with these people. While he may have no firm proof that whoever was in charge here was behind everything that had happened, every instinct he had told him it was so.

"You should leave. Go now," their reluctant host grunted at them.

"Not until we see your boss."

"I am the boss, I have nothing to say."

"Bullshit, you're too small," Sam jibed.

The Spaniard flushed but was stopped from replying by a shout from behind. All three looked past to where a younger man had exited the bullring and was beckoning them forwards.

"Looks like we are welcome after all," said Sam, smiling as he pushed past the fuming Spaniard.

"What was that all about?" asked Tilly as they walked towards the bullring and the more welcoming local.

"Just a chat about the weather," dismissed Sam, forgetting his companion could not speak the language.

Their new host did not bother with any welcome speech, instead simply led them through an opening amongst the steel-framed bullring. Sam had to duck as he followed through the structure before climbing up a steep set of stairs back out into the open air. Taking the last step, he felt the sun bear back upon his uncovered head and found himself stood amongst a spectator stand looking down into a sandy arena. Around them, sat on the wooden benches surrounding the arena, were a small crowd cheering on the spectacle below.

"What the hell?" gasped Tilly in wonder as she stared down at the arena.

"Well, I've never seen anything like that before," admitted Sam.

Below their feet, its great bulk steaming from the perspiring sweat, was a fighting bull, its muscles bulging tightly against its skin. The crowd cheered as the beast made another charge across the arena, only stopping as it reached the steel bars that caged it. But it was the two figures in the centre of the ring that caught Sam's eye. The two men were joined by a length of thick chain wrapped tightly round their forearms, which ran along the sand under a metal ring fastened to the ground.

"What are they doing?" asked Tilly.

The answer came as the bull began its next charge. Lowering its horned head it pelted towards the nearest man. An intake of breath came from the small crowd around them as the two men took the strain of the metal chain, each trying to gain control of the other. Sam watched as the one in the 'bull's-eye' tried to pull himself out of the firing line. His competitor held his ground, keeping the chain tight as its links ran under the metal ring in the centre. The targeted Spaniard now saw his choices limiting as the animal homed in. He had to avoid the bull's charge but he could only move inwards to slacken the chain. Sam held his breath – if the man went too early then the bull would follow, if he went too late then he would face the painful consequences. The tight chain restricted movement, hindering any attempts at trickery to fool the bull's charge. There could only be one way out.

A silence fell on the crowd as the beast charged, the only sound now the clinking chains against the dividing ring. Sam found himself still holding his breath as the man waited until the last possible minute to dive out of the bull's bulk. It was timed beautifully as he stepped in towards the centre and out of harm's way. It would have been a perfect move if it hadn't been for his rival on the other end of the chain who, expecting the move, had responded by pulling hard on his end. The resulting tension caught the evading competitor off balance, dragging him to the floor. Now the crowd roared again as the bull put on the handbrakes to change direction.

"He's in trouble now," muttered Sam.

It had become a foot race between the fallen man and the charging beast, and there could only be one winner. The bull's head dropped, the horns pointing directly at the flailing form on the ground. The Spaniard had almost staggered to his feet, tried to get upright, then stumbled once more to the sandy floor. All around Sam the crowd held its breath. There seemed to be only one outcome as the bull bore down on its victim.

"Oh, God, he's going to be killed," gasped Tilly, grabbing Sam's arm.

Sam agreed – it looked like there could be only one outcome and one which would not end well for the unfortunate man. Instead, Sam was wrong – at the very last moment the man's competitor gripped his end of the chain and pulled again, this time dragging his rival out of harm's way. The crowd gave a huge cheer, men were standing to applaud the spectacle as others dropped down to usher the still-raging bull back inside its pen.

"I hope you enjoyed our little show," a voice said in broken English.

They turned to see sprawled across two benches, a skinny bedraggled figure dressed in a pair of dirty torn jeans under a stained white vest. Lank grey hair grew to his shoulders over a sunken face.

"Is that it?" replied Sam. "I was expecting more fireworks."

"You mean more blood?"

"If that's what you call fireworks around here."

The sunken face split into a smile to reveal a line of dirty teeth. "You will have to forgive our ways, this method of bullfighting has been practised around here for centuries. Our ancestors used to use it as a method of solving dispute, a type of Spanish duelling."

"With bulls that size I'll stick to pistols at dawn."

"Ha, that would be too quick for us, we like our sport to last a bit longer." Their host sat up and reached out a skinny arm. "I'm the Chief, you will have to forgive us the welcome – we are not used to visitors."

Sam considered the hand for a moment but decided to take it. "Sam – and this is Tilly."

The man called Chief nodded and indicated for the pair of them to sit down next to him. "You picked a bad day, the boys down there were only practising one of the smaller animals we have here."

"You call that one small?" said Sam, surprised.

"Indeed, some of our larger beasts would have had those two boys for breakfast."

"If it's bigger than the one just on show then it can only be a minotaur?"

The Chief seemed to like Sam's jest and smiled. "If you'd like I can have one of the boys give you a tour?"

"I'd like that, if it's only to see this larger mythical beast."

He chewed one of his long fingernails causing Tilly to look on in disgust. "So what can I do for you? I take it you're not here only to admire our animals?"

Sam decided there was no point trying anything smart with this man. Regardless of the scruffy exterior on show he could tell there was something else just below the surface. He felt an involuntary shiver trickle down his spine.

"I work for the British government and I'm out here investigating a number of deaths that have occurred recently in the area."

The Chief, looking on over the activity happening down in the bullring as the next spectacle was being prepared, listened impassively as Sam spoke.

"Some of these deaths we believe may not have been due to natural causes."

"Must have kept the police busy then."

"Something like that, but at the moment we are all a little

stumped and I'm hoping you may be able to help shed some light on things."

The Chief gave a loud dry bark of a laugh. "I seriously doubt it, unless they are all bullfighting enthusiasts."

Sam ignored the comment and instead pulled out Selwin Birks's diary from his pocket. Flicking his fingers through the pages he stopped on the list.

"I don't suppose you would recognise any of these names?"

The Chief looked down at the pages opened up below him for the barest of moments before turning his gaze away. "Of course I do, Mr Taylor, and yes, I know who you are and the girl but you're wasting your time."

"I am?"

"Yes, you are, so let me save you some time. Of course I know all of those names, I owned all of their homes as part of an equity release business we ran. You know the deal – we buy the house, let the occupants live in until they die and then take the property back after they are in the ground. There's nothing illegal about it and I would also argue nothing immoral in helping an older generation live out their final years in comfort out in the sun."

"It's just a shame none of them have actually lived these many years of comfort, have they? Most have survived barely months after signing your legal and completely immoral contract," snapped Tilly, speaking for the first time since meeting the Chief, who seemed completely at ease with the implied accusation.

"Ah, so there we go, you're implying that I am going round killing my business partners to help fill my own pockets? Please be reasonable, you can't come here with no evidence accusing me of such things. Tell me, Mr Taylor, which of these unfortunate names have you any evidence of having not died of natural causes? I have seen all of the post-mortem reports, none had any question of foul play. Until now no one from law enforcement has ever bothered to see me as anything other than what I am, a simple businessman."

"My father did not die of natural causes," said Tilly, a coldness entering her voice.

The Chief twisted round on the bench, dropping his feet down from the row in front. He eyed the doctor as if in debate as to what to say. So far in their conversation he had not even bothered to skirt the subject of his supposed involvement in the deaths of his clients. In fact his whole defence had been to take it on, to make Sam and Tilly provide the evidence to back up their accusations. It was not an approach Sam liked. He felt they were being played – as if this man was trying to gauge what they knew rather than vice versa.

"I heard about your father and I agree your father was clearly different to those on Mr Taylor's list. His death was no accident, that is clear. Although that does not help us, does it?"

"Why not?" challenged Sam.

The Chief gave another of his grim smiles. "Because her dad wasn't one of my clients, was he? Not sure how I can be linked to that one. Your whole hypothesis is based on all these deaths being connected to one man and yet as you can see, I never even met your father."

"So you're admitting that you do have links to the other deaths?" asked a surprised Tilly.

Sam, however, was not as surprised – there was nothing to be gained by denying the link, if anything it would only hinder. But there was a big leap between admitting to being business partners, albeit one who stood to gain from the deaths, to actually wielding the knife.

"Of course, it's clear as day that I knew and worked with all of those names but that doesn't mean I had anything to do with their demise. My dear, look, you are going in circles – we already know every single one of those people died of natural causes, clear acts of God. So unless you are insinuating that I am some sort of deity then we are wasting all our time."

"Then it's a good job you have such a good local pathologist in Doctor Serrano, isn't it?" said Sam sarcastically.

That was the key and the Chief knew it. While Doctor Serrano was signing off every death as natural, then this man who called himself Chief could keep on counting the euros.

"I wouldn't know. I've never met the man."

So that's where you draw the line, thought Sam. It was one thing to be seen to benefit from the deaths yet quite another to be seen to be acquainted with the man who signs the death certificates.

Sam sighed and looked out back to the ring down below where a new bull was being exercised by a handler riding a horse. He knew there was no point in arguing with this man, not yet, not without some sort of actual evidence. Perhaps he should simply leave here and give everything they had to the police, let Moreno try to get blood from this particular stone. A thought flashed across his mind.

"How do you meet your clients? I mean, you had a particular type – single homeowner with no dependants – not the easiest person to locate."

For the first time in their interaction the Chief seemed slightly unsure what to say. Eventually he said, "The solicitors, they acted as the go-between, they found them. Nothing to do with me."

You're a liar, thought Sam, that was something to look into, a chink in the impenetrable armour. This whole operation was becoming clearer, the roles of each individual taking shape. Although it did still leave the start of the process. After all, just how did they select their targets?

"Have you any more clients on these deals?"

"No, why?"

"I just wondered if we should check to make sure their life insurance policies were up to date, seems signing up with you isn't that good for your health."

The Chief could not help but smile. "Or private medical insurance premiums."

"You're a grim bastard."

The Chief, now clearly bored by the conversation, simply yawned, stretched and then scratched his groin.

EIGHTEEN

THE MAN they called the Chief lazily slung round from the wooden bench, then stood to reveal a surprisingly tall frame from which his unwashed clothes limply hung. Sam tried to guess the man's age – between the weather-worn face, lank greasy grey hair and a dress sense that would insult a homeless beggar, there still seemed to be a youthful sort of energy within. Even without their suspicions Sam doubted he would have liked their host. There seemed to be an edge to everything he did, as if they had barely scratched the surface of whatever was hiding in plain sight.

"Come on, I'll give you the tour. It's not much so let's start then with our four-legged friends downstairs."

Silently, Tilly and Sam followed their host, there seemed to be little point in trying to continue their questioning. Whatever was happening here was not going to reveal itself to them today. Stomping along the wooden beams the Chief led them along the surrounding stands that looked down into the bullring. Reaching a narrow staircase the tall frame of the Spaniard bent down to take the wooden stairs into the depths below.

Behind him Sam felt a tension in Tilly as they made their way slowly down the steep steps. His own feelings were quite relaxed, his senses told him danger, while not far away, was not awaiting them below.

"Watch your head," the Spaniard grunted as the three of them reached the ground floor of the stand. To Sam's left he could see the open space of the bullring separated by metal bars spaced wide enough for a man to slip through, while preventing any of their pursuing beasts from following. Even before he had taken the last step the smell of caged cattle filled his nostrils. Blinking to get used to the darkened space it took Sam a moment to gather his bearings. He was now standing at the end of a narrow passageway either side of which were individual pens, each containing a caged animal. Sam could feel the eyes of great beasts following him as the three made their way down the line of bulls.

"Tell me you've checked the locks on these?" he called out to the Chief.

"It's all electronic now, there's a control panel down at the end. Just don't press the red button or we will all be squashed. We've found it safer for the handlers to keep a few inches of steel between them and the animals."

"Why do I sense someone learnt that lesson the hard way?" muttered Tilly, looking into one of the cages before jumping back in shock as the animal headbutted the locked gate.

The Chief laughed dryly. "You are not wrong. You see, here we take great pride in rearing some of the fiercest beasts in Spain." He stopped in front of the largest pen. "Take this one for instance, he is my finest, our great *el Rey*."

"The King?" translated Sam. "I didn't know bulls liked Elvis."

"Not even the king of rock and roll would be able to eat this slab of beef," cried the Chief, banging at the steel bars.

In response came a resounding clang of horn against metal as *el Rey*, disturbed from his peace, rattled at the cage. Sam peered into the darkened pen to see a huge black creature silhouetted there. Even in the limited light he could see thick lines of muscle stretching out across every inch of the creature's body.

"Christ, how big is that thing?" asked Tilly, looking over Sam's shoulder.

"Eight hundred kilograms, he's big even for a fighting bull. The next largest animal we have here is only seven hundred and he's considered big."

El Rey, seeing he now had an audience, went still, two black eyes staring out at the faces behind the bars.

"I think he heard you," said Sam, slightly in awe of the bull.

"He hears everything, he is a clever Englishman. The cleverest we've ever had here and I've raised some impressive creatures. I've had people from all over the world come and try to buy him from me, they have offered me thousands to take him away but they don't understand him like me. They would never be able to have a relationship like we have."

Listening on, Sam was surprised to hear the change in the Chief's voice which had softened ever so slightly. "Touching, I didn't have you down as the hugging type."

The Chief, in response to Sam's sarcasm, kicked at the pen's bars, triggering the great bull to a headlong charge into its steel environment. Both Sam and Tilly jumped back in fright from the power of the animal, their eyes ringing from the deafening sound of the undamaged bars.

"No, I'm not and neither is *el Rey*. I should have warned you before but *el Rey* has killed three men and injured six more, now the mere smell of human blood can set him into a frenzy."

"That and the steroids," added Tilly regaining her composure.

The Chief eyed the doctor before letting out a wry smile "I don't know what you mean."

Tilly raised an eyebrow. "I'm a doctor and while not a vet I can see the effects of long-term steroid use. Look at the abnormal muscle growth, the dilated eyes and then the clearly aggressive behaviour. What have you been giving this animal? Is it even legal?"

Their host studied Tilly for a moment before answering. "It is a personal recipe, call it a family secret."

Sam was bemused at his host's nonchalance at being rumbled. "And is it legal?"

"Who knows?" replied the Chief, a slight twinkle in his eyes. "But if I told you that breeders and fighters are more likely to give their animals tranquillisers before a fight would that be more befitting? To give the human even more of an unfair advantage in a fight to the death? No, in my ring it is our animals that are gods of the arena, we mere mortals only come to test ourselves on their altar."

Sam did not respond. Instead, he allowed the Chief to lead them away from *el Rey* and further along the line of pens. Reaching the end they slipped through a line of bars into a small office space where they found the same man who had greeted them on their arrival. The grumpy-looking Spaniard was now manning a control panel underneath a line of screens showing CCTV of the farm.

"You take your security very seriously here," commented Sam.

"We like our privacy," said the Chief.

"Next to the bulls? I take it smiley over there gets used to the smell."

The Chief gave a wry smile. "You see, Señor Taylor, my bulls are my life and I will protect them like my own children. Cesc here knows that if anything happened to my bulls it would be him fighting *el Rey* next."

Cesc, not understanding the English conversation, just glowered up at them. Leaving the confines of the bullring, Sam was grateful for the refreshing air that blew over them as they followed the Chief. Now standing amongst the decrepit industrial buildings Sam asked a question that had been nagging at him since their arrival.

"What else are you into? I mean business ventures. I guess you're involved in a bit more than bullfighting and building a holiday property portfolio?"

The Chief, now rolling a cigarette, answered without looking up. "This and that, I have fingers here and there. The family made its start in fishing, I still own most of the town's trawlers but how many rich fishermen do you know?"

"Not many," answered Sam honestly as he stuffed his hands in his pockets. He looked casually around the open yard and noticed three trailers standing empty to one side. All three were unhooked, their doors wide open to reveal empty insides. The scene was harmless enough, but Sam's interest was piqued by the waiting pallets of plastic water bottles which a forklift driver was preparing to load onto the waiting trucks.

"What are they for?" he asked innocently.

If Sam was expecting his question to have been harmless enough, then the reaction of their host was not in line with his expectations The Chief, who up until now had seemed completely at ease under all of their questioning, suddenly changed right in front of their eyes. His languid body immediately became tense, the shoulders raised in shock. He looked from Sam to Tilly and then to the busy forklift.

"It's nothing, just a friend using our land," he said, trying to dismiss the question.

"What does he need three pallets of water for?" Sam wondered aloud.

The Chief hesitated. "He has horses which he keeps up in the hills, they struggle to get drinking water up there."

Sam, not knowing whether this could even be true, did not respond. True, the land here was as dry as a bone and yet was transporting pallets of plastic water bottles really the best way of keeping their animals hydrated? Sam was doubtful. Added to the Chief's strange reaction, it did not quite add up.

"I think I'm going to have to leave you now, I have a few things I need to take care of," muttered the Chief, still slightly shaken.

Sam, able to recognise when their welcome had expired, took the hint. "I understand, I'm sure a man of your talents has many pressing things to worry about."

The weather-worn face of the Chief seemed to relax as if the shadow cast by the discovery of the pallets of water bottles had faded. Sam couldn't help being still curious, nothing else they had spoken about with this strange figure had triggered anything near the same response. It was as if he had somehow touched a hidden nerve. The Chief, now back to his languid self, led them back to the car. He stopped as the three of them reached the rental.

"If you will let me know if you need anything, I'd be more than happy to help. I don't like thinking there's something bad happening in my home town."

Tilly looked like she was about to say something until Sam gave her the slightest of nudges and she kept quiet. He did not think he could take any more of the man's bullshit in this one visit. Both of them bit their tongues until the car had travelled up the dust-covered track and they were back on the narrow road before the dam broke.

"We found him, Sam, we found the man who killed my dad." Tilly spoke excitedly, the words flying out. "I know he came out with all that shit about just being business partners but I could feel it, I could see it in his eyes. He did it, he killed them all and he just sat there goading us."

Sam shifted uncomfortably in his seat, unsure how to respond to his companion. "For what it's worth I think you're probably right although there are a lot of holes in your theory. Questions which would need answering before we could even broach it with the police."

"I know that, I'm not an idiot. He probably – no, let me change that – he certainly didn't do the actual killing but he's behind it. He gets the solicitor to make all the arrangements, buys the houses at a cut-price offer, right?"

"Right," said Sam, thinking how much this all sounded like he was having a medical procedure explained to him.

"Then the homeless pirate, the captain or whatever."

"The what? Do you mean the Chief?" Sam said, laughing and trying to concentrate on the road ahead.

"Yes, whatever he calls himself. He has the pensioners killed off, has that bent pathologist sign them off as accidents and cuts a nice profit. He probably had Nurse Diaz killed off to protect his prized pathologist."

Sam bit his tongue but then answered, careful not to upset his passenger. "Yeah, I can't fault your reasoning, it's just like I said – there's a few holes you'd need to fill out."

"Like what?"

"One – how do they select their targets?"

"I don't know, can't be many single pensioners out here."

"Two – you'd need to prove a link between the killers and the homeless pirate."

"Right, yeah, I know that."

"Three – and you won't like this – what role does your dad play in all of this? We know he was investigating the names on the list but how did the Chief know that? What tipped them off to have him killed?"

Tilly frowned and looked out of the window as she wrestled with Sam's points.

Seeing the disappointment in her Sam leant over and tapped her leg. "Hey, for what it's worth I think you're right, we finally found the connection. We just need to connect the rest of the dots and we will be able to get him."

Then that would still leave him with the dead MI5 agent and the wrongfully accused au pair, thought Sam sourly. Even with this new lead he felt miles away from actually being able to get back on a plane home. He let his mind wander from the strange Chief and his herd of bulls, back to the old town's police station. Checking his watch he suggested they could still check in on the incarcerated Alex.

"Yeah, no problem, do you fancy eating out tonight?" replied Tilly, her mind moving away from the conundrum of the Chief.

"Only if it's as good as last night."

"Better, there's a tapas place I know in the next town along the coast, we used to go to it when I was younger. Dad knew the couple that run it."

"Count me in." He paused then asked a question he had been pondering. "What did you think of the water bottles? Is that normal to use them on livestock?"

"I've no idea, I mean Dad used to say the water bill was the worst bill to be paid round here, I just thought that was because of the pool. Still, it does seem pretty strange, a lot of effort taking three trucks."

"Oh, Christ, that's it! Why the hell did I not notice it?"

"Notice what?"

Sam slapped the steering wheel in frustration. "Why did they need three lorries for only three pallets of water? Surely it would be easier to just have the one?"

Tilly did not seem as excited by this. "So what? Perhaps they had three herds to cover."

"Yeah, but they would still take the one lorry. Did you not notice how strangely the Chief reacted when we noticed them? He looked like we'd discovered his worst nightmare."

"I still don't see what difference this all makes? I mean what does three lorries of water have to do with my dad's death?"

"Honestly? Absolutely nothing but still are you not curious?"

"I'd rather know why he killed my dad to be honest."

Sam did not reply – instead, he turned his attention back to the road. There were still too many questions left to answer in this strange town. Cresting the final hill before the descent into the main Jávea bay, he mused on everything that had happened to him since leaving that empty plane back in London. Somewhere travelling some far-flung corner of the world was an air stewardess called Joanna and Sam wondered if her life had taken such a strange turn since their departure. Probably not, he decided. The world of aviation probably did not have the same number of corpses to deal with. Perhaps he was in the wrong profession, he should have become an airline pilot. *It wouldn't have been that different to what I do now, would it?* he thought. Travel the world, see some places, all without the trouble that seemed to follow him around.

Tilly brought his attention back to the car. "Still, those bulls were interesting. Did you see what it was packing below? I've never seen one so big."

Not for the first time that day Sam bit his tongue.

NINETEEN

THE LONG RECTANGULAR shape barely made a sound as it dropped into the ocean. To the crew members watching from the side, the shrouded body seemed to hardly break the surface of the rolling waves. The tired faces looked on with barely disguised indifference as the second body was lifted up by two of their fellow crew members, then slid down past the rusting hull and into the blue depths below. This routine had become second nature to a crew now well used to the high death rates of their cargo. They were, after all, simply units of cargo to be transferred from one harbour to another across the Mediterranean Sea. If they died of whatever sickness grew within the confined spaces deep inside the steel hold, what difference did it make to them? The money they received would still be the same. Wages that far exceeded the usual incomes of these Spanish fishermen. So who cared that some nameless refugee ended up in Davy Jones's locker?

At least this is how the majority of the grizzled captain's crew had thought. Until that young fool Carles had decided to grow a conscience. What had he told the youth? Not to concern himself, to keep his mind on the money and yet here they were. He kicked out at the third bundle at his feet and cursed. An anger unlike any he had felt for years simmered under the surface at the circumstances that had led him to this. He could sense the crew members standing round him trying to keep their distance. The day's events having shaken a crew used to the most extremes of hardship.

"Did you want to say anything?" asked one of the braver members of the crew.

"Have I ever said anything before when we've done this?"

"No, but I thought with it being–"

The captain cut in. "No, there is nothing more to say."

The crewman eyed his companions as if trying to find a fellow voice to support his suggestion. Instead, he was met by blank glares, the indifference to death had stretched even to one of their own.

"Just get on with it, drop the bastard in and be done with it."

The two crew members assigned to the burial duties each took one end of the covered body, heaved once and let go. The entire crew watched as the third corpse hit the water. For a moment every one of them stood still, each with their own thoughts. But then one by one, each returned to their assigned duties as they made the final leg of their journey. Only the captain remained. He leant against the rail to watch as his ship sailed past the few remaining ripples that betrayed the last-known location of Carles Casillas.

A voice hailed him out of his trance and he turned to see his second-in-command calling out to him.

"What is it now?" he grunted back.

"The Chief, he's on the satellite phone, says it's urgent," said the man, holding out the phone.

"Shit," the captain grumbled, not in the mood to deal with his superior. "I'll take it in my cabin."

Taking the proffered device he left the deck and headed inside. Once secure in his small private cabin, his placed the phone to his ear.

The voice of the Chief crackled down the line. "I hear you had some trouble?"

Grunting, the captain answered, "It's been dealt with."

"Evidently. What happened?"

The captain debated with telling the man at the end of the phone to mind his own business but decided against it. The Chief was the Chief after all.

"We found one of the crew engaging with the cargo. He was planning on helping them escape. He's been dealt with."

And he had been dealt with thoroughly. He himself had found Casillas in the hold with the cargo, had heard the whispering, the urgent voices echoing round the metal container. Walking slowly along the gangway he had picked up a long wrench left by the ship's engineer, the heavy iron cold to the touch. Creeping slowly along the passage he had come upon the unsuspecting Carles and in one stroke had split the young man's head open. Even in the dimly lit hold he had seen the grey brains amongst the blood staining the end of the tool.

"Good, good, you did well," crowed the Chief. "There's no point in delaying the inevitable. How did the rest of the crew take it?"

"You know the men as well as anyone, I told them we'd split Carles's share between them and they soon shut up."

"Yes, that's fair, I'll make sure they get a little extra as well."

The Chief paused as if expecting an acknowledgment of this show of generosity but was to be disappointed. Eventually he spoke again. "What about the cargo, any more problems with them?"

"None, I think the sight of what we do to our own was more than enough of a warning."

A bark of a laugh came over the phone. "I bet it gave them a shock. How many units have we lost this time?"

This the captain knew was the real question the Chief wanted to ask. "We lost two more today. There's a sickness amongst them, a fever of some sort and without any medical support on board there is nothing I can do. I'm afraid we will lose more before we dock and you will probably lose a few more on the onward journey."

"Goddamn it, this is all I need to hear," the Chief said. "Tell me, what do you need to fix this?"

"We need a doctor, or you will need one to check everyone over before you send them onwards."

"How the hell am I supposed to do that? I can't just walk them all into Dénia Hospital can I?"

The captain rolled his eyes at his master's words. "What about that pathologist you have working for you? Can't you get him to help?"

"He's unavailable at the moment, there's quite a bit of heat over here. In fact I need to talk to you about it."

Here we go, thought the captain, another problem for him to solve. "What type of heat? The police?"

"No, no, nothing like that, those pigs couldn't find their socks never mind us. No, we have a problem with an outsider sticking their nose in. We don't think it would be wise for you to come into dock just yet."

"What am I supposed to do then? I've a tired crew and dying cargo. How long am I supposed to just sit here?"

"Peace, my friend, it is only a short delay. It is just while we deal with the problem and then you can come home. Just stay off the coast and we will come get you. Best to stay off radio and if anyone asks say you're doing a final sweep for some fish."

The captain rubbed his face, this was not the news he had been wanting. They had been only hours away from their home port and now would have to float out to sea until the Chief sorted himself out. But what could he do? The Chief was the Chief.

There was a moment's pause before the Chief added, "And about your medical problem, I think I know where we can get you a doctor. If anything it may help with solving our other problems."

"Fine, I'll cruise north for now and wait till I hear from you. We meet at the same spot, yes?"

"Yes."

"What are you going to do to the outsiders?"

Humour entered the Chief's voice. "Same thing you do to your crew members."

The line went dead and the captain put the device on his desk. Looking out of the circular window he tried to remember his own advice. *Think of the money, just think of the bloody money.*

TWENTY

SAM STRETCHED his legs out from under the patio chair as he sat under the orange glow of the Spanish sunset. He took a sip of the ice-cold Tarquin's gin and tonic and raised his glass in thanks to deceased Selwin for his taste. The man had known his spirits, thought Sam as he looked over the rooftops of the rows of villas that stretched neatly along the hilltop in front of him. For the first time since arriving in the Costa Blanca he felt relaxed, at ease with the world. True, they were still only chasing ideas in the Selwin Birks case and worse, he had made next to no progress in the Chris Kane murder. Even after visiting the incarcerated Alex Coombs again that evening, Sam had failed to secure her release. Not that it worried him too much, he could sleep a little easier knowing at least one person was safely locked away from whatever was going on here.

The sound of his phone vibrating on the tabletop snapped him out of his trance. A message from Emma told him she had failed in her political negotiations with the Home Office and an MI5 colleague of Chris Kane's would be arriving in the morning. The final sentence warning him to play nice. Sam groaned internally, another awkward figure in this circus of players. He had spent much of the early evening thinking about the Kane case, trying to think of any possible angle he could have missed but nothing materialised. Not even one of his crazy impossible ideas, which if only to keep himself entertained, occasionally gave him the breakthrough he needed. The only thing he kept coming back to was the strange behaviour of the widowed Sofia Kane. After meeting that cold cow, he could now say when it came to grief, he had seen it all.

Sam was just debating which of the two characters he had met today were the strangest, the widow or the Chief, when he was interrupted by the arrival of Tilly. She was dressed this evening in a dark pine-green cocktail dress, a single strap running over her shoulder. Her blonde hair had been tied back, revealing her long neck from which hung a silver necklace.

"Are you really going out looking like that?" she said accusingly.

"Yeah, why not? I've put a shirt on," said Sam, looking down at his cargo shorts with a T-shirt covered by one of the new shirts he had bought the day before.

"I didn't mean the shirt, why do you still insist on wearing those god-ugly boots."

"As I said before, you try kicking someone in flip-flops."

Tilly shook her head in despair before turning on her heel back into the villa. Sam drained the remnants of the gin before following her. Dinner had been booked somewhere in the next town down the coast and Sam drove the pair of them along the main roads which led out of the Jávea bay and over the hilltops back down to sea level. They avoided discussing the day's events – instead, Sam listened as Tilly spoke of her time working in the medical profession. How between her and her colleagues they had seen pretty much everything that life could throw at a person.

"Even someone like the Chief?" asked Sam, thinking of the strange figure they had encountered.

"No, you're right. I don't think I've quite met anyone like that piece of shit."

Sam laughed and as he did so his eye caught something in the rear mirror. He looked again and in between the queuing traffic he noticed the grille of a black Mercedes. Something about it seemed familiar. He tried to get a glimpse of the driver, but was limited by the glare of the setting sun on the Mercedes' windscreen. Returning his concentration back to the road ahead he kept looking back up at the rear mirror, eager to try and get a better view of the trailing car.

Tilly noticed Sam's behaviour. "What's got your attention?"

He nodded up to the mirror. "The black Mercedes two cars back, I recognise it."

"There's lots of black Mercedes, what makes you think you've seen that one before?"

"I honestly don't know, maybe the number plate? Call it a hunch."

Tilly rolled her eyes. "I wouldn't worry about it, this is the main road down to Moraira so it's probably just an innocent local on his way home."

"Hmmm," said Sam, still unsatisfied.

The Mercedes continued to follow them along the main road, ignoring the increasing number of turn-offs. As each minute passed with the car still behind them, Sam felt his nerves increase. As they stopped for a set of traffic lights he leant past Tilly and retrieved the pistol from the glove box.

"Seriously?" Tilly sighed.

Sam ignored her and placed the weapon on his lap within easy reach of his steady right hand. After everything that had happened this was not a moment for waiting and hoping for the best.

Reaching the outskirts of Moraira, Tilly directed Sam into a large car park which stretched out from the back of the town to where the bright lights of a fun fair illuminated the dusk. The car bounced slightly over the rough ground as Sam slowed his speed, half searching for a parking spot, half keeping an eye on the approaching Mercedes. He pulled into the first available space, driving through to the front of the next row of cars in case he needed to speed off. Keeping the engine running he swivelled in his seat and waited to see if he had been right.

"Shit," Sam said as the long silhouette of the Mercedes drove down the rows of parked cars. "Tilly, keep your head down."

They both watched on breathlessly as the suspect vehicle made its way towards them. Sam gripped the pistol and cocked it, he was not going to be caught unawares. They would realise he was not a defenceless nurse. He gripped the handle tightly, tensing as the headlights rose up to meet them, then came the bonnet, the dark glass of the interior and then they had driven past. They both strained in their seats to watch as the would-be stalkers drove the entire length of the car park, down towards the lights of the fun fair.

Sam gave a sigh of relief and uncocked the pistol.

"Satisfied now?" demanded Tilly.

"I'm never satisfied," said Sam, climbing out of the car. He indicated the pistol still in his hand. "And I'm keeping this with me tonight."

Tilly gave him a pitying look. "Whatever, can we get something to eat now?"

Scowling, Sam got out of the car, looked down the long car park, but not seeing the black Mercedes, stuffed his hands in his pockets and followed Tilly. She led him between the parked cars and through the gravel-covered ground back onto the main road. Confidently navigating the side streets she led him into a small square covered in tables. A brown sign hung over the door to a glass-fronted restaurant announcing Cava.

"Best tapas in Spain," Tilly announced, smiling as the owners spotted her.

"Tilly!" came the cry from inside. A short-haired woman came flying out and wrapped her arms around the smiling Tilly. "Oh, I'm sorry about your dad."

Tilly gave a weak smile. "I know, I'm sorry too. It's good to see you again, Claire. How's the family? Where's Paul?"

Claire released Tilly. "He's inside running a drinks order, we're busy tonight."

"As always."

"Yes, as always but we've got you a table in the corner over there." She indicated to one side of the square and then noticing Sam, asked, "And who's this? I didn't know you'd finally found a man."

"No, not really. If anything he found me and it's not like that. He's helping to find out what happened to Dad."

Claire raised her eyes. "Ah, the police still haven't done anything then?"

"Nope, but we will," said Tilly, sounding more confident than Sam felt.

Claire led them to their table before returning back to her kitchen.

"The best tapas in Spain ran by the English?" mused Sam.

Tilly grinned. "Beat them at their own game, haven't they been doing it to us on a football field for years?"

"Them and everyone else in the world," replied Sam, picking up a menu, but before he had a chance to open it he had it snatched out of his hands. "Hey, what are you doing?"

"I'm choosing tonight, it's tapas so expect lots of different dishes coming out at you. Just try and keep up."

Tilly was as good as her word, starting with ordering two large German beers brought over by Claire's husband Paul, who like his wife greeted Tilly as an old friend.

"I'll miss playing golf with your dad." Paul sighed as he placed the glasses on the table. "Me and him used to be a right pairing. I'll have to play with that numpty accountant from now on so I can kiss goodbye to any winnings."

Tilly grinned up at him. "Dad used to say he had to carry you round all the time."

"Shut it, you," said Paul, laughing. "Let me know if you need any help collecting his things from the clubhouse, they will reach out to arrange closing his membership and shares. But you know where I am, in fact I'm playing tomorrow so will speak to the secretary and get it moving."

"Cheers, Paul, I would appreciate that."

The first round of plates came, a mixture of covered nachos, quesadillas and prawns, each dish cooked to perfection causing Sam to regret having to share. They spoke of their respective childhoods and family members as if neither of them wanted to discuss the darkness that had brought them together – Tilly of a distant father, Sam of exploring heather-covered moorlands. Just as they were finishing their first round did Sam notice the arrival of a single man. It would have been impossible to have missed him, he towered over Paul as he showed him to the table next to theirs. This newcomer must have been well over Sam's own six feet. He was dressed in a white shirt stretched tight by thick muscles, the top two buttons undone. Long brown hair was tied in a topknot fashion above a narrow, high-cheeked face where small brown eyes looked down over a sharp nose.

Taking the seat alongside Sam on the next table along, the newcomer rubbed his stubble-lined face as he studied the menu. Sam and Tilly made eye contact and gave each other the same awkward glance, although any curiosity was soon replaced as the second round of plates appeared. This time a collection of sliders, curries and pulled pork.

"I'm afraid I have to ask," said Tilly, putting down her fork, "but what do we do now?"

Sam glanced up from his burger. "What do you mean?"

She gave him a glare. "You know – with the cases? We know that this Chief clearly has something to do with my dad's death but we can't prove it. Do we go to the police or what?"

"I honestly don't know. I agree with you that we know most of it, it's just there's still too many pieces missing. There's not enough for the police to do anything, it's all guesswork, hypotheticals. They need something firmer, something they can use to charge them all."

"Them all?"

"Yes, the Chief, his minions and don't forget our good 'doctor death' Serrano. I reckon he's the weak link in all of this."

"What do you mean the weak link?"

"He's the one person who's right at the coalface in all this. Think about it, he's the one that has to front up to the police, to the deceased families and his own medical teams to convince them all the deaths are innocent. All the Chief has to do is claim that it's just coincidence that his business partners keep on dying. They are, after all, old and he has the cover of an apparently neutral doctor telling everyone the deaths were all natural."

"I see what you mean, without Serrano providing air cover the Chief's story would be far less viable."

"Exactly, the only reason he's not been investigated yet is no one thinks the deaths are suspicious. Everyone except your old man. Problem is there's no way to link Serrano to the Chief, well, not at the moment."

"So what do we do?"

Sam ran his hand through his hair as he thought for a moment. "I think we need to try and put some pressure on the good doctor, let's see if he cracks."

"Tomorrow?"

"Why not?" Sam then remembered Emma's message about the MI5 officer that was being sent out. "Although we may have one problem, we will certainly be having company tomorrow."

He told her about the expected arrival making Tilly ask, "Does that mean you're no longer on the Kane case?"

Sam shrugged. "I have no idea, I've never heard of MI5 sending someone abroad like this. It's out of their remit. I guess I'll just have to meet him tomorrow and see what he wants to do. Hopefully he'll see things the same way as we do and get Alex out of jail."

"It's still strange isn't it that this Kane guy dies around the same time as my dad. Could there be a connection?"

Sam sighed and sat back in his chair considering the question. It had been something he himself had tried to reason out. On the face of it, no, there was no connection. What possible link did Chris Kane have to the Chief or Selwin Birks? But like everything else in this place, it was what was below the surface that mattered. Chris Kane had been speaking to the same solicitors used by the Chief on the morning of his death, yet now Sam had to admit that that was a very small thread to go on.

"Maybe, but then again maybe not. Like your dad's death there are lots of things I don't like. I don't like how Alex Coombs has been set up, I don't particularly like the reaction of Mrs Kane and I especially don't like the timing. But I'm just a suspicious character, it's all probably just another innocent coincidence." Sam said the last line with a sly smirk.

"Yeah, right." Tilly laughed back at him. "This is mad, isn't it? I mean, like in the space of a few days my dad dies, we then find out he's one of many, an innocent nurse is stabbed in front of us, a guy gets killed while away boating with his young au pair and now we think a crazy tramp who trains bulls is all behind it. I mean come on, next thing you'll be telling me there's this evil mastermind orchestrating everything from behind the scenes."

A voice interrupted them. "Hi, excuse me."

They both turned in surprise only to see their dining neighbour looking over at them.

"Yes?" asked Sam.

"Sorry to interrupt, please can I borrow your tomato sauce." The narrow face gave a friendly smile as he indicated the plastic bottle.

Sam handed it over to him before returning to Tilly's reasoning. "Yeah, I wouldn't worry about it too much, I've seen stranger things."

"Like what?"

"I once had to rescue someone from a castle."

"Yeah, right."

"No, I'm serious, some big time drug dealer who worked for some organisation called le central had set up camp there. I had to storm in and everything."

Tilly laughed aloud. "You're mad. Honestly, you do talk some rubbish."

"It's true, and I once smashed up a criminal smuggling gang with a dwarf."

"Shut it, seriously you're not funny."

"I'm always funny, but do you know what is bothering me – and believe me, I know it's a bit small fry when you think of everything else that is going on – but the Chief's reaction when we saw the lorries and water pallets. Don't you think he was acting strange?"

"Kind of but surely that has nothing to do with us?"

"Probably not, although for a man who seemed to have answers to everything he came up short when we asked about that. It was almost as if he was caught in a panic."

"I think you should let that one go, it's not as if we've not got much else to think about."

Sam gave up and returned to his dinner. The third course came, again causing Sam to regret having to share but he was soon satisfied by the delivery of Claire's home-made brownie to finish. By that time Tilly had begun questioning him about his time in the army.

"Do you miss being in the army?" she asked him, scraping the remnants of her dessert from the now empty plate.

"Sometimes, it's a type of lifestyle, a vocation. It's not something you can just pick up or drop off. I don't think I'd be able to go back now and enjoy it the same way. Things will have changed since I was there. It's like anything really, it's all about the people who you spend the time with. They will have moved on with their own lives," Sam mused.

"I get that, it's like a chapter you have to close to move on."

"Exactly."

"But still, Captain Sam Taylor, eh? Sounds good, I bet you've used that a few times."

"A few."

"Excuse me." Again the stranger on the table next door interrupted, causing them both to look round. "Did you say you were in the forces?"

Sam studied the tall man before answering. "Yes, Military Police, Second Regiment, Two Twenty-Two Provost Company."

The narrow face spilt into a grin. "Nice, I was in the air force, logistics." He reached out a hand. "Name's Neil Major, Lieutenant if we are using the military terms."

Taking the offered hand Sam felt a tight grip across his own. "Captain Taylor then, er, nice to meet you."

Neil Major sat back in his chair. "Nice place this, isn't it?" he said, gesturing around at the busy restaurant. "First time I've been here, heard it was good."

"The owners are great, cook everything themselves," said Tilly proudly.

Major nodded in agreement. "Now that I can agree with, the food was spot on. I am sorry to interrupt a romantic evening, it is always good to meet a fellow serviceman."

"Oh, there's no romance here," replied Tilly a bit more forcefully than she intended, causing Sam to raise an eyebrow.

Major chuckled then stood up. "Of course not, I get it. Well, nice to meet you both."

They watched as Major wandered amongst the other patrons finding Paul to pay his bill.

"I bet he wasn't allowed to wear his hair like that when he was in the air force," mused Sam, watching him go.

Tilly teased him. "I think you'd look good with long hair."

"Shut it, you've already upset me by claiming there's no romance here. I don't just take anyone out to posh restaurants, you know."

Tilly kicked him under the table as Paul returned with their bill along with two glasses of tequila.

"Compliments of your neighbour, said it would help bring out the romance?"

Sam grinned as he drained the glass in one then waited for Tilly to say her goodbyes. Standing there in the warm night air he felt the alcohol lighten his head, the mixture of gin, beer and tequila making him slightly sleepy.

Tilly returned and pushed over the remaining shot glass. "Here, you take it and I'll drive."

Sam merrily did as he was told and downed the glass. "Yes, ma'am."

Leaving the still-busy restaurant, Tilly led Sam back through the town's back streets out onto the main road, then into the large car park. With his mind gently clouded and his stomach filled with Claire's excellent food, he missed the two men who hurried past as they stopped by the rental. Nor did he immediately spot the twin lights appearing at the end of the row of cars as the black Mercedes came back to life, the shiny black bonnet nosing its way through stationary vehicles renewing its pursuit of the small rental.

TWENTY-ONE

SAM RESTED his back in the passenger seat and closed his eyes, letting the alcohol wash over him. The trapped heat of the car combined with the strain of the past few days sent a blanket of drowsiness to wash over him. Next to him Tilly drove the rental along the main road, then out of the small seaside town back inland where they would cross back over to the next bay. Sam was quite happy to drift off and only be woken when they arrived back at the villa. Suddenly the car came to an abrupt halt followed by the sound of the engine being cut off. He opened one eye in surprise, surely the journey had not been that quick, he thought.

"Are you going to stay and sleep off dinner or are you coming in with me? We need some actual food for breakfast, unless you're planning on living off gin and tequila?" the voice of Tilly asked him.

Blinking, Sam rubbed his eyes to see they had pulled into one of the German discount supermarkets that lined the main road out of town.

"Nah, you're all right, I'll stay and guard the car," he told her, settling back down into his seat.

Tilly rolled her eyes then left him in the car. Sam rested his elbow on the side door and leant his head into the palm of his hand, closing his eyes. He was ready for bed, the thought of the air-conditioned bedroom making him even sleepier than before. Feeling an itch in the corner of one eye he placed his forefinger and thumb over the bridge of his nose and rubbed. Opening them again all his dreams of a good night's sleep evaporated in a rush of adrenaline.

"No bloody way," he said to the empty car as he squinted through the windscreen. "You've got to be bloody kidding me."

Ahead of him, parked to one side of the supermarket's car park was the black Mercedes. Whoever had been driving it had followed them here, he had been right after all. Not that this thought gave him much comfort at this moment in time. Blinking profusely he pulled out the hidden pistol for the second time that night and again cocked it ready for action. He was damned if they were going to take him without a fight. Next, he looked over his shoulder to see if he could spot Tilly. The blonde-haired doctor was still somewhere in the shop.

"Goddamn it."

Perhaps he should go in and get her? No, he told himself firmly, their pursuers were obviously not wanting to cause a scene anywhere too public, otherwise they'd have acted sooner. Either way, Sam had decided they would not be getting the chance, he'd had enough of being caught up in whatever all this was. It was time to start swinging back.

Keeping one eye on the Mercedes he spotted the advancing figure of Tilly leaving the glass doors of the supermarket. She carried a filled shopping bag which she dropped in the boot before returning to the driver's seat.

"Well, you look like you've woken up," she commented, spotting the new alertness in her companion.

"The Mercedes, it's back," Sam said slowly.

Tilly frowned. "What, where?"

"Two rows back over there. I'm certain it's the same one."

Tilly glanced over to where Sam was pointing and shook her head. "You don't know that, it could just be another Mercedes."

"It's not," Sam said curtly, an icy coldness now in his voice.

Tilly swallowed, eyeing the held pistol resting on Sam's lap. "What are you going to do?"

"Right now? Nothing. Too public. But I'd quite like to have a word with whoever's been spending their evening watching us."

"Then what are you going to do? Five minutes ago you looked like you were going to fall asleep, now you want to take out an unknown tail?"

"I sobered up. Come on, turn the engine on or otherwise they will think something's wrong."

She did as instructed then asked, "Where do you want me to go? I'd rather not have them follow us back home if you're going to do something."

Sam thought for a moment, his mind now operating back to its full capacity due to the proximity of the danger. "The Granadella cove? The one with the long winding road. You said it can be reached by a minor road from this side of the headland?"

"Yes, I did, although it's a bloody narrow drive, no one hardly uses it. We'd be all alone if anything went wrong."

"It's perfect. Come on, just do as I tell you."

Still looking slightly uncomfortable at the sudden change of the night's events, Tilly drove them out of the supermarket. She pulled out onto the main road then turned down the way they had just come back into the town.

"They will be wondering what we are playing at driving back towards Moraira," she said worriedly.

"Don't fret, they will think we've forgotten something and then when we drive up the headland that you're just giving me the scenic tour."

Tilly did not look reassured. Instead, gripping the steering wheel more firmly, she navigated her way through the traffic. Sam kept his eyes on the rear-view mirror, desperate to see if he had been right about the tail. For a moment he felt his stomach drop as no black car could be seen leaving the supermarket. Then slowly, almost cautiously it came out onto the main road and began to follow them again.

"Here they come," said Sam but Tilly ignored him, concentrating on the road.

Driving back through the streets of Moraira, Tilly still keeping her thoughts to herself, she drove steadily towards the shadowy headland that rose up from the horizon. Behind them, the Mercedes kept a steady distance, the driver seemingly confident that whichever way home its prey tried, they at least knew the final destination. Sam checked and rechecked the pistol in his hand as the small car began its steep climb up the narrow road that led back towards Jávea. Now they had become the only car on the road as they made their way up the twisting turns. Sam, looking over his shoulder, had seen their pursuer had been forced to drop right back in a pointless bid to avoid detection.

It was only as they reached the summit of the first headland as it dropped down into the Granadella cove with its now empty pebbled beach, did Tilly speak again.

"Sam, what are you actually planning on doing?" she asked, a slight edge to her voice.

"I don't know yet, I'm just going to talk to them."

"Then you don't need a gun," Tilly told him firmly. "You've been drinking and I don't want you to do anything stupid."

"What about if they have guns?" said Sam defiantly. "Have you forgotten what they did to your dad or all the others? These guys don't mess around, Tilly. If they see an opportunity they will take it. You have to be willing to go toe-to-toe with these people sometimes."

"You still haven't told me what you plan on doing?"

Sam thought for a moment then answered, "Drive to the bottom of the cove then make your way back up that long winding road. When you get to a hairpin near the top, stop and put on your hazard lights."

Tilly for once did not argue, instead returned her attention to steering the small car down the steep road towards sea level. Sam looked behind him but could no longer see any sign of the Mercedes as the driver cautiously kept his distance. It was only as they reached the cove's bottom did the sight of headlamps piercing the night's sky tell Sam that his plan was still in motion. They began the journey up the twisting and turning road back up the other side towards the main headland. Looking down out of the car windows Sam could see the sheer drops down to the rocks below grow higher and higher until eventually he instructed Tilly to pull over.

"Put the hazards on and wait in here," he told her calmly.

"What are you going to do?" she asked again, only this time with more urgency.

"I'll run behind us and hide somewhere. Once our friends get here they will see you and hopefully stop to get out and investigate. Well, hopefully," he added as an afterthought.

"Hang on, you want me to do what exactly? Just wait here and be a sitting target?"

Sam shrugged. "I prefer the word bait, but I'll go with your suggestion."

Tilly scowled then held out her hand. "Fine. Then give me the gun."

"What? No chance."

"Do it, Sam, or I'm driving us straight back home."

Sam studied the firm expression that had crossed his companion's face and decided there would be little point in arguing. Sighing, he handed over the weapon.

"You can have that telescopic baton you got all excited about, it's still there in the glove box."

The memory of the expanding baton immediately lightened his mood and Sam retrieved the heavy metal cylinder from the compartment in front of him. He took a final look at Tilly. "Cheer up, it could be the same team who killed your dad. I bet you'd like to have a word with them."

Tilly did not reply as Sam left her alone in the stationary vehicle. The thought that she could drive off and leave him stranded here floated across his mind. He pushed it away. Instead, he jogged back a few metres to where a deep ditch ran along the left-hand side of the road. Above him the rocky clifftop loomed against the night sky as he crouched down amongst the rocks and piles of pine needles freshly fallen from the trees around him. Listening intently he gripped the solid metal of the baton, then using his thumb, pushed the switch which released the spring expanding the pole outwards. He touched the heavy metal ball at the baton's end that gave the weapon an additional weight at its tip. Sam was ready.

Below him the sound of the approaching car increased as the Mercedes made its way up the many twists and turns that led out of the cove. Surely they would stop, thought Sam. In fact, by not stopping it would only add weight to the belief they had been following them in the first place. Why else drive past? Tilly must have been thinking the same thing as she opened the car door to come round and stand at the vehicle's rear. Sam hoped to God she carried the pistol out with her.

The twin lights of the Mercedes came round the final bend, momentarily blinding Sam's vision. It slowed as the driver spotted the parked rental. Sam watched as the driver hesitated for a moment, unsure how to react to this new situation.

"Come on, you bastards," whispered Sam. "Get out and have a look."

It was almost as if the car's occupants had heard him. Whoever was driving pulled the car to a stop a few metres behind where Tilly was now stood waving them down. The noise of the engine died, leaving only the sounds of the night echoing around them. A stillness crept over the small stretch of road as all of the participants weighed up their next move. Sam wondered how he would explain his sudden appearance if the car's passengers were just innocent passers-by. But his fears were immediately extinguished with the sight of the two occupants exiting the car just ahead of him. He watched on in quiet satisfaction as both men loosened hidden weapons stuffed in their waistbands. The revelation of the two weapons was not a worry, he had the element of surprise to counter the numerical advantage.

"Hey, thank you, we've broken down," Sam heard Tilly call out to the two newcomers in English.

The newcomers looked at each other uncertainly as they advanced towards her. Sam guessed neither spoke English, instead the nearest to him called out in Spanish. "Where is the other one?"

Tilly, oblivious to what had been said, continued. "We can't get the bloody thing to start." She leant her head inside the car to a non-existent Sam. "Try starting the engine again, Sam."

The Spaniard tried again in his native language. "Where is the man?"

Sam would have laughed if the situation wasn't so serious. Three strangers all fumbling around in their native languages. Moving slowly he climbed up back onto the road. Ahead of him the two outlines of the Spaniards had come to a halt just ahead of Tilly. Both had one hand clasping the grip of a pistol.

Tilly tried again. "Have you got any jump leads?"

The Spaniard closest to the metal barrier overlooking the cliff edge gave his companion a slight nod causing both to begin drawing their weapons. In the darkness Tilly missed it but Sam, expecting it, did not. He sprinted up from his crouched position and ran, his booted feet hitting hard on the tarmac. The Spaniards must have heard but were too slow in reacting. Sam reached the first of them, swinging the extendable baton hard into the exposed back knee, causing its owner to cry out in pain. His companion stepped back in shock yet not far enough away to avoid Sam's upswing and the weighted end of the baton crashed into his face, the heavy metal thumbing into the eye socket, cutting skin and fracturing bone.

Sam was now in full fight mode, his animal instinct taking over as he crashed his weapon into the first opponent, this time landing a brutal blow to the man's temple, sending him to the ground. The second attacker, half blinded, roared in anger and tried to grab Sam's arms in a great bear hug. Trapped, his arms by his side and his back to the Spaniard, he tried to wrestle himself free, but his grip was too tight. In front of him the other man was slowly recovering, he was almost upright. Sam gave him a swift kick between the legs with his booted foot before returning his attention back to his other assailant. Still unable to escape the iron grip around him, he flung his head back, feeling it hit into the man's already damaged face. He heard a pained grunt, followed by the arms around him releasing slightly, allowing him to break the hold. Leaping free, he turned back on his heel, the baton raised high, ready to strike – when a voice called out.

"Enough, everyone stop there." It was Tilly, holding the pistol out in front of her.

Sam grinned and took a step back. The two Spaniards, while unable to understand the spoken words, certainly got the message of the black muzzle pointed at them.

"Why'd you do that? I was just getting into my groove," complained Sam as he went round and removed both of the pistols still stored in their pursuers' waistbands.

"Do you ever just shut up?" snapped Tilly. "Seriously, you always have to say something, don't you?"

Sam shrugged as he threw one of the pistols over the cliff edge while keeping one for himself. First, checking the weapon, he wandered round to join Tilly standing in front of the now sullen pair. The one whose eye socket Sam had smashed tried to dab at a trickle of blood dripping down his cheek. Next to him his companion stood unsteadily as he tried to put weight back on his damaged knee. Both stared up at their conquerors with pure venom.

"What do we do now?" asked Tilly.

Sam turned to the pair and asked in Spanish, "I take it the Chief didn't want to come himself this evening?"

Neither replied. If he had been expecting a reaction to the mention of their boss then Sam was disappointed.

"Okay, then start by telling us what you were planning on doing to us this evening?"

Again, no answer. Next to him Tilly was shaking slightly as she tried to keep her weapon pointed at the pair. Sam noticed both sets of eyes were following her rather than him.

"Look, guys, this can go two ways – either you tell us what we want to know or you can take a short walk and a long drop." He pointed towards the edge of the road.

Again, neither spoke. If anything, both faces had turned even grimmer.

"Ask them if they killed my dad," Tilly muttered.

Sam, surprised at the question, did as he was told. Still, neither of the two spoke but Sam noticed a slight smile appear at the corner of one of their mouths before it disappeared again.

"The lady asked you a question," growled Sam, stepping forwards to press the gun under the chin of the man struggling to stand.

"We don't know who her father is," he grunted.

"What did he say?" asked Tilly.

"Nothing useful," said Sam, stepping back. Now he had these two goons he was unsure exactly what to do with them. Perhaps he should just let them go, he thought, tell them to pass on a message to the Chief that they know what his game is.

"I want to know, did they kill my dad?" Tilly asked again, this time her voice getting louder. It seemed that the reluctant Tilly of earlier had vanished now she was actually face to face with the men who had maybe killed her father.

"I'd tell her if I was you, I reckon she's probably a poor shot but at this range? I don't reckon it will be a head shot, probably a bullet in the guts followed by a slow death?"

Still neither man spoke, it seemed everyone in the Chief's organisation carried this unspoken confidence. So Sam tried another tactic. "What does he do with the water pallets?"

Like with the Chief earlier in the day this caused a reaction. Both men seemed surprised to have been asked such a question.

"I'll count to three then one of you is going for a jump," bluffed Sam, knowing full well he could not just throw an unarmed man off a cliff without provocation.

"One… two…"

The broken eye-socket man spoke first. "It's for the fishing fleets, fresh water for the trips."

Interesting, thought Sam, either this man was lying or the Chief had not been honest with them. Something about those water bottles seemed to scare everyone they met. He stepped back, considering his next move. As he did so he noticed the eyes of the two Spaniards flicker between him and Tilly. He realised that he should have probably moved her back out of range of a desperate lunge from the pair, but it was too late. Sam saw the feet of the man with the bleeding face move back slightly, then move forwards. Next came the hand released from stemming the wounds to his face, stretching out for Tilly's own outstretched hands. Tilly, her body still shaking slightly, had missed all this, her reactions too slow to respond to the threat. Even worse, she then hesitated to pull the trigger. The second Spaniard had also caught the minute signals and moved almost at the same time for Sam. The years of practice, of training, of being able to spot danger did kick in for Sam, who standing slightly further back, did not hesitate. He fired once, twice and then a further two times into the now prone corpses on the ground at their feet.

TWENTY-TWO

THE CRISP BANGS of the four gunshots reverberated around the rocky cliffs, echoing for an age and back to ring in their ears as they stood there amongst the corpses. Sam lowered the pistol as he crouched down to check his fallen adversaries.

"Sorry about that, I should have told you to stand further back," he said as he searched the pockets of the two dead men. When he received no reply he looked over his shoulder to see Tilly still frozen to the spot, her face white with shock. "Hey, are you okay?"

"You shot them," she gasped, more a challenge than a question.

Sam finished fishing through their pockets but retrieving nothing of interest. "Looks like it, doesn't it?"

"But you killed them."

"I do hope so, otherwise I'd be really questioning all that time I spent on the shooting range back in basic training." He could see his words were not helping matters, Tilly was still clearly in shock. He spoke more gently. "In moments like this it's either you or them. Thankfully this time it was them."

Tilly gave a brief nod, slowly coming to her senses. "Do you think they were the team who killed my dad?"

"Probably, I can't imagine there being that many hired guns working round here."

"Then I'm glad," she said savagely.

Sam put his arm around her shoulder thinking about her earlier insistence at taking the weapon from him in the car. "Come on, let's get a move on."

"What are we going to do? We can't just leave them. Do we ring the police?"

Sam chuckled. "I'm not spending a night in a cell for these bastards." He kicked one of the dead men. "Let's give the scruffy tramp something to think about."

Tilly watched as Sam dragged the first of the bodies to the side of the road where the cliff face fell down to a small rocky ravine. Straining, he tipped the lifeless body over and watched curiously as the floppy limbs bounced between the rocks.

"One down."

After sending the second corpse after the first Sam went back to check on Tilly. Her face had regained some of its colour. "Well, that was easy enough, now for the car."

"You're not going to drive it down there?" Tilly asked with renewed shock.

"No, I've got a better idea for that. Can you drive the rental? I want to find a driveway in an empty villa."

Tilly did as instructed, returning to the rental while Sam clambered into the Mercedes. The moment he sat down in the driver's seat he felt the night's alcohol return to slightly cloud his mind. Shaking it away and being careful not to touch anything he didn't need to, he followed Tilly up to the top of the Granadella cove and back to the headland plateau. Immediately they were surrounded by streets filled with villas and it didn't take long to find one that looked boarded up for the season. With Tilly waiting on the street, Sam parked the car on the empty driveway and wiped down the wheel of any fingerprints before dropping the keys in the letter box.

"If you ask me, that Mercedes is nice but hasn't a scratch on our little rental," he joked, getting back into the passenger seat.

Tilly shook her head but did not reply. In fact, she kept her counsel for the entire journey back to her family villa. Not that Sam minded, he could again feel the return of the light headiness from the night's alcohol as the adrenaline rush faded away. Reaching the comfort of the lit-up villa, Sam followed Tilly back inside where she left him to head straight into the bedroom. Sam, quite happy to be left alone, retrieved a cold beer from the fridge then dropped onto the sofa. A stiffness was beginning to creep in across his joints as the strains of the day took their toll. He closed his eyes, leant his head back against the cushion and tried to clear his clouded mind.

A door opened somewhere behind him and a pair of feet could be heard making their way across the tiled floor. Reluctantly he opened an eye to see Tilly standing there – the dress had been replaced by a long T-shirt which barely reached past her hips. She stood there for a moment looking at him, her hazel eyes seemed to flash in the half-light. He waited for her to speak but instead she leant forwards and kissed him hard across the mouth.

Catching his breath as she moved to sit on top of him, he started to speak but Tilly stopped him.

"For God's sake, just for once don't say anything. I can't take any more of your wit for one night."

Sam did as he was told, waiting until later as they both lay in bed, Tilly resting against his shoulder before daring to speak again.

Tilly finally broke the silence. "How do you do it?" she asked as she ran a soft finger up his chest.

"I mean, I'm glad you enjoyed it but it's not really fair for me to disclose my bedroom secrets after one showing."

She pulled hard on one of his chest hairs. "I told you no more wit."

"Sorry, but seriously, do what?"

"Just kill a person like that and not let it affect you."

Sam shifted uncomfortably at the question. The subject of morality was never going to be a comfortable one. "I don't know. It's like I said, at times like that it's either you or him."

"But don't you suffer from any guilt, any remorse?"

"Honestly, no, not really. People like that know what they are getting into. If they had shot me I don't believe for a moment that they would be sat awake now worrying about it. It is just something I've never really thought about."

Tilly shifted her head down away from him, hiding her face. "You didn't even flinch, you just knew what had to be done."

"Would you rather I hadn't?"

"No, it's just I'm worried that I hesitated, I couldn't do it. Even though I knew I should have pulled the trigger myself."

Sam considered her before answering and then said truthfully, "I really wouldn't overthink it, I've known many in the army who would have done the same. The military spends hours trying to prepare their people to get past that instinct that stops you from killing a fellow human being. Christ, you've spent your whole professional career trying to save lives, of course it would feel alien to do otherwise."

"I guess you're right."

"Of course I am, I bet you wouldn't hesitate to operate on someone to save them, even if it led to the patient dying on the operating table, would you?"

Tilly now rolled over and leant her head on her hand. "No, I guess not."

"And you wouldn't spend your time regretting making that decision or feeling remorse for the deceased?"

"No, but…"

Sam interrupted her. "Well, it's just the same for me."

She frowned at him. "How is that the same? I'm trying to save someone's life."

"So am I, just in this case it's even more important I'm trying to save someone far more valuable."

Tilly looked at him, waiting for the answer.

"Me of course – screw letting those bastards be able to go home to bed over me. Let them rot in the ground instead."

Tilly dropped her head onto the pillow and looked up at him. "Thank you, Sam Taylor, thank you for everything."

Sam woke the next morning to find the bedroom empty. The chair that had been placed against the door to block any potential intruders had been moved back to its position by the cabinet. Tilly was nowhere to be seen. Not that Sam was worried. Instead, twisting his body to stretch out his back, he lay still, thinking of the night's events. From dinner to the two pursuers, all the way to pleasant imagery of the slim naked body that had slept next to him. In the space of a few hours he had experienced two ends of the emotional spectrum.

Groggily he left the bedroom in search of his host. The living room was exactly as they had left it in the early hours, the sofas and cushions still out of place. Rubbing his face, he heard the sound of splashing from outside and he wandered out to the garden. While breakfast had been set on the table ready for him, he only had eyes for the toned shape of Tilly gliding through the pool. The small ripples crashed against the tiled side as she rolled under the water to change direction and push off against the wall. Taking a seat, he poured himself a glass of orange juice as he admired the view. Already the heat of the day was causing droplets of sweat to form at the back of his neck. After all, they had not gone to sleep until the early hours.

A short time later Tilly pulled herself out of the blue water and grabbing a towel she walked up the short flight of stairs to the veranda. Using the towel to dry her long blonde hair she eyed Sam as he sat under the sun.

"I thought you might have come in and joined me?"

"I wish I had now," he said, looking up at her.

"It would have cooled you down."

"I seriously doubt that."

She rolled her eyes but sat down next to him. "It feels like we've missed most of the morning but I didn't want to wake you up."

"Don't worry about it, I needed the rest."

"What did you want to do today?"

Sam was saved from answering by the sound of the villa's doorbell chiming from inside. They glanced at each other, unsure of who it could be.

"Expecting guests?" he asked her.

"No, the pool man doesn't come today and the gardener's not due until tomorrow."

"Great, probably the Chief wanting to know what we've done with his men."

Tilly's eyes flickered. "Don't say that."

The bell chimed again and the two of them stood up from the table.

"I left the two guns in the bedroom, can you go get them?" he asked firmly.

Moving quickly, the pair slipped back inside the villa, Sam heading straight for the front door, Tilly to the bedroom. Reaching the door, Sam peered through the frosted glass and was not surprised to see no one standing in the porch. Whoever had rang the bell was still outside the main gate.

"Here you go," said Tilly, returning with both her father's and last night's assailant's weapon. She had covered her bikini with a black shawl. Whatever reservations she had held around the weapons the previous evening seemed to have vanished.

"Thanks, now step back. If anything happens to me run straight out the back and climb over into one of the neighbours' gardens and keep running."

The doorbell rang again and Sam grabbed the door handle. Slowly he pushed it outwards. Peering round, he looked down the garden pathway to see a lone man standing behind the wrought-iron gate.

Seeing Sam, he waved and shouted in English, "Hello, I'm looking for Sam Taylor and Tilly Birks. Is this the right place?"

"And who are you?" Sam asked instead.

"Ha, I was warned to expect this kind of welcome. Charlie Franks – I used to work with Chris Kane."

Sam looked over his shoulder to where Tilly was watching on nervously. "It's the MI5 guy."

"How can you be sure?"

Sam peered back round the door. "Prove it."

The man at the gate gave a wave of his hand. "How? You can't see my badge from over there."

"He has a point," muttered Tilly, listening from behind. "He is expected, remember, they told you he was coming."

Sam tried to think of some sort of trick question but failed. In the silence Charlie Franks spoke again. "Come on, man, we are on the same side after all. Look, Chris Kane was a friend of mine, we worked in the Financial Crimes team of MI5, his wife is called Sofia who you met yesterday. His au pair is called Alex and is currently banged up inside a rotten Spanish jail cell – where she will remain unless we do something."

"What do you think?" Tilly asked Sam.

"I'm not sure what else we can do, just watch out on what you say. Remember, he's here for the Kane case, not to find out what happened to your old man."

Hoping Tilly had got the message Sam pushed open the door and walked down the stone path.

Charlie Franks stepped back from the gate. "There we go, there's a good man. It's bloody hot here, isn't it? I don't know how you've been managing it."

"You get used to it," replied Sam as he unlocked the iron gate.

"I'll take your word for it. Nice place this, isn't it? I understand it's where the old MI6 lad got killed off."

Sam bristled at the man's tone. "I wouldn't speak like that when you get inside, his daughter may have a thing or two to say about it."

"Of course. I understand."

Sam studied the MI5 agent closely, trying to read whatever intentions lay within. Charlie Franks was tall, even taller than Sam's six foot frame, with long gangly limbs. A sturdy face with high cheekbones and cleft chin looked back at him. He wore his blond hair long, with strands pulled back over his ears. Sam guessed, almost unfairly as he had only just met the man, that he came from a wealthy background, probably privately educated. Whether it was the cut of his shirt, the brown leather sailor shoes, the cream chinos or the clipped accent, Sam didn't know. Pushing the unprovoked thoughts out of his mind he followed the agent back inside.

Tilly was waiting for them in the hallway and Sam introduced Charlie to her.

"How lovely to meet you, Miss Birks, and so sorry that it's under such circumstances. My office did brief me before I left as to your situation. What a shitshow, I don't know how these Dago bastards even manage to tie their shoelaces."

"They are doing what they can," said Sam, still unsure of their guest "Come on, there's seating outside on the veranda."

Tilly led them through the living room towards the patio doors. If Charlie noticed the displaced cushions still strewn across the floor he made no comment. Outside, the three of them sat round the breakfast table and Tilly offered a jug of orange juice around.

"No, not for me, thanks." Leaning back in his chair, Charlie's eyes flickered between the two of them. Sensing the tension he asked, "So then, how do you want to do this? I'm guessing from your cold northern stare-off you are not that happy to see me."

"After what we've been through it's becoming hard to trust anyone these days."

"Fair point, perhaps if you'd be willing to share these adventures then we may be able to find some common ground from which to start off with."

Sam frowned. "What do you want to know then?"

"My friend is dead and his wife has not stopped ringing my office and the police have the wrong person in jail. From what I understand it's your office's job to iron this all out and yet here I am."

"What do you want me to say? There's not much more I can add than what the police should have told you already. I don't think the girl killed him, someone either swam up to the boat or was already on it when your friend was murdered. We swam out yesterday and are no clearer as to what happened ourselves. I'd like to think with the evidence of the diving computer, the call records and the lack of forensic evidence they will let Alex out today."

Charlie leant forwards in his seat. "Then what? Are there really no other leads, no other suspects you are following up?"

Now Sam shifted uncomfortably, he didn't quite want to admit that they had done very little in resolving the Kane case. "I had planned on visiting the station again this morning to see what's the latest."

"Sounds like you're all over it then," said Charlie sarcastically. "Might as well book my return flight now."

Sam did not bite. Instead, he asked about the widow.

"She's holding up okay, I've just come from there actually. She's made of strong stuff that one. But tell me this, it's something I've been thinking about all the way here – is there a connection between the two deaths? Between yours and mine." He indicated Tilly.

Sam hesitated before answering, he did not want to dive into his theories on the Chief and his operations. Instead, he answered, "We are not sure yet, we know they used the same solicitor and that Kane was on the phone to them just before he died."

"There you go then, what did they say when you visited them?"

No one answered.

"Surely one of you have been to see them?"

Sam shook his head. "We've had other leads."

"What other leads?"

Tilly slammed her glass on the table in frustration. "Christ, you two, you're like a pair of chess players each trying to gauge the other out. You can at least tell him what we have been up to, he may be able to help."

Sam did not answer, he still carried a sense of mistrust of this newcomer, even if he could not yet put his finger on it.

Instead, Tilly told the story. Starting with the discovery of the hidden safe, the diary and its list of names plus the mysterious key. She described their suspicions of the pathologist, the murder of his assistant and the discovery of the property buying scheme. Of their visit to the Chief's estate and his denial of everything. She was just about to reach the part of their evening's pursuers when Sam interrupted.

"And we've also had suspicion to believe we've been followed," he added, silencing Tilly before she told him about the killings. She had already said more than he was comfortable with.

Charlie Franks had listened quietly to the whole story, neither asking any questions nor interrupting as Tilly went through everything. He frowned at the retelling of their time with the pathologist but seemed less interested in their dealings with the Chief.

"I get why you don't like this Chief fellow, he sounds a complete piece of trash but I don't think you have enough on him at the moment."

Sam bit his tongue, the memory of the altercation at Granadella still fresh in his mind. He gave Tilly a glance to make sure she followed his lead.

Charlie continued. "I, however, have more concerns over the pathologist. He sounds like the key to everything. It's him that is holding everything together. I think we should be focusing our attention on him."

Sam ran his hand through his hair, studying the MI5 agent. He had repeated Sam's exact hypothesis from the previous night about Doctor Serrano. In fact, almost word for word.

Tilly had noticed it as well. "That's what we said, well, what Sam said last night. What do you think we should do about it?"

Charlie nodded at Sam. "I can see you're a clever fellow to have around then, glad we are on the same page."

Sam said nothing, not sure he was on the same page.

"Well, I suggest we pay our good doctor another visit, perhaps somewhere a bit more private. Have a little heart-to-heart and see if we can't find some common ground."

"And if we can't?" asked Sam dryly.

"Then we help him to find it."

TWENTY-THREE

SAM WAITED with Charlie Franks as Tilly went back into the bedroom to change. The two men attempted to create awkward small talk as the minutes passed by and both were grateful when Tilly returned.

"Ready?" she asked brightly.

"I am," replied the equally bright Charlie.

Sam just grunted, the new arrival having dampened his mood.

They had agreed to visit the police station first and to get the latest information from the investigation team. Sam half hoped they would be able to push for the release of Alex Coombs.

Charlie Franks, picking up on Sam's displeasure asked, "How do you want to play this then? As you know I have absolutely no authority here, I'm completely out of my depth. Remember, MI5 are the domestic branch. I'll be more than happy to just follow your lead."

Sam eyed the taller man, unsure whether to quite trust this seemingly friendly persona. In this line of work, it was rare that any officer would surrender to any other authority so willingly.

"Fine, I'll tell you now it's not like I have any sway over things here either. We are guests of the Spanish after all."

"I'm sure you'll be able to use that delightful northern charm."

Charlie stopped, his face becoming serious. "I've got to ask, especially with everything you've told me, are you armed?"

Sam eyed Tilly then answered, "I am, we have the one pistol between us."

Tilly looked at him, surprised at the lie, but Sam ignored her. By not revealing the second weapon currently carried in Tilly's handbag they had kept at least one surprise held back.

"You?" Sam challenged.

Charlie seemed slightly taken aback by the question. "I'm not sure I'm supposed to have one."

"Neither are we. But that's not what I asked."

The MI5 officer seemed to regain his composure. "Well, keeping all cards on the table, yes I do and I left it in the car. I didn't want to give you any cause to suspect me as having any ill intentions."

The three of them began to head out of the villa as Sam asked his next question. "How the hell did you get hold of a pistol? You've only just arrived, bet you didn't get that through on hand luggage."

Charlie gave a toothy grin as he held open the iron gate for Tilly. "Well, I had a little tip-off things may get a little hairy out here. Seems someone in your team gave someone in my department the heads-up that you generally like to attract trouble. It was easy enough, I just had one our contacts in Gibraltar drive up and meet me at the airport. All under the table, obviously."

"Obviously," answered Sam, brooding on the explanation. It was plausible, he decided, although he would have quite liked to have known who in the office had made the comment about him attracting trouble. Not that he exactly disagreed with the assessment but still.

Reaching the parked rental, Charlie Franks pulled out his keys. "Let's stick to separate cars, that way we can split up and cover more ground if needed."

Unsure what he could have possibly meant by 'covering more

ground', Sam went along with the suggestion, more than happy to have a break from the newcomer.

"He seems nice enough," commented Tilly as Sam started the car.

Receiving only a grunt in reply she continued. "What's up with you? He's done nothing wrong. If anything he just seems to want to help."

"I don't know, I'm probably overthinking things. I'm not exactly the team player am I?"

"You've been fine with me."

"I know you, well, I know what you're doing here, what your connection is to everything. As to this guy, he's just turned up and we've just got to trust him? I wish you'd not told him everything you did. I did warn you."

Tilly ignored the reprimand. "What was I supposed to do? Anyway we've not told him everything, he doesn't know about last night. I see what you did there with the second gun, you didn't want him to know about it, did you?"

"No, it won't hurt to have some sort of insurance."

Halfway to the station Sam had a call from Detective Vega to say she and Commissioner Moreno would meet them at the Arenal marina. Changing direction he soon pulled into the small car park that overlooked the marina, Charlie parking his own rental in the bay next to them.

"Right, we cannot continue mistrusting one another," Tilly lectured him as he switched off the engine. "We need to get this sorted, we've enough enemies without having to fight our own."

Tilly unbuckled her seat belt and even before Sam could respond, was standing outside the car. Sam, bemused by his companion's determination, followed more slowly. Standing up, he watched as she stepped towards the other parked rental. Resting her arms on the small hatchback's roof she called out to Charlie as he, too, clambered out.

"Well, this isn't the police station…" said Charlie, putting on a pair of sunglasses.

Tilly ignored the question, cutting over him, "Hey, so, Charlie, Officer Franks or whatever–"

"I quite like whatever."

"Quite. Look, you may have noticed my friend here hasn't given you the kindest of welcomes. In fact, I would say he's bordering on rude."

Charlie Franks shrugged and pulled at a strand of blond hair behind his ear. "I wouldn't worry about it, he's from the north – they are all like that."

Tilly wasn't to be put off. "Well, you have to understand we've had a bit of a rough time of it and it's becoming harder to trust people."

Charlie stepped back from the car and raised both his hands, palms up. "Seriously, we are going to do this again? What more can I say or do?"

"You say you used to be friends with Chris Kane?"

"I was, yes."

"Then prove it."

Charlie's eyes flashed from Tilly to Sam as if weighing the two of them up. Sam half expected the man to refuse, to become defensive at this questioning of him. Instead, with a simple shrug of his shoulders he reached into one of his pockets.

"Opposite hand," said Sam, remembering the man's claim to having a weapon.

The MI5 man did not argue and using his left hand he reached into his trouser pocket to pull out a phone. Unlocking it, he flicked his thumb across the screen a few times before offering it to Tilly, who, receiving a nod from Sam, took the device.

"You see, how else would I have that if I wasn't friends with him?"

Tilly showed the phone to Sam, still standing on the other side of the rental. Peering over the rooftop Sam could see two faces looking up at him from the screen. The pair of them were sat around a table holding drinks. There was Charlie Franks and next to him holding a half-empty glass of beer was Chris Kane.

"That was us on the office Christmas night out, I forget exactly which bar that was taken but I think it exonerates me, wouldn't you say? Can we all be friends now and get on with whatever it is we are doing here?"

"It's enough for me," said Tilly brightly as she passed back the phone. "Glad to have you on the team."

"And you?" Charlie indicated to where Sam still stood. "Is that enough for even your suspicious mind?"

"I suppose so."

"Smashing, so is either of you going to tell me what it is we are doing here? I thought we were heading to the station."

"Change of plan," said Sam, walking round to some wooden planks that formed the jetty running along the marina.

The three of them headed down the planks, careful to avoid the mixture of holidaymakers and locals. They spotted the two police officers standing on the deck of one of the boats further down the marina.

"I see you've found yourselves a new friend," Commissioner Moreno called out as they walked towards the boat.

"More like he found us," replied Sam. "Commissioner Moreno, Detective Vega, this is Charlie Franks, he used to work with Chris Kane."

The two Spanish officers nodded at the newcomer as the three of them stepped down onto the white boat to join them. The boat rocked slightly as they placed their weight upon the deck. Checking his balance, Sam gave the small boat a look-over. The five of them were stood on the deck of the stern, from which a leather chair stood in front of the ship's wheel. To the front could be seen a spacious sun deck broken only by windows looking down into the cabins below.

"Kane's boat?" guessed Sam.

"Indeed," answered Moreno.

"Nice, in fact very nice for someone working in government."

Moreno raised an eyebrow. "Are you questioning how the deceased could have afforded this vessel?"

"Maybe."

"Then don't. Kane married into a wealthy family. His wife had all the money." Moreno took a seat on one of the benches. "You will not be surprised to know our forensic team have finished all their checks."

"And?" asked Sam, already guessing the answer.

"Nothing, both the girl and the boat are clean of anything suspicious. We found no trace of Kane on any of her clothes."

"So you're going to release her?" asked Tilly.

Moreno looked up at the Englishwoman. "Yes, this afternoon." Then to Sam she said, "But she will need to remain here for the time being while we finish our investigation."

"That could be a problem," said Sam, thinking aloud. "I'm not exactly sure she will be welcome back to the Kane residence. I know Mrs Kane believes in her innocence but it's probably not the best idea she goes back there."

"Agreed, that's where I hoped you may be able to help," the Commissioner continued.

"I'm not sure she can stay with us," said Sam with a chuckle. "I'll ring the office and have them book her a room in a local hotel."

"That is acceptable," confirmed Moreno. "Now then, I guess you'd like to know what we will be doing next with the Kane case."

"Indeed, I'd like to know that very much," said Charlie, speaking for the first time. "My government will not be accepting anything other than a successful outcome in this case."

Moreno twisted her lined face to look up at the MI5 officer. She seemed to consider the new arrival to this strange case, her eyes narrowed as if trying to bring something to memory.

"We are doing everything possible," snapped Detective Vega, her face flushed with anger. "If you have any bright ideas as to what actually happened then please enlighten us. For all we know this could be something to do with your own government."

"And what proof do you have for that?" growled Charlie.

"Enough," said Sam, coming between everyone. "This isn't helping. I know you will all be doing everything in your power to solve this case."

He placed a hand on Charlie's shoulder. "And we have plenty of other things to be worried about."

Charlie's face flickered but he got the message. "Yes, quite."

Moreno also got the unspoken message. "I take it you are still looking into Señor Birks's death."

"Yes, but like you two here, we are getting nowhere."

Moreno sighed then stared out to sea. "What have we come to, two murders and none of us are able to be honest and help each other. I know you're hiding something from me, Señor Taylor, but your business is your own for now."

Sam eyed Tilly whose face reflected his own discomfort yet neither spoke the truth. Instead, he posed the next question to Detective Vega.

"Can I have a look below deck?"

"Why?" answered the younger officer defensively.

"Humour me."

With a nod from Moreno she moved back to allow Sam access to the steps that led below. Tilly and Charlie followed both, not sure of Sam's intentions. Stepping through the small doorway Sam took the small steps down to the lower deck. Standing in the middle of the small cabin he peered round the space, noting the bedroom with its wardrobe, the small kitchen and toilet.

"What are you looking for?" asked a confused Tilly.

Sam just gave her a wink before returning to the open air.

"Find anything of interest?" enquired the commissioner, still seated on the white leather-covered bench.

"Nope, but it does help my hypothesis."

"Hypothesis?"

"Kane's killer was on the boat all along, they hid in the cabins below, probably in the bedroom. They waited until Alex was in the water and then killed Kane," guessed Sam. "Then they swam to the shore, hence why Alex neither saw them nor heard a boat. Both me and Tilly here made the swim ourselves yesterday."

"While it is a good theory, it still does not help us identify who it actually was. It could have been anyone hidden below," retorted Vega, clearly not impressed by Sam's theory.

"That's for you to worry about, interview whoever was around the marina that morning, see who was observed entering the boat. Check to see if there is any CCTV, you know the kind of things the police do."

Vega's face flushed but was checked in her response by Moreno. "We are looking into everything we can and we will give some thought to your ideas. I should say we found no sign of any foreign DNA within the boat's interior. Our team gave every centimetre of this boat a thorough check."

"What do you mean by foreign DNA?" asked a curious Tilly.

"Anybody whose DNA was not supposed to be found on this boat. Kane's family, Alex, friends known to have used the vessel and the local diving master – all pretty standard and expected users. Or to put it another way, all with an alibi as to why they were on the boat before the murder," Moreno explained, her face giving nothing away.

"Then pick one of those out and cross-check their stories surely?" snapped Franks.

Commissioner Moreno rose from the bench and gave the three foreigners a sympathetic smile. "There is only so much lecturing I can take from you, young man, until I, like my friend here," she indicated Vega, "become tired of it and begin to be insulted."

Sam could spot a warning when he needed to. "I'm sorry. I understand how tough it is. I'll speak to the office and have some accommodation found for Miss Coombs. When will she be released?"

"Sometime this afternoon," confirmed Vega coldly.

"What about you three?" asked the commissioner. "What are you planning on doing? I'd like to know more about how your inquiries are progressing. Have you found anything more to shed light on Señor Birks's death?" She lowered her voice. "Or on our mutual friend Doctor Serrano?"

Sam looked up at his companions before answering. Tilly bit her lip while Charlie kept his face blank. "We've had a few leads pop up."

"Pop up?"

"We are still assessing what we should do."

Moreno's eyes flashed. "And will you be sharing these with us?"

Sam ran his hand through his hair. "I think it would be best if we spared you too much of the details. I'm not sure you'd like them."

Now it was Moreno's turn to pick out the warning. The middle-aged police officer gave a knowing nod but said no more. Instead, she turned to her fellow officer. "I think that is a no, don't you, Detective Vega?"

Vega, still frustrated by the conversation, gritted her teeth, turned on her heel and climbed out of the boat. Sam watched as the officer marched down the jetty, grateful not to have received any serious taste of her wrath.

Moreno sighed as she watched her go. "Ah, the confidence of youth, the ability to have absolute certainty in your own actions." She gave Sam a knowing look. "We are here if you need anything, just try not to cause me too much trouble, yes?"

"It does seem to follow me," admitted Sam, getting ready to leave the boat.

The three of them said their goodbyes, again Moreno's eyes narrowed slightly as she seemed to try and place Charlie. But the MI5 officer gave her his most widest smile and clasped her hand tightly before departing.

Away from the Spanish commissioner he said, "Well, I can see the fun you've been having, those two did not seem the most helpful."

"I've seen worse, you have to remember we are on their patch after all," said Sam. "I mean they could make things a lot harder for us if they so choose. Although I wouldn't put it past Vega to find an excuse to cause trouble."

"Do you really think whoever killed Chris actually hid in the boat?" Charlie asked, walking next to him.

"I can't see how else it could have been done. Unless it really was Alex but I find that extremely hard to believe."

"But if all other routes are proven false then surely we have to consider it?"

Sam grimaced at the thought of having to consider Alex Coombs as a murderer. The young girl just did not fit the picture. Then even as he said it he heard his own words come floating back across his mind. *They come in all shapes and sizes.*

TWENTY-FOUR

THE THREE OF them continued past the parked rentals onto Arenal's main walkway. Sam, busy with his own thoughts, kept quiet as Tilly and Charlie debated the state of the cases. His mind was focused on watching the serene scenes around him. To his left the white sand was filled with families, nearly every square inch was covered in beach towels and chairs. A game of volleyball was in mid-flow, the shirtless players glistening with sweat. The very thought of trying to throw himself across the court's sand in this heat made him queasy. Around them the concrete pathway was humming with groups of tourists pottering amongst the different shops, restaurants and bars. Not for the first time since he had arrived, he thought enviously of the retired community of expatriates living out here in the Mediterranean sunshine.

"So what do you think, Sam?"

His attention brought back to the present, Sam stared blankly at his companions.

"What do you think we should do?" Tilly repeated for his benefit.

"What are the options?"

"Charlie here thinks we should visit Doctor Serrano now, he's already got the guy's home address."

Sam glanced at Charlie. "How have you done that?"

"You're not the only one with a support office back home. They rang the hospital earlier but it is his day off."

He shrugged. "I've already said, I still think it would be a good idea to have another chat. I'd like to see what he says about his assistant's killing."

Returning to the rentals the three split up again, Charlie leaving Sam and Tilly alone. Sam let Tilly drive this time, allowing him to call in on Emma as they travelled behind the MI5 officer's car.

The dry Irish tone answered on the first ring. "You decided to call in, I'm honoured."

"Sorry, wrong number."

"Don't start, I honestly don't know how people put up with you when you're out on a case."

The image of Tilly silencing him the night before flashed across his mind. "I don't know what you mean? I'm a delight."

"Of course you are, what have you got for me?"

"Not much, although Alex Coombs is going to be released this afternoon."

"Is she? That's interesting, have the police found a new suspect?"

"Nope, just that they don't think it was Alex."

"Christ, that's a shitshow. If they don't find out who actually killed Kane then they will have some noise coming their way. I take it the MI5 man arrived? Someone called Charlie Franks, yes?"

"He did."

Emma picked up on the tone. "And?"

"He's all right, typical posh boy."

"Ah, and that doesn't sit well with the grim northern sense of class identity."

Sam didn't answer, there was no point in trying to explain his unwarranted sense of distrust to someone hundreds of miles away.

"Right, whatever, I take it if you're bothering to ring me you actually want something?"

"Alex Coombs."

"What about her?"

"She needs somewhere to stay while the investigation finishes, can you get someone to find her a hotel please?"

"Yes, we can do that. Anything else? Have you made any progress on the Birks case? I keep getting calls from Sir Jeffrey wanting to have an update every few hours."

"He knows I don't call in, I don't know why he's wasting his time." Sam stopped and eyed Tilly before continuing. "But you can tell him we know who killed Birks."

Emma's voice tensed up. "You do? Who?"

"Some local businessman called the Chief, seems like he's the one behind the deaths of everyone on Selwin's list."

"Fantastic."

"Yeah, don't get too excited, there's absolutely nothing to prove it. It's based entirely on intuition."

"Damn, what are you going to do?"

"Probably something I shouldn't."

"In fact just stop there, I don't want to know, just stay safe."

Sam gave a hollow laugh. "And keep you updated?"

"Of course."

There was a pause before Sam asked a question which had been bothering him. "I've a bone to pick with you, or someone in the office."

"Only one?"

"For now – who told the MI5 guys that I attract trouble?"

"I've no idea," answered Emma honestly. "It's only me who's spoken to the MI5 guys and I wouldn't want to ruin the surprise of meeting you in person."

Sam smiled at the jest. "Well, someone did."

"It could have been anyone, perhaps one of them has friends in our department. It's hardly a state secret that you get yourself into all sorts of trouble. I really wouldn't worry about it."

Not wanting to get into a discussion about his doubt, he grunted in agreement. Yet it was still in his mind, there was just something that bugged him about the MI5 man, even with the photo of him and Kane. Emma wished him well and hung up, leaving Sam with his doubts.

"What do you think Serrano is going to say?" asked Tilly, interrupting his thoughts.

"Probably not a lot, I'm sure he's more scared of his masters than of anything we can throw at him. Even at my most persuasive there's not much I can really do to him. Our biggest card is to let him know that we are onto him, try and scare him into an early confession to save his own skin. But I doubt it, yet you have to shake a few trees to find monkeys."

Tilly chuckled. "What? Is that a real saying?"

"I don't know, probably but who really knows?" said Sam, joining in the laughter. It felt good to be enjoying Tilly's company again. Ever since they had been joined by Charlie it had felt as if they were unable to relax, to be themselves again. Perhaps another subconscious warning, thought Sam.

They drove back towards the south end of the bay, back into the land of the villas until turning into a street not far from Tilly's own villa, the two rentals pulled in. Looking up through the windscreen Sam could only see a whitewashed wall, its peaks covered by an unbroken line of trees blocking all sight into the house beyond.

"Private sort of place, isn't it?" mused Sam as he stepped out of the car.

"A nice place, that's for certain," answered Charlie, having left his own vehicle. "According to Google Maps the trees cover three sides of the property, with the fourth opening out onto an edge of the headland overlooking the bay."

"Nice views if you can get them," said Sam.

Tilly snorted. "What do you suggest? Can we just ring the front doorbell and he will be happy to see us?"

"Possibly," Charlie replied, rubbing his chin.

"I mean, if it was me and I saw us three pull up I'd be locking myself in straight away," she continued.

"But you're not him, are you?" Charlie reminded her. "He may know you two but he doesn't have a clue who I am. So what do you think? Will he be more inclined to open up to a stranger or two people he already knows and definitely doesn't want to talk to?"

"When you put it like that," mumbled Tilly. "Now what – we just watch as you walk right in?"

"No, not quite. I'll go in and I'll make it so you can follow."

Sam, still suspicious, asked, "And how do you plan to 'make it so we can follow'?"

"I don't know that part yet. Don't look at me like that, have you never had to improvise on the job?"

Sam and Tilly reluctantly agreed with the MI5 man's proposal. Stepping back from the gate leading into the tree-walled property, they watched as Charlie confidently stepped to the green-painted gate. Looking over his shoulder he gave them a cheerful wink then pressed the bell. Standing still for a moment Sam watched as the blond-haired man fidgeted with his waistband, the right hand subconsciously touching the handle of the concealed pistol behind him. Whatever the outside confidence Charlie had shown, he had still gone in armed. Sam very consciously touched his own weapon.

"I don't like this," complained Sam as they stood on the pavement.

"Like what?"

"All of this, it just doesn't feel right."

Tilly frowned. "I thought we had gone through this about Charlie. He clearly knew Kane, you said yourself there was someone coming from his office?"

"Yeah, but–"

"Yeah but nothing, it's not exactly as if you have any other plans."

Sam grimaced. "But that's also a red light, I don't like that he's just accepted our word for everything."

"What did you want him to do? Cause a fuss and be difficult?"

"Well, yeah, most people you meet in this profession are rarely that accommodating."

"You mean you're surprised that not everyone is like you?"

Sam did not answer, instead he watched on quietly as having the gate opened from an unseen switch inside, Charlie walked into the inner sanctum of the property.

"Ten euros it goes okay?" betted Tilly.

"No bet."

The two of them waited in the hot sunshine, the thick tree-lined wall blocking off any possible sea breeze. Already Sam could feel the sweat prick against his new blue shirt.

He opened his mouth to say they should follow, when Charlie's head poked through the wall ahead of them.

"Come on in, it seems our friend is willing to have visitors after all."

Wondering what this could possibly mean, the two of them followed through the gate and into a well-tended garden. Dug-in sprinklers were at work spraying down the flower beds and neatly cut grass. Palm trees were embedded at intervals around the garden. Following the pathway they trailed Charlie onto a covered porch, the door still ajar.

"What happened?" asked Sam, catching the taller man up.

"You'll see," answered the back of Charlie's head.

Not liking the answer, Sam stepped through the door and into the chilled air of the villa. Standing in an open hallway they walked across the flagstoned floor towards the sound of running water. Just in front of them Sam could see Charlie was now holding the pistol.

"What's with the gun?" he asked, now more firmly.

Charlie, not looking back, answered, "A mistake, it seems I misread the situation."

Not knowing what this could possibly mean, Sam hurried his

pace, pushing Charlie to one side to enter an open-plan kitchen. To his left, white sofas sat round an unlit firepit, to his front, bi-fold doors opened to the outside patio. But to his right, standing next to the sink and holding a towel under the cold running water was Doctor Serrano.

The pathologist removed the soaked towel and pressed it to his round swollen face. "I take it you're here to hit me as well then?"

The smell of whisky filled Sam's nostrils, the pathologist in front of him seemed tense, on edge almost. Sweat was dripping down the bald forehead, the small eyes attempting to blink it away.

Sam glared at Charlie. "What the hell happened?"

Charlie seemed none too concerned as he bent down then picked up the pathologist's fallen glasses. "I hit first, the moment he opened the door actually. Thought it was better than waiting to be proved wrong."

"And proved wrong you have been," snapped an angry Serrano, taking back his glasses and putting them back on his face. "I take it you're here to talk to me about the Chief, yes? Well, that's what this buffoon has told me. I'll tell you everything all right, but then I'm off, I'm leaving this godforsaken town."

Standing there still trying to process everything, Sam asked, "What the hell is going on here? What do you mean you're off?"

"I'm leaving, running away, taking my blood money now before I get two new holes in my head." He waved at a pair of suitcases laid open on the white sofas, both filled with clothes and bundles of cash.

Suddenly it hit Sam. "You think the Chief is going to kill you?"

"Of course he's going to kill me, why else would I be leaving? It was only a matter of time before things came to an end, I've had word that my time is up. I am no longer a useful asset, instead I am a liability. Ha!" He spat out the final word. "Me a liability, it is rich coming from that man. But he is the one with the muscle."

"How do you know he's going to kill you?" questioned a still-confused Tilly.

Serrano turned to the woman and removing the damp towel pointed it at her. "Because of you and him." He nodded at Sam. "You two with your questions, it seems you touched a nerve and the Chief has decided to close up. Thankfully I still have a few contacts of my own and I've had just enough warning to get out. I thought this useful idiot had been sent to do the job but thankfully I know all of the Chief's men. It is just a shame he had to hit me."

"Yeah, sorry about that," said Charlie sheepishly. He put down the pistol on one of the side tables. "Then again, how was I supposed to know what was happening?"

"You bloody well ask," snapped the injured doctor.

Sam tried to recall the confident pathologist they had met that day in the mortuary and compare him with this new panicked persona. The man's face looked pale, sweat dripped down his brow. Still holding the damp towel to his face he picked up a glass of whisky from the countertop.

"What are you looking for?" asked Sam, moving further into the room. "Pity? You forget why we are here, Doctor."

"I know why you're here, I'd have to be an idiot not to know that. You are after the evidence that connects me to that bastard they all call the Chief."

"And why is that?" snarled Tilly, her anger at the memory of her father's death returning at the sight of the panic-stricken doctor. "Because you have spent the last few years covering for that murdering pig."

Serrano gazed back at her, his eyes weighing up his fellow medical professional. "I don't deny it, why would I? What have I left to lose? But you won't get what you really want here. Why would I sacrifice myself for your revenge?"

Sam could see where this was going. "Let me guess. You want a deal? Protection from the Chief and a plea deal in return for your evidence?"

Serrano laughed, a horse laugh of a man already halfway through a whisky bottle. "You think those louts in the police could protect me? They are the most incompetent fools in Spain and I should know! I've spent the last few years leading them astray."

"Then what do you want?"

"For you three to piss off while I finish packing."

Sam moved again, this time to block the drunken doctor within his kitchen. "Not going to happen."

Serrano took another gulp of whisky then stared into his deep-blue eyes. Making his decision he slammed the glass down. "Fine, fine, fine, fine. Better you than some half-arsed incompetent police officer. You want the evidence to bring down the Chief, you can have it. But you have to let me go first."

Sam looked from Charlie to Tilly. Her hazel eyes flashed back at him.

"I don't trust him," she said, her voice full of venom. "This piece of shit is the reason why my dad's dead and all of those others."

Serrano shrugged and refilled his glass. "It was not my doing. I did not pull the trigger."

"You keep telling yourself that, what about your assistant, Nurse Diaz? I take it that was nothing to do with you either?"

Suddenly the alcohol-induced haze fell from the doctor and he glared at Sam, his face livid. "Don't you start on me, Englishman, you know nothing. That whore was about to betray me, to sell me out." The Spaniard started moving towards Sam, slamming the now half-empty glass against his chest. "She stole from me, she was going to let me rot in a Spanish jail cell. She deserved everything she got."

Sam couldn't help it, the sickening self-entitlement that emanated from the man was enough to make him sick. As quick as a flash, far too quick for the inebriated doctor, Sam slapped the glass out of his hand sending it flying against the wall. Without pausing he kicked the doctor in the groin causing him to bend over in pain. Then with his left hand he grabbed the collar of the man's shirt, pulled him upright and slammed his fist into his soft stomach. He felt Serrano's legs give way and he released the shirt allowing him to fall to the tiled floor.

"Sam!" remonstrated Tilly.

Charlie just grinned. "I have to say, loving your work, Mr Taylor."

"You shouldn't have done that," chided Tilly as Serrano retched on the floor.

"He had it coming," said Charlie approvingly. "What do we do with him now?"

Sam stared down at the still-retching doctor. "What do you think? Do you think he's telling the truth about having the evidence?"

Charlie shrugged. "Who knows and who cares? If the Chief is after him let's take him down to the station and he can see how long he lasts down there."

"You can't do that," gasped Serrano, wiping vomit from the corner of his mouth. "You may as well kill me now."

Crouching, Sam picked up the doctor by the collar and leant him up against the countertop. "Talk. You have two minutes to convince me not to make sure the Chief finds you."

The pathologist spat out the remnants of vomit from his mouth. "There's a USB stick, it has all of the pathology reports, the real ones. It also has recordings of all my conversations with the Chief over the years. I always knew it would end like this. It's all yours, you can have it if you let me go."

"Where is it? In the house?" asked Sam.

"No, it is in a safety deposit box in town. You can have it. Just let me go."

"How can we trust you?" said Tilly, now coming to stand next to Sam. "You could be lying to us."

"I want to see the Chief banged up as much as anyone, probably more so. So how about this? You remember on your first night here? You stayed in the Birks's villa and had that night-time visitor?"

Sam's eyed widened as he remembered the near-naked fight with the intruder. "Yes?"

"It was me who opened up the window and told the Chief about the safe. I did it all when called to study the crime scene. You see how useful I can be? Why would I tell you that if I didn't want to help?"

Sam ran his hands through his hair as he weighed up the options. As reluctant as he was to let this man go, the thought of bringing down the Chief was appealing, while at least one mystery had been cleared up.

"Then we will take you there, you get the stick, give it to us and then we will let you go."

"No chance, the entire town is watching for you. The Chief's been watching you for days, if he sees me with you then we are all dead."

"He's not watching us now," retorted Sam.

"I bet he is, you just don't know it."

Serrano was adamant, no matter what Sam or Tilly said he refused to leave the house with them. He was convinced the Chief would have them shot on the street rather than risk their plans coming to fruition.

Sam was about to lose the will to live when a voice broke the conversation. "I'll take him, no one knows me yet. Well, not enough to suspect me."

The rest of the room's inhabitants twisted round to stare at the forgotten voice of Charlie Franks. His square face seemed relaxed, at ease with the whole situation, as if it was just another day at the office.

Serrano frowned. "And who are you exactly?"

"And that proves my point," answered Charlie. "Leave him with me and I'll get this stick. If it turns out to be rubbish then I'll make sure the doctor is still able to write his own prescriptions."

Sam paused before answering, the thought of trusting their one breakthrough in this case to a man he hardly knew and still doubted unsettled him. He tried to think of some sort of alternative but failed to come up with anything.

"I think that's a fair plan," said Tilly before Sam had a chance to think things through.

Charlie Franks beamed. "And you, Sam? Are you willing to trust me with this?"

Sam swore under his breath, looked beyond the patio out over the bay. In the distance the looming *el Montgó* could be seen shimmering in the heat. There was nothing else left for him to do. Ignoring the knots within his stomach he answered, "Damn it, okay."

TWENTY-FIVE

SAM HELPED Charlie in a vain attempt to sober up the inebriated Serrano. Picking up the weak-kneed pathologist under the arms, they carried him out from the kitchen and onto the patio.

"I really don't need this," protested Serrano as they helped him down the stairs into the open garden. "They know me well enough in the bank."

"I know but it will make us feel better," said Sam, nodding at Charlie.

With a heave they threw the doctor into the blue swimming pool below their feet. The still fully dressed Serrano landed with a splash before kicking and spluttering. He made his way back to the side.

"You bastards," groaned the Spaniard.

"Tell it to your patients," growled Charlie, pulling him up out of the water.

Returning inside they found Tilly, having herself returned from checking the street for any tail.

"Well, we are still clear, I don't know what Serrano's thinking saying we are being watched." She stopped, seeing the drenched doctor standing between the two men. "I don't want to know."

Sam pushed the wet doctor forwards. "Then we best get a move on. Me and Tilly will leave now and return to the villa, hopefully drawing off any suspicious eyes." Next, looking at Charlie and Serrano, he said, "Then you two can drive down to this bank, get the USB stick before dropping off the good doctor at the train station."

"Right, sounds like a plan," answered Charlie, the look of confidence still on his handsome face. "You two can leave now, I'll go and help this bastard get into something dry. You will ring me if anything happens?"

Sam gave a grim nod of agreement, the suspicion of the MI5 man currently pushed away for the time being.

Leaving Sam and Tilly, Charlie pushed the bedraggled doctor out of the kitchen into the depths of the house.

"Shall we be off then?" said a smiling Tilly. The thought of finally finding physical proof to condemn her father's killer was having a visibly lightening effect on her. Her round face glowed with excitement.

"Come on then," said Sam with a sigh, wanting to return to the comfort of the Birks's villa. He began to follow her out of the kitchen but then stopped as something caught his eye. Pausing, he waited for Tilly to reach the villa door before calling after her.

"I'll catch you up, I need a pee."

"Whatever, just hurry up."

Sam waited another heartbeat, listening to the sounds around him, until, certain the other occupants of the house were busy upstairs did he move. Walking quickly to the side table he picked up the discarded pistol that belonged to Charlie Franks. Quickly checking the weapon he found nothing out of the ordinary. The weapon looked fairly new, the mechanisms that fired the rounds seemed to be in working order. Removing the magazine he counted each of the rounds. There was nothing out of the ordinary, apart from Sam's distrust of the owner. Still debating his next course of action he replaced the now lighter weapon back on the table surface. He pushed out the thought of what Tilly would have said about this.

An unknowing Tilly was instead waiting for him outside in the rental. Sam retook his place in the passenger seat before silently emptying his pockets into the car door compartment.

"Well, that was more successful than I expected," she announced, starting the engine.

"Was it? You're not upset about Serrano walking away?"

"Ha, he won't get far, either the Chief will get him or the police. As soon as we have the USB it incriminates him as much as the Chief. All we've done is given him a head start."

"Remind me never to become your enemy," muttered Sam, looking out of the window.

The drive back to the villa was short, barely three streets away from where they had left Serrano and Charlie. Throughout the journey Sam had been keeping an eye out for any potential tail but the streets were empty. Even their own street was empty of all except one car which sat patiently for them outside the villa.

"Is that…?" asked a surprised Sam.

"Yeah, it is," replied an equally bemused Tilly. "What's Paul doing here?"

Tilly brought the car to a stop behind the Cava owner. The bald-headed Paul was leant against the side of his car waiting for them. He looked slightly embarrassed as they clambered out and greeted him.

"All right, Tilly, sorry to bother you."

"No, you're not bothering me at all, what's wrong? Not like you to be on this side of the hill."

Paul scratched his jaw. "Well, the thing is I've just come up from the golf club. I've spoken with the secretary and everything is in motion with selling your dad's shares." He stopped and looked sheepish.

"But?" prompted Tilly.

"But you know what these pompous bastards are like. They get something in their minds and won't let it go."

"We've met a few like that ourselves," said Sam, coming to stand behind Tilly.

"Yeah, you will," continued Paul. "They asked me to ask you if your dad left any keys with you. Apparently, and I say 'apparently', your dad had an extra locker in the staff quarters, down in the basement. I've no idea why but…"

Sam, seeing where this was going, interrupted. "What key?"

Paul ignored him, intent on finishing his tale. "Well, Selwin must have also taken the spare key to this locker and so the bloody secretary has this bee in his bonnet that if it's not returned he won't start the sale of your dad's shares."

This time both Sam and Tilly almost shouted. "What number key!"

Stunned, Paul blinked before answering. "Eighty-nine, the secretary definitely said Selwin had taken number eighty-nine."

Tilly jumped on the shocked Paul wrapping him in a great bear hug. She kissed the now blushing restauranteur on the cheek. "You are a hero, Paul."

With that she turned on her heel, unlocked the villa gate and rushed inside.

"What was all that about?" asked a bewildered Paul.

"You know when you have a problem that you have no idea how to solve?"

"Yeah?"

"And someone just comes along and provides the answer?"

"Yeah?"

"Well, you've just earned yourself a massive tip next time we are in town. I'll make sure she drops off the key today."

Sam left Paul to find Tilly already upstairs opening the hidden office safe. She reached into the metal box and removed the long-forgotten keys. Holding them up Sam saw the two familiar keys marked eighty-nine.

For a moment neither of them said anything, the look of suspense filling their eyes. Finally, Sam spoke.

"It's like you said, anything important to your dad is at a golf course! I was told your father was old school, liked to keep things written down. You don't think…?"

"That he already has everything we need locked away?"

"I mean, I'm not one to get my hopes up but why else lock up the keys?"

"Exactly. Why all the secrecy?" asked Tilly in return.

Sam took the small pair of keys, examining them in his hands. Had the literal key to everything been in the house this whole time?

Tilly came closer. "What should we do? Should we wait until Charlie returns? He may already have everything we need. We can then take everything to the police."

Looking down at the trusty green Rolex Sam shook his head. "No, let's go now and get whatever's inside. I don't quite trust…" He stopped, not wanting to cause an argument. "I don't quite trust that doctor," was all he could say.

Tilly took on the driving duties, this time pushing the small rental hatchback to its near limits. More than once she caused the tyres to screech as she took a tight corner. The merest hint of a green light was seen as an invitation to force her way through the traffic in her excitement to get to the golf course. Sam gripped the roof handle ever more tightly with each passing mile. He couldn't decide if he was enjoying the thrill of the ride or was desperate to just get out alive.

Reaching the golf club Tilly drove up through the gates and into the half-empty car park. The afternoon heat had driven all but the most hardy of players off the fairways. Now standing amongst the parked vehicles the two companions looked at each other, both thinking the same thought.

"Where do we go now?" voiced Sam.

"I don't know, I've only ever been here once and that was only to meet Dad for lunch."

In the end they decided to start by circling the building and surveying the scene. They walked past a busy swimming pool, a driving range, tennis court, pond and putting green. They drew odd glances from the two golf shop attendants as Sam poked his head round the corner to see if they had missed a hidden exit.

"Paul did say the basement, didn't he?" asked Tilly.

"Yeah, why?"

She pointed down a concrete ramp, a green carpet was inlaid onto it providing firm footing for those walking down its steep slopes. Checking the coast was clear they hurried down into the building's depths. Immediately the heat of the day evaporated as the solid concrete kept out the sun's rays. Reaching the bottom of the slope they stood together at the end of an empty corridor. To either side of them doors led off into unseen rooms, the glass windows frosted to block out unwanted observers.

"I tell you what, if this was in a horror film at night I wouldn't want to have to see what's at the other end," said Sam, pointing down to the far end of the corridor.

The two of them made their way down further into the depths of the building. Both were tense with the expectation of finally finding the answers to all their conundrums. Bypassing the green-keeper's office, the cleaning stores, and boiler room they finally found what they were looking for. A row of dull metal lockers lined up along the white-painted wall where the corridor ended.

"There it is," breathed Tilly nervously. "Top left, three in."

Sam took the key and pressed it into the silver locking mechanism. Applying pressure the lock resisted for a moment before releasing. Opening the locker door they peered inside to find a single item.

"A folder? What's inside?" asked Tilly as Sam pulled out the bound papers.

"Give me a chance. Come on, let's find somewhere to open it first."

"There's a bar upstairs with lots of private offices for the golf club committee."

With Sam clutching the folder tightly, they found their way back upstairs and into the bar of the club. Slipping into one of the side rooms Sam dropped the folder onto the desk before taking a seat.

Joining him, Tilly pulled the folder towards them and opened it. "Christ, Dad, you never did things by half, did you?"

Looking down at the now open folder Sam could see what she meant. The folder was filled with papers, many of which were annotated in a strong flowing script in red ink. At the top, a title page read – *Case Name Octopus: An investigation into the deaths of expatriates in the Spanish town of Jávea and the subsequent criminal undertakings discovered.*

"The title could do with some work," commented Sam as Tilly turned the page.

"Dad liked to write, he could be a bit theatrical in his wording."

The next page began with a summary of the request by Mrs Sheridan to look into the approach by a local organisation to purchase her property. Of how through her natural distrust of strangers and knowledge of a neighbour's recent demise, she had been driven to seek the advice of the retired agent. How piece by piece, Selwin Birks had carefully stalked the murky organisation which they now knew was masterminded by the grim man they called the Chief.

"There's got to be more in here than just the villa scam and murders," said Sam, thinking aloud as he looked at the papers below him.

"You're right, oh my God, you're right," gasped Tilly as she turned the page.

In front of them, written out in black and white was a small diagram. At the start was the word *Octopus*, circled in red with the name *Chris Kane* written underneath. Two arrows led from the circle, the first went to a second box with the name *Chief* written within and the second to a third box containing only two words.

"*Le Central,*" read Sam grimly.

"The what?"

"Le Central, they are a criminal organisation, a big one. I've met them before, too many times. These are bad people, really bad. Think criminal but on a global scale."

"And they are interested in bumping off old ladies?"

"I know it does seem hard to explain, what does your dad say?"

They looked down again at the diagram and at the circled word. *Octopus*.

"Christ, Chris Kane is involved, but how?"

Sam answered, reading the red-inked annotations. "Of course, he's a financial crimes officer, he must be the one who finds out which of the expatriates out here are financially vulnerable. At which point the Chief takes over and does the dirty work."

"Then why kill him?"

"I honestly have no idea, perhaps after learning that Selwin was onto them they decided they needed to shut down the operation. Perhaps it was through Kane that your dad managed to put together the pieces. They certainly killed him because of this folder, so why not Kane?"

"Jesus, Dad, I wonder what he did wrong?"

"Nothing, these le Central people are professional bastards. I guess they were wanting to protect whatever income they were getting from the villa sales."

A weariness seemed to pass over Sam, he rubbed his eyes in frustration. After everything he had got it wrong, he had never even considered that the dead man could have been involved in the criminality at work. Yet now it had seemed obvious from the start, what had he said before? That the only thing missing was how did they find their targets, now it seemed he had found the first link in the chain.

"And le Central?" said Tilly, still studying the diagram.

"I dunno, perhaps take a cut? They do have feelers everywhere."

Again Sam was wrong, almost as wrong as it was possible to be. The next page of the folder changed everything and for a moment neither of them spoke as they read through the expertly collated evidence. Of how the Chief's organisation using presumably the finances of le Central had expanded beyond their own shores. How using their established fishing fleet they were able to cross the Mediterranean and using the very worst of humanity was transporting the desperate of society into an unknown future. Selwin had seemingly gone to great lengths to painstakingly capture his evidence. There were photos of all the players involved, from the Chief and his organisation right through to Kane himself. The only gap being a blank space with the unknown le Central contact.

"I wonder who this?" questioned Tilly, pointing at the blank space.

"Someone very dangerous. I'd be happier if the only le Central representative was Kane."

Taking each page in turn they saw photos of the Chief's farm, the lorries being filled with older water bottles. Selwin had even somehow captured a harbour scene, where a rusty fishing boat was having huge crates of what seemed like stores of fish lifted from its hull. But a further image now zoomed into the open lorry betrayed the huddled forms of people climbing out.

Placing the folder down on the desk Tilly finally broke the silence. "What do we do now?"

"I have no idea. This is huge, far beyond anything I could have expected. I mean, it fits – think back to how defensive the Chief was when we saw the lorries being loaded. He was worried we may have actually stumbled onto his real game."

"You mean the property schemes are not his main focus?"

"Hell no, just look at the money. I'm no expert but I can promise you human trafficking will be a lot more lucrative than swindling some pensioners. People like the Chief are the prime movers in the illegal sex rings, the slave labour workforces and everything else you can force a desperate person into. At best they are just smuggling them onto the continent, at worst they are ensuring they end up exactly where they want them. And believe me, if le Central are involved then I'm willing to bet it's the worst-case scenario."

"So what do we do?" Tilly asked again.

"We have to go to the police." Then Sam paused, thinking aloud. "Hang on, why didn't your dad do that?"

"What do you mean?"

"Well, he certainly had the evidence, why didn't he go straight to Moreno?"

"I can tell you that." Tilly picked up the folder and flicked through the pages, searching for a specific page.

Reaching it she pointed down at the text and read, "'On reviewing the entire case in full I have concerns as to how such an enterprise can operate undercover for so long without attracting the attention of the local authorities. It is my assessment that this is only achieved through the active or at the very least passive support of the very highest levels of police enforcement'."

"So Selwin did not trust the police? That would make sense, but I think he's wrong. Remember what Serrano said? He called them incompetent rather than complicit, at the very least he did not think they were involved. Otherwise why did he go to such lengths to cover up the murders?"

"But my dad…"

"Was not certain, as he said it was only an assessment. I bet he never actually met Moreno and I can't see her allowing this evil to happen in her town. Especially not something like this. People, innocent people dying on her watch. She would hate it, she will hate it when she finds out. I can't begin to tell you how much suffering these types of operations cause."

Tilly rose from her chair. "We need to get this to the right people, same with whatever evidence Charlie has managed to get from Serrano. Surely with that and this we will have enough?"

"We will – and we will make sure that the right people get hold of it."

It was time to shut down the Chief.

TWENTY-SIX

THERE WAS an air of excitement in the car drive back to the villa. Finally for the first time during their stay on the Costa Blanca, both of the occupants felt they were on the front foot. That the tide had not only turned in their favour but had become a tidal wave of progress towards the inevitable success and closure. Even if they returned to find Charlie had failed to retrieve Serrano's evidence, surely Selwin had closed the case for them. Sam was already thinking of the plane home and a future date with Joanna as he drove the rental back onto the villa's quiet residential street. At the same time his mistrust in Charlie had evaporated in the haze of success.

"Charlie's back," said Tilly, pointing to the MI5 man's rental and then at a white transit that was parked next to it. *Danny's pools and gardens* was written down its flanks. "Oh, and the pool man's turned up."

Sam parked in the space between the pool man and rental directly in front of the villa. Turning the engine off they watched as Charlie clambered out of his car. He gave them a friendly wave followed by a thumbs up.

"Looks like we are not the only ones to have had a successful trip," Tilly said, smiling as she unstrapped her seat belt.

"Indeed, if he's got what Serrano promised then I may have to give the posh bastard an apology," grumbled Sam, following his companion onto the street.

"How'd it go?" Tilly called out to the waiting Charlie.

The blond-haired Charlie gave his best, mostly toothy grin and raised a finger indicating for them to wait, then bent down to retrieve something from the car.

"I bloody told you," cried Tilly, elbowing Sam in the ribs. "We've hit the jackpot today."

Sam was saved from answering as Charlie Franks now stepped back from the rental, the blunt black muzzle of a pistol pointing directly at them.

Tilly stopped still on the pavement outside her father's home, her whole body frozen in surprise. "What the hell?"

"We can get to that later," snapped Charlie, his voice now cold with disdain. "Keep your hands where I can see them."

Sam stared blankly up at the taller man and then at the gun. Recognising it from earlier he shook his head and stepped forwards. "Don't be so bloody stupid, you bastard."

For a moment Charlie seemed to lose his confidence, he faltered slightly as Sam moved towards him.

Sam snarled, "If you think I'm letting a jumped-up posh bastard like you screw me over, think again, it's going to take a lot more than you to stop me today."

"Then perhaps this will be enough."

Both Sam and Tilly whipped round to see stepping out of the parked transit a group of men. Sam recognised their leader immediately, the Chief's head of security – Cesc, a revolver held up in front of him. The weapon looked small in the Spaniard's hand. Sam knew the weapons range of accuracy to be minimal but the damage of those bullets at this range would be fatal.

"Bastards," spat Sam as the Spaniard moved in to remove his own weapon.

"And I'll have that." Charlie indicated the folder in Tilly's hands, having rediscovered his confidence.

"I always knew you were a piece of shit."

"But you didn't do anything about it? Silly boy, eh?"

Sam bit back his retort. Instead, Tilly said, "I should have told Sam to smash your face in."

"That's not exactly the sentiments of a caring doctor now, is it?"

Tilly flushed but kept quiet.

"Come on then, into the van please." Charlie indicated for the pair of them to move.

"No," replied Sam firmly. "I don't think we will."

Cesc pushed the cold metal of the revolver into Sam's back. "Get in."

"No, you don't scare me, you scruffy bastard. If you were going to kill us you'd have done it already. You need us alive," said Sam, trying to sound more confident than he felt.

Cesc hesitated for a moment, looking to Charlie for direction. The Englishman gave another toothy grin and held up the folder.

"We only need one of you, Mr Taylor, for our questions, so it's your choice."

Sam swore, it was no use, there were too many of them. Perhaps he could have charged Charlie alone and broken through. If the rest of Cesc's men were armed with the snub-nosed revolvers with their limited accuracy, then he could have had a chance, but even the worst marksman should be able to hit one of two targets. He gave a sideways glance at Tilly and saw the fear in her eyes. This was not the place for a fight.

Charlie seemed to have guessed Sam's thought process and raised his own weapon to now point at Tilly.

"I'll start with the woman."

Reluctantly Sam and Tilly allowed themselves to be shepherded into the back of the van where two pairs of handcuffs were placed round their wrists, tying them tightly behind their backs. Charlie and Cesc watched over as their men pushed the prisoners to the van's floor and against the metal panelling.

Charlie climbed in with them, instructing one of Cesc's men to take the rental. Sam and Tilly watched as their captors made themselves comfortable in the cramped space, Charlie looked particularly pleased with himself as he sat down opposite them. The van shook for a moment as the engine came to life and Tilly was jolted back into Sam as the driver drove onwards.

"I take it you never got Serrano's evidence," asked Tilly, her voice full of scorn. "The pair of you put on a good show, I'll give you that. You certainly had me fooled although I'm surprised he let you break his nose just for us."

Charlie looked at her quizzically. "You think that was all set up?"

"Wasn't it?"

"No, of course not. That bloody fool had no idea who I was. But to answer your question, yes, in fact I did retrieve Serrano's little evidence. The good doctor kept his word and did exactly as he was told right up to the point Cesc over there cut his throat."

Tilly gasped. "What, you mean he wasn't working…"

"For us?" teased Charlie. "Of course he was."

Tilly opened her mouth but no words came out.

Instead, Sam answered for her. "You just were tying up loose ends," he said, guessing the real motive.

Charlie flashed his toothy smile at the pair of them.

Sam shook his head. "We did your work for you, didn't we? By getting him to reveal all his evidence against the Chief we pretty much signed his death warrant."

"Don't beat yourself up, he was a dead man long before he spoke to you. We just needed to be sure first."

Sam shook his head in exasperation, how had he been so stupid? Why had he failed to act on his instincts about this man? There had been so many red flags and yet he had gone on blindly into this trap. An anger flashed through him and he had to fight the urge to kick out at his captors around him. He tried to move his hands, trapped in the metal cuffs behind him, yet only felt the metal dig further into his flesh.

Charlie had moved on to reading Selwin's carefully curated

file against the Chief. "Ah, you two have been busy. I take it this is your old man's work, yes?" he asked Tilly who just glared back at him. "Yes, I see. Well, he was a bloody good spook, wasn't he? Seems to have done a proper number on the old Chief. Well, well, he even linked old Kane's role in everything."

"It's just a shame he didn't work out there were two rats in MI5," snapped Sam.

Charlie looked up at him. "Two rats? Christ, man, I'm not MI5 – don't tell me you believed that cock-and-bull story. I was flown in yesterday as a favour to a friend. We knew we had to get your trust and when it was heard there was a new man coming out from London to join you it made perfect sense."

Sam frowned. "How did you...?"

Charlie shook his head and reached down to a rucksack down by his feet, withdrawing two cloth bags. "I think that's enough questions for now, I have some reading to do," he stated, placing the bags over their heads.

Sam, his world now in darkness, felt Tilly lean in closer to him for comfort. He tried to push the thoughts of recrimination out of his mind, he had to think of a way out of here. The van bumped violently as the driver hit a pothole causing all of the occupants to flail about. Without their arms to steady themselves Tilly and Sam were thrown hard against the floor as those around them laughed mercilessly, Tilly's prone body coming to rest on his legs. No one came to help them back upright and the pair of them lay huddled together on the van floor. Sam tried to estimate how long they had been driving as time had somehow become hazy. Around him their captors spoke in low voices. Every so often he would hear Cesc or Charlie make a comment.

"Where are you taking us?" Sam heard Tilly ask through the hood.

"None of your bloody business, you will find out when you get there," came the hard reply from above.

Sam kept quiet, he'd already guessed where they were heading and his suspicions were confirmed as he felt the van's wheels leave the tarmac onto the rough, uneven track that led down to the Chief's compound. Next, he heard the crunch of the gravel on rubber as the van came to a stop, followed by pricks of sunlight forcing their way through the hood's material as the door was opened. New voices could be heard as the kidnap team all made their way out of the vehicle. The deep voice of Cesc was giving out orders which led to a set of strong hands roughly pulling Sam upright.

"It would be easier if you just took this off us? We have both been here before," he muttered to the unseen faces.

His answer came in the form of a punch to the stomach and he lurched forwards as the air was driven from him. Sardonic laughs greeted his stumble.

"What happened? What did you do?" cried Tilly, unable to see the violence.

"Shut it," came the unseen, sardonic voice of Charlie Franks.

The pair of them were dragged across the yard, until the reduction of the sun's brightness through their hoods betrayed they had entered one of the buildings. Moments later they were forced down onto chairs where unseen hands removed their handcuffs and replaced them with cable ties fastened directly to their seats. A faceless laughter crackled across the room, followed by the pattering of footsteps moving away from them before the sound of a door cut them off.

Finally, silence descended upon them. Still covered by his hood, Sam strained his ears to tell him everything they could. Beyond his own deep breaths he could just about hear Tilly next to him.

"Hey, Tilly, are you okay?" he ventured, conscious they may not be alone in the room.

"Yes," the muffled voice of the doctor came back to him. "What did they do to you?"

"Just hit me. I'm fine, forget it."

"What are we going to do?" Her voice, normally so strong and confident, seemed weaker, more uncertain of itself than at any time since Sam had known it.

"Right now, wait it out. They clearly want something otherwise we wouldn't be sitting here." His words sounded hollow even to him but he had to go on, to try and give her some hope in their survival. "Just keep yourself calm and ready. Trust me, there will come an opportunity to get out of here. We just need to be ready to take it."

"I will have to take your word for it right now. Is this the part when you tell me you've been in lots of scrapes like this?"

Underneath the bag Sam smiled to himself, there was still a spark left in her. "Yeah, all the time. Although last time I was saved by a friend blowing the whole building up."

"If it works I'll definitely take that."

The sound of approaching voices came drifting into the room causing Sam to tense, all his senses suddenly switching back on.

"Listen, Tilly, don't do anything to antagonise them. Just follow my lead and don't panic."

Whether Tilly felt comforted by his words he never knew as he then heard the sound of the door being flung open. Listening carefully, he heard multiple footsteps coming into the room but no voices. He felt someone move close to him, a hand was gently laid on his shoulder before the fabric bag was tugged upwards. Sam blinked profusely as the light of the room blinded his eyes. It took a moment to fully register the face now in front of him. There was no mistaking the slim-framed woman, from the black hair, down to the long neck with its large silver crucifix.

"Sofia Kane," said Sam, his voice full of disgust. "Not quite the weeping widow then?"

Mrs Kane smiled then stepped over to Tilly to remove her covering.

"What the hell?" gasped Tilly, recognising their host.

"I'm sorry to have kept you waiting." The tall woman smirked, moving back from the pair of them. "But we are all here now."

Sam looked past her to see three other people had entered with her into the room. To the left, standing closest to the door stood Charlie Franks, the sly smirk seemingly now permanently etched across his face. Next to him, slouched in a chair, his long lanky legs spread out in front of him was the Chief. The vagabond was still dressed in his ragged vest and jeans. Sofia went to take a seat next to him and the difference between the pair's appearance could not have been more evident. Sofia was wearing a cream dress, every part of her appearance sculptured for its style. Next to her, the scruffy Chief looked even more dishevelled, a feat Sam had presumed to have been impossible. But actually, now they were sitting together side by side there was something about the pair of them…

"I take it you're not going to offer us refreshments?" asked Sam.

"No," answered the woman calmly.

"Then you best get on with it, we've places to be this evening."

"You see what I had to put up with? All this shit," said Charlie from the corner. "You lot should have paid me double for having to listen to him."

"You're getting paid well enough," said a voice.

Sam and Tilly turned to stare at the speaker now sat off to one side of Sofia Kane. For an instant Sam didn't recognise the thickset man with his hair tied in a topknot. Then it hit him.

"You! You were the air force guy in the restaurant last night. Hang on. Major, wasn't it?"

The man called Major gave a brief smile then nodded. "I was, although cards on the table I'm not an officer in the air force. So you can call me Major or Neil, whichever you prefer."

Sam stared into the dark-brown eyes of Major and felt a twinge of fear trickle unbidden down his spine at the coldness that looked back at him. The Chief he knew about and had expected, but this man was something else.

"And what does that make you?"

Major shrugged. "A nobody, just like yourself."

"We will see about that." Sam nodded back to Sofia Kane. "I take it you're over the death of your husband?"

She shrugged. "I will be. These things happen."

Sam shook his head in disgust. "And the children? How are they getting along without their dad?"

"I wouldn't know, their real mother took them back to England this morning. The benefits of being only a stepmum."

"Indeed, so what can we do for you all? I take it you're after something in return for bringing us here?" said Sam.

"Cocky bastard, aren't you?" said the Chief, his head resting back against his hands. "It's almost as if things were the other way around and we were the ones tied up."

"You will wish you were tied up when I'm done with you," growled Sam.

Tilly snapped, the frustration of her situation getting the better of her. "Oh, for God's sake, enough of this. Tell us what you want with us."

"A few things actually," answered Major. "We've been reading your father's excellent report, he really did do a thorough job, didn't he?"

When neither Sam nor Tilly answered he continued. "Let's keep it simple, who else did you share it with?"

Again neither Sam nor Tilly answered.

Instead, Charlie Franks spoke. "There, you see? No one. They were going to be meeting me with it."

Major thought for a moment, rubbing his chin. "Perhaps, but from what you said before, Mr Taylor here didn't quite trust you – who's to say he hasn't already sent a copy off somewhere?"

"Now that would be a problem, wouldn't it?" said Sam. "You said it yourself – Selwin Birks was a very efficient man, probably made quite a few copies."

"Then you can illuminate us before we have to start asking in a less friendly way," continued Major.

"If we are answering each other's questions you can start

first," said Sam, his mind full of unanswered thoughts. "Starting with that piece of shit in the corner."

Major, the Chief and Sofia Kane all turned to look at Charlie Franks who stuffed his hands in his pockets and leant against the wall.

"What do you lot want me to say? I told you everything. I flew in yesterday as a favour to Major, he told me to follow you around a bit."

"But my office knew you were coming. They knew your name and everything."

"Of course they did," snapped Sofia Kane. "They did send the real Charlie Franks out here although unfortunately for you he visited me first."

The Chief suddenly gave out a bark of a laugh. "And now he's at the bottom of the sea below your house."

Sofia Kane gave her neighbour a contemptuous look. "Indeed, it was a straight swap for a man you had never seen."

"You didn't even bother to check my identification, not that it would have mattered. We had already sourced a pretty good fake," added the false Charlie Franks.

Sam cursed himself, thinking back to their first meeting with the imposter. The fake Charlie had waved at them from the street while Sam had been stood in the porch. Sam remembered Franks' feigned bemusement at their inability to read his – non-existent – badge from inside the house. He had never thought to check again.

"But you showed us a photo of you and Kane together on a works night out?" asked a bewildered Tilly.

"Yeah I did, but it wasn't a works night out, I knew Chris through Major over there. That photo was taken in Arenal a few months back. A stroke of genius, if I may say so myself," said the fake Charlie. "That threw you right off my scent. I knew then I had your trust."

Sam looked away from the imposter, the self-recriminations for not spotting the fraud earlier would have to wait. There were other questions to ask. Moving next along the line of faces he stopped at the Chief's languid form.

"I think I know enough about you."

The Chief scratched his groin, oblivious.

Third in the line-up was the recently made widow. Sam went to open his mouth then stopped. It couldn't be. He looked back at the dishevelled form in front of him and then back to the Spanish beauty next to it. One looked like he had spent the last few years sleeping rough, while the other could have walked right out of a Madrid catwalk. But it was there, he was sure of it. In the slim frames, the narrow faces, it was something around the eyes…

"No way," he gasped.

"Pardon?" asked a confused Sofia Kane.

"You two. You're siblings?"

TWENTY-SEVEN

SOFIA KANE RAISED A MANICURED EYEBROW, crossed her shapely legs and sat back in her chair. A look of mild amusement twitched at her narrow lips.

"Not bad, Mr Taylor, a good spot. Not many people have ever managed to make that connection. Well, not many outsiders that's for sure."

"I can see where you get your good looks from," said Sam, indicating the rough-looking Chief.

Sofia's eyes narrowed while her brother chuckled, showing his stained teeth.

"So which of you killed Chris Kane then?" asked Sam, tired of being the one without answers.

"I did," replied Sofia Kane coldly. "We no longer needed him and it was made very clear that if we still wanted to continue our relationship with le Central our friend, my husband, had to go."

Sam involuntary flinched from the coldness of her words. Sofia Kane had almost said them with glee.

She continued. "I sent Chris and the girl to get the oranges, using the time to hide myself in the boat. From there it was easy enough to wait for him to be distracted by the call from the solicitor."

"Which you arranged," added Tilly, guessing correctly.

"And why the police found no unaccounted for DNA on the boat, no one would be surprised to find prints or DNA of the owner's wife on board," surmised Sam.

"Indeed, and then a gentle swim back to shore where I was taxied back to my house."

"Where you were able to play the bereaved widow?"

"Don't patronise me, Mr Taylor, I did what I had to do for the family, like I always have. There may have been some love at the start of the marriage and especially when he introduced us to the world of le Central, but love dies, family lives on."

Sam shook his head, there was no point in arguing with these people. Any attempt to try and question how they could be willing to act in such ways would be falling on deaf ears.

Sofia Kane seemed to read some of Sam's thoughts. "I don't know why you're looking at me like that. I did try to tell you the girl was innocent, I never wanted her to become caught up in everything. She was just a nice distraction for the police."

"Delightful. Lady Macbeth has a conscience." Sam moved his gaze from the brother and sister and back to the man called Major.

"And you? You've been awfully quiet for a man your size."

Neil Major shrugged. "I like to listen."

"Like you did at the restaurant last night? I bet you enjoyed that, a right little voyeur."

Major laughed aloud, his thick muscles straining against his tight shirt. "I did, in fact hearing you two talking about the case made my mind up on Serrano. Knowing you were close to cracking him was just the prompting I needed."

"It must be hard to be the brains of the operation. I take it you're the prick representing le Central?"

"Indeed."

"I can tell, I've met your kind before."

"Funny that I've never even heard of you before."

Sam bit his tongue, refusing to bite. All four of the individuals in front of him made his skin crawl. All four of them could go to hell for all he cared.

Tilly moved in her chair. "What about the nurse? The mortuary assistant, Diaz? Which of you killed her?"

Major glanced down the line of conspirators. "Who?"

"The nurse," answered the Chief nonchalantly. "We did that, she was going to give them evidence on Serrano."

"Oh yes, I'd forgotten that."

Sam's temper snapped and he tried to jump up but the cords on his wrist held him back. "You bastards, you sick sardonic bastards."

"Careful, Taylor, your welfare is not that important to us," warned Major.

"It is to me," growled the Chief.

Major raised his hand. "We will get to that."

Sam wondered what he had done to upset the Chief but was unable to ask as Major continued.

"We've wasted enough time here, as we all now know, thanks to your father's little research, that you are aware of our main business dealings, which puts us all in a bit of a problem, doesn't it? I'll even share with you that right now, we have a new shipment currently sitting off the coast as we speak."

"By shipment you mean people."

"Indeed. Miss Birks, if you'd prefer, we have a shipment of people waiting to come into harbour. We cannot disembark our cargo until we know who else you two have told about our operation."

Neither Sam nor Tilly replied, both just looked on impassively, waiting for their captors to continue.

"Very well, I will share with you that unfortunately some of the said people on board are not at all healthy and I don't think it is an exaggeration to say the longer they stay afloat the more of them will die. In ways, which I'm sure you can imagine are not pleasant. So I have an offer for the both of you and a separate one for Doctor Birks."

"Go to hell," snapped Tilly.

"If you believe in that type of thing, then that's your business," answered Major, still unfazed. "But here is my offer – you tell me exactly who knows about your father's information and then agree to provide medical support to our new arrivals up to their final destination."

"And in return?"

"And then you may walk free, our business completed."

Sam raised an eyebrow in disbelief, he thought the chances of either of them being allowed to walk free were between zero and none.

"You said it was an offer for me, what happens to Sam?" asked Tilly, directing her question at Major.

"He stays here as a guest of the Chief, as insurance."

Tilly bit her lip and glanced at Sam for his support.

"What happens if I refuse?"

This time the Chief answered, sitting forwards excitedly. "Then we'll beat the information we need from both of you and you can spend the last few hours of your lives thinking about all of the innocent people who will perish without adequate medical attention. I think we may have hit ten dead already on this trip."

Sam's mind flickered to an image of a damp overcrowded boat before coming back to his own depressing situation. Before him the four faces were watching carefully. He tried to weigh up the options, his only conclusion being that it was better to delay any physical abuse until as late as possible.

"Deal," he said firmly.

Tilly twisted in her seat. "What? No deal."

"No, it's a deal," Sam confirmed. "Given the choice I'd rather accept that scruffy bastard's hospitality over a beating any day. That is, of course, if he promises to have at least one shower during the time I'm here."

Tilly gaped at him, open-mouthed. "You expect me to go along with them? To help them?"

"Yes."

"You don't believe they will keep their word surely?"

"Nope, but a lot can change before then. Better to live to see another day, eh, guys?"

"Indeed," answered Major, a sly smile etched on his face as he tried to imagine how they could ever possibly think anything would change.

"Sam, no!" pleaded Tilly.

Sam ignored her, anything was better than certain death. At the very worst it gave Tilly a chance of survival. As for him? Well, he'd met worse than the Chief.

"We told no one about the folder. I can't guarantee the old spy didn't have at least one copy somewhere but we never found it. That good enough for you? Great. Now let Tilly loose and do whatever you have to do with me."

Neil Major stood up, rearranged his shirt and put his hands in his pockets. He nodded at the fake Charlie Franks who pulled out a small knife which he used to free Tilly's bonds.

"Very good, Mr Taylor, I can see you're a man of vision. I'll take the girl down to the harbour and prepare the boat. Please radio your crew to meet us at the usual location. We will wait for nightfall then make for land. Make sure you have everything ready for when we dock."

Major gave Sam a gentle pat on the shoulder before continuing. "Until next time, Mr Taylor."

Sam ignored him, the sarcasm was self-evident.

The fake Charlie grabbed the still-protesting Tilly by the arm, dragging her to the door.

"I will not leave him, no, stop, get off me! Sam, tell him, stop him!"

"Tilly, stop and concentrate on helping those people on the boat. I'll be fine, we will meet again."

The words fell on deaf ears as Tilly, kicking and pleading, was half carried out of the room, followed by a still-grinning Major. The room's remaining occupants watched quietly until the door was closed behind the struggling doctor.

"Shall we discuss my accommodation? I'd like to order breakfast for eight each day."

The Chief's eyes flashed. "Really?"

"No, I suppose not. I take it I won't be treated to a hospitable stay while I'm here?"

"Nope."

"And the chances of me being allowed to leave?"

"Zero."

Sam sighed. "It's what I expected, at least the girl's got a chance. What's going to happen now?"

The Chief stood up, stretched his long limbs. Sam was struck by how tall the man was standing there in front of him. The Spaniard gave his seated sister a quick glance before whipping back round to strike Sam across the cheek. Sam was rocketed back in the chair but remained upright, the blow stinging his cheek far more than expected. There was a hidden strength to the Chief.

"Big man striking a tied-up prisoner," spat Sam, launching a mixture of spittle and blood at the Chief's feet. "I would still bet your sister hits harder."

The Chief's response was to pull Sam's head back by his hair and this time land a hard punch, splitting the Englishman's lip.

"You can forget seeing the friend again. Englishman, you're mine now and Major has said I can do whatever I like with you."

Sam grimaced through the pain. "We can start by taking you shopping for something that doesn't stink of bullshit."

The Chief punched Sam hard in the abdomen then pushed the chair backwards causing Sam to crash to the ground. Three vicious kicks followed as he lay helpless on the floor.

"Come on then, let's hear another joke," spat the Chief, stopping to collect his breath. "I can't hear you, what was that?"

Sam held his tongue. While the pain shooting through his body was excruciating, he'd be damned if he showed any emotion to this man.

The Chief bent down and again gripped Sam's hair, twisting it painfully and turning his head round to glare into his face. "Major may have finished with you but I still have one question to ask you."

Sam glared up at the snarling face. "Go to hell."

Another slap followed. "What did you do with my men?"

Sam blinked in a mixture of pain and confusion. What the hell was he talking about?

The Chief twisted his grip upon Sam's head tighter, pulling him up from the floor. "I said what did you do to my men? You know the ones we had following you last night. We both know they never made it home."

"They must have got lost."

The Chief gave a laugh of derision. "You don't know when to stop, do you? I could break every bone in your body and no one would complain. Give me one good reason why I shouldn't?"

Sam, unable to give an answer, kept silent.

"I'll ask again, what did you do with my men?"

"Last I saw of them they were heading for a swim."

The Chief swore, released Sam's hair then kicked his exposed ribs after he fell back to the floor.

"Okay, that's enough," ordered Sofia Kane. She had remained still the entire time as her brother had lashed out. "You have your answer, your men are dead. By the sounds of it probably in the same place as the real Charlie Franks. There's nothing to be gained by wasting your time kicking the stuffing out of him. I thought you were going to give him to the bulls? You promised to give the boys something to watch."

"They can get their kicks somewhere else."

Sofia stood and placed her arm on her brother's elbow. "You promised them, remember this man killed their friends as well. It is only fair they get to see his death."

The Chief made a growling sound before he slowly knelt, took hold of Sam's chair and lifted both him and it upright. Sam had to stifle a groan as the movement sent waves of pain through his bruised body. Spitting out another mouthful of blood he wondered what they could possibly mean by giving him to the bull. His mind flashed back to the fight in the arena, was he going to have face off against one of the great beasts?

Sofia took her brother's hands and ran her fingers over where the blows had damaged his skin. She kissed it gently and stroked his chin.

"I have to go, make sure you keep your word. Give the guys a good show, they deserve it. And for God's sake make sure you deliver for Major this evening, we cannot afford another slip-up."

Stepping away from her brother she gave Sam a final glance but neglected to say anything to him. Turning on her heel, she left Sam alone with the Chief who watched her leave then turned to Sam.

"She has always been the smart one, the one with all the brains."

"Don't tell me – you're the beauty of the family," Sam said with a laugh, flinching from the effort.

The Chief also gave a brief bark of a laugh. "No, I suppose not. Funny how things work out though. So my men are dead then?"

Sam did not see the point in lying. "Yes."

"Very well, I do not take it personally but there is still a debt to be paid."

"The way I see it, you're still winning in the killing scales."

The Chief rubbed his chin thoughtfully. "Indeed, yet I still have a duty of care to my men."

Reaching into his jeans pockets the Chief withdrew a battered penknife and moved towards Sam. Seeing the shine of the dull metal Sam tensed and was surprised as he felt the cable ties release their grip. He immediately rubbed the feeling back into his hands.

"Don't try anything, I have enough guns out there to put you down before you even get out of this building," warned the Chief, stepping back.

"So what happens next? I take it you still plan on giving me to the bulls?"

The Chief flicked a strand of greasy hair back from his face then scratched his groin. "You remember the bullfight happening when you first came here?"

The image of the two chained men dodging the giant bull's horns flashed through Sam's mind.

"Yes," he answered cautiously, not looking forward to whatever the Chief had planned.

The Chief walked away from Sam to the open door. He called to someone outside before turning back to the captive Englishman.

"Good, because today out on that arena, Señor Taylor, you will be fighting me and our great *el Rey*."

TWENTY-EIGHT

SAM WAS DRAGGED none too gently out from the room where he had been held by a pair of the Chief's men. His mind was spinning as he tried to comprehend the imminent challenge ahead of him. The thought of somehow trying to duel with the Chief while at the same time avoiding the charging bull made his stomach churn. The pain from the Chief's beating was throbbing through his body, the taste of blood fresh in his mouth. Around him a sense of excitement seemed to have filled his captors. Guided by the two men on either side of him back out to the main yard, he was greeted by a chorus of whistles and jeers from the assembled crowd of onlookers. The expectation of the late-afternoon's entertainment seemed to have brought out the entirety of the Chief's workforce.

"Nice to see I can still attract a crowd," commented Sam sourly to his captors.

"It's not often we get to see a proper fight," answered one of the guards. "You're lucky, it's even rarer to get to see the Chief at work."

"I'm honoured."

"He's the greatest bullfighter between here and Valencia. You best make sure you don't die too soon otherwise you'll upset a lot of people."

Sam shook his head. "I'll try my best."

"I wouldn't worry, the Chief knows what he's doing, he'll make sure we have a show," said the other guard.

Sam bit his tongue not wanting to give them any satisfaction. They marched across the gravel yard towards the small arena with its enclosed bullring. Somewhere in that collection of metal and wood waiting for him was the animal they called *el Rey*. He thought back to the previous afternoon and his attempt at humour over the animal's name. Back then he had only the Chief to worry about, God knows how he was going to deal with both of them.

Above him the sun had reached its peak and was beginning its inexorable descent towards sunset. It would be nightfall in a couple of hours, that's if he survived long enough to see it. He wondered where they had taken Tilly. That bastard Major had spoken about the harbour, perhaps she would find a way to escape. Even now she could be on her way to find help. He pushed the thought out of his mind, the only help he was going to be getting was from his own wits and skill.

The Spanish guards guided him through one of the arena's entrances and into a passageway that led underneath the rows of benches. The sounds of tens of people clambering across the wooden benches pounded Sam's eardrums. A cloud of dust was forming as disturbed particles fell between the beams. Sam had been brought to a small space separated from the bullring by thick metal bars which ran around the entire circumference. Between each lay a gap large enough for a man to slide through onto the sandy arena. Peering through, Sam watched as a man swept the arena's sandy floor while another checked the thick wrought-iron ring embedded in the centre.

"You're lucky," commented one of the guards.

"I am?" replied Sam, not seeing how his current predicament could possibly be seen as lucky.

"We've got another delivery tonight so we've got to get this over with soon. Otherwise the Chief would have made you stew a little. The last man he fought he had locked up next to one of the bull cages for a week. The poor bastard had to sleep next to the beast that killed him."

"What happened?" asked Sam, unable to stop himself.

"The Chief had him skewed on *el Rey's* horns, took the poor sod an age to die. Left all his entrails spread across the sand."

The two guards laughed grimly as Sam grimaced at the thought of his entrails being laid bare across the sand. He swallowed, sweat was beginning to form on his neck. What the hell was he going to do? Desperately he tried to picture the various tactics used by the two fighters they had watched the day before, but all that kept coming back to his mind was the speed and strength of the charging bull. He was somehow going to have to evade the animal and at the same time try to face off with the man who had orchestrated everything.

Feeling his dry mouth he asked his captors for a drink. A lukewarm plastic bottle was thrown towards him. He caught it, took a long swig and poured the rest over his face in an attempt to awaken all his senses. The sound of feet stamping rhythmically on the planks echoed around him as the crowd's excitement built.

"Any tips?" Sam asked his smirking captors.

"Watch out for the sharp parts, they can hurt a bit."

"Bastards."

One of the guards noticed movement in the middle of the ring. "Time to go," he said, pushing Sam between two of the bars.

Sam allowed himself to be forced through the metal opening and onto the sand-covered arena floor. All around, a host of Spaniards hurled their abuse at him. He raised his arm in sarcastic greeting, it only increased the noise.

"I'm not sure they are cheering for me," he said to his guards.

For answer a great cheer came back as a new figure entered the arena. The Chief, his greasy hair now tied back in a ponytail, had walked out to his people. In one hand he carried a coiled-up metal chain and with the other he waved to the crowd that had gathered to see him kill the Englishman. He nonchalantly strode across the sand, the upcoming fight seeming to cause him little to no concern at all. They met in the middle of the arena, the thick iron ring embedded in the ground between their feet. With a nod from the Chief, Sam's guards turned on their heels and returned to watch from the stands. Without even looking at Sam the Spaniard dropped the chain to the ground then threaded it through the embedded ring. The small links clinked as they were pulled through until half of the chain had passed under.

"Here, take this," grunted the Chief, holding one end out to Sam.

Taking it, Sam saw a leather strap had been fastened to the final link in the chain.

"Fasten it round your wrist," instructed the Chief, fastening the opposite strap around his own.

Sam did as instructed, tying the leather strap tightly around his right wrist. Around them the crowd's excitement was growing as jeers and whistles were directed at him. The sweat was now pouring down Sam's neck and along his spine. His heart was pounding against his chest as he tried to process everything that was happening around him. He still felt sore from the kicking he had already received from the man directly in front of him.

"Would you like me to tell you the rules?" asked the Chief in a mocking tone. His grey eyes looked out from a sunken face, as though an animal surveying its prey.

Not receiving a reply the Chief continued. "You must keep the chain tied to your wrist at all times, if you remove it we will shoot you. The bull will be released from that gate over there." He indicated one side of the sand-covered arena.

"Great," muttered Sam, remembering the Chief previously telling him how they injected steroids into the bull to increase its aggression.

"That is the only rule. The fight will end when only one man remains alive." He said the last part with a sly smile, already picturing Sam's demise.

"To the death then," replied Sam, trying to sound braver than he felt. He still had no idea how he was going to even try and survive the next few minutes. Somewhere behind those bars was over eight hundred kilograms of beef ready to tear him apart.

"Are you ready, Englishman?" challenged the Chief, flexing his arms, causing the crowd to cheer.

"Go fuck yourself, you bastard," snapped Sam in a final act of defiance.

The Chief grinned as he gave the metal chain a flick. "Now we both step backwards, the moment the chain tightens, the bull is released and we begin."

For one of the few times in his life Sam was speechless, the sheer suspense of the moment had wiped away any of his usual wit. The Chief had begun to step backwards, his eyes fixed on his opponent. Sam, mirroring, made his own feet begin the walk away from the Spaniard. A loud bang caused him to look to his right where he could see the silhouette of the bull fighting to escape the metal cage.

"Are you ready, Englishman!" jeered the Chief.

Sam ignored him, not removing his eyes from the thrashing, but thankfully still-caged animal. What would the creature do upon release? Would it charge blindly out at the first person it saw? What should Sam do about the chain now fastened to his wrist? Perhaps he should be watching the Chief rather than the imminent arrival still hammering against its imprisonment.

"Jesus Christ," Sam whispered.

The sense of panic was swelling still further within his chest as he watched the chain grow ever tighter. In barely a few steps the links would be strained and the fight would begin. Three steps, two steps and then the chain tensed, both fighters were trapped together by their mutual bond. Only one of them would be released. Sam turned, watching with suppressed horror as the locks on the bull's pen were released and the giant animal burst out onto the arena floor.

At the exact same time as the animal's hooves hit the sand the Chief sprang into life. With a strength Sam would never have expected, he pulled at the chain causing the Englishman to stumble forwards. The Chief's men sat in the crowd, cheered even louder as Sam lost his footing and fell hard onto the arena floor. To his right the bull flicked his huge head towards him, the whites of its eyes widening in anger. Lowering its horn-tipped head, it pawed at the ground then sprang forwards.

Sam didn't need to see the bull to know it was coming for him. The sound of the hooves seemed to thunder down upon him as he desperately tried to regain his footing. He had managed to get upright just as the animal was pounding down upon him. Panic gripped him, causing him to drive back to ground to avoid the charging bull. Sand from the arena floor now caked his sweat-covered face and his lungs were straining against his ribcage desperately trying to take in more air. Above him more jeers and abuse was being thrown down from the stands.

Rolling to his side, he crouched, looking for the bull's next charge. The giant animal had driven through to the other side of the arena and was now turning, ready to make its next pass. Somehow the creature seemed even larger when seen without the safety of the cage. Sam tensed himself waiting for the next charge. The bull shook its head then flung itself towards Sam. This time he was ready, his whole body was prepared to fling itself away from the incoming horns. He took a step to his left, readied himself to twist right but just as he was about to make his move the chain round his wrist tensed. He had forgotten the Chief at the other end.

The Spaniard, knowing this sport's every possible nuance had ran round behind Sam and waited for his moment. Sam was flung backwards onto his backside by the jerking chain just as the bull came in for the kill. His only option was to roll out from under the incoming hooves but he was not quite quick enough. A heavy foot smashed into his outstretched leg as it thundered past sending Sam spinning on the ground.

Again the crowd cheered, excited to see their champion land the first blow. Sam cried out in pain as he came to a halt, the sand now in his mouth. His leg felt like it had been smashed with a bat. The voice in his head screamed at him to move, but all he wanted to do was curl up on the ground. Gingerly he attempted to look up to see where the next attack was coming from, hoping that the bull had changed targets. It had, the giant creature having bypassed the fallen Sam, and it now spotted the Chief. Sam watched as the creature now charged his opponent, who simply pivoted past the incoming horns.

"You see, Taylor, you have to understand the animal, to feel it, to become one with it."

"Oh, do shut up, you scruffy bastard," groaned Sam, staggering back to his feet. Gently putting weight back onto his injured leg he stumbled slightly as he found his balance.

Whether it was due to the rubbish spouted from the Chief or the pain in his leg, for the first time since the fight had begun, Sam felt his mind begin to clear. Something in his mind was beginning to tick, the instinct to survive, honed over years of surviving moments like this. The pain in his leg was intense but it wasn't broken, he could still fight.

Across from him the bull was turning. It paused for a moment as it took in the scene before it, then stamped its front hoof and snorted before again making towards Sam. This time he was ready for it – and the Chief. The bull charged straight for him and Sam immediately leant his weight away from the Chief causing the chain to tighten. Using all his strength he pulled at the links forcing the Chief to meet the challenge and pull back. The Spaniard was laughing, thinking Sam was trying to run from the incoming charge. Instead, waiting until the bull was almost on him, Sam released the pressure on the chain and allowed himself to be pulled to safety by the unsuspecting Chief.

Sam watched with pleasure as the Chief stumbled backwards,

waved his arms for balance then fell flat on his back. His pleasure was short-lived, however, as his own leg buckled from the pain of the previous blow and he, too, again fell onto the sand. Once more he did not need to see the bull to know it was charging down on him and he rolled to his left, this time narrowly avoiding another kick. The bull charged on past Sam straight at the Chief, who, still on the ground, barely had time to avoid a thrusting horn.

"What happened to becoming one with the animal?" Sam called out as he knelt on the ground.

The Chief's response was to spit out a lump of sand. Around them the crowd had quietened slightly, no one had ever remembered seeing the Chief on the floor.

The voice inside Sam's head spoke. *Ignore the bull, take the man.* He blinked, once, twice and then wiped the sweat from his face. Time seemed to slow, he could hear the blood pounding through his eardrums. The bull wasn't the key to ending this, only by killing his opponent could he ever hope to walk out of here. A smile crept across Sam's face, the trace of an idea forming in his mind. He just needed the right opportunity, the right time to strike. Reaching down he grabbed a handful of sand before gently rising to his feet. The chain in his right hand was slick with sweat, but that didn't matter now, he could still find a grip on the smooth metal.

Flicking his eyes around the arena he searched for the bull. The drugged-up animal was running round the edge of the ring, its black eyes watching both Sam and the Chief. Forcing himself to look away from the bull he turned to stare at the Chief. The tall, lanky, grey-haired bastard had stopped smiling, his lined face dripped with sweat. What had the bastard said? The only rule had been not to remove the chain? Sam smiled again, causing the remaining colour to drain from the Chief's ugly face.

Without even glancing back at the bull, Sam gritted his teeth from the pain in his leg and charged right at his opponent. The Chief froze in shock as the Englishman sprinted across the arena and launched himself forwards. Sam threw the handful of sand straight into the Chief's face, immediately blinding him. An instant later he dived onto the unsuspecting Spaniard, forcing him backwards. Still using the shock of the sand, Sam slipped behind the struggling Chief, used his left hand to grab the loose chain and with his right hand still in its strap, wrapped it round his enemy's neck. The Chief flailed desperately, trying to get a grip on the tightening chain as it dug deeper into his neck. Sam almost gagged at the smell as the Chief's greasy hair was thrown into his face.

Looking past the struggling Chief, Sam saw *el Rey* had stopped pacing. Its black eyes were focused on the two men, locked in their desperate struggle. It lowered its head.

Sam kicked the back of the Chief's knee forcing him to the ground. Gripping the chain even tighter he bent forwards and whispered into the Chief's ear, "Long live the king, you dirty bastard."

The great *el Rey*, the king, the bull that had already killed, charged. The Chief tried to speak but the metal links cut off anything legible. He tried a final desperate attempt at escape as Sam twisted the metal chain tighter around his wrist. Only then did Sam realise his mistake – he, too, was going to be caught up in the bull's charge, not that he had any time to rectify it. The bull smashed into the pair of them, the left horn piercing into the Chief's stomach and driving on through his body until the point split through the back of his dirty vest. Sam, caught up in the blow by the chain across the Chief's neck, had to twist to avoid being skewered along with his enemy. Releasing his grip on the chain, he let himself be thrown backwards and away from the carnage. Landing heavily on the ground, he looked up to see the still-writhing Chief, the blood-tipped horn skewered through him.

TWENTY-NINE

THE CHIEF SCREAMED. A gasping, choking sound that seemed to echo around the shocked stands. Sam watched in sick amazement as the giant bull twisted and spun in an attempt to dislodge the dying man from its horn. Flecks of blood were being flung across the dry sand as the Chief's body was finally set free from the piercing horn. A silence had fallen over the watching crowd, the only noise coming from the now gasping Chief, as his lungs fought against the blood that was now filling their airways. No one moved to help, it was as if the entire crowd had become frozen in shock from the spectacle that had befallen their master. Sam forced himself to look away from the scene, if ever there was going to be a moment to escape this was it. Slipping the strap from his wrist he staggered to his feet, pausing he gazed around at the filled benches above him. The crowd was beginning to come round from the scene they had just witnessed. A deep, low rumbling noise was starting to reverberate about him.

Sam did not need to be told twice. He spun round and ran to the spot between the metal bars from which *el Rey* had entered the ring. Finally, the more quick-witted of the Chief's men were climbing down cautiously from the stands, careful to watch the still-prowling bull, its left horn dripping blood. Slipping through the iron bars he found himself once again in the same corridor that the Chief had taken him and Tilly through the day before. All around him the remaining bulls smashed up against the cages that held them in check. Something seemed different this time, whether because of the smell of blood or some other unknown reason, all of the animals seemed more aggressive in their confinement. The bars all around Sam seemed to echo from the sound of the huge creatures' attempts to escape.

"Taylor!" a voice shouted out through the darkened space.

Sam looked up to see the weather-worn face of the Chief's security guard, Cesc, under his mop of untidy black hair. His eyes were full of uncontrolled rage as the stocky Spaniard ran towards Sam. Stopping just yards away he raised a small snub-nosed revolver and fired a round at the Englishman. Sam, having anticipated this, had already flung himself into an empty cage, slipping slightly on the floor of hay and excrement. Grabbing the metal bars for support he felt his hand press against a plastic box fitted outwards of the cage.

Cesc moved forwards, screaming, "You think you can just run away, Englishman! You pig, you scum, you—"

Whatever else Sam was he didn't get a chance to hear it. Standing back upright, he pushed his hand round to the front of the plastic box, flipped open the cover and pressed the release button. Immediately each of pen's gates opened, the mechanical wince lifting the heavy bars up and releasing the inhabitants. Cesc stopped moving, looking round in fear. He had barely enough time to register the charging bull as it slammed into him. The helpless security guard was driven hard against the iron bars and fell limply to the ground, his lifeless body soon lost to the stampeding hooves. Standing in the empty pen, Sam watched as the herd of animals stormed onwards through the passageway and out into the open air.

Only as the last animal exited the arena did Sam follow, pausing to look upon the corpse of the now nearly unrecognisable Cesc, his body squashed to pulp by the pounding hooves.

Stooping down, he picked up the fallen revolver, pocketed it and muttered a soft "Olé" over the dead man. *Two-nil to the bulls*, thought Sam as he left the arena for the last time.

Stepping out in the open yard area, he could not help but take a moment to enjoy the chaos around him. The Chief's empire was crumbling before his very eyes. The vengeful crowd had exited the stands just as the angry bulls had escaped their confinement. All about him groups of Spaniards were being chased by enraged animals from one end of the plateau to the other. Sam smiled as he watched one of the creatures send a man cartwheeling into the air. Another had forced a group of frightened men up onto the roof of a metal container, each desperately trying to help more to safety.

Reluctantly Sam pulled himself away, the thought of the captured Tilly fresh in his mind. He needed to find some sort of transport. What had Major said? Something about the harbour? Surely he must have meant Jávea's small harbour rather than the small Arenal marina. Perhaps if he was lucky they may not have left. If he could just somehow find a phone? Ring the police? No, he had been wrong about Charlie Franks and there was still no guarantee he could trust Moreno's officers just yet. There was also the boat full of innocent people to think of, if anything went wrong then there would be even more lives lost. He was going to have to do this alone.

There was no point looking round the farm buildings for a vehicle. The only one visible was a battered pickup truck which was currently receiving further damage as one of the rampaging bulls crashed into its side. Skirting round the chaos about him, Sam ran across the open yard and up to the chalk track which led back up to the main road. If only he could flag down a passing car. Ignoring the dull aches from across his battered and bruised body he began to jog along the rough roadway. Behind him he could still hear the sounds of the bulls wreaking their havoc on the Chief's hapless men. Sam grinned grimly as the memory of the dying Chief flashed across his mind. One of the four captors down, only three more to go.

A white pickup truck turned off the main road and onto the track ahead of Sam, who, seeing the approaching vehicle, immediately stopped running. Raising one arm in greeting, he used the other to withdraw the pocketed revolver before hiding it behind his back. The driver of the truck spotted Sam, slowed the vehicle and wound down his window. Sam let out a dry laugh, he recognised the face staring back at him with the broken nose. It was the same man who had broken into the Birks's villa on his first night.

"Who the hell are you?" the driver demanded, then recognising Sam, he tried to drive off, but was too slow. Sam rammed the small revolver into his shocked face, once, twice and again, the third time once again breaking the man's nose.

"Now that will teach you for waking a man up in the middle of the night," said Sam, opening the car door and pulling out the now unconscious driver. "You see what happens when you fight a man with his clothes on?"

Sam unceremoniously dumped the limp body to one side. Climbing into the cabin he slammed the gears into reverse and took a final look at the still chaotic plateau in front of him, before reversing back up the track and the open road. Immediately Sam's thoughts again fell upon Tilly. Where was she now? Surely they would have treated her well until they had got what they needed from her? Otherwise what had been the point in keeping her alive? Sam kept telling himself this as he drove through the foothills and back down into the bay. It was, after all, his fault she had been taken. Peering through the windscreen he could see the blue sea in the distance, the dimming sun shimmering across it.

Sam forced the truck onwards. He tried to estimate how long since Major and Tilly had left the farm. What had it been? An hour? It could not have been more than two at the most. How long did they need to get the boat ready? Gripping onto the steering wheel even more tightly, Sam sped the truck through the outskirts of Jávea towards the harbour, the pain from his beating from the Chief and the bull's kick fading into a dull ache as the pressure of finding Tilly grew. Bypassing the old town, Sam brought the pickup to a stop not far from where they found the body of the unfortunate Nurse Diaz, the group of small palm trees hanging limply in the still evening air, their shadows the nurse's final resting place, spurring a flame of anger deep within him.

Around him groups of tourists were mixing with locals on their way home for the day and Sam had to push his way through the crowds towards the harbour. Turning a final corner he now ran through a packed car park then stopped as he looked over the mass of moored boats. To his right were tied three industrial fishing boats, their decks covered in rolled up netting and baskets. To his left, nestled under the clifftop, lay rows of smaller private vessels, lined up along wooden jetties. A mixture of warehouses, office buildings and bars surrounded the entire harbour.

Sam swore and ran his hand through his hair. Neither the fishing boats nor the small private boats gave him much hope. He doubted Major was the type of person happy to slum it in a fishing boat and all the private ones seemed too small. Praying he had not arrived too late, he made his way further into the harbour, all the time searching for any sign of his prey. Heading to his left, Sam travelled towards the rows of jetties with their smaller boats moored alongside. Ahead of him more buildings appeared, some restaurants with tables and chairs outside and next to these stood a couple of warehouses surrounded by more boats, dry-docked and ready for servicing.

For a moment Sam debated asking someone if they'd seen the missing threesome but then stopped. He caught sight of a dark-grey hull peering out from behind the dry-docked boats. Hope restored, Sam ran through the rows of hulls, each resting on their sides waiting for whatever servicing they needed to return to the water. Reaching the final row of boats he finally saw what he had been looking for. Moored against the far seawall of the harbour, its sleek black-and-grey hull gently bobbing in the still waters was a stunning yacht. It must have been over a hundred foot in length with long panoramic glass windows embedded along its side.

There must have been three full decks of floating luxury in front of him.

A familiar voice echoed from one of the decks causing Sam to step back into the cover of the boats. "What is taking so long now? You useless sacks of Spanish shit, we were meant to have gone half an hour ago."

Peering round, Sam could see the distinct figure of the fake Charlie Franks screaming at a couple of dock workers as they scrambled out of a hatch that must have led to a lower deck. None of the Spanish workers seemed to have been able to understand the spoken English, but they had registered the meaning. They turned abruptly back down into the boat's interior and out of sight. Deciding to risk it, Sam began to make his way round to the moored yacht, careful to use the harbour's other obstacles as cover. There was no sign of either Major or Tilly, only the lurking presence of the fake MI5 man standing over everything from the highest deck.

Stepping behind a low wall, Sam ducked his head from view. There was nothing now between him and the yacht, any move he made now would be seen by anyone standing on deck. There was no other option but to wait. Steadying himself, he listened for any sign that his watching enemy had moved from his overseeing of the dock workers.

Suddenly Sam heard the hated voice call out, "Yes, goddamn it, I'm coming down."

Then, peering round the low wall a final time, he saw the coast was clear. Walking as quickly as he dared without raising suspicion, he headed towards the immaculate vessel. Stepping down onto the wooden jetty and then up again onto the lower swimming deck of the boat. No one had seen or noticed him. There had been no cry or challenge, the vessel's occupants must all be inside. There was no point in revealing himself until he was certain that he knew the whereabouts of the fishing trawler with its human cargo, otherwise they could simply sail to another port or worse, dispose of the cargo. He dropped down the open hatchway where he had last seen the disappearing dock workers. The smell of the engine hit his senses, a mixture of oil, diesel and sweat filled his nostrils as he took the rungs of the ladder downwards.

Reaching the floor below, he paused, taking in his surroundings. Standing there in the middle of the boat's engine room he debated what should be his next step. The two dock workers were busy tightening something on one of the two engines just ahead of him. Neither noticed his arrival, their concentration fixed on fastening a valve back into place. Deciding that he could not stay here, he gambled on repeating the false Frank's arrogance.

Speaking in English he demanded of the two turned backs, "What the hell is going on here?"

The two Spaniards jumped in surprise, evidently not used to seeing the management in such a place.

"We fix it, we are good now," came the reply in broken English.

Trying to give his best impression of his two arrogant former captors, Sam barked, "Well, that's not good enough is it? I wanted to have been gone by now!"

Giving the two scared workers a final look of disgust he walked straight past and through a door leading out of the engine room. He was on board and still undetected, although for how long depended on his next choice. Reaching down, he gripped the handle of his revolver in one hand, the snub-nosed weapon would be lethal in such close quarters. Looking forwards, he saw he was in a corridor that seemed to stretch the length of the ship. To either side of him were what he presumed were guest bedrooms, their doors bearing small silver numbers. He listened intently, hoping to hear something, anything that could tell him where to hide.

Deciding against the guest rooms, he walked to a door marked *Crew*. He was doubtful Major would have risked having a large crew on board, he pushed the door open and stepped inside. He was inside the crew's living quarters, a small kitchen and seating area surrounded him. It was empty, the limited crew aboard must have been preparing the vessel for sea. Careful not to make a sound, Sam walked through the living area and pushed on through to find three bedrooms, all filled with bunks. Two rooms showed obvious signs of being lived in; two sets of personal belongings were strewn around. While the third was empty, the two bunks stripped of any bed linen.

It would do, decided Sam, carefully shutting then locking the door behind him. As the door closed to he felt the judder of the engines gently shake the yacht to life; they were moving. Taking a seat on one of the bunks, Sam listened to the noises emanating from around him. He tried to discern the different number of voices but gave up as they merged together. Seated comfortably for the first time in what seemed an age, he gingerly rubbed the growing bruises along his body. A small window showed that they were now moving away from the harbour wall and out towards the open sea. Placing the revolver on the cabinet next to him, he checked his watch, sat back and crossed his legs. Somewhere above him his enemies sailed onwards, unaware that below their feet he awaited them. The time for vengeance was nearing.

THIRTY

SAM SAT motionless as the yacht sailed away from the mainland. Thus far he had managed to distinguish two additional voices, which he guessed must have belonged to the crew. He had once heard the distinct voice of Major, but only to call out to see how far they were from their destination. Of Tilly or the fake Charlie Franks, he heard nothing. A new thought crept unbidden into his mind as he sat feeling the yacht's bow beating against the sea's waves. What if Tilly wasn't on board? What if they had left her on land somewhere, waiting for an influx of trafficked migrants. He pushed the thought out of his mind. It was clear the evil bastards needed to get medical attention to the sick as soon as possible or risk losing even more money on the trip.

Without warning he felt the sound of the engines die down and then stop. Looking out of the window he could see their speed in the water had slowed. A red sunset was beginning to shimmer over the restless waves as Sam stared outside. It was time to act. Picking up the revolver he checked the remaining bullets and stood up. Pressing his ear to the cabin door he listened carefully to the sounds outside. From somewhere beyond his own cabin he could hear footsteps making their way down a flight of stairs. They were coming closer. Next, he heard the sound of a door being opened and whoever it was stepping into the crew's living quarters. Sam tensed slightly, worried his location was about to be discovered, when he heard the sound of the door opposite being opened and shut. A crew member taking a toilet break, he decided.

Cocking his weapon, he quietly stepped out of the cabin and gently tapped on the toilet door.

A voice called back angrily, "Occupied, get lost."

Sam tapped again, this time more urgently.

"I said get lost, I'm taking a crap."

Sam ignored the man and tapped even harder.

"Seriously, there's another toilet, you impatient bastard," complained the voice as the toilet's occupant attempted to open the lock.

"I'm going to bloody kill you," grumbled the crew member as he pulled back the door and then stopped. His eyes widened in fear as he looked right into the muzzle of the revolver. "What? Who?"

Sam raised a finger to his lips and spoke quietly. "Shh. I'm not going to hurt you, at least not yet."

It wasn't that he felt any queasiness at killing anyone involved in what was going on on board, it was more the moment he squeezed the trigger it would give up his position.

"Where's the girl?"

The guard mouthed wordlessly, as if his brain was trying to comprehend the situation it had found itself in.

Sam repeated the question, this time with more threat in the words. "Where is the girl?"

"Upstairs, she's on the deck with the bosses."

"How many are on board?"

"Three of them and two of us, me and the captain up top."

The two voices he had heard earlier.

"Are there any weapons on board?"

The crew member nodded. "But locked away, you cannot get to them."

"Yeah, but neither can they."

"What are you going to do to me?" whimpered the man.

Sam considered the crew member for a moment, debating what to do with him. He lowered the gun, then savagely kicked the man in the groin. The crew member went down, clutching between his legs, presenting Sam with the opening he needed. With a sickening crunch he smashed the butt of the gun down on his exposed head, knocking the owner unconscious.

"Well, at least I didn't shoot you," said Sam, lifting the limp form back into the toilet then he pulled the chain to flush it. "And at least I got rid of the smell for you. I bet your mates on the fishing boat don't do that."

Pushing the door closed, he smashed the lock to pieces ensuring the man inside was trapped. *One down*, he thought, turning through the crew's living space. If Tilly was outside on deck with Major and his mate then that made things easier. Moving as quietly as possible he opened the door out of the crew quarters and walked back onto the lower deck. He spotted a set of stairs and keeping his weapon pointing upwards began to climb. Reaching the main deck he poked his head up just high enough to see through onto the room beyond. A fine dining table filled half the space, followed by a lounge area facing out onto the open deck. He could just about hear voices coming from outside.

He crept quietly up the remaining stairs and walked silently to the next set of steps just to his right. These were steeper than the previous ones and he had to use his free arm to steady himself as he made his way upwards. Reaching the top, Sam was pleased to see the back of the yacht's captain looking outwards through a set of binoculars, oblivious to his arrival. For the first time he was beginning to regret wearing his boots as the hard rubber soles seemed to make excessive noise as he moved forwards. Tensing his body, he took a final breath then launched himself at the unsuspecting seaman.

The captain spoke, thinking it was his crewman returning.

"Looks like our friends are on time, they are just on the horizon now."

Sam did not reply. Clamping one hand over the man's mouth, he wrapped the other arm round his open neck. The captain fought desperately in an attempt to shake Sam off but he held on tight, squeezing the pressure to the man's windpipe ever harder. He could hear the man's muffled shouts, smell the man's aftershave as he gripped on firmly to the now weakening body. Giving the backs of his legs a swift kick, Sam brought his opponent down to the deck and held him there until a stillness crept into his limbs. Slowly, he released his grip and rolled off the unconscious captain.

Taking in deep lungfuls of air Sam gently checked the man's pulse and finding it still beating, was grateful. There only needed to be two deaths this evening. Straightening himself up, he looked around the ship's bridge. Amongst the various controls and dials he quickly spotted the radio and a satellite telephone. He looked out from the bridge and saw the approaching fishing vessel as the captain had said heading towards them. Part one of the operation was complete at least, he now knew where the traffickers were heading. Taking up the satellite phone then checking the coordinates on the digital map in front of him, he dialled a number. *That will please Moreno*, he thought, replacing the phone. He reckoned it would just give him time to complete part two before the cavalry arrived.

Leaving the bridge he headed back down the steep staircase to the main deck. The voices at the stern of the ship were still talking. The sound of laughter echoed back through the room as their owners relaxed, unaware of what was coming. Sam checked the revolver a final time and walked forwards.

Ahead of him he could see both Major and the man he knew as Charlie Franks stood by the yacht's rail looking out to sea. Major was holding Tilly's arm, pointing a champagne flute out to sea where the fishing trawler was heading towards them. No one had even noticed the sound of Sam's footsteps walking towards them. Quietly he took a seat on a sofa directly behind the trio.

"And you see, my dear, you'd be amazed how many we can fit into that piece of shit in just one run. Our friend the Chief, while for all his faults, does have a knack for this business."

"He's still a dirty bastard," grumbled the man Sam had known as Franks, also looking out at the approaching ship.

"Yes, well, perhaps we can try to groom that out of him."

"I wouldn't worry about that, the dirty bastard won't need it where he's going," said Sam softly.

The impact of his words would stay with him forever. The reaction from the two men was almost in slow motion for Sam as he sat watching. Charlie Franks, upon seeing Sam, desperately dropped his glass flute and reached for his gun. Neil Major took a second longer to realise who had spoken. The moment the words registered he twisted round, pulling Tilly's slim body in front of him as a shield.

Sam could have laughed at it all. He waited until Charlie Franks' gun was almost pointing at him before firing a single round into the man's chest. The bullet crashed into his ribcage, splintering bone on its way through tissue, muscle and more skin as it went straight through him. He was dead before he hit the floor. The gun fell from his lifeless hand and spun along to the deck to stop by Major's foot. For a moment silence fell on the three people still left alive.

"Go on," said Sam, calmly watching as the big man's eyes flashed downwards. "Pick it up."

Major studied him for a moment, weighing him up, before taking in the small pistol and the struggling Tilly still in his grip. He must have decided that the revolver in Sam's hand was not accurate enough to risk shooting him while he had hold of Tilly. Smirking, he bent down, taking the shaking doctor down with him.

"That's it, pick it up," encouraged Sam. "Now we can talk."

Major wrapped his fingers round the gun and stood upright,

sweat was pouring down his face. Instead of pointing it at Sam he jammed the muzzle into Tilly's cheek.

"So you lived, I take it then you killed the Chief?"

Sam shrugged and placed his own revolver onto the sofa, Neil Major's eyes following his every movement. "I don't think I can take all the credit on that score. He ran into a bull that disagreed with him, nasty business."

"I told him to just shoot you and be done with it."

"Sensible, although I don't think the Chief had a sensible bone in his body."

Major steadied himself, tightening his grip on the frightened Tilly. "You're an arrogant piece of shit, you know that, don't you?"

"Coming from you, I'll take that as a compliment." Sam flicked his eyes to Tilly. "You all right? Did they do anything to you?"

She shook her head, her eyes wide in fear at Sam's apparent disregard for his own weapon.

"That's good, otherwise things would have gone very differently."

"And how do you think they are going to go? That I'll just let you walk away and forget about this?" sneered Major, his small eyes flashing dangerously.

"Mate, we are in the middle of the sea. No one is walking away from this, swimming maybe."

Tilly's mouth dropped as she shook her head. Sam could already read her mind, at her amazement that even now he was making stupid comments at a time like this.

Speaking directly to her he said, "Don't worry, this will soon be over."

Major laughed. "Yes it will, sooner than you think."

The tall dark-haired man moved quicker than Sam had expected. Flinging Tilly to the floor he turned the gun directly at Sam still sitting still on top of the sofa and pulled the trigger. Nothing happened. A confused Major tried again, he squeezed the trigger but again no bullets left the muzzle. Twisting it round he looked down at the weapon in surprise.

Sam bent down to pick up Tilly. "You see, I've made many mistakes in my life, but not fully trusting that lump of meat down by your feet will not be one of them. If you're going to shoot someone at least make sure the gun's loaded next time."

Major tried to stammer something. Sam cut him off.

"I know what you're going to say and yes, I emptied your friend's gun back in Serrano's house. I should have known then he wasn't who he claimed to be. No MI5 agent would take such little care of his weapon."

Tilly glared at him, now finally exasperated. "How did you know he'd not reloaded it? You were willing to risk both our lives to what? Show off?"

Sam sat back into the deep cushions of the sofa next to his own loaded gun. "Come off it, these arrogant bastards would have loved gloating at me if they'd found out what I'd done. The moment neither mentioned it back in our little interrogation meant I knew I was safe." He reached out and took the ice-cold champagne bottle and poured himself and Tilly a glass.

Major watched on, still standing against the rails, his face full of disgust.

Sam noticed his enemy watching. "Can I get you one? One for the road perhaps?"

"What are you going to do with me?"

"Do with you? Absolutely nothing, I'm sure your le Central friends will have their own plans for you. I'm just going to let you go. I've already rung the authorities, they should be here just before that rust bucket over there."

Major glanced over to the still-approaching fishing trawler then back to Sam. "You're just going to let me go?"

"Yes, although like I said we are in the middle of the sea and it's a long way back," said Sam menacingly.

The realisation of what Sam meant hit Major in that moment and he turned nervously to the west where over the horizon and the setting sun lay land. "I can't swim that…"

"Far? Well, there's only one way to find out."

Major looked as if he was about to argue then stopped as Sam finally picked up his weapon. "It's your choice."

His huge frame shaking, Major gulped then stepped towards the edge of the yacht.

"Oh, yes, sorry I forgot," said Sam coldly then fired a single shot into Major's leg causing the man to scream and stagger against the railings. "That was for Nurse Diaz, it will make sure you remember her next time."

Still staggering, the le Central man fell backwards, landing into the blue surf. Sam and Tilly peered forwards to see the sopping wet hair break the surface, its narrow face looking up at them.

"Land's that way." Sam pointed towards the horizon before returning to fall into the sofa's embrace.

Tilly stood for a moment watching the now bobbing head of her former captor before coming to join Sam on the yacht's sofa.

Passing her a glass he said, "I could get used to this. A nice little runaround yacht. Iced champagne on tap. Beautiful sunset. Good-looking girl next to me – and look – a show," he added, indicating the struggling Major.

Tilly stared at the Yorkshireman unable to find the right words. His deep-blue eyes sparkled as the handsome face grinned at her. All of the strains of the past few days seemed to have vanished. She had never quite met a man like him, someone so determined to succeed, to see it through to the end. But she could also tell there was a spark within him, a force that somehow enabled him to look into the face of adversity and to simply smile back into it. Here was a man she could never fully understand, or in reality put up with. Looking at him here on this yacht, her own pains of the shared adventure seemed to fall away. Her shoulders relaxed and she leant into this man who had come and saved her, who had avenged her father and all the others.

Moving closer into him, a thought crept into her mind. "What did you actually do to the Chief?"

"I taught him the value of becoming a vegetarian."

EPILOGUE

THE TWO UNIFORMED police officers stepped forwards and banged the octopus door knocker down hard. No one answered. Officers Mata and Picque turned to look at Detective Vega for further instruction. The blonde-haired officer gave a curt nod and the pair tried again. The three loud bangs seemed to reverberate around the driveway, echoing into each of the waiting officers' ears.

Sam, standing slightly behind the group of uniformed officers, asked calmly, "Are we sure she's still in?"

Vega twisted round to glare at him. "Of course I am, we've had the place under surveillance since last night."

"Perhaps she's sleeping?"

The detective gave him a withering stare. "At eleven in the morning?"

Sam shrugged. "It could have been a heavy night."

Vega gave an audible grunt and gave the orders to the assembled officers to spread out and make their way round the building. Sam, purely a witness to this arrest, stuffed his hands in his pockets and followed Vega as she walked. No one was truly worried, the clifftop villa had only one exit.

Stepping onto a garden path Sam stifled a yawn as the

weariness of the previous days' activities hit home. Ever since he and Tilly had watched the dark head of Major fall beneath the waves a final time and greeted the stunned coastguard boats, they had hardly stopped. From seeing the wide grin of satisfaction on Commissioner Moreno's face as she awaited them on the harbour's edge, to the sense of relief emanating from Sir Jeffrey over the phone as they told him his friend had not died in vain. The last few hours had been extremely memorable, even Detective Vega had managed a smile. Now as Sam headed round the side of the villa, the final piece of the puzzle was about to be wrapped up. One last final loose end about to meet their fate.

A shout came from one of the officers ahead of them and caused the rest to speed up, breaking into a run as they raced round into the back garden. The police officers surrounding him came to an abrupt halt as they came to the end of the property and Sam saw her. She was as glamorous as the day they had met in this very place. Even in her final moments as a free woman, Sofia Kane seemed determined to make a statement.

Perched on the pillared wall that separated the pool area from the sheer clifftop beyond, the woman who had killed her husband in cold blood barely registered their arrival. Her stern face was looking over the deep-blue sea below. Detective Vega, not wanting to have to bring in a corpse over a live witness, quickly ordered for her men to return to their positions at the front of the house. Only as the last uniformed officer moved out of sight did the widow speak.

"You took longer than I expected."

"We had a few other things to attend to," answered Vega nonchalantly.

Sofia glanced contemptuously over her shoulder. "I wasn't talking to you. I was talking to him."

Vega eyed Sam, then slowly, not wanting to cause a scene, indicated for Sam to move forwards.

"I wanted to get some breakfast first," he answered reluctantly.

This was not the conversation he'd had in mind when he had asked to accompany Vega.

"No, you fool, I meant about the case. I warned them you would work it out, the moment I met you I knew."

"I'm flattered, although I thought I did pretty well considering I did it inside three days."

Sofia scoffed. "You were slow, you allowed Major and my brother to play you. I take it you killed my brother."

"Not me, I just gave him a little push."

"Poor Jorge, he never did see the danger."

Sam raised an eyebrow, it had been the first time he had heard the Chief's Christian name. "He didn't see the bull either, which is strange considering how bloody big it was."

Behind him Vega cleared her throat. Sam ignored it. Slowly he walked towards the seated widow. Her legs dangled over the side.

"You know it's over, don't you? There's nothing left," he told her firmly.

"Yes, I know."

"You will be pleased to know Alex Coombs is currently on a plane home."

"I'm glad."

Sam doubted that. He looked back towards Vega who mimed for him to grab her. Taking a couple more steps he was almost level with Sofia. Staring out past her, over the waves below he asked, "Did any of you ever know how many died in the crossing?"

Sofia Kane gave a dry laugh. "Of course not, why would we?"

"Or what became of them after you handed them over?"

"No."

Sam sighed and nodded his head, moving closer. "And the people you killed for the houses? Vega's team have already found more properties in the family name. I take it they were obtained the same way."

"Yes." The single word was almost whispered, as in confession.

Sam grimaced and muttered sourly, "Outstanding."

She again turned to look at him, her brown eyes met his deep blue. Understanding crossed between them. Sam noticed she was still wearing the silver crucifix.

Twisting round, Sofia Kane turned to look at Vega then pointed up at the villa. "Everything you need is in there, Chris kept everything inside the office."

Vega, following Sofia's outstretched arm, also turned to look up at the villa.

"What do you mean everything is in there?" she asked, still staring behind her, then turning round she shouted, "No!"

Vega blanched then ran to the wall where now only Sam stood, one arm resting where Sofia Kane had sat.

"She's gone," gasped Vega, looking over the edge to the rocks below.

Sam casually joined her in peering down for the missing Sofia. "So she has, she must have jumped."

"Jumped?" challenged Vega, her face flushing.

Sam rubbed his chin and waved his hands. "I mean she must have become overcome with remorse. I've seen it before."

"She didn't seem overcome to me," accused Vega.

"That's your problem, Detective, you're just not a people person like me."

Leaving the car back with the rental company, Sam and Tilly walked through the multi-storey car park, across the bridge and into departures. They turned to each other a final time as Sam put down his bag. He smiled at her beautiful face with its large hazel eyes and wide smile. A face which since the closure of the Chief's operations five days ago had become very familiar. Almost too familiar, making this parting far more difficult than he had expected.

"I guess this is it then, Doctor."

"Indeed it is, Captain."

Bending forwards, Sam kissed her a final time, a long lingering kiss which ended reluctantly. She gave him a knowing smile, placed her hand on his cheek.

"Give me your phone," she ordered.

Sam did as instructed, curious to know what she had planned. He watched as she tapped away at the screen then handed it back to him.

"There you go, call it a poor attempt at paying you back for everything."

"You don't need to pay me anything back."

"I do, let's leave it at that."

They paused as an announcement over the tannoy interrupted them.

"Is anyone meeting you at the airport?" she asked him.

Sam flinched, remembering the image of Sir Jeffrey and Emma standing there in arrivals. "Good God, I hope not. If they are I'm on the next plane out of there."

She smiled again, a final picture for him to remember her by.

"In which case see you around, Taylor."

"Indeed, Birks."

With that they parted, Tilly back to her father's villa and he to whatever awaited him back home in London. It was not until he had got through security and had ordered a final gin and tonic in the terminal bar, did he remember to check on whatever she had done on his phone. Flicking open the screen he found the messages app open and a new conversation started.

> Hey Joanna, I'm back – dinner tomorrow, 8pm? Anything but tapas.

Paris, France

The Pont des Arts, known to many as the 'Love Lock Bridge' crosses the river Seine between the Institut de France and the central square of the Louvre Palace. Its wrought-iron railings were traditionally the place where lovers would fasten padlocks as a gesture of locking their love for one another. Now after a crackdown by the local authorities, only a few rebellious locks remained.

Not that the figure leaning against the cold railings much cared for such acts. The pedestrian walkway was just simply a convenient meeting place for clandestine conversations such as this one. He looked down at his watch, seeing the minute hand creep nearer to the hour mark. Night had fallen over the city of lights, the heat from the hot summer's day beginning to fade into the darkness.

Leaving the railings, the figure moved to one of the benches lining the wooden planks below his feet and sat down. A group of runners jogged past, able to finally exercise under the cool of moonlight. He listened as the sound of pounding feet on wood died away, only to be replaced by a new sound. Single footsteps this time, sharp heels landing hard upon the ground.

"You're late, my lady," the man commented as his companion sat down next to him.

"You told me to finish my dinner first. It would have been rude of me to leave the CEO of one of France's largest banks before he had at least paid the bill."

"Where is he now?"

The newcomer indicated the east side of the riverbank. "In a taxi somewhere waiting for me, probably telling some lie to his wife about why he won't be home."

"Then you best not keep him waiting. Tell me, what is it you have for me?"

"Jávea." She said the single name cautiously, as if expected a rebuke.

Instead, the man just clasped his hands, placing them on his lap, waiting for her to continue.

"Major's dead."

"That's a shame."

She gulped, clearing her throat. "We will have to shut it all down, it's over."

The man made no reaction, instead looked down at his fingers. "It happens, do we know how?"

"An Englishman. Someone called Taylor killed them all. The name, it is…"

"Familiar?" asked the man. Indeed the name was familiar to him, far more familiar than even she knew.

"Yes, he's the one who stopped our Amsterdam operation and our drug line in the south."

The man looked away from his hands and up to the Paris skyline. In the distance the Eiffel Tower shone against the darkness. A tourist boat glided past, its passengers staring at the famous landmarks around them all.

"And?"

The woman noticed the danger in his voice, she was unsure how to approach it.

"What would you like us to do? Surely this man is purposely hunting down our operations? We should have him killed."

Her companion let off a tight, grim smile. "No, no, my dear lady, we do not need to do anything like that yet. I know of Mr Taylor, he is just a lost pawn in a game far beyond him. He plays no part except what is given to him, we do not bother with pawns. Forget about Spain, it is done. We learn and we move on. Major was a useful idiot, that was all. You should return to your banker, he will be waiting for you."

The woman frowned, as if she wanted to continue the debate. Not that anyone could debate with this man. Instead, bowing her head, she took her leave. Standing, she straightened her dress and was about to walk off when the man spoke again.

"Forget about the name Taylor," it commanded in a deep, firm voice.

Confused, she opened her mouth to speak, then decided against it. Saying no more, she turned on her heel and was gone into the Paris night.

Left alone on the bridge, the man stretched his legs out and wondered. He rubbed his chin and considered the name that had now thrice interrupted his business dealings. The thought dangled in his mind, he tried to push it away but it stubbornly held on. Now that was the question, the one which he would now have to consider. One which would determine more than one person's destiny. Just how much did Sam Taylor really know?

THE END

AUTHOR'S NOTE

Code Dead is the first Sam Taylor adventure set outside one of the main cities of the world. Unlike both Amsterdam and Berlin, Javéa is not the most recognisable of places. That being said, I have lost count of the times I have met people who have visited the small coastal town in the heart of the Costa Blanca. It does, however, hold a special place in my own heart and deserves a few extra lines to highlight its many charms.

Nearly every location described in the book is based on reality. From the bustling Arenal, the quaint old town and the visually stunning Granadella cove, each is well worth a visit to stop by and imagine our protagonist's brooding presence. I have always tried to stay true to the feel of the place, the mixture of the old and new. It is an unspoken but clearly visible balance between the tourist and the local. While not being a local myself, I have always felt the people of the town have always managed the balance quite well.

The description of the Moors and Christians festival is also accurate, although words do not do the event justice. The sheer effort that goes into the whole event by the local community is worth the visit alone. I would also recommend the reader do a quick internet search of *el Montgó* mountain. I promise you, there

AUTHOR'S NOTE

really is a distinct shape of an elephant's head formed by the ancient rock formations.

Talking of recommendations, both of the described restaurants are genuinely incredible places to eat. The Azorín is located near the harbour and is a perfect example of local cuisine, make sure you try the paella. Just off the main street, if you do not know it's there, then you do not know what you are missing. Cava is also a genuine tapas bar in the next town along the coast. Right in the heart of Moraira, the restaurant is run by Claire and Paul and both are two of the loveliest people you could hope to meet. The description of all the menu items are correct and trust me, you never know what to order. Please let the author make two recommendations, the home-made brownie and the German beer...

The centrepiece of the story, the villa *Esmerelda*, is also a real place. In this case, my grandparents' holiday home! A location of many happy family holidays over the years, I will apologise now for giving my grandma nightmares of dead bodies every time she walks into her living room. My own memories of playing golf with my grandad out there will live with me for the rest of my life.

Our fictional owner of *Villa Esmerelda*, the impressive former MI6 spy, Selwin Birks, is an amalgamation of two of my grandparents' friends who have sadly passed: Selwin Smith and Geoffrey Birks, who were two equally impressive men. I felt it was only right that it was Selwin Birks who took ownership of their beautiful and much-loved home.

These days, I continue to make my own memories with my girls around the town. We have spent many hours throwing stones on the pebble beach of the Granadella together. So if you see a family of four with two little blonde-haired girls, with the father looking particularly stressed, playing on the beach, then come say hello – it could well be me!

Until then, there are still plenty of places for our hero to visit, many gins still to be drunk, and with le Central circling ever closer in the shadows... Sam Taylor will return.

ALSO BY BEN BALDWIN

Code Red

Spy Code

ABOUT THE AUTHOR

Ben Baldwin is the quintessential Yorkshire man lost down south. Having grown up in the foothills of the Pennines, right in the heart of the Last of the Summer Wine country, he can now be found in Buckinghamshire living with his girls: wife Kimberley and their two children, Ella and Megan.

If he's not writing, working or chasing the kids, he can be found exploring the Buckinghamshire countryside on his bike or hacking holes into it while playing golf.

A management consultant in the professional world, he would be first to admit it is only to fund their adventures in the family motorhome 'Henry.'

His journey into writing has been called 'a hobby that got out of hand' by his wife and the Sam Taylor series is his first foray into the literary world.

He can be contacted at www.ben-baldwin.co.uk.

A NOTE FROM THE PUBLISHER

We hate typos. All of our books have been rigorously edited and proofread, but sometimes mistakes do slip through. If you have spotted a typo, please do let us know and we can get it amended within hours.

info@bloodhoundbooks.com

www.ingramcontent.com/pod-product-compliance
Ingram Content Group UK Ltd.
Pitfield, Milton Keynes, MK11 3LW, UK
UKHW040815191125
9056UKWH00036B/320